DRAGON IN EXILE

DRAGON IN EXILE

A New Liaden Universe® Novel

SHARON LEE & STEVE MILLER

Dragon in Exile

A Baen Books Original

Baen Publishing Enterprises
P.O. Box 1403
Riverdale, NY 10471
www.baen.com

ISBN: 978-1-4767-8071-9

Cover art by David Mattingly

First Baen printing, June 2015

Distributed by Simon & Schuster
1230 Avenue of the Americas
New York, NY 10020

Library of Congress Cataloging-in-Publication Data

Lee, Sharon, 1952–
   Dragon in exile / Sharon Lee and Steve Miller.
       pages ; cm
   ISBN 978-1-4767-8071-9 (hc)
   I. Miller, Steve, 1950 July 31– II. Title.
   PS3562.E3629D73 2015
   813'.54—dc23

                                                     2015005946

10 9 8 7 6 5 4 3 2 1

Pages by Joy Freeman (www.pagesbyjoy.com)
Printed in the United States of America

MANY THANKS...

...to Alma Alexander, for the Right Word

...to Jo Clayton, who left us too soon, but gave us Skeen before she did

...to Janet Kagan, wherever you are, for *Hellspark*, one of our favorite books, ever

...to Gus Fleischmann, who volunteered to create, and bravely curates, the Liaden Wiki (liaden.wikia.com)

...and to all the Scavenger Hunters on Facebook and LJ—you guys have Awesome Search Skills

DRAGON IN EXILE

PROLOGUE

. . . .

THE NURSERY SLEPT IN MOTTLED TWILIGHT.

Night-dims spotted along the walls lit a muted pathway to guide the nurse, should one of the babes wake within the deep night and call out. There were darker shadows along the edge of Nurse's path, that a child's half-waked imagination might populate with any number of creatures, fell or fair: Dragons might easily reside in such shadows; black cats, pirates, wolves, or flutterbees.

At this hour, the shadows sheltered only one habitant—another shadow, slightly darker than themselves. It had for some while stood motionless, listening to the sounds of the sleeping nursery. Now, it moved, black against black, resolving briefly into a grey silhouette as he crossed the lighted path, melting once more into the darkness beyond.

He ghosted past the alcove where lay the slumbering twins; his foot gliding soundlessly over the tuned board at the entrance. The twins were not his target—that lay further on—and in another moment he had achieved it.

She lay quiet and to all appearances deeply asleep, a star-decked blanket twisted about her legs, and a determined fist locked 'round the tail of a well-chewed plush cat. A strand of light from the night-dims straggled into the crib and brushed her hair, sparking copper.

That she was asleep now did not mean that she would remain so. He must take care, and be quick, for she was bold, even so

1

young; to extricate her without waking her—or the house—would be a challenge.

He bent close over the sleeping babe, and touched the stubborn fist, coaxing it gently open. The other hand he held ready, should she wake.

The child's name was a compromise, as so many matters must be compromised, when two cultures married. The mother had wished for "Lizzie," in order to honor her Terran foster-mother. The father...had wished to provide options. Thus, he had suggested a name which was inarguably Liaden; an old name, belonging, one might say, to no one.

Talizea, which might, in the Terran way, be *shortened* to "Lizzie," and thus both cultures were served.

The shadow froze, breath-caught. Talizea yos'Phelium muttered under her breath, sighed, squirmed...and sank back into sleep, her grip on the toy slackening.

Smiling, he drew the cat away, reached into his pocket and withdrew a dark muffler, in which he quickly wrapped his small target. He raised her, sleeping, and pressed her firmly against his shoulder.

A moment, then, he paused, listening. He heard a body shift, and blankets slide—the nurse. A step brought him into deep shadows, where he waited, but she settled without waking, and in another moment, he was at the nursery door.

It closed silently behind him.

· · · ✳ · · ·

Elsewhere in the house, beneath a skylight framing a study in black velvet, lit by distant, sullen stars, the child's mother stirred in her bed. She extended an arm toward her partner, and slipped back into sleep.

· · · ✳ · · ·

The former nursery shadow settled his back against living wood, and sighed. It was warm here, under Tree—much warmer than the supposed summer evening beyond the canopy. He crossed his legs and settled the baby onto his lap, folding the blanket away from her face. For a wonder, she slept on. Talizea was not usually so sound a sleeper. One might almost suspect Mrs. pel'Esla of drugging her charges—and one might, also, sympathize.

Val Con yos'Phelium sighed once more, lightly, and stroked his daughter's bright hair. So must Miri have been, as a babe, even to the spangle of freckles across the small nose.

There had, of course, been no need to steal like a thief into his own nursery and pad away with his daughter in arms. Well, excepting that it was late, the children, and their long-suffering nurse, asleep and better to remain so. The nursery schedule was not made to accommodate those nights when dreams or old memories woke him beyond any hope of finding a second sleep.

Many times, on such nights, he walked alone in the garden, or sat here beneath the Tree, where one of Korval was never truly alone, or sought the music room and his omnichora.

On some nights, however, he felt the need of Talizea, who was, after all, the delms' heir, who would take up the management of Clan Korval, or whatever else they may have become by the time he and Miri judged it time to pass the Ring.

He had felt the need of her tonight, young as she was, because there was so much...

...that he hoped she would forgive him.

"To the best of my knowledge, Talizea," he murmured, leaning his head against the warm bark of the massive tree at his back, "you will be the next delm of Korval. As your immediate predecessor—your mother would say, as *half* of your immediate predecessor—I wish to abase myself, and to ask that you...make your best effort to forgive me for the rare hash I have made of matters. It is true that there are many years yet before the Ring will pass to you, but our estate—Korval's fortunes are already altered beyond recognition. I was born into a clan well-established on Liad, one of the wealthiest worlds in the galaxy, comfortably situated, and our *melant'i* impeccable, if...odd.

"Less than a Standard after taking up the Ring, I had fired upon the homeworld and seen Korval banished, our name written out of the Book of Clans."

He smiled slightly, looking down at his daughter, sweet still in slumber.

"I will not hide from you that it had been the desire of...several Korval delms—including your grandfather, whose acquaintance I hope you will make very soon—to remove the clan from Liad. That I accomplished what had long been the Will of Korval, that was done well. My methods, however...were...perhaps...inelegant."

Talizea yawned suddenly, raising her fists above her head, and subsided with a small chuckle.

"Yes, well. It relieves me that you are able to find humor in the situation. I was, myself, considerably amused—as was your mother, and your uncle Shan. I do not hide it from you, Talizea: our humor is not *quite* in the common way."

She made no further answer, and after a little silence, he continued.

"So—banishment, for crimes against the homeworld. We would at that juncture have been homeless, save for your cousin Pat Rin. He had been approached by agents of our enemy, the Department of the Interior, who had sworn that all his kin were dead. They wished to set him up as Korval, you see, and have him do as they bid.

"Well, you will say that they could not have thought the matter out, or they would have recalled what fate most usually befalls those who seek to leash a Dragon. I can do nothing but agree. I think, perhaps, that they forgot our shield—the Tree-and-Dragon—is...not a metaphor. Or perhaps they were complacent, believing that they dealt with the Least Dragon.

"However it came about, they made an error. Your Cousin Pat Rin dealt with the Department's messengers as they deserved, and—thinking himself quite alone, you know, and with all of our deaths upon him to Balance—well, there's no dressing it up in clean linen, is there? He subjugated an entire world to his purpose. It was very wrong of him—a violation of so many regulations I dare not count them—but we must make some allowance for his natural grief.

"In any case, he made this world—this *Surebleak*, as its native people have it—his base, and he hunted our enemy, the Department of the Interior, to Liad itself, where they kept themselves hidden beneath Solcintra City."

He sighed.

"Which is how Clan Korval came to fire upon the homeworld, taking blameless lives, in order to rout our enemy. I do not wish you to think that this was some accident or misunderstanding on our part. We were quite in earnest, and we accomplished our goal.

"One might say—indeed, our official position is—that we rid the homeworld of a threat to its well-being. The Council of Clans took another position."

Talizea made a small complaint. He picked her up and cradled her against him. She subsided with a sigh.

"Yes, you do well to ask more nearly about the Department of the Interior. Their destruction was necessary. I say this not only as your father and your delm, but as one who was pressed into the service of this Department: They are a blight upon every joy in the galaxy. Their methods of training are...reprehensible; they seek to make each of their operatives care only for the Department and its goals. They compel...terrible things. You are young; I will not say what they required of me. I feel—again, I beg your forgiveness!—but I feel that I will never tell out all of the things that I did, in their service."

His eyes were burning. He closed them, lest the tears fall onto Talizea and wake her.

"Well. To bring that particular history into the present day, our strike did not destroy the Department entirely—one could hardly hope for that. We had supposed that the blow we dealt was sufficiently severe to require the Department to retire from the lists. In that, we were in error. The Department continues, though much diminished, and now they have as their object Korval's utter destruction. Indeed, we hold...several agents in our care, which is perhaps—no, it is surely not wise. Best to put them beyond any further cruel usage. Yet...well. I fear your father is not always wise, and the delm thus far has been lenient with a fool."

He opened his eyes, and looked down at his daughter's small, unformed face.

"All of this, course, comes at a time when we are ourselves diminished; wrest from the homeworld to this Surebleak, which perhaps may have a use for Korval, but surely does *not* require interference from the Department of the Interior. It is my intention that Korval survive, and that Surebleak survives. And, most of all, that you survive, daughter, whether there will be a Ring to pass on to you."

Talizea opened her eyes, and smiled.

Heart tight, he smiled also, and turned his head toward the sound of a light footstep on the grass.

"*Cha'trez?*" he called softly.

"Right here," she said, stepping under Tree and dropping to her knees beside him in one smooth motion.

"Reading Lizzie the riot act?"

"Bringing her up to date on the current situation," he corrected. "After all, she is our heir."

"Can't start too young, I guess," his lifemate said, though her tone was dubious. Her hair was loose, falling in copper waves down past her waist.

"My father used to talk to me about the delm's business, when I was far too young to understand it," he said. Talizea had closed her eyes; he lowered her again to his lap. "Did my absence wake you?"

"Prolly just time to wake up," she said, and looked up as the leaves above them moved noisily, as if in a sudden breeze. She put her hand out, and two seed pods fell unerringly into her palm.

"Well, there," she said with a smile, holding a pod that he knew without a doubt to be *his*. "Have a snack."

CHAPTER ONE

. . . .

Jelaza Kazone
Surebleak

BREAKFAST WAS AN INFORMAL BUFFET LAID OUT IN THE MORN-
ing parlor, where early risers and late served themselves at their
leisure.

Val Con had breakfasted early, with Miri, and seen her into
the car, Nelirikk acting as driver, security and general aide, a
duty he ceded to no one, save occasionally to Miri's lifemate,
and that grudgingly.

After the car had cleared the drive, he retired to his office, it
being his day among Korval's paperwork and correspondence,
while Miri sat first board at the Road Boss's newly constructed
office at the port. He had worked with commendable diligence
for several hours, when a particularly annoying letter from Clan
Vishna's First Speaker opened him to the realization that a cup
of tea would be very pleasant.

The breakfast room was occupied when he entered; two ladies
sat at a small table by the window, speaking together in High
Liaden. The elder of the two ladies was a native speaker, and
sat in a position of tutor over the younger lady, who had made
strides in her command of the language since her arrival, some
local weeks ago.

High Liaden was scarcely the easiest of languages to master,
and, despite her strides, the younger lady found errors a-plenty
on which to lay her tongue. However, the elder lady's patience

7

remained unruffled. She mildly corrected those infelicities of mode produced by her companion—and, generally, Val Con thought, one ear on the conversation as he poured a cup of tea, the errors *were* of mode, rather than word choice. Not particularly surprising; Terran learners as a race tended to find High Liaden mode markers baffling, if not outright lunatic.

Teacup in hand, he plucked an apple from the bowl, and turned toward the door.

"Good morning, sir," the younger lady said, as he passed the little table, "I hope you have arisen into a joyous day."

Unlike some of her other utterances, the mode of the formal morning greeting to those not of one's clan was pitch-perfect. Val Con paused and inclined slightly from the waist in the small bow permitted between kin.

"Certainly, I hope for joyous things upon the day," he returned, speaking slowly and clearly in the Low Tongue. "However, we are kin; you need not stand so high as *sir* with me."

The lady—Kamele Waitley, in fact; his sister Theo's mother—frowned, her fair brows pulling together, an extravagant expression no native-born Liaden would ever allow upon her face.

"Are we," she asked, her mode wavering considerably, "kin?" A smile, every bit as immoderate as the frown, appeared. "Or should I say, *how* are we kin?"

"In the most straightforward manner possible!" he told her. "You are Theo's mother. Theo and I share a father. While it's true that Theo did not come to Korval at birth; yet she did not go to another clan. Liaden custom therefore allows us to be siblings. You and I trace our kinship through Theo."

His reasoning was a little rocky, given that, according to Liaden custom, a person of no clan was considered dead; and he saw the elder lady—Kareen yos'Phelium, his father's sister, and therefore Theo's biologic aunt—frown, a far more subtle expression on *her* face. For a moment, he thought she would protest, scholar of the Liaden Code of Proper Behavior that she was. But she let the matter slip past, merely inclining her head politely, and murmuring, "Nephew. I see that you are quite in spirits this morning."

He smiled at her, broad enough that Kamele Waitley would see and know him for a jokester.

"I am in the best of good spirits, Aunt; I thank you."

"I wonder," Kamele Waitley said, speaking more quickly than

the conversation warranted, "I wonder if you have heard from Theo."

"Nothing yet," he answered gently.

Theo's situation at last report had been...risky. They—he and his brother Shan, to whom Theo and her ship were formally under contract—had separately called her home. Regrettably, along with Korval's talent for piloting, Theo's patrimony had included a full measure of stubbornness. It was yet to be seen if she recognized any authority save her own, when her ship was in danger.

"We hope to hear from her soon," he told Kamele, which was still possible, if increasingly less probable. "Or, she may, you know, just ship in, and the first we know of it will be a call from the port, asking that a car be sent."

In reality, Korval would know the moment *Bechimo*—Theo's ship—entered Surebleak orbit, but there was no reason to trouble Kamele with that information.

"Indeed, my impression was that Theo is as impetuous a pilot as Korval has ever produced," Aunt Kareen put in. "It will be just as Val Con says—we will know that she has arrived when she does, and not one moment sooner."

Kamele smiled, wistfully, or so it seemed to Val Con, and murmured, "Impetuous."

"I fear so," he said, and bowed slightly, teacup in one hand, apple in the other. "If you will excuse me, I have an enormously irritating letter awaiting my attention."

"Please," Kamele said, with an earnestness utterly at odds with the mode, "do not let us keep you from your work."

Generous permission in hand, he left them.

Vishna's letter had not become less irritating during his break; not even the apple could sweeten it sufficiently to make it palatable.

In a word, Vishna wanted assurances.

Assurances that the trouble pursuing Korval would not touch Vishna. Assurances that continued alliance with Korval would not damage its other alliances upon Liad itself.

Vishna wished to be held without liability, should the alliance falter, and Korval to accept all risk in any venture they might undertake together.

"After all," Val Con muttered, "Korval brings nothing but risk to any venture."

Teacup in hand, he leaned back in his chair and closed his eyes, mentally reviewing the alliance with Vishna.

It was reasonably long-standing, having first been negotiated by his grandmother, Chi yos'Phelium, though it was certainly not among the longest, or the strongest, of Korval's alliances among the clans.

Indeed, his grandmother had negotiated this particular alliance—now, he recalled the entry in the Diaries!—in order to deny it to Clan...Ochrad, had it been? He would need to check the entry. It had been a chess move, the alliance with Vishna, and ought to have been reviewed some time since. Only, it had caused neither party any real effort to maintain it; Vishna saw a slight profit from the arrangement, and if Korval did not see a profit, certainly, it had seen no loss.

"Well," Val Con murmured. "That casts a far different shadow, does it not?"

He leaned to the keyboard and typed a request that Ms. dea'Gauss, Korval's *qe'andra*, review the arrangement with Vishna and their latest correspondence, and advise him as to the desirability of a continued association.

That done, he called up the Diaries, keyed in Vishna's name—

The comm chimed: not the House tone, but that assigned to Scout Administrative Commander ven'Rathan, she who held Korval's captives—Korval's *prisoners*—in what were thought to be escape-proof rooms, with Healers on-watch at every hour.

Commander ven'Rathan called but rarely, though she filed a terse written report every local week, the text of which scarcely varied, which was also the case with Korval's prisoners.

Something must have...changed.

Stomach tight, he opened the line.

"Good morning, Commander."

"Good morning, Commander," she answered, giving him the courtesy of his own Scout rank, and continued with scarcely a pause. "I have been asked to extend...an invitation to you."

Val Con frowned. An invitation? Could it be that the Department sought to negotiate for the freedom of its agents? *There* was a thought that exhilarated—but, no. Every one of the Department's operatives, from courier to Agent of Change, held it as a certainty, that the Department would not seek in any way to rescue them, should they fall into the grasp of the Department's enemies. It was, in the worldview produced by training, a matter of pride, that one was expendable, while the Department's great work continued.

"You intrigue me," he told Commander ven'Rathan.

"And now I will proceed to baffle you: Melsilee bar'Abit extends her compliments to former Agent of Change Val Con yos'Phelium, and wishes to ally herself with his purpose."

Melsilee bar'Abit was a Senior Field Agent: wily, resourceful, and utterly dedicated to the Department's work.

"It's a ruse, of course," Val Con said.

"So I thought, as well. Therefore, I brought forward not one, but two of our Healers, and had them scrutinize her. Both report that she is sincere in wishing to align herself with your purpose. Both report that her state of mind is serene and clear. One asked if she was sane, but neither Healer would commit to so much."

No, neither would. Training...left scars. Those who had broken training, of which there were, by his precise count, two, were forever changed. Those who had broken training and who had in some measure been Healed—of which there were again, those exact two—did not reclaim their former selves so much as they created a new self, somewhat reminiscent of the old.

And that line of thought...gave pause. Two *had* broken the Department's training—himself, and Rys Lin pen'Chala, who had also been a Senior Field Agent. Why, then, could there not be another? What prevented Melsilee bar'Abit from becoming the third to contest training, and prevail?

It was excitement now that burned in him, so brightly that he closed his eyes and mentally reviewed the calming and focusing exercise known as the Scout's Rainbow.

"Commander yos'Phelium?"

The Rainbow spun in a wheel of color behind his closed eyes. He breathed in, deliberately, and let the breath go in a sigh.

"Yes, forgive me. Please extend my compliments to Melsilee bar'Abit. Tell her that I will come to her there."

"She is serene and calm," the Healer murmured. "It may be that she is meditating. I find nothing of subterfuge, or violence. She is...at peace."

Val Con looked to Commander ven'Rathan. "I will go in alone, and speak with Agent bar'Abit. Healer, please monitor her. Commander..."

"The room will be filled with gas at the first hint of a mis-
step," she said flatly. "It is, being a gas, not able to distinguish
between friend and foe, so allow me to regret now the headache
that will greet you upon awakening. This is to be a first conversation only, with, as you have said, the Healer monitoring, and the
session recorded. If it is proven that she is sincere in her desire
to change alliance, we will craft a staged removal from the cell
to ... secured quarters."

Val Con bowed. "I concur."

"Will you allow me to set up a video meeting instead of this
face-to-face confrontation?"

They had discussed that approach when he had first arrived, and
he had insisted on the personal meeting. Still, if their roles were
reversed, he supposed he would argue for a conservative course,
as well. It was what was rational, and would give the Healer
nearly the same opportunity to deep read the agent. However ...

"Trust must begin somewhere. She has extended a hand. If I do
not meet it with goodwill, we may well lose something precious."

Scout Commander ven'Rathan sighed, but she stepped back,
signaling the guard to open the door.

Melsilee bar'Abit sat cross-legged on her cot in the small room.
She opened her eyes when the door snapped shut, and regarded
him without expression.

He bowed, briefly, as one of superior rank to one of lesser.

"I am Val Con yos'Phelium Clan Korval," he said. "You had
sent me a message."

She was a compact woman, her light brown hair wisping around
her head in soft curls. Her eyes were blue-grey, large, and set
slightly too close together.

"Why, yes, I did send you a message," she said, her voice as
wispy as her hair. "I asked you to come and talk with me."

"So you did," he said, gently.

He had spoken with Melsilee bar'Abit when she had first come
into Korval's care. She had been acerbic and savage, nearly a
complete turnabout from this uncertain demeanor. Which could,
so he thought, be an effect of having broken training. She had
accomplished what he and Rys had, but alone, with neither lifemate
nor brothers at hand to catch all of the pieces when everything
she had known, and been, broke apart.

She unwound from the cot, and stood in her stocking feet, prisoners being disallowed boots. Carefully, she bowed, as one acknowledging a debt.

"Thank you, for coming to me," she said. "I regret that I must ask—do you recall my message?"

He felt a frisson of disquiet, and made careful answer.

"Your message was that you wished to ally yourself with my purpose."

"Ah," she said softly, very nearly a sigh.

She bowed once more, deeply, hands expressing gratitude, admiration, and sincerity even as she lunged into a throat punch.

He dropped, leapt up, saw her spin, and blocked the second blow, recognizing the beginning of the sequence, as he spun away from the third, and launched an attack of his own, meaning to disable her even as she leapt to meet him, fully committed to the kill, and there was no choice—there was no *time!*

His body knew the answer, and provided it, firm and hard. The sound of her spine breaking was loud—and final.

He dropped to his knees beside her, his fingers going to the pulse point on her throat—but no; he was far too competent to have botched a kill so straightforward as the Fist of Malann.

The door opened while he was still kneeling, weeping over her body.

CHAPTER TWO

. . . .

Audrey's House of Joy
Blair Road
Surebleak

"THIS HALLWAY!" THE GENTLEMAN DECLARED. "THIS HALLWAY cries out for Queterian carpet!"

It was a handsome hallway, at the moment made more handsome by the rich, rare sunlight flowing in from the mid-hall window. The highly-polished plastic floor positively glowed under the suasions of the sun; the pale pink walls were as rosy as love's first blush.

The gentleman's companion, some Standard years past her first, and even her fifth, love, laughed fondly down at him, and shook her bright head.

"You think I didn't *look* at them catalogs you brought me?"

"Of course, you looked at them. Given your final order, I would go so far as to say that you had studied them thoroughly."

The gentleman smiled. The sunlight was less kind to him than to the floor and walls; it struck true silver from his hair and wantonly traced the fine lines about his eyes and mouth. The lady dyed her hair, so the sun got nothing but false gold there, and had its revenge among the lines of her face.

It was an interesting face, round-cheeked and pale; the shrewd eyes a pure blue, the chin truculent, and the mouth a little hard. The gentleman's eyes were kinder, and grey; his chin decided; his mouth firm and sweet. Together, they made a pleasant picture,

15

there in the sunlight: she the taller; he the slighter, obviously very much at their ease with each other.

"I studied them all right, back and forward, and back again. So, I'll take leave to tell you that I know how much Queterian carpet costs."

"But do you know," the gentleman mused, his eyes dreaming on the wide, gleaming hall, "how much it costs, wholesale?"

"Strange to say it, I do. And it's still outta range. Even if I hadn't just bought a whole house full of new carpet and furniture—which I have done, and you well know!"

"The upgrades to the house are good for business," the gentleman pointed out.

"Agreed! Queterian carpet, though—that's what we here on Surebleak call ice on top the snow. It's nice to dream on, but—"

"But you are in the business of dreams!" the gentleman said, tucking the lady's arm through his. They proceeded amiably down the hall toward the stairs.

She laughed. "Luken, I thought you knew what my business is!"

"I do," he said promptly. "You are in the business of comfort, and joy, and dreams. Ephemeral goods, and all the more precious for being so. Such things must be offered and received in an environment of beauty and grace. Thus, the new furniture, the new paint, the new rugs. Your house may now stand with any other house of delight on any port I have visited. Indeed, you already enjoy custom from Surebleak Port—from persons of wide experience."

"That's so; we had to upgrade for those folks, but here's the thing we can't lose sight of: the local folks—those fancy dreams and comforts you'll have me selling—the local folk *need* those things, maybe more'n the port custom. I gotta be careful not to price myself outta their paychecks."

"You must, of course, continue to care for your core clients, but there may be..."

They had reached the head of the stairs, and he paused, bringing her to rest beside him. He gestured, as if strewing flower petals across the treads, inviting her to enjoy the modest and graceful descent to the floor below.

"This, too," he murmured, "in Queterian."

She sighed, for a moment seeing it in her mind's eye, the distinctive pattern of browns, oranges, and reds swirling down her staircase, like a dance of autumn...

With a half-gasp, she shook her head, stepping away from the pretty illusion.

"We're a couple of dreamers, right here," she said. "What we need is breakfast to hold us down to ground."

"Doubtless, you are correct," Luken said, beginning his descent, his free hand lightly gripping the rail. "You are a wise woman, Audrey."

She laughed, and hugged the gentleman's arm.

"Now, there's a thing that's rarely said! I'll tell you what, Mr. bel'Tarda; I think you're a flirt."

"Nonsense, I'm an honest businessman," he said, and smiled when she laughed again.

As the house told time, it was early; Audrey and Luken had the breakfast room to themselves. They chose from the breads and fruit, cereals and juices on the sideboard, and settled companionably into what had become their preferred table in the back corner.

Audrey sighed as she settled into her chair, and sent a considering glance around the pleasant room.

"Is there some trouble?" Luken asked, and she almost sighed again. Such a sweet man; he couldn't be any more attentive to her if she was paying him. The fact that she *wasn't* paying him had the power to surprise her, as did the notion that she held of him, as a *friend*.

But, there, she'd left the man without his answer, and she'd already seen what he was capable of, when he decided something needed to be fixed.

So, she smiled at him, and shook her head. "No trouble. More like I haven't had enough breakfast to weigh me down to ground, yet." She broke a roll onto her plate, and reached for the jam pot.

"What were you dreaming, then?" he asked, spoon arrested over his cereal bowl, his gaze on her face.

"A window," she said promptly, and waved her hand toward the far wall. "No sense to it, really, the room being where it is, but it just came to me, seeing the sun in the hall upstairs, that we got so used to the possibility of a shoot-out in the streets that we built without windows mostly, and, for extra protection, made all the gathering rooms interiors."

Luken smiled at her. "You were wishing for a window onto the street?"

"That's it," she said, well pleased with him. "A fancy, you'd call it, and not anything like trouble."

He looked about the room, as if weighing its merits, and returned his attention to her. "I think you are very right to think that a window would improve the appeal of an already pleasant room. Why not indulge your fancy?"

He meant it for a tease, maybe, and not a serious question at all, but it caught her that way, so that she took her time spooning jam onto another piece of bread, frowning as she felt along her thoughts and memories.

"I've been on Surebleak all my life, here on Blair Road 'most all it," she said, slowly, keeping her eyes on her spoon. "I've seen Bosses come, and I've seen Bosses go, and—fond as I am of our current Boss—this *boy* Pat Rin of yours!—and as much as he's done already here... I can't quite shake the feeling that... this is another one of those dreams I been having lately, and I'll wake up one morning to find out..."

Words failed her—*and a good thing, too!* she scolded herself. *What kind of talk is that for a man at his breakfast?*

"You fear that you will wake up one morning to find that my boy has failed," Luken said, merely matter-of-fact. She looked up and met his eyes. He inclined his head, seriously.

"We must all fear the same thing; and those of us who esteem and support my boy must fear it most of all. And yet, I think, Audrey, that you may have overlooked an important difference between our Boss Conrad and those other Bosses you have known."

She eyed him. "What's that?"

"Pat Rin is not working alone; he is not merely working with one or two other like-minded Bosses. He has brought all of the allied Bosses of Surebleak to his side, and committed them to his projects. In addition, he has the whole of Clan Korval—what is called here the Road Boss's family—at his back. Even in its present circumstances, Korval is formidable... and will grow more so, as we settle in to our new home and customs, and the delm mends our alliances." He paused, as if struck by some other thought or consideration, then moved his shoulders in that fluid not-shrug that meant *some*thing, Audrey thought, though sleet knew what.

"Setting aside even his allies and his kin, Pat Rin has done something... extraordinary. Something that no other past Boss even attempted. He has opened the port and made Surebleak an acceptable destination, an up-and-coming planet where trade is growing. He has brought *the galaxy* to Surebleak, and while Surebleak may change because of it, it will not, I think, return to those days that you recall."

Luken leaned forward and touched her hand lightly.

"You must of course please yourself, in the matter of the window."

She gasped a laugh.

"We'll just put it on the back burner for right now," she said, and they returned to their breakfasts in companionable silence.

What thoughts occupied Luken were for him to know; Audrey, however, continued along the lines he had set down for her.

True enough that Boss Conrad, who had apparently been born to the name Pat Rin yos'Phelium Clan Korval, on the high-rent planet of Liad—true enough that the Boss had let the galaxy know Surebleak existed; and the galaxy had seen opportunity.

There were a lot of folks coming on-world, through that new-opened, and expanding port. Surebleak being by population a Terran world, it was maybe a little odd that most of the new immigrants were Liaden, riding in on the Road Boss's coattails. Oh, there were Terrans coming in, too, but not in near the same numbers.

The incoming Liadens, they brought their own culture with them, naturally enough, and it wasn't anything near Surebleak culture. Still, it wasn't as much of a mess as it could be—not yet, anyway—because most of them who had followed the Road Boss were a subset of Liaden called Scouts, a corps of galactic explorers and general busybodies, as Audrey caught the signal, who specialized in studying, and getting along in, other cultures.

Things were really going to get stirred up, Audrey thought, when more of the regular folks looking for a better place to be came in. They'd expect that all civilized people acted the same, and that's where things would start to rub. There'd already been some of that, but the Scout-to-regular-citizen ratio had so far kept upset to a minimum.

Well. That wouldn't be for a few years, yet. In the meantime, the Scouts were teaching classes. She'd signed up for one, herself—Introduction to Liaden Culture. It didn't look like anybody was offering an Introduction to Surebleak Culture...yet. She figured she could teach one herself, if it went too far along without anybody more qualified than the proprietor of a whorehouse stepping up. Though she had a notion that she'd draw Scouts; and that Scouts would know exactly what questions to ask—and get way more out of the answers than the so-called teacher would ever know.

Still, she told herself again; they had time. Trade might be growing on Surebleak, but they were still on the various lists that mattered to those who traded planet to planet as a *world in transition*, and an *emerging market*.

She reached for her juice glass, and glanced up at her companion, surprising a pensive look on his face. There were a couple things that she knew about which could bring that expression to him, and she picked her target not quite at random.

"I'm behind on asking," she said softly, so as not to jar him from whatever he was thinking, "if there's been any news from your daughter."

"Nothing, no," he said, his expression smoothing. "But, you know, it is a delicate business and a delicate time. She doubtless has much on her mind."

Audrey wasn't clear on the precise nature of the delicate business that Luken's daughter Danise was engaged on, with the support of her younger sister, but she did know that the circumstance of Clan Korval getting kicked off Liad wasn't making her work any easier. That was, Audrey thought, the trouble with families: one branch goes off and does something like blow a hole in the homeworld and it wasn't enough that *they* got thrown off-world, like the Road Boss'd been. Nope, the whole family got trouble splattered all over them, too, though they'd been miles away from the explosion.

"In any case, it is a matter in which she and her sister are much more invested than I. Whatever the outcome, I will remain on Surebleak." His smile this time was whimsical. "It's so *very interesting* here."

Audrey laughed. "You could say so, though other words come to mind."

"A place may be many things, as an individual may hold many *melant'is*," Luken said, placidly.

Melant'i, that was one of the things that Liadens had brought with them—it was like honor, only a lot more complicated. People died of *melant'i*. She was hoping her Liaden culture class would cover it. In depth.

"Would you like some more juice?" he asked, rising.

"Thank you." She handed him her glass, and stacked their used dishes to one side while he made the trip across the room and back.

When he was settled back into his chair and they had both had a sip from their glasses, Luken leaned back.

"Audrey, I wonder if you might agree to Queterian carpet in the upper hall, and the center stairway."

She frowned at him.

"Didn't we decide I can't afford that?"

"We decided that it was dear, at retail and at wholesale. However, I believe I may unite house and carpet at well under wholesale."

"Mind if I ask how that's going to be accomplished?"

"I would be disappointed if you didn't ask," he assured her. "Here is the case. You are aware that I am a rug merchant?"

"You might've mentioned it once or twice."

He smiled. "Well, perhaps I have. In any case, I have recently received news of my stock, which has been recovered from safe storage and will soon be with me here. Among the recovered stock is a quantity of Queterian carpet, which I have held for a certain member of the Liaden Council, for the last six Standards."

Audrey started to ask what that had to do with her, but managed to keep the question on the back of her tongue. *Give the man a chance to tell it, Audrey.*

"Every *relumma*, this particular individual would make a payment to me, in order that I not sell the carpet to anyone else. Half of the option payments went toward purchasing the carpet; half went to warehousing and inventory costs. At the time that this individual cast his vote in Council to banish Korval from Liad, he had purchased two thirds of the carpet. The cost of one third of the carpet may, I believe, be well within the means of your house. I am willing to wait upon payment, or to work out a schedule that will not overtax your treasury."

She saw it again, the stairs dressed in elegant autumn carpeting—and blinked her way back to sense.

"Why?" she asked. "Why not just sell it to somebody else at full price? Or—here's an idea both of us should've thought about—why not put it down in your new digs? I'm gathering you're telling me that the original arrangement fell through and you got to keep the rug and your money?"

"I am telling you that, yes." He extended a hand and put it over hers where it lay on the table. His palm was cool and smooth.

"As to why here and not elsewhere...Let us say that I would find it particularly satisfying if the carpet intended to grace the formal gathering room of one of Liad's fifty High Houses should instead ornament a house involved in the business of joy."

She thought about that.

"It's revenge, then?"

"It is Balance," Luken corrected. "I grant that it is my Balance and not yours, but I hope that you will be able to indulge me."

She wanted that carpet so bad she could taste it, and yet... Balance. Balance was damn near as dangerous as *melant'i*.

"Let me sleep on it," she said.

Luken gave her a pretty little seated bow. "Of course. There is no need to make a hasty decision."

CHAPTER THREE

Surebleak Port

"I AIN'T DRUNK AN' I AIN'T GOIN' NOPLACE WITH YOUSE!"

The first assertion was untrue; Hazenthull could smell the drink on the woman's breath. Her stance was commendably steady; her hands were curled into fists, and Hazenthull could see the scars of past encounters across her knuckles.

So, this was one of those who drank to release their inner belligerence, then sought the joy of battle. Tolly had explained this to her during their first shifts together. She had doubted him, but she had by now seen enough of these sorts during her shifts on Port Security to understand that Tolly, as usual, had spoken with accuracy.

Had she been walking her shift alone this afternoon, she would have merely knocked the woman across the head, thrown her over a shoulder and taken her to the Whosegow to be booked and fined.

But, she was not on-shift alone. Tolly was with her and Tolly's preference was not to go to the "trouble" of lugging unconscious drunks halfway across port. Tolly's preference was to find one of the belligerent's troop and convince them to take her in charge.

So it was that Hazenthull watched in resignation as Tolly walked toward the inebriated woman, hands upraised, truncheon swinging from his belt, gun holstered and peace-bonded.

"I ain't drunk!" The woman snarled again, and raised her fists.

"Sure you ain't," Tolly said easily. "Just a little under the weather, like they say here."

"I ain't sick, neither!" She lunged, Tolly stepped aside, Hazenthull watched. The combatant kept her feet, and came back around to challenge Tolly again.

"You scrawny runt! Call me sick, will you? C'mere and I'll show you who's sick!"

Hazenthull understood very well the place of the ritual insult in battle, and in disputes between troop. In her opinion, the belligerent woman lacked style, as well as sense. Tolly would not be drawn by such weak stuff.

"Hey, hey, nobody's calling anybody sick," he soothed, showing the palms of his empty hands. "Just something the locals say, that's all. Means tired; the weather's pretty heavy hereabouts. Nothing the matter with being tired. Happens to all of us. So, what I wanna know—you gotta crew mate around somewhere, somebody to make sure you get into your bunk?"

"Think I need a keeper? Think I ain't capable?" The woman lunged again, unexpectedly on target. Hazenthull's hand twitched, but Tolly ducked under the driving fist, and came up behind the woman's right shoulder.

Hazenthull sighed. He could have easily grabbed the wrist as the fist went by him, thrown the woman, and ended the matter. This preference of his was time-consuming, as well as risky. Sometimes, she wondered if it was the risk that drew him, for Tolly, when he could be persuaded to it, was a focused and effective fighter.

The drunk threw another punch, far wide. Hazenthull had no concern for Tolly's safety, unless he slipped in a puddle of beer and the woman fell on him. She let her eyes wander. The noise had attracted attention—it always did. That was part of Tolly's method. It was likely that one of those attracted would be of the troublemaker's troop, and compelled by honor to prevent her disgrace.

And, there! A grizzled man wearing a stained and unfastened jacket had twitched toward the action, as if he would interrupt— then settled flat on his feet, and shoved his hands into the pockets of the jacket.

So, he was not fond of the belligerent woman, and he thought he'd let Tolly teach her a lesson, Hazenthull thought, as the woman lunged, and Tolly dealt her the lightest of taps on the head as she staggered past him. The man tensed, but did not take his hands out of his pockets.

Obviously, he needed a reminder of the duty owed a comrade.

The woman was showing Hazenthull her back; she had adopted a wide-legged stance, as if she was now ready to stop toying with Tolly, and deliver genuine damage.

Perfect.

Hazenthull's hand dropped unerringly to the truncheon on her belt. She had it off its hook, and stepped forward, arm swinging high, her attention on the back of the woman's head...

"Stop!" came a hoarse cry, and the man in the dirty jacket ran heavily forward, ducking under the arrested truncheon, and grabbing the woman's arm.

"Stop it, Hannit! You wanna go down for hitting a Peaceman? You know the cap'n said she wasn't goin' to stand no more fines! You're into t'ship so deep already 's'wonder you had any drinkin' money!"

"Jerry?" The drunk turned to peer into his face. "T'ell you doin'?" She jerked her arm as if to break away.

The man not only kept his grip, he shook her by the arm he held.

"Stand down, you damnfool! 'Pologize to the Peaceman now, an'..."

"No apology necessary," Tolly said quickly. "Just doing my job, that's all. You'll be taking her in hand now? See she gets safe back to her ship?"

Jerry looked like he wanted nothing less, but he nodded, jerkily. "I'll do it, small thanks I'll have."

"But you have my thanks," Tolly told him cheerfully, "and the thanks of my partner, who didn't really want to strike a defenseless civilian. Did you, Haz?"

Hazenthull had no objection at all to striking a fool, but Tolly had coached her on this. He said that Port Security needed *good PR* to make their jobs easier.

So, then...

"Of course not," she said, hanging the truncheon back on her belt. The drunk woman had turned to stare, eyes wide. Hazenthull gave her a grin, showing teeth. The woman paled slightly.

"Okay, Jerry, sure," she said. "Time I get back, I guess."

Jerry gave another one of his jerky nods, to Hazenthull.

"Sorry for the trouble," he muttered, then he moved, hauling his comrade by her arm and stamping off through the crowd, which gave way before him.

"Okay!" Tolly clapped his hands, spinning around on a heel. "Okay! Show's over! Everybody! As you were!"

Slowly, they dispersed. When they had done so, Tolly caught her eye, and jerked his head toward the door. She nodded and they walked away together.

"Why do you?" she asked, as soon as they were outside. The day was bright, for a change, and blisteringly cold. Hazenthull fished her gloves out of her pockets and pulled them on.

"What else should I have done?" Tolly asked, which he always did.

"Take her to the Whosegow—"

"Escort a drunk across port, book her, and fill out the forms."

"That is standard procedure, as given in—"

"As given in the book, yeah, I know. But, see, Haz, one of my rules is: *never fill out forms.*"

"Why?"

"Good question. Because forms give information. Where were we, when were we, what are our names, our badge numbers? All that, on the forms, and our friend there would've gotten a copy when she paid her fine. I'm not real keen on somebody who gets drunk and likes to fight having my name and badge number. What if she wakes up tomorrow thinking that the only way to save honor is to track us down and kill us?"

"That one had no honor."

"If you say so. Thing is, this way—she knows our faces; she knows we're Port Security. If she comes in tomorrow with a complaint, as drunk as she was? She wouldn't be able to pick me out of a lineup."

"She would, me."

"Yeah, that's true. Maybe I should partner with somebody less obvious."

This was Tolly's humor, Hazenthull had learned. She was meant to laugh and forget. But, she had another question. A serious question.

"Why do you not?"

He grinned up at her, blue eyes glinting.

"'Cause I like you, Haz. We make a good team. Were you really going to cane that drunk?"

"I was getting bored," she said, which was *her* humor.

Tolly laughed.

"Next time, I'll make it march," he said. "C'mon, let's take a walk through the Emerald; get out of this wind."

The Emerald Casino had its own security. There was no reason for Port Security to perform a walk-through or any other check, there.

Tolly liked the place, though, and every shift made sure that they walked through at least once. More often than less, he would meet someone he had known from a previous duty cycle or on another world, and they would exchange some words, or a bow. Early in what Port Security insisted was their *partnership*, of an evening when they had met no less than eight of Tolly's acquaintance on their casino walk-through, she had demanded to know if he had held duty down the length and breadth of the galaxy.

"Near enough," had been his answer. "I started young, see."

"I, too, started young," Hazenthull had replied, pleased to find this similarity between them, and thinking of the tests that had brought her out of the creche for extended training, in addition to basic weapons work. When at last she had achieved it, her rank had been Explorer, which had as its counterpart among Liadens, Scout. She had never heard that there were Terran Scouts, but she had lately learned that the troop had not known everything there was to know.

"What was your rank?" she'd asked Tolly, this notion of Terran Scouts in her mind.

He'd given her a smile, blue eyes flashing in what she had already known was mischief.

"Specialist."

Explorers and Scouts were Generalists—they knew a little about a vast number of things. Specialists knew a very great deal about a very narrow field. They were important to the troop, and especially to Explorers. She had herself consulted numerous Specialists in the pursuit of her duty, but found that they were uninterested in anything beyond their narrow vision. They were not, perhaps, quite as stupid as Common Troop, but there could be no real camaraderie, as between Explorers.

Or as between Scouts and Explorers.

Despite his rank, Tolly continued to act more like a Generalist than a Specialist, and Hazenthull had at last come to terms with

the discrepancy by deciding in her own mind that Command
had required a Specialist and Tolly had tested weaker than the
rest of his cohort in Generalist tendencies.

"Afternoon, folks," Herb, the midday bartender, waved them
over to the bar. He often did so, to offer hot coffee and tea,
"for their trouble," as if this pleasure of Tolly's was of service
to anyone save himself.

"Good afternoon, Herb," Hazenthull said, looking down at
him from her height. Herb, a sturdy Terran male, was broader
than Tolly, but much of a height. She, a former Yxtrang Explorer,
female and undergrown, still overtopped both.

Tolly smiled, but she refrained, having noticed that, while Tolly's
smiles calmed, hers unnerved. She didn't wish to unnerve Herb;
she liked Herb, and respected his abilities with the blackjack he
kept under the bar. He was not a soldier, but he knew his weapon
and used it effectively.

"Afternoon, keeper," Tolly said, speaking the Surebleak dialect,
which Herb did. "Every little thing going fine?"

"I got no complaints. Wanted to let you know though, there's
a fella askin' after a Tolly Jones. If that's you, you'll find him at
dice."

"He got a description, this fella?"

Herb shrugged. "Liaden."

Tolly laughed. "That narrows it down."

The barkeeper grinned. "Yeah, don't it? Redhead, ain't missed
any meals lately, got a glitter-bit in his left ear; limps a little off
the right leg." He paused, considering. "No leather."

Leather on a Liaden meant Jump pilot, or Scout. Or both.
Usually. There were those who were unwise enough to wear
leather they had not earned. Port Security was sometimes called
to officiate at the disputes between those false troops, and the
pilots or Scouts they had insulted.

But Tolly—Tolly had gone still; and his face had lost what she
had considered, when they first were teamed, the smile of an idiot.

She felt a prickle of energy between her shoulder blades. It had
been . . . a long time since she had seen serious action. Though she
enjoyed her sparring matches with Nelirikk Explorer and Diglon
Rifle, there was a satisfying savor to facing a real opponent on
the field that was absent from pleasant practice sessions with
comrades.

"Well, he don't sound like anybody I know, nor anybody I got a hankerin' t'meet," Tolly said, smile back, and lean muscles loose. "Might be we'll just go out the way we come in. That okay by you, Haz? If Herb'll forget he saw me?"

"No trouble there. Worst memory on port. Known for not being able to remember my own name, hardly."

"I have no objection to leaving," Hazenthull said, disappointment replacing the pleasant anticipation of battle.

"Great, then let's do that. Thanks, Herb."

She held her tongue until they were outside, heading for the Surebleak Bazaar. "I will be pleased to stand at your back, when you meet your enemy."

Tolly looked up at her, frowning briefly before the smile flashed back into being.

"Now, that's real nice of you, Haz. But I don't know that guy."

"You knew him," she said, with certainty. "You froze like a soldier taking cover from a drone."

He gave her another look, neither frowning nor smiling.

"It's not a good thing, to lie to your partner," he said slowly. "Especially when she's smarter'n you." He sighed. "Sorry, Haz; you're right. I knew him. He used to have the ordering of me, but he doesn't now, which is a fact he finds harder to accept than I do. It's not a dueling matter." A pause, then, "That's what you thought I was going to do? Set up a duel?"

"Or an ambush," Hazenthull said. "I did not know in what way he had earned your displeasure."

"Oh, about a thousand ways," Tolly said, in the light tone that meant he considered the topic closed. "But maybe none of 'em were killing offenses. Look fierce, now."

They went in by the Bazaar's public door, showed their badges to the scanner, and entered.

Though it, too, staffed its own security, the Bazaar and Port Security thought it wise that there be multiple patrollings up and down the busy aisles.

"The more cops they see, the less trouble there'll be," said Port Security Chief Lizardi. It was a theory not entirely supported by fact, but Hazenthull had learned long ago not to quibble with Command.

And, she enjoyed the Bazaar, with its distinctive aroma that was the roiling together of many diverse aromas, and its bright displays of foodstuffs, and carpets, and metalworks, juices, and wines. It was said that the planet Surebleak had nothing to offer anyone who did not live on Surebleak, but that was plainly not so. There were things here that the troop would pillage for; that soldiers would duel to possess.

The aisles were crowded this morning; though way was made for herself and Tolly, and they completed a circuit in good time and order.

It was then that they entered the second area: a common room, where those who had purchased samples of local food and drink might consume them, and where others might sit down and work out arrangements of sale, or where still others might rest quietly for a moment.

The common room was considerably less crowded than the Bazaar floor. Hazenthull went to the left, Tolly to the right, marching in truth, making a show of detailed scrutiny of each occupant.

"Yxtrang!" The scream was as raw as a war cry, and she reacted to it as she would have done, had she been on the field of honor.

She spun, knees flexed, sidearm in her hand, scanning the crowd—it was all instinct and reaction; her body completed the moves before her brain recalled that *she* was no longer Yxtrang, *she* was a member of the yos'Phelium House Guard, serving under Captain Miri Robertson and Scout Commander Val Con yos'Phelium.

She had him in her eye now—a man past the prime of his life, with lank grey hair, dressed in an insulated orange coat.

"Yxtrang!" He yelled again. "Killer!"

Carefully, she straightened to her full height, and slid her gun into its holster.

"I am not an Yxtrang," she said, trying for Tolly's tone of calm reason. "I am attached to the household of the Road Boss, and I am employed as Security by Surebleak Port."

"Road Boss ain't nothing but a killer hisself!" the man in orange coat jeered. "Allya oughta be shot for war crimes, or run off-planet. Start with you, since you're here. Hey! Yxtrang on port! Who's gonna help me, here?"

"I'll help you, friend," said a calm voice. The sound of a safety being released was very loud in the quiet area.

The man in the orange coat froze; Hazenthull saw the whites of his eyes.

Tolly moved, gun pointed at the man's chest.

"What you want to do is put your hands on top of your head, slow and easy, or else I might think you were going for a weapon and I'd have to shoot you. That's my first bit of help."

"Yeah, okay, I get it," the man in the orange coat said with a grin. "Joke's gone too far. I'll be gettin' on."

"No," Tolly said, his voice hard, and sounding so un-Tollylike that Hazenthull turned her head to stare at him. "You'll put your hands on your head and you'll stand there while my partner searches you. If you don't do that, I'll consider you a high-level threat and I will shoot you. Got that?"

The man stared, then, slowly, put his hands on his head. He was, Hazenthull saw, starting to sweat.

"Haz, you wanna search this guy?"

She moved forward, staying out of Tolly's line of fire, and divested the prisoner of the weapon on his belt, and the folding knife in the pocket of his pants. Neither weapon was of professional grade, or even particularly clean. She patted him down, not gently, ignoring his, "Hey, watch it there; I need that!" and stepped back.

"He is clean," she told Tolly.

He nodded. "Cuff him."

She shot a glance at him, saw his tiny nod, and stepped forward again to cuff the man's wrists behind his back.

"Hey, gimme a break! It was a joke, all right?"

"In fact, it's not all right to try to call a lynch mob down on a Port Security officer during her rounds. It's not all right to assert that a Port Security officer in pursuit of her duty is a *killer*."

"Well, fine me, then! Ain't nothin' here for cuffs! Just playin' a joke, like I said. Friend—" He stopped, and Tolly tipped his head slightly.

"Friend?" he prompted.

"Nothin'. Slip o'the tongue. C'mon, Security, get these things off me. I'll pay the fine."

"Not my call," Tolly said. "You can tell it to the Port Security Chief. You might find it interesting to find out how she feels about random port scrum calling down mayhem on one of her officers as a joke." He moved the gun, very slightly.

"Let's go, Haz."

"Yes," she said, and nudged the prisoner. "Walk."

CHAPTER FOUR

. . . .

Jelaza Kazone
Surebleak

"SHE *THANKED ME*."

It was the first thing he'd said in over an hour, after a terse report of what had happened with Melsilee bar'Abit. He'd shut down after that. The pattern of him, that she could see in her head, gone dark and...off-center in a way she could see and feel, without being able to quantify.

Not for the first time, she wished that the lifemate link was stronger on the details, and less...definite on the emotions. If there'd been anything useful to the punch in the gut she had gotten out of nowhere this afternoon—about the time, so she knew *now*, that he'd been ambushed—she couldn't figure what it was.

Knowing that he was upset—horrified, she guessed covered it—wasn't necessarily a bad thing, though she could probably have figured that out for herself, after hearing him tell it.

What would be *really useful*, though, was if she had any clue about what was going on inside that twisty mind of his, while he sat silent, face averted, in the corner of the couch.

Still, she figured it was a win, that he stayed with her, instead of vanishing into the music room, or the garden—or, worse, down into town—even if he wasn't talking.

And now he was talking again—and it was new information, which meant he'd been sitting there turning the situation over and over in his head, sifting through the details *again*—but that's what he'd been trained to do, in every part of his life: as a First-In Scout, as the delm's heir, and, yeah, as an Agent of Change. Details killed. Details saved. A smart man—and let there be no doubt about who wasn't the dummy in the room—a smart man ignored the details at his very great peril.

So.

"She thanked you?" she repeated, soft-voiced.

He turned his head to look at her straight for the first time in more than an hour.

"When I first entered her cell, she rose, and bowed in acknowledgment of a debt, and she thanked me, for coming to her."

Miri blinked—and blinked again as she suddenly got what he was telling her. "So she knew you were going to kill her?"

"Her whole intention was that I kill her. She planned the entire thing, meticulously."

"How'd she hide it from the Healers?"

"That is where we see brilliance."

She saw tears start to his eyes; he drew a hard breath and looked away. When he met her eyes again, his were dry.

"Melsilee bar'Abit began to meditate; the Healers report this. Very likely, she was meditating in order to reaffirm her purpose as the Department's tool. Possibly the discovery of the protocol by which the Department imbeds the phrase that may be used to control . . . recalcitrant agents—possibly that was an accident. I am not, you understand, inclined to accept *accident* or *happenstance* with regard to anything touching the Department's training."

"So she could've gone looking for it."

"Indeed. We cannot know if that was the case, and for the purpose of the final sum, it does not matter. She located the protocol, and she used it to embed a control phrase."

Miri nodded. An Agent of Change had tried to use a control phrase to bring Val Con back under the Department's influence, way back on Vandar. Would've worked, too, except Val Con had done some meditating of his own and replaced the Department's code with his own.

"Once she had the control phrase in place, she used her meditations to hide what she had done from her waking mind. That procedure produced a trance state, which the Healers saw as tranquility, and calm.

"When all was firm, she sent a message to me, with the control phrase embedded. She asked, after she had thanked me, if I would remind her why she had wished to see me. Whereupon, I gave her the phrase that released her to action."

He closed his eyes again. "I am a fool."

"No, you ain't. She was a smart woman, and she didn't have nothing to do all day every day except sit and think how was she going to get out of this mess she was in. You'd've done the same."

He looked at her, face bleak.

"I would have intended to escape. Her whole intention was to die. She knew my level; she knew that she could not prevail in a confrontation between us. It was necessary to her purpose that I not withdraw before the telling blow had been struck. She therefore needed to guide my responses, which she did, until there was only one choice possible. The Fist of Malann..." He took a hard breath.

"It was well chosen."

Silence fell again, though he seemed less...askew; more centered.

That was a good thing. Good enough that she decided to push a tiny bit toward normal.

"You want a glass of wine?"

He smiled slightly.

"A glass of wine would be pleasant. Shall we sit out?"

"Why not? After all, it's summer."

• • • ❀ • • •

"A joke's all it was, Chief. Guy gives me twenty cash, says to rib the big port cop. Call 'er Yxtrang, he says, that always gets 'er laughing. She'll know where it come from, that's what he said. Ain't my fault her partner's got no sense o'humor. You don't arrest a man for having a joke."

Port Security Chief Liz Lizardi considered the man in the orange coat as one might consider an insect found in a half-eaten ration bar.

"I might not arrest a man for having a joke. But I do—and I require my security officers to—arrest people who are inciting to riot and disturbing the peace of this port."

"Riot! I wasn't no such—"

"Shut up," Commander Lizardi told him.

He did so, his red face getting redder.

"The actions of my security officers aren't in question. They saw a clear threat to the peace and security of the Bazaar and they acted to contain it. That's their job, and they did just fine. You, on the other hand—you're ass-deep in slush, friend. What was the name of this fella with the sense of humor?"

He shrugged, and jerked his head at Hazenthull, where she stood at guard by his side, directly before the commander's desk.

"Ask her; she's the one s'posed to know all about it."

Commander Lizardi glanced at her. "Security Officer? You know who this guy's talking about?"

"Commander, I do not," she stated.

"Nobody you got a standing joke with, about you being an Yxtrang?"

Hazenthull shook her head and stated, "No, Commander."

She hesitated, considering troop wisdom with regard to volunteering, and decided that additional information would be helpful to this case. "I am not known for my sense of humor, Commander."

She heard a small sound from the other side of the prisoner, as if Tolly had sneezed. Commander Lizardi pressed her lips together firmly, and nodded.

"Thank you, Officer," she said gravely.

"I believe my officer," she said. "She served under my command in action, and I know her to be a truthful and stalwart soldier. You, though"—she glanced down at her screen—"you got quite a record on port, Mr. Kipler. Petty thievin', havin' a few too many beers and busting stuff up, decking security at the Emerald. Spent the night in the Whosegow for that one, I see, *and* paid the fine."

The prisoner laughed suddenly.

"Is that what this is about? You want your piece? Why'n't you just say so? The cash is in my left inside pocket. You can gimme change."

The commander sighed and shook her head.

"You're not getting it, Kipler. I've got you on conspiracy to start a riot in the Bazaar. That goes right up to the Bosses, on account the Bazaar's counted as Surebleak turf, not port turf. Conspiracy to riot is something the Bosses take real serious, and unless you come up with the name of that free-spending fella, you're gonna take whatever they dish out all on yourself." She paused, head to one side, as if considering.

"Seems a lot to take on, for twenty cash."

The prisoner's shoulders tensed as he tried his strength against the cuffs, but they held firm.

"I *dunno* who it was," he said, voice urgent. "Some guy, is all. Twenty cash for doin' nothing much—you don't turn that down, now, do you?"

"But it turns out not to be nothing much," the commander pointed out. "Was he Liaden?"

"Nah, no! Sleet! What do I gotta do with Liadens? Guy was as local as me."

"Now, there's something useful already. If you cooperate with the Bosses, they might let you off light. Officer Jones?"

"Commander Liz?"

"Will you and your partner please escort Mr. Kipler to the Whosegow and see him signed in. Tell the watch officer that he's in custody of the Council of Bosses."

"Yes ma'am," Tolly said. "Okay, Mr. Kipler, let's go. Turn around."

The man in the orange coat hesitated, as if he would argue—or as if he had thought of something else useful to tell the commander. He turned at last, however, shoulders slumping.

Hazenthull fell in behind, with Tolly ahead and slightly to the left, the prisoner between. And so they left the commander's office in good order.

· · · ❋ · · ·

They were on the balcony. Neither had felt like moving chairs out, so they were sitting on the floor, companionably hip to hip, legs dangling over the inner garden, enjoying a soft breeze that was considerably warmer than the summer air outside the walls. Val Con's theory was that the Tree was influencing the garden temperature, as for years it had influenced its ecosystem. The tree, in Miri's private opinion, was way too fond of meddling with stuff that ought to be outside of a tree's natural concerns.

"Commander ven'Rathan counsels us to end the prisoners' suffering," Val Con murmured.

That meant, Miri translated, that Commander ven'Rathan had come down on the side of killing the six remaining prisoners. She had a point; they were dangerous; they were expensive; and their training gave them protection against much that Healers did. Anthora and Natesa had managed to break loose a name or two, and a couple of locations, but that was the extent of the information they'd been able to harvest.

Though, as far as Val Con was concerned, it wasn't about the information that could be gotten from the agents.

It was about the agents, themselves.

"What do the Healers think?" she asked.

"They think that the prisoners cannot be restored to their former...selves. They think—because they have seen it happen—that any attempt to forcefully remove training...kills the agent. Horribly."

He sighed, and raised his glass for a sip of wine.

Eventually, he spoke again, his voice expressionless, the way it was when he cared too much about something.

"The Healers, in a word, believe that continuing to hold the prisoners under such conditions, knowing that they can never be cured, is a cruelty. Master Healer Mithin herself sends to me that she will undertake the...necessary releases. She waits upon the Delm's Word."

Miri had been a soldier. She'd seen executions; she'd been, a couple times, part of a firing squad. There wasn't much objective evidence supporting the supposition that the prisoners in hand were innocent of any particular crime that could be named. They were a drain on resources, and an unacceptable risk with every breath they drew.

And yet...

If they killed—terminated, *released*—the prisoners, they weren't any better than the DOI.

And that small flaw in the pattern that was Val Con, inside of her head—that would never be mended.

She sighed, like he'd done, and sipped her wine.

"Let's sleep on it," she said.

• • • ❈ • • •

"He said he was collectin' insurance, Boss."

Vessa Quill had been among the first to move into Boss Conrad's turf when the tollbooths were closed. She had immediately set up a bread bakery in a storefront half a block away from the Boss's house, and proceeded to capture a respectable clientele. Conrad had spoken to her only a few weeks ago, during one of his walks through his turf, and her plans had all been for expansion: hiring another baker, and perhaps branching out into pastries.

Now, she was angry, her arms crossed over her chest, and her pale face hard. Nor did the Boss particularly fault her for being angry.

"We do not collect insurance," he told her, keeping his voice smooth. "None of the Bosses on the council collect insurance. It is, in fact, illegal, to collect insurance."

"Illegal" was not, perhaps, a concept that sat easily with Baker Quill. Indeed, to most of the residents of Surebleak, the concepts of allowed and disallowed behavior were...alien to their everyday lives. The reality of the streets had, for several generations, been that strength prevailed. The strongest of all—in terms that favored brute force over mindfulness, or even mere cleverness—rose to become Boss.

In a rational system, the Boss would have then exerted herself to protect those weaker than herself. On Surebleak, however, the Boss had preyed upon those she should have held safe in her care. In particular, Bosses sold *insurance*—protection from their own spite—and made examples of those who did not, or could not, pay.

The sale of *insurance* had been the very first thing that the Council of Bosses had forbidden in its new table of laws.

"He said," Baker Quill continued, as if he hadn't spoken. "He said he'd burn down my place, if I didn't have the vig when he come back, in two-day. He'd take some of it in bread, he said, but he wants six hunnert, cash. I ain't got that kind o'money, and if I did, I wouldn't pay it. My mam, she paid the insurance money, and what'd it get her? Broke *an'* made a zample, 'cause the Boss's 'hand put 'er money in his pocket an' tole the Boss she didn't pay."

He bowed his head slightly.

"I am sorry to hear of your mother's tragedy. You are very right to bring this matter to me. The Bosses no longer collect insurance, and there is a law"—another uneasy word—"that forbids the collecting of insurance. Anyone caught doing it will be taken up by the Watch, and will be assessed fines."

"Fines," she repeated, and he could believe that she was measuring *fines* against the loss of her livelihood, and possibly her life.

"There are other deterrents, for those who persist, but yes, for a first offense, fines. Now. You say that this insurance salesman has promised to return for his payment in two days?"

"That's what he said." She hesitated, then added, "My old turf, sometimes they come back early; and if you didn't have the money, they added a *surcharge*."

Gods, what a planet.

He nodded.

"Here is what we shall do, if you will consent to it. I shall ask Mr. McFarland, my head 'hand, to assign one of my own security staff to you. This person will leave with you this evening, and will remain at your side until the insurance collector returns for the money. At that point, my staff member will remove this person from your orbit, using what force is necessary, and will bear him to the Watch, where he will be imprisoned until the Bosses call upon him to explain himself."

He paused, considering her set face, and asked, gently, "Does this proposed course of action satisfy you?"

To her credit, she took time for consideration. He folded his hands atop the desk and waited.

Eventually, she said, "That'll cover, 's'long's he don't have backup. If he's got backup..."

"You are correct; that is something which should not be left to chance. We will not leave you without protection. Instead, your security will call the Watch to retrieve the insurance sales-man, and will remain with you until it had been ascertained that he is either working alone, or his partner has also been apprehended."

She nodded once, decisively. "That'll do it, then."

"Excellent. Let us bring Mr. McFarland in our conference."

He touched a button on his desk. The office door opened almost immediately, and Mr. pel'Tolian stepped within.

"Sir?"

"Please tell Mr. McFarland that we have need of his expertise in my office. And please ask Cook if we may have refreshments."

"Yes, sir; at once."

Mr. pel'Tolian withdrew.

"Is there anyone else—a family member, or a close friend—who might also be in danger from this person who is selling insurance?"

Baker Quill frowned.

"I'm by myself," she said slowly. "But it comes to me, Boss, that fella must've been up and down the whole street with this; not just me."

"Indeed," he replied. "We shall make certain of that tomorrow."

"Yeah, but why am I the only one here, talking to you about this?"

That was an excellent question and likely had something to do with enculturation. or an instinct toward denial, or . . . Val Con would be able to tell him. It would, perhaps, be useful to know. For now, he could only offer the simplest probability.

"Perhaps they were afraid," he said to Baker Quill, and turned his head as the door opened to admit Cheever McFarland's not inconsiderable bulk.

"Evenin', Boss. You wanted to see me?"

Mr. McFarland had taken the baker away, leaving him blessedly alone. He closed his eyes, leaned back in his chair, and wondered if Natesa had returned home yet, from her tasks in town. Perhaps they might have a quiet dinner, alone. Quin was with Luken, helping with the arrangement of the port annex shop . . .

The door to his office opened.

He opened his eyes and in the same instant snapped to his feet—and relaxed, feeling foolish, as his lifemate closed the door behind her and turned to face him, elegant brows arched above ebon eyes.

"Did I wake you?"

"Very nearly," he answered, going across the room to her.

She entered his embrace with enthusiasm and kissed him thoroughly. Arm in arm, they walked toward his desk.

"I wonder if we might dine in our room," she said. "I am . . . somewhat weary."

He laughed softly. "I was only just thinking the same thing. Yes, of course—Quin and Luken will be dining at the port. But, what has happened to tire you?"

Natesa rarely admitted to weariness; to hear her say so concerned him . . . not a little.

"Stupidity tires me," she said. She released him and sat on the corner of his desk. He sank into his chair, looking up into her face.

"What happened?" he asked again.

"Why, some fool had declared an entire street to be *Juntavas turf.* She proposed that all the shopkeepers would henceforth pay her a percentage of their business, and further let it be known that she had the means to enforce this. I heard of it from Jerfin Marx when I stopped by to find if his son had fully recovered from his misadventure. She had apparently only left him, but she moved fast. I found her three blocks distant, informing a bewildered greengrocer of these new arrangements, and asserting that she had the whole might of the Juntavas behind her.

"Naturally, I needed to hear more, so I took her aside to ask for her code number. She denied having any such thing. I then asked for her handle, and she denied having one. She is now being held by the Watch until the answer to my inquiry through the Judges' office is answered."

She sighed, and closed her eyes. "I fear that we are beset by amateurs, my love."

"I fear it, also." He rose, and took her hand. "Come, let us retire. I will ask Mr. pel'Tolian to bring us a cold dinner and a bottle of wine."

"Two bottles of wine and you have a bargain."

"Done!" he said, with a grin, and raised her hand to his lips.

CHAPTER FIVE

Jelaza Kazone
Surebleak

IT WAS SNOWING, DESPITE IT BEING SUMMER: A GENTLE DRIFT of dainty flakes sparkling against the twilight sky. "Farmer's friend," they called such warm-weather flurries on Surebleak, where snow was always possible, and *warm* an exercise in relativity.

The man at the door stood with his hands in the pockets of his coat, listening—to the wind, to the dwindling whine of the taxi's motor, to the rapid pounding of his heart.

The door was of dark wood, and of a considerable age: the carved edges of the Tree-and-Dragon that adorned it were smooth, as if every member of every past generation of Korval had run their hands over it, on homecoming. He felt an urge to do so himself, for was he not a son of the House?

Well...no. In point of fact, he was clanless, which was to say that he stood as the sole survivor of his clan. He had, however, been declared a *brother* of a son of the House, a dubious and dangerous honor that he had accepted only after taking counsel of his grandmother, and his...other...brothers.

The ties that bound him to the delm of Clan Korval were of a bitter forging, but no less compelling for that. Who, after all, could know the heart of a man returned from hell as well as one who had made the same journey?

So it was that, having prepared a brother-gift appropriate to their bond, he had dressed in the finest clothes that could be found for him, and gone out alone from the *kompani*, down the road, and away from the city, to this ancient house from another world, where now, facing the door and the clan sign, his courage failed him.

Rafin would scarcely credit it, he thought wryly, the fingers of his right hand curling inside his pocket. Nor did he suppose that this door, of all doors on the planet of Surebleak, was unwatched.

Surely, the security system knew he was here. If he did not gather himself to ring the bell within, so he suspected, the next dozen beats of his craven heart, he could expect that the system would act to protect the house.

Well.

He took a breath, feeling his resolve, if not his courage, firm, and considered the door anew.

A palm pad was set into the right side of the door's frame—an awkward placement, though it was certain that the house had his imprint on file. He recalled it being taken, during the time he had been held here for interrogation.

At the left side of the door was a simple rope, attached to a brass bell, now frosted with snowflakes.

He raised his hand, grasped the cold rope and pulled, once.

The bell clanged, loud enough to hurt the ears. Before the complaint had died away into the fading twilight, the door opened inward, and a man dressed in Korval livery stepped into the breach.

"Good evening, sir," he said, speaking the High Tongue in the mode of doorkeeper.

"Good evening." He answered in the mode of visitor to the house, for he was that, as well. "I am Rys Lin pen'Chala, and I am come to speak with my brother Val Con yos'Phelium."

"Certainly, sir. Please, come in out of the weather."

The butler stepped back, and Rys stepped forward, into a wide hallway that was more comfortable than grand; wooden walls and floor gleaming under soft yellow lighting.

"May I have your coat, sir?"

"Certainly."

He slipped out of the overlarge garment, and surrendered it to be hung neatly on a wall hook next to what might have been the butler's own coat.

"Follow me, sir," he said, and Rys did, down the hallway, passing closed doors of what must be the formal receiving rooms, and into an interior hallway.

A stranger would not be brought so far into a clanhouse, unless accompanied by a member of the House. But he—he was the brother of a son of the House. *Melant'i* attached to such persons.

Another turn, and the butler opened a door with a bow.

"Here you are, sir. And, may I say—welcome."

It was the sort of thing an old retainer might say to a returning son, but almost too warm for the brother of such. It disturbed him—and then he forgot the matter as he stepped into the room—

And stopped, heart stuttering.

He was in a small, informal dining room, where all the family who were to House had apparently gathered to share Prime meal...

...Every one of whom was looking at him.

"Rys!"

A tall, slim man rose from the table and came forward, hands outstretched, smiling broadly. Brown hair, green eyes, a clan ring glittering from one of those shapely hands, by which he would be recognized as Delm Korval.

His brother Val Con.

"Well come! *Well* come!" His shoulders were gripped and held in a brother's emotional embrace. Tears started to his eyes, as shocking as they were unexpected; he blinked them hastily away as he looked up into his brother's face.

The other man—his age, more or less, and like him, much older than mere years could account—the other man's smile softened, as if he understood. But of course he did understand. Val Con yos'Phelium had been an Agent of Change, a man shaped by torture and dark arts into someone—something—*other* than who he had been. Terrifyingly other. A man who betrayed and killed effortlessly, without remorse, without shame.

Very much the same as Rys Lin pen'Chala.

"Forgive me," Rys said, soft enough for a brother's ears. "I had no wish to disturb the evening meal."

"The arrival of a brother is no disturbance. There is a place for you at the table—indeed, you find us much reduced this evening, with so many away on the clan's business.

"But, here! You have met my sister Anthora, and her lifemate, Ren Zel dea'Judan; the lady next is my aunt Kareen yos'Phelium, and next to her, my sister's mother, who guests with us—Scholar Kamele Waitley. Beyond her is my lifemate, Miri Robertson Tiazan. All—here is my brother Rys Lin pen'Chala."

As introductions went, it had more the feel of the *kompani* than a Liaden High House, but no one seemed put out; the elder lady aunt was not best pleased, and not just, he thought, by her nephew's rag manners. From her frown, it would appear that he, himself, offended her sense of propriety, a point of view with which he had some sympathy.

By the standards of the *kompani*, he was splendidly attired, but a costume comprising an emerald green shirt with sweeping, dramatic sleeves worn under a black vest lavishly embroidered in scarlet, yellow, and brilliant blue, and a gold-tasseled scarlet sash did render him . . . rather obvious. Something modest, such as his brother Val Con's pearly shirt, would have more likely gained an elderly aunt's approval.

He bowed carefully, convenably, to the room. Straightening, he murmured, "I am informed and honored."

"Also, hungry," the red-haired lifemate of his brother said, in Terran, her voice too fine for the harsh Surebleak accent. "Bring the man down here and give him his dinner."

It would appear that this was a strong hint to all present to return to their own interrupted meals. They did this, and voices began to take up the threads of suspended conversations. Rys went down the room on his brother's arm, and took the chair next to Miri Robertson Tiazan.

A dish of clear soup appeared before he had gotten his napkin to his knee. The others at table had already moved on to the next course, but apparently he was to have a complete meal. Shaking his sleeve back, Rys reached for the soup spoon, then simply put his hand flat on the table, and sat staring down at his own gleaming fingers, shivering.

What in the names of the unfeeling gods was he doing here, in this house, among these people? He was not High House. His clan had been seated upon an outworld; their livelihood gotten from the growing of grapes and the making of wine. Gone now, all save Rys Lin pen'Chala, destroyed in an Yxtrang raid. And Rys Lin pen'Chala destroyed as well, in a far more fearsome disaster . . .

"Little too much bold action, there?" Miri Robertson Tiazan said quietly from his side.

He took one hard, deep breath, lifted his head and met candid grey eyes.

"I fear that I had not...properly regarded the hour."

Had he stopped to consider, he might easily have realized that a visit at this time of the evening would intrude upon Prime. However, he had not considered—or, he had only considered that, having taken his decision and in possession of the fruit of his labors, he must at once place it into the hands of the man who would know best how to use it.

"Take your time," she said. "If it'll help, I'll just talk in your direction, so your conversational duty's covered."

That was...kind. He felt tears rise again, and blinked them away.

"I am grateful," he murmured, and picked up the proper spoon. The soup was excellent.

"I wonder if you might advise me," he murmured, looking again to his host.

She tipped her head to show that she was listening.

"Yes. I...believe that I will not do justice to a full formal meal. At...home, we are accustomed to simpler fare."

"Just eat what you want. If the soup's enough, that's fine; maybe with some finger food, to fill in the edges. If it'll ease you, we ain't doing full formal—hardly ever do. Tonight we got the soup, the main course, and dessert. Which is pretty informal." She looked momentarily owlish. "So they tell me. Kareen ain't comfortable unless we dress, else you'd've caught us in Surebleak motley, and you all prettied up!"

He smiled. "My grandmother would not have me shame the *kompani* by calling upon my brother in less than the best I might wear," he said.

"Very proper," came the overly clear voice of the elder aunt.

He raised his eyes to look at her, and she inclined her head.

"One has naturally been informed of the circumstances of the delm's brother. May one inquire as to your grandmother's name?"

"Indeed." He met the lady's eyes firmly, his experience of such being that anything less than firmness would mark him as dismissible.

"My grandmother's name is Silain Bedel. Her title, by which it is proper for those not of the *kompani* to address her, is *luthia*."

"I thank you," the lady said, with sharp, but seemingly genuine sincerity. "One makes a study, you understand, of modes of politeness. I would not wish to err, nor to give offense, should I have the honor of meeting Silain-*luthia*."

"One's grandmother holds similar views," he murmured, glancing down to find that his empty soup dish had been removed, replaced by a plate of small savories, and another of warm rolls.

"Politeness smooths many paths," the pale-haired mother of his brother's sister said in laborious Liaden. She smiled, open and utterly Terran, and he felt an immediate affection for her, as one might for a child.

"Please"—this was again the elder aunt—"commend me to your grandmother, if you will. I am Lady Kareen. It would be my very great pleasure to have Silain-*luthia* to tea, perhaps also including Scholar Waitley, if she does not object. I do understand that we are inconveniently located, here at the end of the road. Rather than demand such a journey from the *luthia*, I would be pleased to host her at the house of my son, in the city. Or perhaps she may recommend an appropriate bakery or tea shop where we might meet as equals."

He inclined his head.

"I will take your message to my grandmother, Lady," he murmured, careful not to make any promise on Silain's behalf.

"Thank you," she said, bestowing a cool smile upon him, and turned her attention to the scholar.

Rys gave a silent sigh of relief to have lost her scrutiny, reached for his glass, and sipped, carefully. The wine was white, floral, with an afternote of lemon. He smiled, and sipped again, enjoying the simple vintage.

"Good evening, Rys," came a voice he knew very well, indeed.

He looked across the table to meet the silver eyes of Anthora yos'Galan, known to some as "Korval's Witch." It had been Anthora yos'Galan who had read his mind and his heart during his questioning by Judge Natesa. It had been Anthora yos'Galan who had certified that he had regained what the Department's training had left of his former self; and that he was no further danger to Korval, or to himself.

He owed Anthora yos'Galan...more than his life, and he would thus remain forever in her debt.

"Good evening, Lady," he said respectfully.

"No, now that you are come as Val Con's brother, I must be

Anthora," she told him, and looked to her lifemate, sitting modest at her side. "Must I not, Ren Zel?"

"Surely that is for Master pen'Chala to decide?"

"Is it?" She frowned slightly, as if considering the proper protocol. "Well, perhaps it is, at that. But I may hope that he will decide in my favor, may I not?"

"Indeed; as I will also hope, on my own behalf. I think, though, that he must come to know us a little better."

He looked to Rys, brown eyes betraying mischief. "I am newcome to the clan, as well," he said. "There is a learning curve."

Rys smiled, warmed. "I see that there might be. For myself, I am well situated with my brothers and sisters of the *kompani*, and do not foresee coming into Korval. However, it is my... belief—newfound—that one cannot have too many brothers."

"So I believe, as well," Ren Zel answered, his smile gentle. "Already, we find common ground."

Beside him, he heard his brother's lifemate chuckle.

"Ren Zel can charm the portrait off a cantra piece," she said, and used her chin to point at what was left of his plate of savories.

"Dessert's coming. You want fruit, or a sweet?"

· · · ❋ · · ·

"I believe we have accomplished wonders," Luken said.

He waved his assistants toward the back wall, and himself walked to the center of the showroom. There, he slowly turned on his heel, surveying the display walls with small rugs hung in a flow of texture and tone; the bright carpets scattered across the gold-toned wooden decking, like autumn leaves scattered on the forest floor. He looked at the sample book set discreetly upon a creamy ceramic pedestal—there was nothing so crass as a *sales counter* in Luken's showroom—at the carpets hung on wooden rods, and the small refreshment table against the back wall, and lastly at Villy and Quin.

He smiled.

"We have, indeed, accomplished wonders," he stated. "Never has a man had two such willing and able helpers. I had hoped that we might achieve enough today that the shop might open in two or three days. With your help, we may open tomorrow."

"Who will tend the shop, Grandfather?" Quin asked, coming forward himself and glancing about. It looked good, he thought.

It wasn't, of course, the equal of Grandfather's former shop in the Solcintra High Port, but then, Surebleak was hardly Solcintra.

"Do you know, I had intended Kensi al'Findosh—you recall her, boy-dear; she had assisted in the old shop for the last few years—I had intended that she should manage the port annex. It still seems a good notion to me—she is entirely knowledgeable, personable, and shrewd. Sadly, she had been detained by the necessity to show her delm that this proposed move of hers to an outworld will profit the clan. I have had a letter from her recently which indicates that she has been successful in that project, and will be joining us here as quickly as might be. I suppose, therefore, that I shall tend the annex until she arrives."

Quin frowned slightly.

"That would mean slowing the work at the primary location," he said. "If I promise not to make an entire muddle of the business, I might stand in until Merchant al'Findosh arrives."

"Why, what a generous offer, Quin dear!" Luken smiled. "I have no concern regarding *muddles*. Certainly, between your father and I, you've received a thorough education in rugs."

"I am no match for you," Quin said, holding his hands up, palms out, and laughing slightly. "I hope you will keep yourself available, should I need to call the shop's expert."

"Gotta charge extra when you call in the expert," Villy observed, drifting into the center of the room. "Mr. Luken, this is everything that's grand."

"And it could not have been achieved without your assistance," Luken told him warmly. "I am very pleased."

He turned about once more, slowly, and came to rest with a sigh.

"Excellent. Come, let us make ourselves presentable. I believe that such an accomplishment calls for the best dinner the Emerald can provide." He glanced at Villy, and added, "As host, the honor of paying the bill falls to me."

Villy's face relaxed. "I *am* hungry," he admitted.

"Then we must not delay a moment longer! Please, take a moment to order yourself, while Quin and I review the security system."

"Thanks," Villy said, and headed for the back room.

The walkway was crowded, and they were obliged to walk in a staggered line, Luken somewhat to the fore, Quin and Villy following.

"Port's jumping tonight," Villy said. "Summer's got everybody feeling spry."

Quin, who had turned the collar of his jacket up, for warmth, and tucked his hands into his pockets, sighed.

"I thought summer was a warm season."

"It is warm!" Villy said smartly. "We don't hardly ever get snowstorms in summer!"

"At—on Liad, we never got snow at all," Quin said ruefully, "except on the mountains."

"I dunno I'd like that," Villy countered. "By the end of winter, I usually figure I can do with less of it, but getting rid of *all* the winter—that just doesn't seem right."

"It is one of the many things that I find myself enjoying about our new home," Luken said, addressing them over his shoulder. "The weather is so interes— Ah!"

"Grandfather!"

Quin leapt forward, knocking the stranger who had slammed into Luken back with a hard shoulder. He raised his fists, braced and ready to take an attack.

The man staggered, in no wise steady, blinked blearily, and seemed to register Quin's attitude. He raised his hands to shoulder height, showing palms and spread fingers.

"Hey, hey, no worries, kid. Jus' a little..." He shook his head and raised his voice a little. "Sorry, Pops. Sorry! Not so steady right now. Ain't hurt, is he?" This last apparently addressed to Quin.

Drunk, Quin told himself. He's only drunk; and he fell. It had been an accident, not an attack. He took a deep breath that failed to bring inner calm, and managed to lower his fists, though he kept to his station between Luken and the stranger.

"I am quite unharmed, Quin," Grandfather said from behind him. "You may stand down."

"Go!" Quin snarled, and the stranger backed up, his steps tangling together. He fell to one knee, leapt up.

"I'm gone!" he said, and was.

"Sleet, you're scary when you're mad," Villy said, slipping his arm through Quin's. "Just a drunk, s'all. Mr. Luken, he's fine."

"Indeed, I am," Grandfather said calmly, taking Quin's other arm.

Quin tried another deep breath to cool the burning need for action.

"Hey, it's okay..." Villy said softly, pressing against him gently. "Easy... that's it, just breathe deep, right?"

In fact, the third breath seemed more calming. Quin sighed it out, feeling his muscles begin to relax.

"That's the ticket," Villy murmured. "No sense bein' all mad."

"There," Luken said. "That is more in the mode. Shall we proceed? I believe we have all earned a glass of wine."

CHAPTER SIX

· ·

Jelaza Kazone
Surebleak

DINNER DONE, THE TWO REPAIRED TO HIS BROTHER'S OFFICE. VAL
Con poured a glass of the jade for each.

Rys sipped—and sighed, as much for the finish as the vintage.

"Will you start a vineyard?" Val Con murmured, so softly it
could have been his own thought.

Rys moved the glass, and watched the wine swirl.

"As it happens, one of my sisters—an avid gardener—has
brought me into an endeavor with grapes. It is very much in
the nature of an experiment, and I do not entertain...very high
hopes of the outcome. Still, the subject interests her, and it would
be unbrotherly, to refuse what aid I can give."

He raised his eyes and met Val Con's gaze.

"Truly, I never thought to work among the vines again."

"And I had never thought to remove Korval to Surebleak. You
may yet discover a grape hardy enough for the climate, which
can be made into something drinkable. I mention this, as your
brother, for our cellar will not last forever."

Rys laughed. "I see that you mean to be a tyrant."

"Only when necessary. And, now, if it is not precipitate—will
you tell me how I may serve you?"

For a moment he had no answer, for surely there was nothing
he wanted, or needed, that was not provided by the *kompani*...

Then he remembered himself.

"I have a gift for you, Brother."

Val Con raised his eyebrows. "A gift?"

Rys nodded, and reached into his vest for the three tiles in their silver frame, the whole no larger than his palm.

Val Con moved forward, but he did not take the gift. Instead, he looked closely at the palm on which it rested.

"Am I permitted to say that your hand is a work of art, Brother?"

"Beautiful and fully functional." Rys smiled. "Rafin insists that his creations be both. Truly, I am fortunate in my brothers."

"As I am fortunate in mine. Now, tell me—what is this? An ornament?"

Rys shook his head. "It is a dream."

He drew a breath, trying to slow himself, but the fever— temporarily cooled by the demands of courtesy—the fever was upon him again, to see the thing well on its way, now that he had completed his part, and he rushed onward.

"I will tell you that the gift comes to you only so that you may use it in the service of those . . . those others, who are yet what we were, and who are held in your care."

Val Con's face closed like a door slamming.

Rys gasped—and shook his head even as surety rose. Those who had been held beneath the Dragon's wing . . . surely he would not, who had been . . . who knew—and yet, what choice had he, with a clan to keep, his resources straitened . . .

He was beginning to shiver, and his eyes were damp again. The hand and arm that Rafin had built for him could not tire, but the dream chimed softly against his metal palm.

"Peace."

The tiles were plucked from his hand, and a warm arm slipped 'round his shoulders. He was guided downroom and pressed softly into a chair. The glass was taken from his hand and placed on the table at his elbow.

"Peace," his brother said again, settling into the chair opposite. "You caught me on a new wound."

"Forgive me," Rys murmured, while he mourned them in his heart, who had not had the chance . . . He had been too slow!

Val Con moved a hand in dismissal. "It was nothing you could have known," he said, and held out the tiles. "Now, please, tell me what you have done. I will undertake not to become the ogre."

It was useless now; those he would have benefited gone ahead, as Silain would have it, into the World Beyond. Yet, he reminded himself, Korval had captured eight only; the Department enslaved many multiples of that number. Perhaps there would be others...

"Rys?"

He looked up, startled out of his thoughts, and smiled wryly.

"Your pardon," he said. "I would order myself, but you see how it is with me." He picked up the glass from the table at his side, and sipped, letting the wine soothe him.

"So." He met Val Con's eyes once more.

"After you released me into the care of my brothers, I had time to think while Rafin repaired the leg brace, and created my new arm. I thought... a very great deal about what you had said to me, on the occasion of our last meeting—that we two alone have broken the Department's training and won back to... to some semblance of our former selves. And I realized what I—what *we*—had done, in order to achieve it. I... prayed with my brothers, and with the *luthia*, who taught me the art of dreaming. When I was proficient, she guided me—in very small sessions, for to relive what I had done was... distressing in the extreme—she guided me in making this dream."

He leaned forward, holding his brother's gaze.

"I believe that it can be used to... to offer a moment of choice, such as came to me, to those still in thrall." He paused, and added, softly, "I regret, very much, that I have come too late."

But Val Con's eyes were bright with tears, and he was shaking his head. "No," he said, his voice low. "You have come in good time."

"But—"

"The decision was upon us—tomorrow, the delm would have sent their word. There seemed no other choice." He raised the tiles again. "You have brought me a choice."

Rys stared, suspended between disbelief, joy, and anguish. He wanted to dance; he wanted to weep. In the end, he sipped his wine, and recruited himself to calmness, and looked up again to meet his brother's eyes.

"You agree, then, that the question must be put?" Somehow, he had never doubted it: of course, Val Con would wish to liberate the agents, if it were possible. There was debt.

He—they—had done so much that was terrible; lives ruined, lives cut short—if either of them attempted an honest accounting, their debt books would be soaked in blood. But here was a chance to Balance the harm they had done...surely that would compel a bold-hearted man who had once, perhaps, been kind?

"Of course, they must have the chance—and the choice," Val Con said. "May I review this thing you have made?"

"Yes, certainly!"

Val Con held the dream up between them, the silver frame gleaming like ice in the yellow light.

"What protocol for access? I lack an Old Tech reader."

Yes, of course. Rys reached again into his vest and brought forth the box and cable Pulka had constructed.

"This is an adapter." He displayed the cable link. "My brother Pulka believes that it will jack into a standard sleep learner. The tiles are inserted here." He showed the box.

"Ah."

"You may also—Silain-*luthia* herself offers this—you may also at any time come to her and dream in her own tent. She naturally guarantees the safety of my brother."

"Of course."

There was a long silence, while his brother apparently took thought. And well he might think long and deep on this chancy gift, Rys thought.

"Well," Val Con looked up with a faint smile. "I will—and I suspect that you will also—need to talk this business over with Miri. How fare you, Brother? Are your reserves high, or would you rather engage with your sister my lifemate come morning?"

Rys stopped in the act of reaching for his glass and looked up into serious green eyes.

"Tomorrow morning would mean another trip out from the city, which I would rather not—"

Val Con moved a hand, cutting him off.

"In either case, you will of course guest with us tonight. Your room has long been made ready for you."

He thought to protest, but, really, it was only sensible that he rest this night in his brother's care. Especially as he suspected that he would have a companion on his return to the *kompani*.

"If we speak with her tonight," he said, to his brother's waiting eyes, "we may make an early start, tomorrow."

Val Con laughed.

"Well spoken, bold heart! Finish your wine, then, and let us seek the lady in her parlor! On the way, we will stop in the kitchen, and you will tell Mrs. ana'Tak what she must put into a basket for your grandmother."

· · · ✳ · · ·

There came a knock at the door to their suite. Natesa was still drying her hair, so it was Pat Rin, his own hair still damp, who opened to Mr. pel'Tolian and the cold dinner.

"Thank you," he said, and stepped aside, experience having taught him that he would *not* be allowed to take the tray and bear it halfway across the room to the table. Mr. pel'Tolian had standards, which included the close-held belief that those of the serving clans *served*. Any attempt by Pat Rin to take the tray would be seen as nothing less than a usurpation of Mr. pel'Tolian's proper duty.

The tray disposed, his man turned, but did not immediately depart.

"Because I refused to disrupt your evening by putting her call through to you, I was charged with the message that Chief Security Officer Lizardi wishes you to be aware that a person named Kipler attempted to incite a riot at the Bazaar this afternoon. He is being held at the Whosegow, awaiting the pleasure of the Bosses. A courier will soon deliver the tape of the interview. I agreed to take charge of it myself and be certain that it was on your desk tomorrow morning."

A riot in the Bazaar imperiled the port at large: crews, ships, workers, business...Pat Rin bit his lip, wondering if he ought to call Liz, just to...

The rustle of fabric caught his ear, and he looked aside, to spy Natesa just inside the doorway to the 'fresher, her sun-yellow robe yet unbelted, and her hair tousled from the towel.

He turned back to his henchman with a small bow.

"Thank you, Mr. pel'Tolian," he said. "I will look forward to reviewing the tape after breakfast."

Mr. pel'Tolian did not so far forget himself as to *smile*; he conveyed his satisfaction with this reply with an austere salute—*to the lord of the house* it was, and moved toward the door.

"Good evening, Master Pat Rin," he said. "Good evening, Ms. Natesa."

The door closed soundlessly behind him.

Pat Rin strolled over to the table—the tray bearing enough dinner to feed them for a week, comprised entirely of favored foods, and the requested two bottles of Natesa's favorite, from the cellar.

"I'll pour, shall I?" he said, and reached for the wine knife.

· · · ※ · · ·

His brother's lifemate was found in the so-called "ruckus room," with the heir. Mother and child were on the floor: the child crawling in energetic circles, the mother observing progress and offering the occasional dry comment on form.

She had waved them to her, and they joined her on the resilient carpet, the baby altering her course toward Rys.

"That's polite," Miri said, approvingly. "Lizzie, this is your Uncle Rys. Rys, be careful; she's a menace. Don't let her near your hair."

He smiled, and extended his natural hand.

"Hello, Lizzie," he said in Terran.

The child paused in her forward motion to consider his fingers; after a moment, she resumed her progress.

"Talizea ignores Liaden as well as she ignores Terran," Val Con said from his side. "I would not have you consider her unpolished. Also—yes—mind your hair."

"She's gonna grow up talking some language all her own," Miri said. "Taking bits of that and more bits of t'other, whichever fits best. Never mind not knowing what her name is."

"I grew up in a three-language household," Val Con said, "and no harm came of it."

"If you say so."

Lizzie had reached his knees, stopped, and rocked backward until she was sitting, looking up into his face. Her eyes were moss green.

"Is there a thing I ought do for you?" he asked her in Low Liaden, as one spoke to children. His chest tightened as she leaned forward and patted his knee. Though he had not given the clan his heir before the Yxtrang destroyed all, there had been children in the house—the heirs of his sisters, brothers, and cousins. He had been fond of children.

This time he extended only his natural forefinger and Lizzie wrapped all of her fingers around it.

"You are strong," he said, waggling the finger a little. "Be careful not to break me."

She laughed, and squeezed harder.

"What is that, a necklace?" Miri asked, and Rys looked away from the child for a moment, as Val Con bent forward and placed the tiles in her hand.

"Rys has made a brother-gift," he said. "This is a dream, *cha'trez*. It has . . . the potential, so he believes, to rehabilitate those we hold in our care."

There was a pause, growing longer, while Miri considered the thing she held. Rys held his breath. He had not considered that Korval's delm might be . . . divided on the matter of the agents' fates.

"I think that I have not seen a dream before," she said, her Low Liaden cool, and carrying the accent of Solcintra. "However, I have seen tiles like these, and I have been warned away from them."

"They do seem to be Old Tech," Val Con answered. "Rys's kind brother, Pulka, has created an adapter that he believes will allow the tiles to function with a standard sleep learner."

Another pause.

"I think I am about to learn that this is not something that will simply be administered to the agents."

"It would be best, I think, if I reviewed it, before . . . administering it."

"Of course you do." She turned to Rys. "Is it *necessary* that he review this . . . protocol?"

He met her eyes, which were chill as fog rising from mounded snow. "Not . . . necessary. Prudent."

That drew a laugh, and a shake of her head. "Prudent. What is this?"

"It is an immersion protocol; it is how the Bedel learn from the past, or from another's unique experience. We say, 'I will dream on it,' when we wish to learn; thus, the means of learning becomes a dream, in the language. I have myself dreamt . . . several times, and taken no harm. I believe that the equipment is not . . . quite Old Tech." He offered her a smile.

"The Bedel can make anything. It is possible that a brother saw an Old Tech learner and said to himself, 'I can build that—I *will* build that! But I will pull its teeth, and win its heart, and make it a part of the *kompani*, so it will never seek to harm us.'"

"Silain-*luthia* extends the safety of her tent for my dreaming," Val Con said. "Thus, I would be using the proper equipment, rather than an adapter that—no disrespect to Pulka!—may not precisely interface with the House's learning units. In addition, I would be in the care of the foremost expert on, and the possible ill effects of, dreaming on the planet."

"And if it breaks you, in spite of all this care?"

Lizzie shouted, her voice high and clear. Scarcely thinking, Rys bent forward and gathered her against his shoulder with the arm that Rafin had made. She pounded on him with tiny fists, then grabbed a handful of his hair.

"You *are* strong!" he said, reaching up to work her fingers loose.

"Warned you," Miri said, in Terran, and returned to her lifemate.

"You notice I ain't trying to talk you out of this harebrained stunt. But I want assurances. Rys Lin pen'Chala."

He froze, his fingers and Lizzie's tangled in his hair.

"Yes."

"You come to this house," she said, and it was High Liaden now, chill and clear. "You come to this house bearing that which you know will not be turned aside. You come at a time when we are beset, when our numbers are reduced, and when those of us who are left are hounded by an enemy who will not call truce. Do you guarantee the proper function of this device?"

"Yes," he said.

"Then hear me. If you fail to return Val Con yos'Phelium to his clan, alive and unharmed, your life is forfeit to me and to my will. Do you agree?"

It was usual to ask for sureties in the event of a risky undertaking. A life for a life was not particularly unusual in such matters. If Val Con died of the dreaming—but he would not. There was no risk, or very little.

And thus no reason not to give his word.

"I agree," he said. "If my brother Val Con is rendered unable to return to his clan or his duty, my life belongs to the surviving delm, to dispose of as she finds good."

She held him for a moment inside that long, foggy stare, then nodded once, and looked again to her lifemate.

"Let's show Rys to his room," she said. "He must be tired, after all this excitement."

Which was, he thought, finally working his hair free from small, grasping fingers, a clear indication that Val Con still had many questions to answer, and of a sort that were best not heard, even by a brother.

"Yes," he said gently. "I am tired, and would welcome my bed."

CHAPTER SEVEN

The Bedel

"YOUR PARDON, *LUTHIA*." ISART WAS BREATHLESS WITH HASTE, his voice louder than necessary.

"Pulka bade me tell you that Rys is come back to us by the Eighth Gate, and brings his brother with him."

Silain the *luthia* looked up from her mending and gave the lad a smile.

"You have done well, Grandson," she said, and the boy's bony face flushed with pleasure. "Go back to Pulka, now. Rys will bring his brother to me by the path he was taught."

"Yes, Grandmother." Isart was gone on that instant, feet pounding.

Silain folded her mending away into the basket beside her, adjusted her shawl, and folded her hands upon her lap. Rys would be some few moments yet, the Eighth Gate being somewhat more remote than other of the *kompani*'s gates.

She had time enough, to pray.

"Grandmother, good morning," Rys said softly.

Silain raised her head, and found him before her, handsome in his finery, his dark curls wind-tousled and sparkling, here and there, with captured droplets. And if that finery which became him so well at the height of his young manhood had blessed Udari as a boy, what matter that?

Behind Rys's right shoulder stood a man slightly taller, though

61

by no means so tall as Udari. His hair was dark also—brown, rather than black—also jeweled with moisture. He wore a black leather jacket with the collar turned up 'round his ears. His face, thus framed, was grave and thin.

"Rys, my child. Who do you bring to my hearth?"

He gestured very slightly with the hand that Rafin had made for him, and the other stood forward, moving with sweet, silent grace.

"Grandmother, here is my brother, Val Con yos'Phelium Clan Korval, of whom we have spoken. Brother, here is Grandmother Silain, the *luthia*."

Val Con yos'Phelium bowed, supple as a sapling. Straightening, he looked boldly into her eyes. His were green. "Grandmother Silain, I am pleased to meet you."

"Brother of Rys, be welcome at my hearth," she replied, which was more formal than her usual style. She saw the side of his mouth twitch toward a smile, as if he knew it.

"Val Con comes to dream," Rys continued, "in the safety of the *luthia*'s tent and heart."

"If you please," the other added, eyes smiling at her from beneath long lashes, the rogue. "I do not, under Tree, have the proper reading equipment to hand. Pulka, the brother of my brother, was kind enough to send an adapter that he believed would function, but I thought it best to seek equipment that was known to behave as it ought."

"I am pleased to guard a dreamer's rest," Silain said. She considered him, and added, "You are wary. That is wise, for I will tell you that this dream Rys has made is cruel, nor has he flinched from the worst of it. Know that the dream cannot harm you; but it may be—and in this instance, I say, *will be*—hard to bear. I will watch, and ensure that you are safe."

"I am grateful to the grandmother for her care," he said softly. "In pursuit of my duty as a pilot, I am sometimes required to fly what we call *sims*, which allow me to fully experience the flights of other pilots, in order to note either error or excellence. My brother Rys would describe this dreaming as something very much like a sim." He bowed his head slightly.

"Flying a sim may also be distressing, for not every pilot survives their error."

"You are prepared, then. Will you drink tea before dreaming, Val Con, brother of Rys?"

"Grandmother, acquit me of discourtesy, but I think tea only if it will ease my way into the dream."

"In fact, tea after dreaming may be best," Rys said.

"I bow to my brother's wisdom," Val Con said, and looked again to Silain. "There is another thing that you should know, Grandmother. My lady has said that, should I not survive this..."

"Harebrained stunt," Rys murmured.

His brother smiled. "Indeed. Should I not survive what she feels to be an ill-advised and unnecessary adventure, she has claimed Rys in Balance."

Silain sat up straighter. She had heard tales of the headwoman of the People of the Tree. She was a warrior so ferocious the Yxtrang revered her as a hero; a lover so skilled that she had captured the heart and hoard of a Dragon; a woman who gave her word but rarely, and always kept her promises.

It was that last which concerned Silain; after all, there were irresistible lovers and fiery warriors in plenty among the Bedel. But promise-keeping, that was dangerous.

"She will take your life?" she asked Rys.

"Grandmother, so she said."

"And you agreed to this?"

"Yes." The face he showed her was unafraid, yet Silain felt a shiver, as if the breeze from tomorrow had stroked her cheek.

"Unless he is inexcusably clumsy," Val Con murmured, "it is doubtful that she will murder him. My lady has a gift for making use of people, waking talents they barely knew they encompassed, and pushing them into extraordinary action. Very likely, she will only make him into what was lost."

Now was Rys alarmed, too long after agreeing to the head-woman's bargain. His hand gleamed when he moved it, as if pushing the words away.

"I am not fit to be Korval!" he protested.

His brother caught the gleaming hand and held it gently, one dark brow out of line with the other, and a half-smile on his generous mouth.

"If it comes to that, neither am I, fit to be Korval," he murmured.

Silain shook her head.

"If you have agreed to this, Grandson, then it will be done, and the Lady of the Tree will make of you what she will."

"Yes," Rys said again. "But Val Con will return to his lady."

Despite what she had said, in order to ease his natural qualms, dreams *did* sometimes kill. Especially such dreams as this one. And it was true that dreams would sometimes open old, or mis-healed wounds.

Silain extended her hand then, imperious. He who would dream released Rys and turned to meet her eyes.

"Grandmother?"

"Your hand," she said.

Cool fingers met hers and she saw it, clearly, the damage that had been done. It was a pattern well known to her; she need only extend her other hand to Rys to see its twin. Someone skilled had taken up the healing of him, and done their work well; he was strong and whole, and if there remained a flaw, it was too small for her old eyes to detect. She was about to release him, when she caught a glimmer of living color, on the very edge of her Sight.

Color? Or flame? She averted her Sight, much as one might avert the outward eyes, in order to see some ghostly thing more clearly. The colors intensified, flowing into an arc. A whisper of melody tickled her Inner Ear.

"A bridge of flame and music springs from inside your soul," she murmured, barely hearing her own voice. "What is the name of the one you are linked to?"

There was a hesitation; she felt him weigh the need to disclose his secrets—and felt him understand that this secret had already been breached.

"Miri. My lifemate. But," he said, his voice taking on an edge of worry, "she agreed to shield herself from this."

"The base of the bridge where it springs from your soul is at the far limit of my Sight. I think I am only able to see it because I hold your hand. Your lifemate may have kept her word, young dreamer, but shielding against such passion as I am able to see would be like drawing a cobweb over a bonfire."

"She has assistance," he said, and she felt that he attempted not only to answer her, but to soothe himself. "My sister and her lifemate are skilled in these matters."

"Well, then," she said softly, "it will fall out as it does."

She released him, patting his cheek as if she comforted a child, before turning to Rys.

"You will do well," she told him, feeling the weight of her words.

And truly, it was unlikely that the man who had survived even the healing of such wounds would die of Rys's dream.

"I believe that I understand the risk," Rys's brother said quietly. "I do not come to this unarmed, or naïve. I have, indeed, some knowledge of horror."

"So I have seen. It will be as it will be, my children. Are you ready to dream?"

"As much as I may be. I would have it done quickly."

She nodded. Rys offered his natural hand, and she accepted his help, rising a little stiffly, and beckoned them toward her tent.

· · · ☀ · · ·

Val Con tucked himself, birdlike, into a nest of blankets smelling not of smoke, as he had expected, but of flowers. When he pronounced himself comfortable, the grandmother bent over him, a crown of flexible golden mesh held between her hands, and settled it upon his head.

He closed his eyes, and extended himself in that way which was perfectly natural, and utterly indescribable, questing after the lifemate link, the complex music of Miri's soul.

His questing met only a damp coolness, like fog.

Excellent, he told himself. *She is shielded.*

In the normal way of things, they did not hide themselves from each other. But this—there was real danger here; he knew it, and he had pressed her hard, until she had agreed to accept assistance, and remain shielded until he returned to her. That... was not to his credit, but he would not, for his life, expose her to any portion of a sim reflecting what it was, to be one of the agents of the Department of the Interior.

"Attend me," Silain said, and he opened his eyes to look up into her face.

"First," she said, "there will be a tone. This tone will put you into a deep sleep. Once asleep, you will dream. You may wake from the dream at any time, or I will wake you, if you seem to me to have become dangerously distressed. Do you understand these things, Val Con, brother of Rys?"

"Grandmother, I do."

He breathed in, breathed out, and brought to mind the Rainbow, the calming and centering exercise that is the very first thing taught to novice Scouts.

"Yes," he heard Silain murmur, as if she had seen the colors whirl and lock. "Excellent. Use what tools you have."

He felt her touch on his hair, lightly, perhaps being certain of the connections; heard the rustle of cloth as she reached to the device—and abruptly felt himself short of breath.

"Brother," he said suddenly. He freed his arm from the blankets. "Your hand, if you will honor me."

"Of course, Brother." Rys dropped to his knees by the cot, and clasped him firmly with his own, natural, hand. "You are safe with me."

Bold words. Would that *he* felt so bold, of a sudden.

"Are you ready, Val Con?" asked the *luthia*.

"Grandmother, I am as ready as ever I will be."

He took a deep, deliberate breath.

Somewhere, a chime sounded, bright and hard.

CHAPTER EIGHT

Jelaza Kazone
Surebleak

"YOU AGREED TO STAY SHIELDED!"

Anthora came to Miri's side, and placed a hand on her shoulder.

"I *am* shielded," Miri snapped. "Though why I let myself be talked into any part of this—"

"No, I see; it is an action of the bond; it seeks to reestablish itself," Anthora murmured, probably to herself. She was looking somewhat over Miri's head, her eyes unfocused—or, say, focused on something she could see and Miri couldn't. Though she could *feel* it, assuming "it" was the lifemate link she shared with Val Con. In fact, she could even sort of see it, through the fog of the shield—an interlocking pattern of color and shape, fluid and persistently fascinating.

"Miri, do you require assistance?" That was Ren Zel, soft-spoken and gentle. She grit her teeth and pulled the shield back together the way they'd taught her.

"Nah," she said, feeling a pang as the pattern was lost once again in the fog, "I'm good."

She had agreed to stay shielded, yes, she had.

If she'd been only half as smart as she'd needed to be, she would'nt've agreed to any bit of shielding; nor agreed to let him trust his brain and his life to Old Tech.

She'd agreed because he'd been so damn afraid when he thought of what it might do to her, who had never been an Agent of

67

Change, nor much of anything, except a street rat and a soldier. Afraid it might break her, that'd come through; afraid it might *taint* her, which she might've laughed about, if she hadn't been half-sick with his fear.

So, in the end, she'd agreed, though she'd made him work for it, and given him time to think of another way, if there was any other way at all...

'S'what you get, she told herself wearily, *for coming to a skirmish unarmed*. She closed her eyes and reached for an exercise to calm her jangling nerves. She'd lost last night's second round of...negotiation when they were still in the ruckus room.

Because she'd felt, right then, just how much this chance to maybe redeem the remaining agents of the Department of the Interior they'd captured meant to him. It was like each one of them, strangers all, held a piece of his soul, and if he didn't release them from their training—the training he'd had and that Rys had—if he didn't at least buy them a chance to get back what they'd lost, he'd never fully heal.

She'd never had the training, but she'd seen what the training did; she'd *felt* the shadowy echoes of what the training did, and it filled her with a sort of cold and helpless fury, that it had been done to Val Con.

And all that was why she'd agreed to remain muffled, cut off from the one sense she'd never thought to have, or want, that had become the center of her own life. To stay here, calmly at home, playing cards with Anthora and Ren Zel while Val Con...

...risked his life.

You knew he had this hobby before you took him on, Robertson. So she had.

"Miri? Will you play another round?" That was Anthora, sounding not quite as flutter-headed as usual. In fact, she sounded a little strained.

Right, then. She wasn't the only one in the room who was worried.

"Sure," she said, walking over to the table. "Another round it is."

Ren Zel dealt. She took up and considered her cards. They were using a Liaden deck, which almost didn't throw her anymore, playing pikit, which required a fair amount of attention on the cards, especially three-handed. She could have wished for something even more demanding of her brain power, and space knew there was work to do, but both Ren Zel and Anthora had advised against making any difficult decisions until the link was reestablished.

Miri sighed, and made her discard.

Fine, then. She'd stay shielded and busy while Val Con got on with risking his brain and his life.

She just wished he would hurry up and get it over with.

· · · ✳ · · ·

He strode down a dark, odorous hallway, floorboards uneven beneath his determined feet—twelve steps, a brisk turn, a sharp halt before a peeling door.

His off hand came out of his coat pocket guided by neither his thought nor his will, and knocked, three sharp raps, before falling lifeless to his side.

It came to him that he was shivering far more than the frigid hallway demanded. It came to him that he did not want to be here; and that he *certainly* did not want to meet whoever was about to open the door.

He turned—he *tried* to turn, but his feet were rooted to the uneven floor; nor could he move his gaze from the warped portal before him.

Home. He thought it; his thoughts, at least, were his own. In his mind's eye, he saw their apartment, Miri kneeling before the fire, heavy copper hair falling in waves around her, pale skin glowing between the strands.

He threw every ounce of his will, and every erg of the terror that filled him into a simple command: *Go!*

. . . and yet he remained there, shivering and stupid, yearning to be gone, until . . .

. . . the door opened.

A stranger came forth, regarding him with a polite absence of expression, while he stood there, heart pounding, and afraid.

She smiled, then, and spoke his name. Neither her face nor her voice were familiar. He wished to tell her that he was come to her door in error, but his voice was dust in his throat.

The woman stepped forward, and cupped his face in her hands, as if they were kin, or lovers, or—no. As if she were delm and he the least of the clan. As if she *owned him*. Her smile widened, and she spoke again; his ear didn't quite process the sounds.

But it was no matter; terror slipped away from him, all desire to be elsewhere with it. He was abruptly and completely content. This was where he was wanted; where he was needed; he had duty, and one to direct him.

And, indeed, she directed him, and he willingly obeyed her; pleased to be of use once more.

· · · ✳ · · ·

His brother cried out, but he did not choose to wake. Rys, on his knees at cotside, felt his hand gripped so violently that he feared for the bones.

Silain glanced at the face of the device, and the meter that measured how long the dream had run.

"He has been reacquired," she said, from her seat on the blanket at the cot's further side, one hand resting lightly on the dreamer's shoulder, the other atop the dream-reader, ready to cut the feed off, if it seemed necessary.

Rys marked how pale Val Con had become, his dark brows pulled tight, sweat—or tears—gleaming on his cheeks.

He teased a kerchief from his pocket, raised it in shining metal fingers, and gently wiped his brother's face. Caught in the dream, the other did not notice, and neither smiled nor recoiled.

It is too much, Rys thought, watching his brother's chest heave as if he were sobbing. *No one can bear this—not twice. His heart will break.*

"Grandmother, the switch!" he said hoarsely, but Silain shook her head.

"A moment, and the choice will arise. Courage, Grandson. Trust your brother's strength."

· · · ✳ · · ·

Miri was cold. Well, of course she was cold, she was on Sure-bleak. Speaking of idiotic moves. She'd get up after her turn and get another sweater from—

The fog between her and Val Con burned away in a blare of agony so encompassing that she didn't hear her own scream. It was like—it was like hot lead being poured directly into her heart; it was like a million knives slicing into her brain, excising memories, stitching in patches with burning needles...

"Miri!" Something cool wrapped her, only to evaporate inside the boiling pain, and she was disappearing; she was being remade, by blade and fire, and everything she'd ever known was twisted; *she* was twisted, and there was a stretched, agonized time that might have been measured in centuries, when she thought—when she *knew*—she would shatter like a sheet of ice...

A bucket of cold water crashed over her head, she was wrapped in fog a mile deep and more, so thick that she barely felt Anthora's arms around her, holding her steady; or Ren Zel, when he picked her up, carried her to the sofa, and laid her down, while a blanket shook itself out, and drifted down to cover her, where she cowered and cried.

· · · ❄ · · ·

Orders came; he bent his whole self to obedience; he accepted directives with neither qualm or question. There was work, a great work, to be accomplished. He was important; he was *vital* to the success of the plan; no one but he could do what was required. Pride in his abilities joined his complacency, his contentment in orders. He took the rifle that was given to him, and went to the place she had designated. There were deaths required, but that did not concern him. He had dealt death before, many times. It had been necessary.

It was a wonderfully clear and freeing thing, duty. His was simply to obey; to do all and everything that was required of him. He was therefore content, as he knelt at the window, and made sure of the rifle, one more time.

He checked the sights, and smiled, satisfied. All was well; his weapon would not fail him.

Soon, the targets would appear. Soon, he would do what duty required: two deaths. He was skilled at dealing death; he felt satisfaction, recalling this.

There! The targets were approaching. As had been foretold, a man, and a woman with long red hair—

No! he heard his own voice inside his head, even as he brought the gun to position.

No! his voice screamed again, destroying his contentment, his satisfaction.

His hands shook; he thrust the voice away, found his focus, and sighted.

"NO! That's Miri!"

He brought the rifle down; he lifted it—and hurled it away, sobbing . . .

. . . ✻ . . .

There was silence in the tent, save for his brother's ragged breathing. Rys used the kerchief again, gently, pity warring with guilt.

"Now," Silain whispered.

Val Con screamed, every muscle rigid—and collapsed, boneless as a cat. The anguished grip of his fingers relaxed, though he did not entirely relinquish Rys's hand.

He drew a breath, deep and unsteady. Another. And another.

His form blurred, and Rys raised the cloth to wipe his own eyes.

"He has chosen," Silain said, and touched the switch at last.

. . . ✻ . . .

Duty was gone; purpose deserted him.

He was alone in a darkness so complete he could not see his own soul.

Gasping, he thrashed, a drowning man flailing after the lifesaving rope. He threw himself—forward, backward—knowing that it *must* be near; knowing that she would not leave him alone. Her strength would rescue him; he needed only to find the link . . .

But it remained outside of his grasp.

. . . ✻ . . .

Silain leaned forward, carefully removed the mesh crown from his head, and draped it over the box.

"Wake," she said, the full power of the *luthia*'s will resonating in her voice. "Wake, Val Con yos'Phelium, and greet your brother!"

There came another breath; a twitch of dark brows; the gleam of green eyes behind thick, sheltering lashes.

"Gone." His voice was a ragged whisper. *"Gone."*

He flung himself into Rys's arms, weeping.

CHAPTER NINE

· ·

Blair Road
Surebleak

"CAN'T SAY HE SOUNDS LIKE THE SHARPEST KNIFE IN THE KIT,"
Cheever McFarland commented, after Liz's tape had run out.

"'Course, you'd want that, with this kind o'job."

Natesa laughed, and shook her head.

"But, why?" Pat Rin asked. "Where is the gain?"

"To disrupt the port, and throw those who maintain order
into disarray? If it had been well planned, there would have
been much for...someone to gain. Including the overthrow of
the Council, eventually."

"Clearly, however, it was not well planned."

"Might be a rock thrown over our heads," Mr. McFarland
said. "Fair warning, so to speak. Might just be somebody out
for simple mischief."

"It might," Natesa said, "be a test."

Pat Rin looked at her. "A test of whom? Or what?"

"Security," Cheever said. "How good are these guys?"

"Possibly," Natesa agreed. "Someone may also have wished to
ascertain how good Hazenthull is, specifically."

Pat Rin frowned. "You mean a strike at Korval."

She moved her hand in the pilot's sign for *maybe/maybe not*.

"In this case, multiple strikes could be delivered with one
blow: Hazenthull, her partner, Security, Korval, and the Council
of Bosses. Or it could have been something simpler.

"A test, as Cheever suggests, to find how Hazenthull comports herself—or to mark any weakness in the working relationship between the partners, which might be exploited."

She sighed and shook her head.

"Again, had they been more organized"—she threw Cheever a half-smile—"or chosen a sharper blade, they might have created a situation that pulled other Security teams away from the real target. As it is...Chief Lizardi is a canny woman. She will already have put her officers on alert. I am in the port this morning and can easily stop by and talk with her regarding potential targets."

Pat Rin sighed, irritated. "Ifs and maybes."

"'S'what keeps life inneresting," Cheever said. "What do you want to do with this Kipler, Boss?"

"There is a council meeting tomorrow evening. Mr. Kipler may continue to enjoy the hospitality of the Whosegow until he may be brought before all of the Bosses to explain himself. We will schedule him as light entertainment."

"I will mention that to Liz when I see her," Natesa said, rising. She stepped to the side of the desk and bent to kiss his cheek. "I will be back in good time for dinner."

He caught her hand, and looked up into ebon eyes.

"Be safe today, my love."

"Always," she said lightly, and left them.

"Okay, then," Cheever McFarland said, after the door had closed behind her. "What's on the schedule that's fun, today?"

· · · ☀ · · ·

They sat 'round the hearth, the grandmother, her grandson, and his brother. Tea had been brewed and poured. Sensing that the brother of her grandson yet needed some time to order his thoughts, and himself, Silain had opened the basket they had brought, and exclaimed over the contents. She directed Rys to cut and butter three of the rolls, to go with the tea, while she continued to loudly, and perhaps, just a little outrageously, praise the giver of the gifts.

"Certainly, I am everything that is virtuous and good," Val Con yos'Phelium said at last, a smile lurking at the corner of his mouth. "Even the Bedel must fall under my sway."

"No," said Silain, well pleased with him. "There, you go too far. The Bedel may love you, and the Bedel may find for you this precious thing or that. But the Bedel go their own way, as we always have."

"Now, come," she continued, returning the various packets of food and spice, and scented soaps to the basket. "Tell me what you think of this dream Rys has made."

He swallowed some of the strong black tea, and smacked his lips, as if he was of the *kompani* in truth. Then he set the cup by his knee and let his gaze touch Rys before he looked to her.

"It is a...powerful dream. I do not think that I would have had the strength to have made it. However, I wonder how Rys knew to make the assignment...peculiar to myself, let us say."

Rys frowned, as well he might, who knew so little of the technicalities of dream-making.

Silain, who knew very much of such things, leaned slightly forward. "There are codes that the one who tends the recording device inserts at the proper points. The core lesson is marked out by a fixed set—that never changes. Certain details are malleable. The assignment, for instance, must be tuned to the dreamer, or dreaming is all for nothing. The technician sets the code."

"I understand you to say that every dreamer will receive a different assignment," replied Val Con.

"Peculiar to herself," Silain said, nodding. "Yes."

Val Con took a deep breath. It seemed to Silain that he was... distressed. She sipped tea, waiting for his next question, which was not long in coming.

"May one ask how this is done, on the level below the setting of codes?"

"That," Silain admitted, "goes beyond me. I know that dream and dreamer interact, but the mechanics of that interaction..."

"I will ask Pulka for the way of it," Rys said. His mouth quirked into a half-smile, "though you risk having another dream given you, Brother."

Val Con shook his head. "In that case, allow me to consult my own resources, first. One would prefer not to disturb Pulka at his work."

"That is wise," Rys agreed solemnly.

"My question then becomes—can the dream be...edited?" He looked fully at Rys. "Understand me, I do not wish you to dream again! You have done enough. I only wish to know if the existing...experience...may be manipulated."

Rys looked to Silain; she nodded.

"We may copy the dream," she said. "We may extract segments, or rearrange the whole. What is in your mind?"

"The segment in which we are . . . recaptured and bound anew. Those we seek to rescue have been acquired and remain in thrall. I believe that all we need do is offer the choice."

"Yes," Rys said, before she could speak. "It is the choice that is key. But choice alone . . . may be too abrupt. There must, I think, be some context."

Silain nodded again.

"That is so, else the choice will merely seem a random thought, and easily ignored. If you wish to free slaves, the dream must be real."

"I understand. Let me think on this, and take counsel of my sister." Val Con reached to the common plate and took up a portion of buttered roll, which he ate with every appearance of enjoyment.

Silain drank what was left of her tea, and handed the mug to Rys for refilling.

"As I sit here reflecting with you, my child, I wonder . . . should the choices offered be three?"

"Three?"

She accepted her refilled mug from the gleaming hand of her grandson and leaned forward slightly.

"The dream offers the choice Rys was given: allow the nightmare to swallow him entirely, or stand as the man he had been. To say, 'No. I, Rys Lin pen'Chala, do not murder schoolchildren. I will not perform this action, and I will do everything in my power to prevent it being done by another.'"

"Yes." Val Con was watching her, green eyes intent.

"As you say, those who are in your care are already wrapped in nightmare. They may not have the strength to stand against it, but they may very much wish to leave its service."

His face hardened, and when he spoke, his voice was flat and chill. "You counsel me to offer them death."

"I do, and I ask you this question: During your own time caught in the nightmare, if your death would have deprived your masters of the single weapon of yourself, would you have chosen it?"

He sipped tea, giving himself, so she thought, time to consider the question fairly. When he met her eyes again, his were solemn.

"Given that I had the ability to understand my situation, yes; I would far rather have died."

"And so might others, too weakened in will to accept the burden of freedom."

"I concede the point. I have already allowed two of those under my protection to die."

They pained him, these deaths. He had failed those he had taken into his heart to save. Good men cared about such things.

"The first one, how did she die?" she asked softly.

He moved a shoulder, his mouth hard.

"Her . . . core self was isolated from the Department's training—without reference or warning. The programming therefore decided that she had been compromised, and chose for her."

"And the second?"

"The second? I killed her, by her intent. I had thought it was the programming, again, but, perhaps . . ."

"Perhaps she had taken the third choice," Silain finished for him. "You will not know that until you put the question to her, when you meet in the World Beyond. The first . . . you say that she was given, at the last, no choice, and so died a bad death. But you have forgotten that we pass into the World Beyond without wounds or pain."

She put her hand on his knee and looked into his eyes. "Death freed her to herself again. The nightmare did not win."

Tears sprang to his eyes; they glittered like jewels in the hearthlight, before he bowed his head.

"May it be as you say, Grandmother."

He did not believe; young men rarely did. She patted his knee and withdrew.

After a moment, he raised his head and looked to Rys.

"I wonder, Brother, if you wish to be . . . involved further in this project."

Rys frowned. "Is there more that I might do? I stand willing, but you must guide me."

"I must think, and consult, with my lady, and with my sister. It is enough, today, to know you are willing. How may I contact you?"

"A message sent with Kezzi will find me," Rys said, naming the *luthia*'s apprentice, and the sister of one of the younger members of Clan Korval.

"That is well, then."

He rose, and Rys with him; Silain remained seated, and looked up at them, two handsome men, each stronger than he knew.

Val Con bowed, deeply, which was pretty of him, and showed a proper respect for the *luthia*.

"Grandmother; my heart is full. I hope to meet you again. Now, I must return to my lady."

"I look forward to many meetings, Brother of Rys. Please carry my well-wish to your lady under Tree."

He bowed again, less deeply, as light as a kiss upon the cheek, before he turned, Rys with him, and left the hearthside.

· · · ❊ · · ·

"Certainly, I see no impediment," Pat Rin said, looking from Luken to Quin. "Quin is perfectly able—after all, you taught him, Father."

"Who're you taking for backup?" Cheever McFarland asked Quin.

Quin wrinkled his nose.

"The shop is directly on port and I've registered hours of operation with Security," Quin said. "In addition, there is a security system installed. Surely, I'll have no need of backup, Mr. McFarland."

"That's nice to hear. Tell you what, humor me and take Skene with you; she ain't been gettin' enough street time, and she'll be glad to step outta the house. Next week this time, let's you and me and her get together and reassess."

In the normal way of things, Quin and Skene were friends; she had served as his security on more than one occasion.

Still, Pat Rin saw the stubborn set of the jaw. One did not like to accept personal security. Indeed, it seemed that particular dislike was a family trait.

"If you please, Quin," he said. "Do Skene a kindness."

His son laughed, and bowed—junior to master.

"Certainly," he said to Mr. McFarland. "I'll do Skene a kindness."

· · · ❊ · · ·

He entered the house by the side door, and ran up the back stairs, Miri's song echoing inside his head. The song was one of the many facets of their lifemate link, the first that had manifested and the most... comforting.

Miri alive... Miri well...

That was the surface, cheery and bright. If one listened more closely, other melodies and themes were found, fascinating and enticing. He sometimes sank into those deeper flows of music, and never rose, but that he felt...energized and...lighter. Occasionally, he had tried to play the deeper themes on the omnichora, but his skill failed him; the reproduction was never as invigorating as the original.

Now, though...

In his confusion, after the dream had done with him, he feared that the link had broken. The song had returned soon enough, and with it the recollection that he had insisted that Miri shield herself from the link's input.

It was only after he had reclaimed his car from Nova's keeping, and was driving out of the city, toward Jelaza Kazone, that he noticed something...different in the song. A new subtheme: dark and toothy.

As soon as he was clear of the city, he accelerated. Possibly, he accelerated too much, the song's new edge gnawing at him, until he abandoned the car on the apron beside the house and crossed to the door, not running. Not *quite* running, but moving as quickly as a pilot might, who had urgent business in hand.

The song drew him to her. He slapped the plate on their apartment door, crossing the threshold with no break in stride.

Miri was in her rocking chair by the window that overlooked the inner garden. It had become a favorite chair, a favorite view. He walked toward her, more moderate now, the new theme slipping into the background.

"Hey, Boss. Good thing the peacekeepers don't give out speeding tickets. You'd've won three, at least."

"I...felt that there might be a difficulty, at home," he said. "Miri."

She turned her head, then, and looked up at him, her face set in grim lines, grey eyes stormy and damp.

He checked, then snapped forward, lifting her out of the chair by her shoulders, staring down into her eyes, grieving and horrified—

"You broke your word?"

He could scarcely credit it. Anthora and Ren Zel were to have been with her; surely *they* had not—

"Where are my sister and her lifemate?"

"Calm down." She gripped his wrists, hard.

He took a breath, deliberately calming himself, and she nodded, her grip loosening.

"Better. And you're right; I didn't keep my word. I *couldn't* keep my word. The link's ... too strong, and it don't want nothing in its way. It took Anthora and Ren Zel together to fog me up; they had to work hard to do it, and even then, bits kept flowing in around the shield." She smiled tiredly. "I think I got the high points. When it seemed like the fireworks was over, I told the pair of them to retire to quarters and take a nap."

The link ...

"Gods, *cha'trez*." He stared down into her face, her song in all its depth rising into his consciousness. "You dreamed ..."

"I missed the intro, if there was one. Came in on the slash-and-patch job." Tears rose again, and spilled over. "That's—they did that to you, didn't they? It wasn't just a sim, *or* a dream ..."

"Today, it was a dream. Before ... yes, they did that. Miri, I would never have had you—"

"Right, I got that." She leaned forward and he gathered her to him, felt her arms go around his waist, tight.

After a time, she spoke again.

"Those people we're holding—they're living that, right now."

"Yes," he whispered.

"Then you and Rys—you're right. If we can give them a way out, we gotta do it." She sighed; he felt her shudder as he held her.

"Wanna know my favorite part?" she asked.

He caught his breath, but managed to answer easily. "Of course I do."

"Right there near the last, where we were being pushed and pushed to give up the last bit of ourselves?"

"I remember."

"Well that's my favorite part, right there. 'Cause we didn't break."

She twisted slightly, and he let her go, and she looked up into his face, raising her hands to his cheeks.

"*We didn't break,*" she repeated. "That's the take-away."

"Yes," he said, and touched the corner of her eye, feeling dampness there. "But you took harm."

"I got understanding. I knew it'd been bad; I didn't know ..."

"There was never any reason for you to know!"

"Nope, there you're wrong," she said, shockingly calm. "I think.

Anthora offers to smooth things over, if it turns out the system got disrupted. But what *I* think is that the system worked just like it's supposed to. The link—it's growing, and we're changing."

"Yes," he said again, and for a moment he wanted to excise the link before it caused her any more—

"No, you don't," Miri interrupted, apparently snatching the thought out of his head. "And neither do I. What I *do* want is for you to sit here in this chair..."

She pulled him over to the rocker, and saw him seated. He sighed and looked out over the garden. Flowers bloomed—it seemed that all the flowers bloomed at once, in celebration of Surebleak's short and chilly summer.

Miri sat on his lap, leaning in and tucking her head down on his shoulder, so she, too, could look out over the garden.

"Okay, now. Tell me how we're going to use that dream to break those people loose. And what we're gonna do with them, after."

CHAPTER TEN

· ·

Jelaza Kazone
Surebleak

"YOU ASK A DIFFICULT QUESTION," KAREEN YOS'PHELIUM SAID. "My brother and I were not—how is it said in Terran?"

"Close?" Kamele suggested.

"Ah, yes, of course. *Close*. An apt word, in the case, for in truth my brother and I could scarcely have been less close: I am his elder by every one of a dozen Standards. Such a gap in age does not, of course, preclude *closeness*. I believe that Sae Zar—a cousin of my own age, in the yos'Galan Line—Sae Zar made an effort to ingratiate himself with the boys, and they were undoubtedly fond of him, with what fondness they could spare from each other."

"Boys?" Kamele asked. "Jen Sar—Daav—has . . . a brother?"

They were sitting together in a small, slightly shabby parlor, the predominant color of which was a faded mauve. There was a firebrick in the hearth, and the little room was almost too warm for Kamele's taste, though Lady Kareen seemed inclined to be chilly, still. It was the hour they had set aside to converse in Terran, in order that Kareen might perfect her skill. They also met for the morning meal, and spoke entirely in Liaden, in order that Kamele might practice what she had absorbed the previous evening, during her session in the learner.

"Daav had, as I did, an age-mate of the yos'Galan Line. Er Thom yos'Galan. It was not possible to see one without seeing both." Kareen smiled, a cool expression on her austere face. "Daav and Er Thom were *close*. In Liaden, the relationship is described as *cha'leket*, which I have been told comes into Terran as *kin of the heart*."

"I understand; I'm a partner in such a relationship myself. I had no sisters, nor did my friend, so we grew to be sisters."

"Exactly," Kareen said. "In the particular case, it was the Delm's Word that produced two children, one of each Line, so very near in age. It was necessary to avert a crisis of inheritance, as the delm's first child had proved inadequate."

Kamele blinked. The delm's first child, as she had learned early in their conversations, was Kareen yos'Phelium; and a more adequate woman would be difficult to find. Kamele had not yet discovered all of the lady's accomplishments, but it was plain that she was a scholar of considerable talent.

"May I ask?" she asked carefully. "I don't wish to cause you pain..."

Kareen moved a hand, deliberately, though the meaning of the gesture was lost to Kamele.

"It is scarcely a secret; all the world knows—knew—that Korval's Ring passes only into the keeping of a first class pilot, and testing proved that I was no pilot at all. The delm had placed all of her coins on one marker, which was not like her, and thus found herself in need of a more appropriate heir. Nor could she accept the risk of producing a second inadequate child. There is no piloting test for newborns; the proof cannot be made until the child is—or nearly approaches—halfling. So, she ordered the thodelm of yos'Galan to bring a second child to the clan, while she herself did the same."

She paused and sent a sharp glance into Kamele's face. Whatever she saw there, and Kamele hoped sincerely that it wasn't the pity she felt, convinced her that more explanation was necessary.

"yos'Galan has never yet failed to produce a pilot. If Daav had not proven, Er Thom would certainly have done. The Ring would have passed to him, averting Korval's crisis."

"But Daav proved to be a pilot."

"Ah, yes; a most excellent pilot. Very nearly a natural. It seemed that he was recalling the equations, rather than learning them for the first time, and there was no one, save Er Thom, could match him for speed."

"And Val Con is also a pilot?"

"As good as or better than his father, as I've been told."

Kamele considered. Kareen's conversation often produced more questions than answers, and today she had opened several enticing query lines. She was herself a scholar and ached to pursue each, but their hour was more than half done. It would be best to ask something that would produce a more-or-less straightforward—

"You wonder, perhaps, that, as Daav wore the Ring, how—or do I mean *why*—he left the clan?"

Kamele frowned slightly.

"Jen Sar rarely spoke of his life before coming to Delgado. I'd always thought that something...very painful had happened to him, that he didn't want to...revisit, or remember."

Kareen inclined her head. "Your instincts are good. Has my nephew shown you the portrait hall?"

It seemed an abrupt, nearly whimsical, change of conversational direction, and while Kareen was often abrupt, she was never whimsical. Therefore, the portrait hall had a bearing on...something.

Kamele shook her head. "It's a large house, and Val Con has many demands on his time."

"True. I will, therefore, take this pleasant duty from him. Would you care to see the portraits? It is a little distance to walk, but I, for one, have been sitting too long."

"We'll run over our hour," Kamele warned.

Kareen smiled.

"If so, then we may usefully segue into an additional hour of Liaden, if that would also find your favor."

Well, that was something, though there was the very real danger that Kamele would miss important information, as her abilities in Liaden were not nearly as advanced as Kareen's were in Terran.

A scholar, however, did not flinch from learning. Kamele inclined her head.

"That sounds very agreeable," she said.

Kareen offered an arm; Kamele took it, and they strolled out of the warm little parlor, entirely at ease with each other.

· · · ※ · · ·

"What do you want, Rys Dragonwing?"

Neither question nor tone were welcoming, but that was Droi's way. That only her voice was sharp, very nearly betrayed pleasure.

"Only to sit with you, and talk for a moment."

"What have you found to talk about, now?" she wondered, never lifting her eyes from her task. Rafin must have brought her his latest gleanings, for she was sorting cables, like to like, out of a tangled, untidy pile.

Rys sat down on the other side of the pile and teased a thin yellow cable loose from the mass.

"I have been to visit my brother under Tree," he told her, keeping his eyes lowered, so that she would not find him too bold and be compelled to strike him for his impudence.

"How did he value your brother-gift?" she asked. He had told her of his struggles with dream-making on previous visits.

"High. I believe he will use it to good cause."

"Well, then he is not a fool. That is well. It is very trying when one's brother is a fool."

That was perhaps directed at him. He ignored it, placed the coiled yellow cable to one side, and reached again to the pile.

"I slept overnight in the house of my brother," he continued, "and met his blood kin."

Droi said nothing, though he could tell by the tilt of her head that she was listening.

"I met his lifemate."

"So? What is she like, the headwoman under Tree? Very beautiful, I suppose, in the *gadje* way, with sweet words in her mouth?"

"She is very like you," Rys said, smiling at the cables. "Beautiful in her own way, and of a . . . decided temper. Her daughter will be another such, I do believe."

"How old, the daughter?"

"She creeps, and tests her grip; she is able to detect a stranger in her orbit." He smiled slightly. "She has a fascination with hair."

"Who could resist Rys's curls?" Droi asked the cable she was slowly extracting from the tangle of its cousins.

There was certainly nothing he might say to that; to point out that untold numbers demonstrably held the ability to resist him seemed false modesty among a people for whom boasting was an art form.

He freed and rolled three more cables before Droi spoke again.

"I have been meditating upon the child we made together."

He looked up, expecting to find her face averted, and so met her eyes, which were only black, if their gaze was sharp, with no touch of red or *veyness* about them.

"Our child is well?" he asked, around a sudden lump in his throat. Droi was Sighted, though she rarely Saw kindly things.

Droi snorted lightly.

"You are a fool, Rys Dragonwing."

"I am, yes. A fool who has lost much and would lose no more."

"You lose nothing in this hour. Our child is robust. She tells me that she will have curls and black Bedel eyes. So here is another who cannot resist Rys's hair."

He smiled, though he felt the prick of tears.

"She," he repeated.

"That pleases you?"

"Very much."

"Well, then, my purpose is fulfilled; Rys is pleased." That was plainly waspish; Droi was nearing the end of her patience with him.

He finished with the cable in his hand, and set it aside.

"I am bound for the World Above," he said, keeping his voice light. "Is there anything that I might find for you?"

"A wise man who has lost nothing."

"I do not think that such a man exists," he said, coming to his feet. "Yet, if he does, I dare not bring him to you."

Droi looked up at him. There were two tiny red flames far back in her eyes.

"Why not?" she demanded.

"For then he would lose his heart, and that would be cruel."

For a moment, it hung in the balance, whether she would snatch up one of the several knives on her person and let fly at him. Then she looked down, and reached for another cable.

"Go away, Rys."

There was nothing to be gained in trying her further. He bowed, gently, and left her.

· · · ❈ · · ·

"All of the delms of Korval are represented here," Kareen said, turning the knob and opening the door. The lights came up in the room beyond, and Kareen, as befit her age, stepped over the threshold first.

Kamele followed, and stopped, one step into the room, staring.

"When in company, one does make the attempt to keep one's face smooth," Kareen murmured. They had crossed into the extra hour of Liaden lessons during their stroll to this room full of treasure.

"Would the host not take offense, at my indifference?" she asked, slowly, taking special care with the markers for mode.

Kareen looked at her sharply.

"That is an interesting insight," she said. "I thank you. To your point, if the host is Liaden, she will be more distressed by a... frank display of emotion. She might think you—forgive me—a little foolish. Far more dangerously, she may think that you are uncivilized and thus not due those courtesies that are owed to the civilized."

"Thank you," Kamele said. "I will attempt to be... civilized."

Kareen was seen to smile slightly.

"You have demonstrated that you are civilized; you have, thus far in your visit, been everything that is convenable," she said. "It is merely the accessories that you must acquire." She turned, moving a hand as if to encompass the room and all it contained.

"But come, there is a particular portrait that I wish to show you, which has to do with your instinct regarding my brother. It will be near the bottom of the room."

She again offered an arm, and Kamele took it willingly.

The pace she set was leisurely; from time to time, she spoke a name, rarely two—"Jeni yos'Phelium, Edil yos'Phelium and Var Ond ter'Asten, Theonna yos'Phelium..."—which might have been informative, had Kareen made any indication of which picture she was identifying.

Kamele felt she must look foolish, indeed, moving her head from side to side, trying to seeing each portrait. She'd have to come back, with a lunch, maybe, and take the proper time to study everything that was...

Kareen stopped.

"The eighty-fifth delm of Korval," she said, her voice perfectly level. "Daav yos'Phelium and Aelliana Caylon."

Kamele stared.

Jen Sar Kiladi, born Daav yos'Phelium, had been well into his late middle years when Kamele had met him at a Dean's reception, more than twenty Standard years before. His demeanor had been grave, his manner gentle. He could deliver a stunning setdown, and his humor had been sly, but he had been... civilized.

The man in the portrait was... feral. His eyes were fierce and black under well-marked brows; his lean face was hard; his mouth firm, and his chin decided. His hair—Jen Sar had kept his greying hair cut short—this man's hair, so dark a brown that it might have been black, had been braided and let to hang over his left shoulder. From his right ear swung an ornament of silver wire, twisted into a primitive design.

Kamele remembered to breathe. She realized that she was holding Kareen's arm rather tightly, but her companion made no complaint, nor spoke at all.

Jen Sar had worn a single ornament, always, on the smallest finger of his right hand. An old silver ring—a puzzle ring, he'd told her when she asked, and then turned the conversation.

The man in the portrait wore a ring on the third finger of his left hand; the same ring that Val Con now wore: Korval's Ring, that passed from delm to delm.

Next to him, holding his hand...

Where he was dark and fierce, the woman beside him was fair and open. Her pale hair had been pulled back into a complex knot; her face was thin, the green eyes direct, her attitude suggesting both intelligence and delight.

She wore, on the hand that held his, a large and inordinately ugly ring, all gemstones and gaud. On her other hand, she wore...

The old silver puzzle ring that Jen Sar had never put off.

"She was murdered," Kareen said, in Terran. "Shot and killed as they arrived at the theater."

"He witnessed..." Kamele began, but Kareen flicked the fingers of her free hand.

"Far worse than that, for one of my brother's proclivities. She understood the situation instantly—she was, of course, also a pilot. She realized that he was the target, and she leapt up before him." Kareen took a deep, deliberate breath. "He lay unconscious for many days; it was thought that he would also die. When he woke, it was plain that he would never recover himself fully. He made a credible attempt, but in the end, he gave the Ring and his heir to Er Thom, and left us."

History was littered with deaths. Even the most civilized scholar became hardened to the murders and betrayals revealed in research. But to have witnessed such violence, to have been so close to death that one woman's desperate leap was everything that had preserved him...

"His... *proclivities*?" she murmured, her eyes still on Aelliana Caylon's face, and her joy-lit eyes. Really, the artist had been extraordinarily talented. Or, perhaps she had been inspired by her subjects.

Beside her, Kareen sighed.

"You will understand that the delm is the . . . embodiment of the clan. Delms spend lives, when necessary, but, crucially, they husband the clan's resources, and protect the vulnerable. This was Daav's training, as the delm's heir; training that reenforced his natural inclinations. He failed in his most basic duty; he failed his own nature, and he lost, as Er Thom once felt it necessary to inform me, that which was dearer to him than his own life."

Kamele managed to move her gaze from the portrait to Kareen yos'Phelium's face.

"But she—Pilot Caylon—was also delm."

Black brows lifted, perhaps in surprise, before Kareen inclined her head.

"So she was."

"She must have been . . . remarkable," Kamele said.

"We were not friends," Kareen answered. She looked at the portrait, her brows drawn, as if trying to recall why that had been. "However, yes. Before she came to piloting, she was, like yourself, a scholar. Her field was Sub-rational Mathematics, where she held place as one of the foremost practitioners of the art. When she was yet quite young, she revised a crucial piloting tool—the ven'Tura Tables—subsequently saving the lives of many pilots. An extraordinary mind. There are of course copies of her work in the house library, should you wish to peruse them."

"Thank you."

Kamele glanced beyond Kareen to the portrait next to that of Aelliana Caylon and Daav yos'Phelium: a woman whose bright hair was cut comfortably short, pale blue eyes secretly smiling. There was much in her face that recalled Kareen and, to a lesser degree, Kareen's brother.

"Ah." Kareen turned, and afforded the portrait a light bow.

"The eighty-fourth delm of Korval, Chi yos'Phelium. One's parent."

"Forgive my ignorance," Kamele said. "But I wonder if she remained in an . . . emeritus status, after the Ring was passed to . . . Daav."

"She might have done so," Kareen said, as one being judicious. "However, she was another taken untimely from us—murdered by assassins, and my age-mate Sae Zar with her. Daav then rose to the Ring, too soon, as he had always contended, and which I believe to be true."

The room was suddenly too warm. Kamele took a breath, and felt her arm taken anew.

"I have distressed you. Forgive me. It was my intent to inform."

"Yes, and you have ... informed me. But—Delgado is a Safe World. Two murders in two generations is ... an aberration. Two murders—three!—in two generations *in the same family*—is unprecedented."

"Korval has always had enemies," Kareen said, as if this were perfectly natural, and not at all disturbing. "Some more deadly than others. But come, let us walk down to the morning room. There should be tea at this hour."

She turned them, and they moved up the room, toward the door.

"Now, tell me, if you will, about this concept, 'Safe World.' I believe it is outside of my range."

There were almost to the door, and Kamele's eye was caught by a small frame set somewhat apart from the rest.

"Ah," Kareen murmured, apparently following her eye. "Yes, that will be of interest. Here, let us come closer."

The frame lit as they approached, highlighting what appeared to be an identification card, complete with a fuzzy flatpic of a woman's face, no more than a suggestion of pale hair, long nose, pointed chin. The words on the card were not in a language that Kamele read.

"The founder," Kareen said, "Cantra yos'Phelium."

Kamele had been doing her research; here was a name that was familiar.

"The pilot who brought the Liadens to Liad?"

"Precisely so. One would have liked a clearer image, but a smuggler would not wish to be remarkable."

Kamele sighed, suddenly weary. "A smuggler would have also led a violent life?"

"One does not suppose so, in normal times. Surely, the primary wish of a pilot working the dark markets would be invisibility? Only see the card; I wager that she might have had a better likeness, but it would not have served her nearly so well.

"That she was thrown into violence, and into the role of a hero-pilot—well. The times were ... unsettled. I have a book about

Cantra's life. I read it over and over, when I was a child. If you like, I will gladly lend it."

Her reading ability in Liaden *might* be up to a children's history book, Kamele thought wryly. She bowed slightly to the other woman. "I would like it, thank you."

"Certainly."

They turned again toward the door, and exited, Kareen taking care to close the door behind them. "Now," she said, reverting to Liaden as they turned down the hall. "You were going to tell me about Safe Worlds."

CHAPTER ELEVEN

· ·

Jelaza Kazone
Surebleak

"SHAN'S WORK HAS TAKEN NO DAMAGE, NOR HAVE YOU."

Anthora sat back in her chair. The grey-and-white kitten somebody had named Fondi looked up expectantly from his curl by her feet.

"It is precisely as if you had experienced a nightmare, or ridden a fatal sim. You were naturally distressed and unsettled, but in the waking world you have taken no hurt."

"The link between Miri and I . . ."

"Functioned precisely as it ought." That was Ren Zel, sitting next to his lifemate in the double chair. "If there was error, it is shared among us, for believing that such a force, once activated, could be circumvented."

He bent down to pick up Fondi, placed him on Anthora's lap and looked up with a slight smile.

"I accept the greater part of the error, for I have on several occasions remarked how like your link is to the other . . . strands of event that I perceive. Neither is to be tampered with, except at great peril."

Miri shivered.

Anthora was only one of the three most powerful *dramliz*—that was Liaden for *wizards*, or maybe *witches*—of the current and two preceding generations. She was a Healer, like her brother Shan. Unlike him, she also held a full hand of weird abilities, among them telepathy, telekinesis, and clairvoyance.

93

Anthora was unsettling enough, but her lifemate was down-right terrifying.

Ren Zel, sweet-tempered, calm, rational Ren Zel, could see—*could manipulate*—what he explained as "the lines that hold everything together," in which "everything" equaled "the universe."

When she'd realized that meant he could unmake the universe as easy as untying the bow on a birthday present, Miri had seri-ously weighed whether to shoot him dead on the spot. It was a thought that occasionally revisited her, and it always dismayed her, not the least because she happened to like Ren Zel.

To hear that the link that bound her and Val Con was made of the same material as the bindings of the universe—that didn't surprise her as much as it should have, given this morning's fiasco.

All that, though, was secondary to the discussion, which was what to do with Rys's dream.

She nodded toward Anthora.

"If the dream Rys made is only a dream, and has no power in the waking world, that means it can't be used, as we had hoped, to free the agents we hold."

Anthora frowned, wrinkling her nose. She looked down at the kitten in her lap, and tickled him under his chin, to the accom-paniment of loud, gravelly purrs.

"I would not dismiss Rys's work out of hand," she said slowly. "It seems to me, when I gaze upon one of those whom the delm has taken under their wing, that I am seeing the mind of one who is caught in an intense state of dreaming." She glanced to Ren Zel. "Does it seem so to you, Beloved?"

He frowned in his turn, eyes narrowed as if he were indeed seeing into the mind of one of the agents.

"My Sight is not so deep as yours," he said at last. "I would agree that they dream, though with . . . reinforcement . . ." He turned his empty hands palms-up in a gesture in which Miri had no trouble reading frustration. "I have no words."

"You would say that training is merely a dream-state?" Val Con demanded, his voice betraying disbelief.

"No," Ren Zel answered. "Not *merely* a dream-state. A dream-state multiplied by many factors of twelve, and lashed into place—" Again, he showed his palms. "Forgive me; *reinforcement* is inadequate, and yet it is the word available."

"The *dramliz* are often at a loss for words when attempting to explain that which only we can see," Anthora told him. "We use metaphor, and approximations, and occasionally, we say, *trust me.*"

She turned her attention to Val Con.

"In the case, *reinforcement* is a good approximation. The state in which the agents live and function is potent. There were, as we know, several steps necessary in order to produce an agent. First, there are the tangible tortures which are applied during training. Once the proto-agent is in a malleable state—confused, in pain, and frightened—someone with the necessary skill binds them to an . . . an alternate reality—"

"To a *lie*," Ren Zel said, his normally cool voice hot with anger.

"A lie, yes; very apt, Beloved. I very much fear that this someone must be one of the *dramliz*, though I cannot deduce whether she was herself corrupted, or came willing to the work." She moved the hand not occupied with kitten in a broad sign for *wrong course.*

"I diverge from the topic, forgive me. The *dramliza*'s part in this process would be to bind into the frightened and abused mind of the trainee the belief that she joined the plan willingly, that she accepts the teachings of the DOI, and that she performs with her whole heart every assignment and atrocity demanded of her."

"It is the lie that *they chose* which keeps them bound into the dream, and to the Department."

"This," Ren Zel continued when Anthora fell silent, "is where we see Rys's genius. He has understood that one may be bound unwilling, and that, at the core of each agent, damaged and dreaming as they are, is the last shred of the person they had been prior to their acquisition. He has understood that there is a stress point—a particular, painful, and provocative moment where real choice is not only possible, it is *necessary.*"

"The trigger must resonate strongly," Anthora added. "As with Rys, who refused to oversee the wholesale slaughter of children."

Miri turned to Val Con. "That's different than how it was for you."

"Yes," Anthora said, before Val Con could answer. "And also no. When the two of you—each one half of a wizard's match, and neither whole without the other—when the two of you met, what happened?"

Miri laughed.

"We ran from people who were chasing us, fought with each other, took up with Edger, interfered with an Yxtrang recovery raid, and about got killed."

"All of that," Val Con said, frowning, "but, in terms of *choice*...
I *chose* to ignore the Loop. Instead of killing you, I *chose* to tell
you the truth. I *chose* to tell you my name; I *chose* to take you
with me—"

"So I could have a new name, new papers, and a new face—I
remember."

"Yes. And I continued to make you a priority, refusing to
abandon you, or murder you, or betray you. Again and again, I
chose to tell you as much of the truth as was available to me..."
He paused and extended a hand. Miri took it.

"Until," he said slowly, "the Loop—the program—concluded
that I was fatally compromised."

"Which is when it told you that you were dead," Miri finished,
squeezing his fingers. "I remember that, too."

"Yes..." He looked to Anthora.

"This dream—made with Old Tech—plucked that from my
memory, and wove it into a choice unique to me. It gave me a
target..." Miri was holding his hand; he *knew* it had been a dream,
though a very powerful one, and still he shivered with horror.

"My target was Miri."

Anthora's mouth thinned, but she asked the question calmly.

"And the choice?"

He took a hard breath, his grip on Miri's hand painfully tight.

"The choice was... difficult, because *I very nearly did not
recognize her.*"

"No worries," Miri murmured. "You recognized me in time."

"A heartbeat longer..."

"Near is not a hit," Anthora said sharply. "Which you know
very well, Val Con-brother!"

Val Con stiffened, then gave her a small, seated bow, which
she acknowledged with a bare inclination of her head. It looked
to Miri like she was shivering, too—and it must've looked that
way to Ren Zel, because he moved closer to her on the chair and
put his hand on her thigh.

"The choice *must be* terrible," he said slowly, meeting Miri's
eyes. "The effort of will required to assert that *I do not allow*
cannot be less than... terrific. Nothing less than a horrific choice
can be sufficient to shatter the restraints and the dream-state."

Anthora sighed, and leaned against her lifemate's shoulder even
as she tucked both hands around the kitten.

"Rys has been very brave, and very clever. He has shown us the way, but we do not want a sim for this—most especially, I think, we do not want a sim created with the Old Technology. At least one of those held in the delms' care is an expert in such technologies, and I would not willingly place a tool in her hand."

"Surely," Ren Zel murmured, "between you and I and Master Healer Mithin, we can create a scenario, and a choice targeted at one heart alone."

"I believe that we can," Anthora said solemnly. "We must speak with Master Mithin and take her counsel."

"Master Mithin," Val Con said, "awaits the Delm's Word so that she may put those in our care beyond further anguish."

"Assuredly, then, we must speak with her," Ren Zel said, and hesitated, before adding, "I ask."

"Ask," Miri told him.

"Yes. The delm understands that we may well, in our efforts, achieve only what Master Mithin can bring about this afternoon, without even the speaking of a word."

Val Con bowed his head. "This may, indeed, be an overstep. We may be guilty of inflicting more pain than necessary, and for an identical outcome. The only thing that makes the course we undertake acceptable is that we offer the chance that some of them may survive."

"I understand," Ren Zel said, and Anthora added, "We will do our best."

"We are confident of that," Val Con said, and stood, indicating the end of the meeting.

The rest of them got to their feet, as well. Anthora handed the kitten to Miri before turning toward the door, with Val Con beside her.

"Hey!" Miri muttered, as Fondi extended sharp, kitten claws, and began to wriggle energetically.

"Here," Ren Zel said, holding out his hands. "If we put him on his own feet, he will cease to be a menace."

"I fear I don't have the touch," Miri said, letting him take Fondi and place him on the floor.

"Kittens are easily offended," Ren Zel said, straightening. "Miri."

She frowned at him. "Yes?"

"You and I are of one mind in this matter of the Lines. It is far too much power for one man to hold. I would only ask that you allow me to tell you, when the time has come for you to kill me. May we make that agreement, between us?"

She considered him: eyes calm, face earnest, and not looking particularly suicidal.

"Have you Seen something?"

He moved his shoulders. "Perhaps I have, but, if so, even I am not certain, yet, of its shape."

Somehow, that soothed her more than a detailed list of the day, time and location of his upcoming murder would have done. She nodded.

"We have an agreement," she said, and he smiled.

· · · ✳ · · ·

"You actually made money from a rug shop in your old port?" Skene asked.

Given the day's business—or, rather, lack of business—it was, Quin reflected, a fair question.

"You must remember that Grandfather's *rug shop* at Solcintra had built its client list over fifty local years," Quin told her.

"Don't think I knew it to remember it," she said. "So, how'd he build up bidness on day one—or, say, day two, since we can maybe figure he did part o'day one like we did, with checking the systems and fine-tuning the lights an' all."

Quin leaned against the back wall, arms crossed over his chest, and frowned.

"He had business from the first," he said slowly, though he had been told the story of how Grandfather had found his trade many times.

"My great-aunt, who had been the clan's elder Master Trader, brought him rugs to sell on commission—*that* was how he began. When he had finished with his schooling, he sold rugs at Korval's booth at the port—much as we are doing..." He saw her grin, and shook his head, his mouth twisting into an unwilling answering grin.

"Much as we are *trying* to do. When he had experience, and people knew his face, he purchased his own inventory, and opened the shop. My great-grandmother, who was delm at the time, bought one of his carpets and had it installed in one of the public rooms at Jelaza Kazone. When her guests admired it, she had no hesitation in telling them where she had purchased it. There were those who came to look at the shop, and those who came to purchase just what Korval had—because there were always those—and there were a small number who came and looked, and talked, and who came back later with a special request, or who sent someone his way."

Skene shook her head.

"You was a big snowball on the old world, hey?"

He frowned, then grinned again.

"Clan Korval was, yes. I don't believe that Grandfather ever thought of himself as a big snowball."

"Well, he wouldn't, maybe," she said, and looked up, her hand dropping to her belt, as the door opened, and two Liadens in ship livery entered the shop, weapons showing on their belts.

The woman wore a trader's ring—respectably garnet. The man had a security stripe on his collar.

Quin walked forward to meet them gently, not a hurrying, hungry shopkeeper, but a man who was pleased to welcome guests into his home. So had Luken always approached his customers.

"Trader, welcome," he said when he had achieved a proper distance. "I am Quin yos'Phelium. How may I serve you today?"

The trader bowed as one who was pleased to accept service.

"May I ask, young sir, if you are in fact Quin yos'Phelium Clan Korval, heir to Pat Rin yos'Phelium Clan Korval?"

"Trader, I am," he said, bowing acknowledgment. "I fear you have the advantage of me. May I know your name?"

"You may—indeed, you must." She bowed once more... as one seeking Balance.

An alarm bell, sounding very much like the collision warning from the sim he and Padi had trained on, back at Runig's Rock, went off inside of Quin's head.

"I am," the trader announced, "Beslin vin'Tenzing Clan Omterth. When Pat Rin yos'Phelium Clan Korval fired upon Solcintra City, he deprived Clan Omterth of one of its precious children: Kyr Nin vin'Tenzing, my heir. I hereby deprive Pat Rin yos'Phelium of his heir, in full and equal Balance."

Her hand dropped to her gun.

A shot cracked.

Trader vin'Tenzing cried out and spun, crumpling to the floor, even as Quin dove, giving Skene room to work, his hideaway leaping into his hand as he rolled. He came to his knees, gun leveled...

The security officer was facing Skene over her weapon, his hands held away from his body, palms out and showing empty.

"Sir, please say to your guard that I would place my weapon in her care, and go to the trader."

"Skene, he says he wants to give you his gun and tend to the woman who is down," Quin translated.

"Tell him to put the gun on the floor and shove it over to you," she said, her voice calm and businesslike. "Then you find out for me does he have any other toys. After we know he's clean, he can check on his boss."

He translated that, too. The security officer surrendered his gun, submitted to being patted down, and did not object when Quin confiscated his boot knife.

"You may see to your trader," Quin said, stepping back. He was starting to shake, he noted distantly. There was blood on the trader's jacket; she was, he saw with a jolt of pure relief, breathing.

"Port Security'll be here in a sec," Skene told him. "I hit the panic button when she started in with the speechifying."

"Why?" he asked her.

She shrugged.

"Looked like a desperate woman to me, and her backup wasn't happy." She threw him a sharp look. "You okay, Quin?"

"I'm a little"—he reached for the word Villy used—"shook."

The security man was kneeling at the fallen woman's side. He looked up at Quin. "Please, is there a first aid kit?"

"Port Security has been summoned," he said. "They will have—"

The door slammed open, bell screaming protest at rough usage.

"Security! Everybody freeze!" a big voice bellowed in Terran. Immediately after came a woman's cultured voice, speaking Liaden: "Port Security arrives. Everyone stand where you are."

· · · ☀ · · ·

Rys had found a packet of dried red beans, and another of rice, which he would give to Jin, thus insuring that the *kompani* continued to eat. He had also found a fleece shawl that folded into a pouch no bigger than his hand, which he would give to Silain. He had first thought of it for Droi, but it was risky to bring Droi things she had not asked for, and he had no wish to try her patience further. Best that he and she were friends. He thought that: *friends*. By Bedel tradition, they were brother and sister, a relationship predicated upon their membership in the same *kompani,* rather than any genetic connection. By Bedel tradition, brothers and sisters might take comfort from each other, even, as he and Droi had done, make a child. Indeed, it was preferred that those of the *kompani* seek comfort within the *kompani,* leaving Those Others, the *gadje,* to themselves.

Bedel tradition did allow one of the *kompani* to make a bond of brother- or sisterhood with those who were not of the *kompani.* He was not the only one of their group to have done so—nor even the only one of their group to have formed a kin-bond with one of Korval, whom the Bedel called the People of the Tree. Silain's apprentice, young Kezzi, had accepted as her brother Syl Vor yos'Galan Clan Korval. Kezzi, destined to be *luthia,* benefited by learning that the Bedel, while naturally superior to all *gadje,* were not the only race, nor Bedel tradition, the only tradition.

The gods alone knew what Syl Vor learned from the Bedel, but the son of a House which routinely sent its children to the Scouts could only benefit from early exposure to another culture.

Rys's meandering thoughts brought him back to his brother, who had been a Scout, and who had expressed a desire for a local Surebleak vintage.

Rys was many years from the vineyard, though wine must run in his blood, so long had his clan tended the vines. He looked about him, taking note of his location, and turned to cross the busy street.

Three blocks south, there was a media center. Perhaps he would find a book there.

· · · ✳ · · ·

Security had called the medics and a second team; they had taken Trader vin'Tenzing and Security Officer pen'Erit away. The first team tarried to question and record Quin and Skene, requesting after that they keep themselves available for more questions, if any arose. Then, they, too, left, and Skene locked the door.

"Wanna call your dad?" she asked.

Quin sighed.

"I would rather not."

"Ain't the sorta thing you can keep from 'im," she pointed out, reasonably, and made the tongue-clicking sound that locally signaled regret. "Does look like Cheever's gonna stick you with me, though. Sorry 'bout that, Boss."

Quin looked at her, sharply, and sighed.

"First, I will clean the blood out of that rug," he said. "Then, I will call my father. Then, we will reopen the shop."

Skene glanced over at the pale green rug with the damp red stain on it.

"That's gonna clean up, is it?"

"Oh, yes," Quin said blithely. "It only wants a damp towel. I'll take it to the back."

"Good idea," she said. "While you're doing that, I'll call in some supper from the Emerald. All right?"

"Yes," he said, bending to pick up the rug. It occurred to him then that he had been behind.

"Skene," he said.

She turned, comm in hand. "Yeah?"

"You did well," he told her, and smiled. "Thank you."

She snorted. "Welcome. Sorry I made a mess."

"It will clean," he said, and carried the rug through the door to the workroom.

It closed behind him with a snap, and he continued onward until he reached the workbench.

He put the rug down, and stood for a moment, deliberately checking his heartbeat, his breathing, the steadiness of his hand.

When he was satisfied that he was in good order, he dampened a cloth in the sink and put it over the stain, pressing gently, but not rubbing.

Balance, he thought, thinking of the trader, who had lost her son in Korval's strike against its enemy.

His father was going to be furious.

CHAPTER TWELVE

· ·

Tantara Floor Coverings
Surebleak Port

"DID YOU INTEND THE SHOT TO DISABLE?" FATHER ASKED SKENE.

"Yessir."

"And your reasoning?"

Quin, sitting beside Skene in the back of the shop, took a quiet breath. Father was being rigidly courteous, which meant that he was...very angry, indeed. He might be angrier at this moment than Quin had ever seen him, and he could only be glad that fury was directed elsewhere.

"Didn't seem a killin' matter," Skene said, her voice so calm as to be almost expressionless. Sensibly, she wished not to draw fire upon her, but she did not make the mistake of either averting her eyes, or of abasing herself. That, Quin thought approvingly, was the way to deal with Father in a temper.

He moved his hand now, brusquely, signaling Skene to continue.

"Yessir. What I saw was a woman keyed up—I'm thinking she'd maybe had a beer or two before finding us—and her backup wasn't on the same page. I had the range, so I took 'er down. If I'd waited for her to commit, Quin woulda had to deal, and he was so close, he'd've had to kill her. I hit the panic button to make sure Security got here fast as could be, because any way it sliced, we was gonna need Security in it."

"Thank you, Skene," Father said, cold, but courteous. "Well reasoned, and well done. Quin."

103

"Yes, Father."

"You delayed calling me?"

"No more than necessary, sir," he said stoutly, ignoring what sounded like a chuckle from Cheever McFarland, who was on the front door. He met his father's eyes.

"First, it was necessary to deal with Security, and clearing the shop of the wounded. There were questions. After—the trader had unfortunately fallen onto a rug, which required attention."

Father frowned. "Which rug?"

"The pale green Pairute occasional with the cream fringe."

"Ah. I hope that the fringe escaped damage?"

"The angle of the fall was fortunate," Quin assured him. "The fringe was quite untouched, and the Pairute of course gave up the stain."

"Excellent."

"Yes, sir. After I had seen to the rug, I called you. Natesa had been on port, and heard of the incident from Chief Lizardi." He nodded to his father's lifemate, who stood behind his chair, one slim hand on his shoulder. "She arrived in time to share the meal Skene had called in from the Emerald."

Father sighed, and looked up into Natesa's face.

"So, it ended not nearly so badly as it could have done."

She nodded.

"Liz remanded the case to the portmaster," she said. "We should hear her ruling—soon. In the meanwhile..."

"In the meanwhile," Father said sharply, "this is a matter for the delm."

"The delm!" Quin repeated, aghast. "But—why?"

"The trader called Balance upon me, did she not?"

"Yes, sir. She said, as you had deprived her of her heir, she would serve you the same."

"Is that what that was about!" Skene interrupted. "No wonder her 'hand looked sick."

"It is a legitimate Balance," Quin said, sure of his footing on this point as only Kareen yos'Phelium's grandson could be.

"What's it fix?" Skene demanded. "'Stead of one dead kid, we got two. How's that better?"

"The theory is that the two identical losses will cancel each other out," Natesa said in her cool voice. "And thus the universe will be returned to Balance."

Skene took a breath, and Natesa spoke again, quickly.

"It is a social geometry that is very important to Liadens. Universal Balance is at the heart of their culture. If you have questions, Quin's grandmother is an expert on such matters. Your best course is to apply to her."

Skene subsided, and Quin saw her decide not to bother Grandmother with questions. He leaned close to her ear.

"Later, I can try to answer. I'm not an expert, but Grandmother taught me the Code."

"Quite right," Father said. "To return to *your* question, my son—when the Council united to exile Korval from Liad, and struck our name from the Book of Clans, they also guaranteed that these actions put paid to all and any Balances arising from the insult to the homeworld. We are no longer a Liaden clan, and thus we are beyond Balance."

Quin stared at him, and suddenly regretted even the small meal he had eaten. They were *beyond* Balance? How was that possible?

Natesa's belt comm chimed. She brought it to her ear, murmuring her name, listened and said, "Thank you, Portmaster," and pressed the off switch.

She looked to Father. "The portmaster has confined Trader vin'Tenzing to her ship until it may lift. That will be at the portmaster's discretion, and soon. *Habista*, out of Solcintra, has been listed as a known violent ship. That rating will follow it until it has seen a dozen ports without another incident. She has also reported the trader to the guild."

Father took a hard breath, and nodded.

"It is a portmaster's decision, and it is not out of the way. The larger matter—that goes before the delm, who will, I very much fear, be required to carry it to Liad. Quin—"

The front door chimed.

Quin was out of his chair before he had taken thought, and found himself between his father and the door, which was quite idiotic on at least three counts.

Not the least of which was that the person entering the showroom, with Cheever McFarland's sizable permission, was no greater threat than Villy Butler.

He paused just inside the shop, glanced up into Mr. McFarland's face, then at each of them in turn.

"Evenin'," he said courteously. "Boss. Ms. Natesa."

He turned back to the large man beside him.

"Cheever? Should I be goin' now?"

"Depends on your comfort level. You come by for a reason, right?"

"Sure I did. Me and Quin got a date."

He glanced over his shoulder, blond brows pulled slightly together.

"You okay, hon? You're lookin' a little peaky."

"Somebody tried to kill him a couple hours ago," Cheever said before Quin could answer. "I'm guessing he's still a little tense."

"No wonder there. Quin? You wanna reschedule?"

"I would rather not," Quin said. "But you may not get much use from me. I fear Mr. McFarland is correct; I am stupid this evening, else I would not have jumped into Natesa's line of fire."

"No harm," Natesa said from behind him. "Pat Rin, do you go to the delm tonight?"

"Yes," Father said. "Best done at once."

"Does Quin also need to be present, or may you, as his father, conduct all necessary business?"

Quin turned slightly, so he could see the pair of them: Natesa in profile with her head bent, and Father looking up at her.

"You have a plan?"

"I do. *Habista* may be scheduled for short-lift, and Trader vin'Tenzing forbidden the port, but there remains the possibility that she has friends on-world who may be . . . sympathetic to her case. I would prefer that the townhouse be free of targets this evening. A precaution only. If Audrey will take Quin and Luken behind her security, while you and I accept the delm's protection . . ."

She looked up. "Cheever?"

He nodded. "No sense making it easy. We don't expect another attempt, but—we didn't exactly anticipate Trader vin'Tenzing, either."

"We could all three accept the delm's protection," Father said. "Quin? Have you a preference?"

He took a deep breath, weighing choices: face Delm Korval in full formal mode, before he had a chance to think about being *beyond Balance* . . . or spend a pleasant evening with Villy?

"If you please, I would prefer to honor our date, if Villy will have me."

"No worries, there," Villy said. "You come home with me, sweetie; we'll get you smart again in record time."

"Very well," Father said, rising. "The delm may well wish to speak to you, later."

"Yes, sir. But...not tonight."

"I understand entirely. Skene—"

Quin straightened his shoulders.

"Father, I would like Skene..." He didn't quite sigh. After all, it was better—for him and for Skene—to ask for the inevitable, rather than have it thrust upon them.

"I would like Skene to be assigned permanently to my security," he said, meeting his father's eyes.

Father inclined slightly from the waist, allowing a certain amount of irony to be seen.

"I believe that the necessary adjustments in schedule may be made. Skene, is this assignment acceptable?"

"Yessir," she said.

"I am pleased," he said. "You will tomorrow work with Mr. McFarland to identify your backup. In the meanwhile, please continue as you have begun."

"Yessir," she said again.

Father stepped forward, and put his hands on Quin's shoulders, and looked closely into his eyes. Quin tried to keep his face open, noting that Father's anger seemed to have burned out. Now, he only looked tired.

"It might have been a *legitimate* Balance, my son, but it would not have been an *acceptable* Balance. Stay safe." He kissed Quin on the cheek, squeezed his shoulders, and then he was gone, Natesa at his side, nodding to Cheever McFarland as they went through the door and out onto the port.

"Okay," Cheever said, looking around at the three of them. "Let's get this place locked down, so Skene an' me can get you young fellas down to Audrey's for your date. Sound firm?"

Quin looked at Villy, who nodded, and at Skene, who gave him a thumb's-up.

"Sounds firm," he said.

• • • ✳ • • •

It came to Rys, as he browsed the offerings at the media center, that—as the delm's brother, and in pursuit of a task for his brother—he had call on the library and other resources of the house. It was, of course, some distance to the house at the end of the Port Road, but he had paid for one taxi ride, and he supposed he could pay for another without doing violence to the Bedel ethos regarding money.

The delm's brother, he thought, a little dizzy with his presumption, might encompass a *melant'i* sufficient to request that Nova yos'Galan—or Boss Conrad himself!—lend him a car; though his courage might be...less than sufficient.

And, truly, he could walk to the house under Tree, if required; it was scarcely on the other side of the world.

So it was that he came away from the media center with two readers tucked into an inside pocket of his coat, and a half-dozen books. One reader and most of the books would go to Kezzi. The other was, for now, his, and he had found for himself a volume of Liaden children's stories. Surely, the Bedel had their own stories—a multitude, even in his limited experience—but he did not wish his child—his daughter!—to be wholly ignorant of those tales his grandmother had given to him, as a child.

He would, he thought, read the book first, to refresh his memory. He had time. At first, he might tell her the stories, but later, he would show her the words in the book, and teach her how to read. He remembered learning to read, just so, following along with Ifry, his next-eldest sibling, as she found old friends on the page, and discovered new ones.

The night wind woke him from these pleasant digressions, as he rounded the corner toward the nearer gate. Summer it might be, but this late into the evening, the wind was sharp and chill.

He bent his head to protect his face from the cold caress—and heard, behind him, the sound of stealthy footsteps.

Rys slowed, as if the wind pushed him, and listened closely.

He heard three...four?...sets of footsteps: slow-moving and achingly light. So much for his fleeting hope that he was by chance preceding a number of his brothers to the gate. Those of the *kompani* walked firm upon the world, unless they wished to pass unnoticed; then vanish they did and none could mark their passing.

The gate was scarcely a block distant. He would, he thought, walk past, and lead those following up the hill to Boss Conrad's tiny shipyard—Korval's first on Surebleak. Once there, *he* would

elude the security guards, while ensuring that those who followed...did not.

Plan formed, he walked on, passing the gate to the *kompani's*
keeping with neither a glance nor an alteration in pace.

Not so, his followers.

They began to run, feet pounding, as if they had some notion
of what they wanted—and where it was located.

Rys struck the heel of his leg brace hard against the roadway,
activating the pneumatics, and—jumped.

He dared not jump too boldly, for only one leg was augmented.
If he were a fool, he would spin in a circle; or leap, and break
his whole leg on landing.

His jump, though not everything it might have been, gave him
a lead on his pursuers. Best, perhaps, to simply outrun them, and
circle around to another of the gates. But if those following had
been *looking* for a way into the Bedel's world below...

A subtle sound disturbed the air behind him, followed by a
spinning hiss.

Rys jumped again, not high enough, unless the thrower had
meant the cords to kill. As it was, they wrapped his legs, rather
than his throat, and he went down, hard, and rolled.

Footsteps pounded. He grabbed the cord and yanked it free,
snapping to his feet with the thing already spinning in his natural
hand, turning to face the four pursuing shadows. He loosed it at
random, and spun to run on, but the fall had cost him precious
seconds. Three steps only he managed before the leader jumped,
and knocked him down.

Rys kicked with his augmented leg, felt something give, heard
his opponent grunt—and he was on his feet again, knife out, facing three tall Terrans. He took a deep breath, recalling all too
clearly the last time he had been outnumbered and cornered—and
thrust the memory from him.

There was a wall at his back, a blessing and a curse. It would
prevent an attacker from getting behind him, but they could box
him in. Indeed, they were moving into position now.

He danced forward, feinting with the knife. The bearded man
took the bait, leaned in, staff spinning—and Rys slapped him
lightly with his metal hand.

His opponent shouted in pain, staff falling from senseless fingers, but Rys had moved on to the next target, leg flashing out,

bootheel catching a knee, and that was one down who would stay down, though if he had a gun or a throwing blade...

The next backed away, in a knife-fighter's crouch, blade weaving, eyes wary.

Rys slid closer, seeking an opening in the other's defense, and spun as the hiss warned him, thrusting his metal hand up to entangle the bola, ducking as the weights flashed past his head.

The kick landed well, in the center of Rys's back. The knife flew from his fingers as strong arms went around him and held him open for the knife-fighter's thrust.

He brought his heel down hard on his captor's foot, and again, not minding the screams, taking all the thrust the brace could give him, the spin breaking the other's hold, momentum sending him hard against the wall. Rys continued spinning, taking the edge of the knife on the metal arm.

The knife-fighter dropped the blade, and swung a fist, catching Rys in the side of his head.

Light flared, ears rang; he dropped back a step; the other pressed his advantage, and there was the wall against Rys's back.

He raised his metal arm, hand fisted, cocked back and ready to—

"No!"

The voice was familiar, especially at volume, and it was Udari who grabbed the knife-fighter and snatched him close, holding him with a blade laid across his throat, and Rafin who thrust forward, grabbing the metal arm above the elbow, and pinning it to the wall.

"Stop!" Rafin bellowed. "Tell me that you will stop!"

"I will," Rys panted, "but they—"

"They are held by your brothers. You are safe, now, little one. Struggle no longer. So. I release you, yes?"

"Yes," Rys agreed, and Rafin let him go, patting him on the shoulder in a way that was perhaps meant to be soothing, and turning him to face his four erstwhile pursuers, now each in the care of one of his brothers.

"*These,*" Garat said, "we have seen these several times. Why do you come to this district, *gadje?*" he snapped, shaking the man he held by the back of the neck.

"There's—there's a city down there, under the warehouses," the man gasped. "We figured prolly you wanted to share."

"Pah!" Rafin said. "We do not share with thieves."

"So," said the man with the crushed kneecap, "there *is* a city down there."

"*We* are down there," Rafin said. "And others much like us, only more fierce."

"The Bosses have given us the place, which is *our* place," Udari added. "Should we come to *your* place and sit down at your table? Will your wife share her bed with us?"

"We can find you," Garat said. "We *will* find you. And we will watch you."

"We will do these things," Rafin said, sounding almost cheerful. "And maybe your food will taste a little strange, sometimes, only sometimes. And maybe your head will hurt—but not always. We will think on these matters, among brothers. But, I get ahead of myself! First, there is something you must know." He put his hand on Rys's shoulder.

"You think that I stopped my brother from striking you because I was afraid for him, eh?"

The knife-fighter swallowed, Udari's blade lying sweet against his throat.

"Yes," he croaked.

Rafin slapped his knee.

"I knew you for a fool! No! I stopped him because I did not want him to kill you. Not because I love *you*—I do not think I could love you, though you have some little skill with a knife—but because I love *him*, and I would not have him mourn your death."

"*Death*," one of the others muttered.

"You doubt?" Rafin asked. "Here, we will show you!"

He released Rys and stepped aside, reappearing in a moment with the staff one of the attackers had dropped.

"Ironwood," Rafin said, hefting it. "Good. Now, you will see why I stopped this, my brother, from striking you with his fist."

He placed his feet firmly, flexed his knees, and held the ironwood staff between his two gloved hands, across his body.

"Brother, I ask that you strike this staff as you had been about to strike the fool your brother embraces."

Rys took a breath, looked 'round at the men who had been trying to kill him, and then into Udari's face.

His most-loved brother smiled, and nodded slightly.

Rys folded his metal hand into a fist, cocked his arm back, snapped forward one step—and struck the staff.

Splinters flew as the ironwood shattered. Braced as he was, Rafin rocked back. One of his attackers cursed in the local dialect.

Rafin turned slowly about, empty hands held high, slivers of ironwood caught in the palms of his gloves.

"*That* is what you must remember from this encounter," Rafin said. "Now, we will return you to your places, and you will tell the tale of this night among your brothers. You will warn them that we will not be preyed upon. And that even the smallest of us is deadlier than you can know. Brothers, please."

Shadows shifted. The man with the broken kneecap was flung, not gently, onto the back of the knife-fighter, who staggered under his weight.

"Brothers," Udari said, and they turned with their captives, leaving Rys and Rafin alone.

"How are your hands, Brother?" Rys asked.

Rafin shrugged.

"They sting. Without the gloves, I would have broken fingers."

Rys swallowed, thinking about the force of that blow, and what he might have done to the knife-fighter's face.

"If you had not run, we would have come to your side sooner," Rafin said.

"I did not want them to find the gate."

"So said Pulka, and Udari, too."

Rafin dropped a heavy arm around his shoulder, and pulled him into a rough hug.

"Come, now, Brother. Let us go home."

· · · ✳ · · ·

"What do you want to try first?"

Quin was lying on his side across the wide bed, his head propped on his hand; Villy sat beside him, cross-legged, one hand on Quin's knee.

"Do I need to go at them one at a time?" he asked. "I was thinking of a—" he frowned, fair brows pulling together, then smiled.

"I was thinking of a multistrand approach."

"Excellent," Quin said. "A multistrand approach lends itself well to the Trigrace curriculum. If we choose well, the strands will reinforce each other. So"—he smiled—"what do you want to try first?"

"Well, if you put it that way...protocol lessons is important. We're getting more Liadens and not-Surebleak folk coming in. My job's to make them feel good, but if I stand too close, or not close enough, or if I touch what I shouldn't, then the customer won't be happy. And...if I can do or say some added little thing that makes them feel warm and homey—that'll go a good way toward making them feel happy, already."

Quin nodded.

"So, basic kinesics, with a concentration on Liaden protocols. What else?"

Villy looked aside, and it seemed to Quin that his pale skin had taken on a rosy tinge. He held his breath, wondering if he should notice the blush, or ignore it.

Finally, he said, softly, something he'd heard among Father's staff when one was shy of offering an...unsophisticated notion.

"I promise not to laugh."

Villy turned his head so fast, his hair fell into his eyes. He shook it back with a soft chuckle.

"That's fair. I wanna go forward with my math, see?"

Well, of course he did. In Quin's experience, *everyone* wished to go forward with their math.

"You will have to take a placement test," he said, "so that your course of study will begin at the proper level. What else?"

"Is there something—broad? Something that'll give me an overview, at the same time letting me figure out what else I'd like to know?"

"General studies, basic," Quin said promptly. "That is a good choice."

He rolled over onto his stomach, and reached down to the floor, where the portable computer sat.

"I will set up the basic curriculum," he said. "It will take a few minutes. You may begin general studies and kinesics immediately. You must complete the tests before you may begin math."

"Right," Villy said, his hand on Quin's shoulder now as he peered down at the computer screen. Quin set up Villy's student account, with himself as tutor, moved the necessary modules, and showed Villy how to access the learning space.

"You may begin at will," he said, rolling over onto his back. "I had notified Director Faro that I will be tutoring, so all the necessary files will be available to us."

"That's good," Villy said, and then, "Quin?"

He looked up. "Yes."

"Do you need a hug, sweetie? You're still lookin' peaky."

He took stock, but all that came to him was that he was tired. However, Villy was a *hetaera*, and therefore sensitive to the needs of others.

"*Do* I need a hug?" Quin asked.

Villy frowned. "I'm asking," he said.

"And I am asking," Quin answered. "You are the expert on pleasure and comfort in the room."

Another frown, this one thoughtful, followed by a decisive nod.

"Okay, then. The expert says, yeah, you could use a hug. Come on up here to the pillows."

He obeyed, coming to rest on his side, his head on a pillow lightly scented with something agreeably sweet. The bed shifted, and he felt a long body press gently against his back. Villy settled one arm over Quin's waist and gave a deep sigh. Without meaning to, Quin echoed it, feeling his muscles loosen.

"There we go," Villy murmured. "You comfy, hon?"

"Yes," Quin answered softly.

"Me, too. You don't have to worry 'bout anything, right? Just relax, and let all that trouble go."

There came another deep, satisfied sigh, that Quin repeated, following it into sleep.

CHAPTER THIRTEEN

Jelaza Kazone
Surebleak

EVERYTHING CONSIDERED, MIRI THOUGHT, IT HAD BEEN AN instructive interlude, starting with Pat Rin's arrival last night in a towering fury, and demanding immediate speech with the delm. Lucky for the delm, she and Val Con'd gone for a walk in the garden before heading upstairs, else the delm would've heard all about how Quin had only nearly escaped being an Object of Balance, and the members of the Liaden Council of Clans deserved, each one, nothing so rigidly proper as having each of *their* heirs threatened at gunpoint, while snuggled up in Val Con and Miri's warm robes and fuzzy slippers.

Mad as Pat Rin was, that's how cool Natesa'd been, but . . . well, Natesa didn't get mad; she got even. Which was pretty much where Pat Rin stood, give or take an edged phrase or six—along with an extra dollop of outrage because the Council of Clans was in violation of the contract in which the terms of Korval's exile were set out.

"An entire *katrain* of *qe'andra* to craft it," Pat Rin had said, "with an eye toward Balance between all parties! Read before the entire Council; every delm receiving a copy of the final contract with the instruction that it was a Document of Common Cause, and all members of all clans were to be made aware of its contents— And a woman walks into a rug shop on Surebleak Port with the express purpose of Balancing the death of her heir, dead of Korval's necessity!"

115

Yeah, it had been quite the sound-and-light show.

The delm had heard the whole business, including that Quin and Luken were overnighting at Audrey's, an arrangement that struck Miri as particularly sensible; promised action after due thought, and all the rest of the formal rigamarole, which actually seemed to calm Pat Rin down a considerable bit.

After all that, the delm left the room; they all four shared a glass of wine, and so to bed.

Anyhow, a certain amount of temper was expected in the day orders, it being a family of hotheads, and herself marrying like to like.

What Miri *hadn't* expected was the spit-and-hiss they'd gotten from Ms. dea'Gauss when they'd brought her in after breakfast to dump the whole mess into her lap, which, her being Korval's *qe'andra*, was exactly where it belonged.

"That is in clear violation of the terms negotiated!"

Those were fighting words, right there, and never mind the snap that fair shattered the polite coolness of the High Tongue, or the two spots of darker gold high on her cheekbones, which could only be attributable to anger.

Miri'd been nothing short of flabbergasted, but apparently Val Con had been expecting something like this.

"Indeed," Val Con had said, keeping to mode, "it could hardly be plainer. We rely upon you to handle this matter in the most advantageous manner possible. Please draw upon House resources for whatever you may need. The pinbeam is of course open to your needs. A Korval ship and a pilot are yours to command at any hour, should you be required to travel to the homeworld."

"Yes, thank you. First, I will send this information to our office on Liad. It may be possible that one of the elders dea'Gauss who remained with their clients on-world will be able to take this to the Council in proxy. If not..." She moved a hand in a sharp, off-with-their-heads gesture.

"I anticipate. First, the transmission. Then, whatever is necessary. They skirted the edge of honor and called for a skewed Balance at the beginning of this, when the delms' lives were called in forfeit.

"That wiser heads prevailed does no honor to the Council, or to Liad. Korval chose not to contest the order of exile, and the *katrain* worked to restore some measure of correctness to the order and the terms. Had there been true Balance present in the proceedings, the Council of Clans would have commended Korval for its service to the homeworld, and the Captain for his care of the passengers."

"However," Val Con said, his voice about as warm as a deep winter dawn, "that is not how matters fell out. We must play the cards in our hand."

"Indeed, indeed. Forgive an unseemly passion. I will see this matter properly rectified." She bowed, from servant to lord, and left them, the door closing softly behind her.

Miri sighed, gustily.

"And I thought Pat Rin'd gotten up a head of steam."

Val Con looked to her. "You think it an overreaction?"

"Seems to me that what we got is one grief-struck mother deciding on the edge of the hour to hurt somebody just as bad as she got hurt. Pat Rin and Ms. dea'Gauss are acting like it's a conspiracy on the part of the Council of Clans to unilaterally wipe us out." She grinned. "Which, if it is, they gotta stand in line."

"There are, indeed, many before them," he agreed. "And that is why we must be certain that all we are confronted with is one distraught mother. If the Council has failed of some portion of its agreements . . . if it has failed of ensuring that every clan member of every clan has been made aware of the facts of Korval's exile; if it has failed to make plain that there are very real penalties attached to ignoring the guarantees the Council gave on behalf of all Liadens, then those matters must be rectified."

He smiled.

"It would be best, if the line stabilized."

It would be best, she thought, but did not say, *if the line started to shrink.*

"Well." She stood. "I told Kareen I'd talk to her this morning about this job we gave her. What've you got?"

"Mr. Brunner and I are scheduled to speak. He wishes to keep us abreast. Also, I have some papers to review on Shan's behalf."

She paused.

"They find the deed to that island he likes?"

"Ms. dea'Gauss believes so. If so, then we must suppose the Council of Bosses to be the heir to the Gilmour Agency. How convenient, that Pat Rin is in-House."

She laughed.

"He might not think so."

"Or he may. I believe there is a Council meeting this evening. If there is room on the agenda, we might have this settled quickly."

"And since we gotta be there anyway, to give the Road Boss report..."

"Exactly," he said, and came to his feet. "Will you and Talizea do me the honor of joining me for lunch?"

"It sounds good. I'll swing by and talk to Lizzie. If her schedule's not too full, sure—we'll both be there."

"Excellent."

He bent and kissed her lightly on the lips.

"Until soon," he murmured, and left her.

· · · ❄ · · ·

Baker Quill jumped every time the door to her shop opened, which, given the fact that her shop was one of the best things about this end of the street, and got a lot of traffic, made for a lot of jumping.

Still, Bosil couldn't blame her, with Baker Quill's ma havin' got burnt out and then made an example. Boss Conrad and the rest of the Bosses, they didn't allow none of that bidness no more... but it was hard to remember that when a guy come in demanding the insurance.

They was, Bosil thought, just too used to the old ways, yet. The new way, it looked pretty good, but, problem was...it was new. Hard to believe it was gonna stick around.

He'd tried to explain to the baker that there was Patrol all up and down the street, checking in with the other shopkeepers and asking them did a guy come in for insurance, and if the answer was yes, how come they hadn't called the Boss or the Watch on it?

Prolly, Bosil thought, they'd been afraid—remembering the old ways. And there it was, right there, if the streeters didn't start believing in the new ways, and actively *wanting* them to stick around, then...the old ways would come back.

He was thinking about that, and trying to work out how to get the streeters behind the new ways, when for all they knew, sooner or later Conrad would get retired, and the next Boss would start in, just like Moran—the guy Conrad'd retired—and the old ways would come back again, only worse...

Thinking about all that, he got took by surprise, some.

The bell over the door clanged, like it'd been doing all morning, and he didn't even look up until he heard a man's voice say. "You got your insurance ready, Baker?"

"No, I ain't," she said, and Bosil heard her voice quaver, even as he slid off the stool he'd been perching on in the front corner of the bakery. "I ain't paying you no insurance."

"'S'at right?"

The guy was your typical insurance collector—big and mean and not too bright. Didn't have to be bright to scare people and take their money.

"How come you ain't payin'? Your little toy here not makin' any money?"

"I ain't paying on account of it's illegal to collect insurance money."

The guy blinked, and then laughed right out loud.

"*Illegal*? Says who?"

"Says Boss Conrad and the Council of Bosses," Bosil said, bringing his gun up, and unhooking the binders from his belt. "You're under arrest."

The guy turned quick enough, gun in hand. He brought it up, not even bothering to aim. The pellet hit the window by Bosil's head and shattered it.

Bosil ducked, throwing his arm up to shield his face from flying glass, and by the time he was in position again, the insurance guy had shot three baskets full of bread sticks and rolls off the shelves, and was aiming for the clock hanging on the front wall.

"Pay your insurance, or you get made an example," he said over his shoulder to the baker. "That's how it works."

His mistake was that he didn't *look* over his shoulder, too, so he never even saw the rolling pin she brought down on the back of his head with every ounce of strength in her.

Bosil jumped over to where the thug was crumpled up on the floor, grabbed the fallen gun, then got the guy's hands bound behind his back.

"Sorry," he said then, to the baker, who was standing behind the counter, flour on her forehead, and her mouth pressed tight.

"Sorry, Ms. Quill; I shouldn't've ducked."

"Winda blows up in your face, 'course you're gonna duck," she said, still staring at the guy on the floor. "This is my shop. He don't get to shoot up *my shop*. And he don't get to make me a zample. I don't care if it's legal or not legal, or what the Boss does or says—*I ain't havin' it!*"

She looked like she was going to either laugh or cry, or maybe both. Either way, Bosil figured her for mostly all right, so he got on the comm to call the Street Patrol.

· · · ✸ · · ·

On Delgado, at the house on Leafydale Place which had belonged to Jen Sar Kiladi and which she had, for most of their life together, futilely tried to resist thinking of as "home" . . .

At Leafydale Place, Jen Sar had planted a garden in the walled yard adjacent to the house. It had been, so he had assured her, a minor affair, as gardens went: a few herbs, some vegetables, and other *useful plants* to Balance, as he had it, the flowers.

Being an avid and conscientious gardener, he had tended the *useful plants* well, and spared nothing to assure their good health.

But he had doted on his flowers.

They'd filled the tiny space, overflowing their beds, running wantonly down the walkway, and climbing the rough stone wall that sought, vainly, to contain them. The mingled perfumes had been intoxicating on midsummer days, when sunlight pooled inside the walls, turning one's thoughts from scholarship to . . . more elemental activities.

She, born to a scholar mother and raised inside the Wall—she'd known nothing of flowers. Jen Sar's garden had been a revelation, unique in her experience, and, for everything she had known, in the galaxy.

But here at the house of Korval, she had found the model for Jen Sar's tiny walled garden; many times larger, its boundaries marked by the walls of the house itself, its center dominated by an enormous tree.

There was a tree in their garden at home—a *paizon* tree, that gave sweet fruit the size of her palm. One of the *useful plants*, it resembled the giant at the center of Korval's garden as closely as—as Delgado resembled Surebleak.

Kamele sighed, and pulled the borrowed sweater closer around her shoulders.

Certainly, her journey had been educational, and had given insight enough for a lifetime. What remained was to decide how she ought to proceed, now that she had found Daav yos'Phelium, returned to the family he had years ago forsaken, at the end of Jen Sar Kiladi's sudden abandonment of his scholarly duties...

...and his *onagrata* of long-standing.

Of too-long-standing, by the mores and custom of Delgado. Kamele sighed again as she followed the path 'round another overgrown curve. There, before her, was a bank of what looked, to her untrained eye, to be bluebells, Theo's favorite flower in Jen Sar's garden.

Pausing, she smiled, and closed her eyes so that she could better enjoy their subtle fragrance.

The question remained, now that she knew—far from being coerced and held against his will by Clan Korval—that Jen Sar had gone home to stand with his son and family during their time of transition...what *ought* she to do?

Officially, she was on sabbatical. She could—she *should*—return to her studies. As much as she would like to see Jen Sar—Daav— again, it had come to her that perhaps he would not feel the same. She had never known him to be careless in his interpersonal dealings. Surely, then, he had ended their relationship so abruptly for a reason. She might guess that the reason had been to shield her from these "enemies" that Kareen spoke of so casually. A man who had lost his mother and a favorite cousin to foul play, and who had seen his lifemate murdered, might be careful of the safety of any others to whom he had formed...an attachment.

Intent upon her role of Avenging Scholar, she had undone his good work, and exposed herself to danger. Best, then, to fade back into academia, where she would be one scholar among a host, safe in anonymity. Bestleaze, where the primary sources for the paper she had in mind were located, was not a Safe World, but it was one of the major research universities, charged with the guardianship of many precious documents. No one was permitted inside who was not properly credentialed. She would be protected, there.

Perhaps she could ask Kareen to write her, when...Daav yos'Phelium returned home from the care of Korval's "allies." He had been wounded; she would like to know that he had recovered well. That he was...happy.

...or perhaps it was best not to know. Best, perhaps, to begin, however belatedly, to heal herself of what Ella had maintained all along was an unnatural fascination.

Yes, she thought. It was time to let Jen Sar go, fully. He had made it quite clear that their lives were no longer running in parallel. Perhaps she would take a new *onagrata*, when she returned from her sabbatical. The house was too big for only her and the cats.

Or perhaps she would ask Ella to live with her...that might be best of all.

First things first, however. She should inform her hosts of her intended departure, which meant researching the ships due in to Surebleak Port and which might be going...

"In a green study, Scholar?" came a voice lately very familiar to her.

Kamele opened her eyes, and turned on the pathway to smile at Kareen yos'Phelium.

"In a sense. I was thinking that, my concerns having been put to rest, it's time for me to continue with my studies, and leave the house in peace."

Kareen tipped her head, her dark eyes quizzical.

"I had not observed any lack of peace generated by your presence. Indeed, it may be said that the honor of caring for a guest has imposed a certain degree of...cohesiveness in the face of our changed circumstances. And—forgive me!—was it not your purpose to speak with my brother?"

"It had been," Kamele admitted. "You must understand that his departure was very irregular and not what I'd come to expect from him. In my ignorance, I became concerned that he had been...coerced, or otherwise stood in need of a friend. Now that I've seen that he chose to return, and is in no need of—of a rescue..."

She faltered, her cheeks warm.

"Though he may yet stand in need of a friend," Kareen murmured. "However, it is perfectly comprehensible that you may find time hanging upon your hands, when you have been accustomed to having occupation. Indeed, it is precisely that realization which moved me to come in search of you. I wonder if you might accompany me into the city."

"Certainly, if I can be of use..."

"I believe that you may be," Kareen said, offering her arm. They turned toward the house.

"The case is that I intend to set up my own establishment, such as I have been accustomed to having on Liad. My son believes that this is unnecessary; and in any wise has been too busy with his duties to assist in locating something suitable. The fact remains that I am inconveniently fixed here, if I will continue *my* work, which I certainly must do. I therefore applied to an associate for her assistance. Today, she sends word that she believes she may have found something which will answer my needs, gives an address, and proposes to meet me there in two hours, local.

"I wonder if you would do me the honor of bearing me company, and also of giving me your opinion of this house that Audrey has found."

She had, Kamele thought, been wanting to see more of the city. Such as it was.

"I'd be delighted," she said.

CHAPTER FOURTEEN

· ·

The Bedel

"ARE THESE ENOUGH GRAPES TO MAKE WINE?" MEMIT ASKED, eying their small arbor doubtfully.

Rys laughed; a mistake that made his bruised face ache.

"No, not nearly enough. For wine, there must be an excess of grapes—five kilograms will yield about four liters.

"However, we have enough to give to Jin, to make jelly, or to offer raw, as part of the evening meal."

Memit nodded, her eyes on the arbor, and her mind obviously on the subject of grape production. "Will the harvest increase?"

In truth, he doubted it. He had doubted the packet of vines that Memit had found, engineered for quick growth in poor soil, would yield grapes at all. He had been wrong in that; the vines *had* grown quickly, putting forth pale red fruits almost too heavy for them, whereupon he and Memit built the arbor to support the fragile tendrils. He had still half expected the fruits to kill the vines. That they had managed a harvest at all was notable, and Rys suspected that one harvest was all the engineered plant was capable of producing.

"Grapes," he said now, "are difficult. I told you how my clan grew row upon row of grapes, halfway up the side of a mountain. They were a special grape we had nurtured, that loved the mountain soil, and the cooler air. There were other grapes that loved the heat and the dry soil of the near desert. Each variety had its preferences; each yielded its own flavor, and chose its own form.

125

"The desert grapes were small and green and tart; ours, children of the mountain, were round and red. The desert grapes made a white wine that tasted as fresh as the clouds in a summer sky. The wine that came from our vineyard was as red as heart's blood and as sweet as love."

Memit had turned to look at him, a soft smile on her thin, hard face.

"Our Rys bids fair to become a poet."

He felt his cheeks warm, and shook his head, carefully.

"I fear I am eloquent only on subjects dear to me."

"Well, that's as should be, isn't it? But tell me now, Rys Silver-tongue, are these grapes jam or are they supper?"

"There's only one way to be certain." He reached up and plucked a small bunch, and offered it to Memit. She took two, and he did. He raised his as if they were a glass and he offering a toast. Memit copied him, and they each tasted of the pale fruits.

It was as he had feared; the skin was strong, the pulp grainy, and the taste...bland. Even had they produced enough to make the attempt, there was no heart in these grapes; nothing from which to make any wine worth drinking.

Nor were they table grapes. Oh, they could be eaten at table well enough, but they would scarcely provide counterpoint to a salty cheese.

He sighed, and looked up to find Memit watching his face.

"Jelly?" she asked.

"Raisins," he said definitively. "I will speak with Jin."

Memit nodded.

"Maybe," she said, "there are other vines—vines like your family knew, or even the desert vines—to be found."

"Maybe there are," he said, "but we have neither a desert nor a mountain." He hesitated. "It was said to me that Surebleak ought to have its own vintage."

"Is that possible?"

"It may be. I must...dream upon it."

Memit nodded at this prosaic answer, and dusted her hands off on the knees of her pants.

"Well,"—she used her chin to point at the cluster he still held—"might as well bring that along to Jin."

"Yes," he said. He added the grapes to the harvest basket

and swept it to his shoulder, grimacing slightly at the protest of hard-used muscles.

He and Memit left the garden together.

They were at the edge of the common when they were joined by Kezzi, Silain's apprentice. For a wonder, her braid was neat, and her clothes not *much* askew.

"Rys, the *luthia* sends that you should have dinner at her hearth."

He paused, looking into the child's brown face. A summons from the *luthia*, of course, was not to be ignored.

"Say to the *luthia* that I will gladly come to her as soon as I have brought the basket to Jin," he told Kezzi.

"I'll take the basket," Memit said brusquely. "Don't keep the *luthia* waiting."

"The raisins—"

"I'll give her the grapes and tell her what you told me. After the *luthia*, you can talk to Jin about raisins. Kezzi, are you going with Rys?"

"No, I'm to take the meal at Jin's hearth."

Memit gave him a stare, as if this were significant. He surrendered the basket to her, and turned his steps to the *luthia*'s hearth.

"Grandmother? You wished to see me?"

Silain looked up from the tangle of beads and ribbons on her lap.

"Rys, my child. It comes to me from Pulka that you were attacked in the World Above yesterday. I wonder why you did not tell me yourself."

He knelt at the edge of her rug and looked into her face, spare and beautiful with her years.

"It was late, and I had taken no lasting harm; there was no reason to break your rest. Rafin made sure of my hand, and my leg, before Udari returned and we retired to our tent. This morning, we went early Above, to find meat for the evening meal, then I was promised to Memit, in the garden."

"You are tender of an old woman's rest."

She raised her hand and touched light fingers to his face. He flinched, then sighed when a gentle warmth eased his bruises.

"You have experienced no ache in the head, or confusion of your purpose?"

"No, Grandmother."

"That is well, then. Will you share the meal with me?"

"I am glad to share the meal. Shall I fetch it from Jin's hearth?"

"No need; Jin sent a basket early. It's in the warming box. If you'll serve it out, I'll put these away."

"Certainly," he said.

Carefully, he brought the bowls out from the box, and carried them to the hearth. Silain's he gave to her; his, he placed by his rug while he fetched tea, in two metal cups.

"Ah, that is well!" Silain said appreciatively, using a piece of flatbread to scoop up the saucy ground meat.

Rys tasted his, and agreed. He had doubts, when he and Udari had found the joint. It had been dry, and tough-looking, which accounted for its place near the back of the butcher's bin. It had been a large piece of meat, and Udari had no doubts at all, so it came back with them, to the *kompani*, and was given to Jin, who had frowned, and said, "Stew."

Apparently, it had been too tough even for stew, thus the coarse grinding and mixing with spicy sauce.

"Tell me," Silain said, scooping up more meat, "about this attack."

He obliged her, seeking to be matter-of-fact, and neither downplay nor overstate his danger.

"It troubles me that these men knew of a city below the warehouses," he said.

"It troubles me, as well," Silain said serenely. "Alosha has spoken to me of men who loiter near this gate—looking, waiting. So, not all of our secrets are known, but it is worrisome that any have escaped. Alosha thinks that new gates will buy us time. He ponders the question of whether these men might be let inside, to meet with ghosts and monsters."

"That might not be . . . wise, for that would assure them that there *is* something beyond the gate."

"So he also reasoned. The headman will do nothing rash."

The headman was, in Rys's opinion, a thorough thinker. He would dream, and talk to those of the *kompani*, and dream, and think until he had found a solution.

"What else have you been about?" Silain asked.

"I have spoken with Droi. She tells me that we have made between us a daughter. She will have curly hair."

Silain laughed softly.

"Droi's Sight rarely deceives her. What took you Above, yesterday?"

"I wished to find what there was to be found," he said. "I had intended to come to your hearth this evening, or perhaps tomorrow. I found a thing for you, and another thing for Kezzi."

In fact, one of the readers he had found had been broken during last night's affair. The unbroken one, he had decided, upon learning of this casualty, would go to Kezzi. He could easily find another, for himself, the next time he was in the City Above.

"I look forward to receiving your gift," Silain said gently.

She set her plate aside, and he did the same.

"Grandson, there is a thing that I want you to do."

He looked up into her eyes.

"I will be pleased to do whatever is required of me."

She smiled, and extended a hand to touch his knee.

"You're a good boy," she said indulgently. "It's not so much of a burden. I only want you to dream for me, Rys."

He blinked. The Bedel archived their knowledge and their skills in dreams; thus, to dream, was to learn. In the time since he had been returned to his soul, given back his life, and been accepted as a true son of the *kompani*, he had dreamed many dreams, including the Bedel language, and the mysteries of those devices that Pulka constructed, that his brother Val Con dignified as Old Tech, with a certain edge of...distrust. In order that he become a more able assistant to Memit, among the plants, he had dreamed vistas of indoor gardens, which had led him to pursue dreams of lighting systems...

...which had sent him again to Pulka, dragging his unwilling brother to the garden level to discuss light tubes and gamma tuning...

Hastily, he brought his attention back to the moment.

"I will be pleased to dream as the *luthia* directs," he said.

Silain smiled. "That's well. But you must know that these dreams I would have you dream must be anchored in your waking mind. So, you will also come to me every day." She paused, as if considering, then smiled. "You see that I heap new burdens upon you. Have you taken your turn escorting your sister Kezzi to her brother's house?"

"Not yet, *luthia*. Shall I?"

"Yes. Beginning tomorrow morning. You will tell your brother Vinchi that the *luthia* has put this upon you."

"Yes," he said, wondering how walking Kezzi to catch the car to school would net him a lesson with Silain.

"Yes," she repeated. "And when you have seen her and her brother off, you will return here, to this hearth, where we will share tea, and do what else is needful."

Well, that hadn't been difficult, had it? Rys thought, and smiled.

"I will do as the *luthia* has said," he promised. "However, if I am to find my brother Vinchi with this message, I will need to leave you now..."

Because Vinchi watched the entrances until the hour after the common meal, whereupon he betook himself to their sister Bazit's tent, and he would not be pleased to be interrupted there.

"That is well," Silain said, smiling at him. "I'm pleased to have shared a meal with you. Here, now." She reached into her sleeve and brought out a set of tiles in their silver frame.

Rys took it in his natural hand, and stowed it carefully in a pocket of his vest.

"May I refresh your tea before I go, Grandmother?" he asked.

"That would be a gentle kindness," she said, handing him the battered metal mug.

He rose, poured the tea and brought it to her, pausing to consider the plates, in need of washing, and Jin's box...

"Kezzi will tend to it," Silain told him. "Go, now. Find Vinchi."

"I will," he said, and bent to kiss her cheek.

• • • ❉ • • •

The back seat of the so-called "landau" was warm and spacious; the seat cushions took Kamele's shape immediately. Compared to the taxicab she had ridden in from the port to Korval's house—well, there was no comparison, really. The taxi had been a utility vehicle, serviceable, practical, and well matched to its tasks.

The landau was...perhaps practical, if it was necessary that its occupants arrive at their destination in a state of unruffled euphoria. Indeed, if there was fault to be found, it was that the temperature in the passenger compartment was just slightly too warm.

The large armsman, Diglon, was at the controls in the front of the vehicle. In order to accommodate his length, the driver's seat and the window between the passengers' compartment and the driver had been moved back, so Kareen had told her.

"Are you comfortable, Scholar? I fear we are somewhat cramped with the new arrangement."

Kamele laughed.

"I think that the two of us could work together comfortably in here all day long," she said. "I'm not at all cramped; in fact, I'm feeling quite decadent."

"You are kind to say so," Kareen answered, settling back into her chair with a sigh. "It is so very pleasant to be properly warm."

"Is Liad a...warm world?" Kamele asked.

"It is a temperate world, with what our good weatherman, Mr. Brunner, styles a *moderate* climate. Mr. Brunner, you understand, does not approve of *moderate* climates; they offer no scope. One gathers that Surebleak holds greater challenges to one of his calling. Those of us who do not aspire to Mr. Brunner's proficiency found the climate...unremarkable. Indeed, I rather miss the tedium of the moderate, when all I might need to consider, upon walking out, was whether or not it was raining."

The car began to move down the drive; Kamele looked out at the browning lawn, and heard Kareen sigh again.

"We will have Surebleak grasses in place by the next growing season, the gardener tells me. She thinks it a good thing, as I shall, if the lawns will be green again."

This was more complaint than she was used to hearing from Kareen.

"Is it permitted to say that I enter into your sadness, for the loss of your home?" she asked, carefully.

Kareen turned her head away from the window and met Kamele's eyes. She was silent for so long that Kamele began to worry that she had overstepped badly. Kareen was normally the most patient of teachers; really very like Jen Sar in her approach.

"It is permitted that one offer condolences upon the loss of kin," she said slowly. "Other, more minor, losses, such as those taken at dice, or cards, or from the 'change—those are not mentioned, being too trivial. Unless, of course, one deliberately wishes to push a point."

"I—"

"Peace, I do not think that you wish to play *melant'i* games with me," Kareen said, and smiled her cool, slight smile. "And

I must confess to you that it is not done, that one will publicly lament such a loss as we have taken—of our home, and our climate, and our culture. Such things are spoken of with kin, or with close friends."

There was a small pause, while Kamele tried to think of something inoffensive and soothing to say.

"Then, I'm sorry for your losses," she said slowly, "but pleased that you're able to share them with me. On Delgado, we said that a burden was lighter, for being shared."

Kareen's eyebrows had risen, and Kamele paused. Had it been Jen Sar, those eyebrows would have given notice that she had surprised, and perhaps not entirely pleased, him.

It may have been the case with Kareen, as well, for she did something else that Jen Sar sometimes did, when he considered a conversation had meandered too far in a direction he did not wish to pursue: she inclined her head and murmured a polite nothing.

"My thanks, Scholar. We say a similar thing: *Many hands make the work light.*"

The car entered the Port Road, and continued onward, apparently hitting none of the potholes or frost heaves the taxi had discovered on the way out to the house. It was like sitting in one of the parlors, back at the house, quiet and conducive to napping.

To fall asleep would certainly be an insult to her host, and Kamele cast about for a topic that might give Kareen's spirits a lift.

"I am interested in your field," she said. "I think you said it was social protocols?"

Kareen tipped her head.

"In a manner of speaking. My work lately has been to codify social and ethical behaviors, rectify them with those protocols put down in the Liaden Code of Proper Conduct, update the Code as necessary and see to its reprinting and distribution.

"However, since the relocation, my work has been redefined. The delm requires me to observe the society in which we now find ourselves, and compile a plan for the clan's new direction, now that the Code no longer . . . constrains us, as the delm would have it. I prefer *informs us.*"

Kamele frowned.

"But surely, ethics and moral behavior are constants!"

Kareen smiled, fully, warmly.

"I would venture to say, Scholar, that you are not a Scout."

"No, of course not. But—"

"But, the Scouts hold—and they are in some measure correct—that all custom is valid; and all law is just—inside the society which formed them. It is therefore my task to discover the ethos and the rule of Surebleak—the core of its custom—and codify it, not only so Korval will find its place more easily, but so that Surebleak will know itself again.

"We have, in Surebleak, as the history is related by certain of the native Bosses, a traumatized society even before my son descended upon it to impose his will and his necessity. While I understand what he has done, why he has done it; and while it is not my place to argue against necessity; it is my duty to deduce Surebleak's society before it is fractured yet again, and its core is hidden forever under the rubble of multiple disasters.

"This is why I must be located in the city."

"I understand your mission with regard to Surebleak," Kamele said slowly. "In fact, I understand it very well. I am, as you know, a scholar. I am very familiar with primary sources and interview techniques. If I can be of assistance to you on that front, I willingly offer my services." She hesitated, recalling her earlier resolve. "At least until I must leave."

"You are kind," Kareen said, "and I willingly accept your offer of help."

Kamele smiled.

"Thank you; I do like to be busy. But there's something I still don't understand."

"You wonder, perhaps, why Korval, which, as a Liaden clan, brings the Code with it, would wish to reshape itself to Surebleak's mores?"

"Yes."

Kareen shifted slightly in her seat, and folded her hands on her knee.

"Society," she said slowly, "is like a tightly packed cube of blocks. Each block is held in place by the pressure of the blocks surrounding it. Remove a block from the gridwork and you accomplish two things:

"First, you destabilize the entire structure. That is perhaps recoverable, depending upon the size or the number of blocks that have been removed, and the pressure of the remaining blocks. Had Korval alone been removed from the gridwork of Liaden society, there would have been very little change. While the grid might have flexed, another House might, or might not have, expanded to fulfill Korval's function in addition to its own; or perhaps matters would have moved along perfectly well with a little space between one set of blocks. A society as old and as rigid as Liaden society might never notice the removal of *one* block."

"But other clans left Liad, too," Kamele said, "and came here to Sureleak."

"Indeed they did. I would venture to say that Liaden society is going to experience—is already experiencing—a change greater than any which has taken place since the Migration itself.

"However, the future shape of Liaden society is outside the scope of my duties. My attention is directed toward the second effect—the forces which act upon the block that has been removed from the gridwork. Without cultural support, the block may crumble; it might ossify; it might, to state an extreme case, explode. For its own health, it must find another grid to support it and which might benefit from its presence."

Kamele frowned.

"Won't Clan Korval and the other Liaden clans simply form an . . . emigre society?"

"It is possible that they will do so, and such a subculture might well serve a useful purpose, as additional support for the larger culture. But there we find cause for more concern. The Sureleak societal grid is scant; there are too few blocks in it; and far too much room between them, so that many of the existing blocks have fallen over. If we are to raise the fallen, and strengthen the whole, it will perhaps be best to marry the society we brought with us to the society that—barring the catastrophe which left it as Pat Rin found it—ought to have been Sureleak's."

"Producing a new gridwork . . . a cube built on the strengths of both former grids?"

"It is an attractive proposition, is it not? However, we cannot know that we ought even make the attempt until we can discover what Sureleak was meant to be."

She sighed, turned her head to glance out the window, then back again to meet Kamele's eyes decisively.

"There is another risk, not inconsiderable, for what functions on a large scale also functions at the clan level. Since Korval was formed, it was yos'Galan's sense of propriety and ethics that guided the clan. For the first time in the clan's existence, we are in a situation that favors yos'Phelium's strengths over yos'Galan's. The delm foresees that the clan itself will change, and while they acknowledge that change is inevitable, and even, perhaps, to be desired, they wish to guide it as much as they are able, to minimize damage, and to be certain that the clan's obligations are met, whatever new form the clan may assume."

Kamele closed her eyes, thinking, feeling the shape of the problem, and how she'd lay out the project grid, if it was hers to undertake, and how many grad students, underfaculty, and emeriti she would need to complete it in a timely fashion.

She opened her eyes to find Kareen watching her with patient curiosity.

"That's quite a project," Kamele said.

Kareen laughed, which Kamele had never heard her do. It was a full, pleasant sound.

"It is, indeed," Kareen said at last, "quite a project. But, there, we are alike! I, too, am most content when I am busy."

INTERLUDE ONE

. . . .

On Luminier Plain

"DO YOU REMEMBER, *VAN'CHELA*, THE BOY ON AVONTAI TO WHOM we brought the dulciharp?"

Her voice was sharper than a mere reminiscence would call for. Perhaps he had drifted off. He feared that he had done so. Well. At least he had waked for her. He did not think he had many more such wakings left.

But the question... from very early in their time together, their first courier run, in fact. He smelled clove and spiced brandy; saw a surprised, round face; light oiling ivory keys, and turning harp strings to silver; he heard three sweet notes, and a woman's anguished question.

"Indeed," he murmured, in this fleeting present he shared yet with his lifemate. "I remember."

"Of course you do."

He felt something... her hand smoothing his hair. It was, he thought, a measure of how far he had journeyed, that he might feel the hand of the dead caress him. Perhaps, when he was done with his own dying—no, *surely*, when he had passed beyond waking, then he would rise up, his strength renewed, to take her hand. He would look down into her face and they would share a smile before they ventured on, together.

That was, he thought, beginning to drift again, a pleasant fantasy, and if it never came to pass, how would he know?

"And do you remember, *van'chela*," Aelliana insisted, still in that sharp, bright voice, "that, when we left, after making our delivery, you led us to a different door to exit, rather than return to the entrance? I asked you why, and you did not know, only that it seemed best."

Had he done so? He did not recall it.

"It sounds very like me," he murmured, and raised a hand—tried to raise a hand—to catch hers.

Her fingers were warm, by which he knew that he was cold.

Very cold.

He drew a breath—he thought he did. He was sleepy; these questions exhausted him, though the sound of her voice was a joy and a comfort.

"Daav!" That was sharp, indeed, and he felt her fingers tighten on his. "Listen to me!"

"As long as I am able..." he breathed.

"I am cruel," he heard her say, and felt her lips brush his.

"Daav?"

"Yes."

"I have found us a different door, *van'chela*. You must trust me."

Trust her? He trusted her before he trusted himself.

"Yes," he agreed.

"Yes. You must walk—only a very little way."

Walk.

He remembered walking. He had come to himself, walking, slowly, uphill. There had been some sparse vegetation, and overhead a sky as pitted and grey as hull plate.

Further walking had discovered only minor improvements in the landscape, while he tired far out of proportion to his labors until, at last, he had achieved the summit and a pasture, as grey and terrible as every other thing in this place, and, only a few steps before him, a door.

He had been puzzled, a little, to find a door by itself at the top of this arid hilltop. An old door, surely, of rich, dark wood, with the Tree-and-Dragon upon it. He had smiled, then, recognizing the front door of Jelaza Kazone, and set toward it with renewed energy.

Six steps out, perhaps six steps from the door itself, he—struck a wall.

Struck it, and fell, into a swoon.

When he again came to himself, and opened his eyes, it was

to unrelenting greyness, and his lifemate at his side. He had
been glad of that, but so...very...tired. Korval's door was gone,
hidden from him by a thick mist, as dry and dusty as the...
material...he lay upon.

"Daav?"

"Aelliana, I think that...walking is beyond me."

"A very little way," she repeated. "I will help you."

He wasted no more of his meager strength in protest, but
instead, when her arms came around him, used it to rise,
clumsily. He was shivering and ill by the time he gained his
unsteady feet, but he did rise, because she wished it of him.
He had never been able to, nor wished to deny her, anything
she might ask.

When he had rested, only a labored breath or two, she urged
him to take a step...a second...a third—and he managed it.
In this, he was assisted, not only by Aelliana's embrace, but the
strong breeze that had sprung up all a-sudden at their backs,
pushing them gently; then not so gently. Shoving them, in fact,
toward two glowing tunnels around which the dry mist swirled.

"What is that?" Panic brought clarity, and a tithe of strength.

Aelliana's arms were not around him anymore—there was no
need; the wind kept him upright. She squeezed his hand.

"The different door," she answered.

"There are two doors."

"There are two pilots," she said, her voice calm. "Daav. Trust
me."

He trusted *her* implicitly—his pilot, his lifemate, his love. But
those glowing portals he trusted not at all. He tried to pivot, to
let the wind rush past him, but he was too weak for such tactics.
Aelliana's grip on his hand kept him from falling to his knees,
even as he realized that there was no denying the wind now;
he—they—*would* enter the portals.

"You will not lose me!" Aelliana told him, her voice as strong
and relentless as the wind. "Daav, I swear it!"

No, of course he would not lose her; how could he? They were
one, or not completely so, though she was always with him...

There was an edge of blackness to his thoughts, and he recalled,
laboriously, that he was dying.

Before them, the portals flared; the wind blasted. His soul
shivered at its moorings. He staggered. Perhaps he fell.

Above him, before him, a portal sprang open. Beyond was a tunnel, suffused with raging white light. And, almost, he laughed.

So, he thought, it is into a sun, after all...

The wind gusted; he flew forward...

And Aelliana let go of his hand.

INTERLUDE TWO

. . . .

Tactical Space

STRATEGIC ACTION HAD FAILED TO PRODUCE RESULTS. THE PROB-
lem was therefore transferred to Tactical.

The problem...was not simple. It was, in fact, Jeeves thought
with uncharacteristic impatience, precisely the sort of complex and
dangerous situation that could only be produced by a lack of proper
consultation with the probability engine and Strategy Module.

Not that he expected Captain Waitley—or any organic person—
to have access to such things. Indeed, Captain Waitley was new
to her station, and new to her ship. Her situation had been desperate: crew were in peril, and all of her necessity had been to
liberate them with their lives intact, preserve the integrity of a
space station, and neutralize an implacable enemy.

It was not Captain Waitley who had been at fault, though
one might wish her to be somewhat less dependent upon tactical solutions. The organic young were result-oriented, and their
ability to plan at true long range was...limited.

But, no, the fault here lay with *Bechimo*, Captain Waitley's vessel, who possessed a very fine and nuanced probability engine, if
Jeeves's reading of his specs was correct, and a grasp of strategy
that rivaled—and that Jeeves suspected at root specifically *was*—the
Uncle's own.

Bechimo should have not only made his captain aware of the
resources at her command, but briefed her on the likeliest long-
term results of using those resources.

Certainly, *Bechimo* could have crafted a low-impact solution that achieved the goals of his captain in regard to her crew, the station, and the enemy. Yet, for reasons beyond Jeeves's ability to parse, *Bechimo* had allowed Captain Waitley to download—download!—a newly-wakened independent intelligence into the computational resources available among seven ancient starships. One intelligence, distributed among thirteen cramped and faltering computers— surely, *there* was a recipe for disaster that even an organic brain could grasp! Added to the circumstances of being downloaded, rather than properly installed into a tuned and ready environment, and the violence to which the new intelligence had wakened . . .

It was hardly a wonder that *Admiral Bunter*, as the newborn had named himself, was confused.

An intelligence distributed among seven ships, several of them heavily armed, ought never, in Jeeves's considered opinion, be confused.

Which brought the tally of errors 'round to Jeeves, himself, who had originally assigned the problem to Strategy.

The most recent direct communication from *Admiral Bunter* had made it entirely, horrifyingly plain that a tactical solution was required to answer the mess that tactics had produced.

Pirates undocking. Will pursue and destroy.

Pirates? Jeeves queried, thinking that Jemiatha's Jumble Stop seemed peculiarly prone to pirates.

His response had been a record of a transaction between Stew, the station's head repair technician, and a woman in worn and outmoded leathers, her face scored by the passage of years.

Stew was seen to put a crate of parts on the counter. The woman rummaged through it, and indicated that a piece was missing. Stew returned to the back room.

The woman snatched three parts out of the crate, shoved them hastily into her pockets, and ran.

Stew returned to the counter, the requested part in his hand, looked about, called—and shrugged, dropping the new part into the crate, and putting everything aside to be dealt with later.

The woman had already reached her ship and undocked by the time the record of the transaction reached *Admiral Bunter*. The ships had immediately brought guns on line.

That is not a pirate, Jeeves had sent. *Only a petty thief. Stop her; do not fire upon her.*

Pirates are thieves, came the answer, followed by: *Target destroyed.*

INTERLUDE THREE

· ·

Vivulonj Prosperu
In Transit

REBIRTH IS A BRIEF, CHANCY GEOGRAPHY, A TENUOUS BRIDGE between two absolutes.

The Uncle had attended many rebirths, most of them simple crossings from material that was aged and outworn to a fresh, new environment. He had assisted in extractions from material so badly mangled it must have been thought that all hope was lost. He had guided captured intelligences, long accustomed to the bodiless state, into warm and waiting flesh. He had himself died and been reborn, countless times.

But never before had he attempted to extract two intelligences, two personalities—two *souls*—who had for many years cohabited a single body, each into its own vessel.

The shared body had taken terrible wounds; wounds from which it had not, and despite the best efforts of others of the Uncle's devices, could not, fully recover. He had considered simply allowing the body, and its occupants, to die the real death. But that death—*those deaths*—would have created... difficulties with Clan Korval; for the treasured elders of the clan had taken their wounds while they had been—he rejected, as he suspected the primary of the wounded pair would also reject the phrase—*in his care*. Certainly, however, they had been partners in the same task, and it would not escape Korval's notice that the Uncle reposed in the rosiest of good health while their elders were far otherwise.

143

He expected that the decision he had taken, to oversee these chancy rebirths, would find only slightly more favor with the Dragon—and that only if he returned to them both elders, intact.

His hope lay in the fact that he had not made this decision by himself. He had received input and, he dared hope, support from a source that Korval would consider unimpeachable.

The Tree—Korval's Tree: Korval's damned, *meddling* Tree, as some would have it...

The Tree had given into the care of the primary, Daav yos'Phelium, former delm of Korval and father of the present delm—two seed pods. The Tree, as the Uncle understood the matter, often bestowed such treats upon the members of Korval, who individually and together stood as its protecting Dragons. It would have been second nature for Daav to have eaten the pods when he received them.

However, in this instance, and according to the man himself, one of those two pods had been intended for Aelliana Caylon, Daav's lifemate, assassinated more than twenty Standard years ago, who had been existing since in the pathways of his brain, or in the cloud of his mind, or in a hidden palace in his heart.

So, one pod for Aelliana...and the second pod, offered to Daav in the hope that the Tree's largesse could heal what the Uncle's devices could not?

"Not ripe," the man had said. It had amused him; it was Korval's humor to savor such ironies, the more so if one's life was the stake.

But—*not ripe*? Did the Tree gamble in futures?

Could the Uncle, who had seen very many strange things down the course of a long and oft-times perilous life, afford to suppose that it did not?

The subjects were entangled, to what degree he could only guess, lacking any instrument that might measure such a thing. He had only the Tree's...assurance?...that they would be able to separate themselves. Blanks were expensive. Yet, he was in unknown space. He could not know if a single blank could accept or, ultimately, nurture two intelligences; that ability might well be unique to Daav yos'Phelium's brain chemistry, which the Tree had without a doubt...adjusted.

And how, indeed, if the Tree were correct: that Korval's elders had both the ability and the desire to separate—and found only one likely receptacle waiting? He might destroy both in such a wise, or force the unthinkable upon them.

Better—much better—to be generous, and hope that the Tree knew what it was doing.

So, the Uncle made his decision as much from courtesy as certainty; two birthing units were prepared with fresh medium—blanks; undifferentiated bipedal shapes; hairless, sexless, dermis the color of unbaked dough.

There had been, in the case of the primary subject, genetic material a-plenty with which to seed the blank. When he emerged from the birthing unit, to ingest what the Uncle very much hoped would be his ripe seed pod, Daav yos'Phelium would look—*would be*, according to any test that might be administered—precisely himself, though rather younger in appearance.

Aelliana Caylon, however . . .

There had been no genetic material for Aelliana Caylon available within the Uncle's considerable reach; therefore, he improvised. Research had garnered the trivialities of eye color, hair color, height, weight. Her body memory, if she still retained it after so long a time as a ghost, would impose something like her former face upon the bland and agreeable features of the blank. She would, in time, *look like* the Aelliana Caylon who had been, but, genetically, she would be a patchwork thing; a monster, to lineage-obsessed Liadens.

He hoped that Aelliana Caylon could be brought to see the advantages of her situation, though he expected it would be a shock to her.

And he very much hoped that Korval could find its way to be . . . practical in the instance.

Or, the Uncle thought, as he considered the transfer status board, Korval might need do nothing more than accept its deaths and mourn them.

For it appeared, given the lack of activity among the various dials and gauges, that Daav yos'Phelium had turned his face away from rebirth.

The Uncle sighed, and bowed his head.

It was, after all, for each to decide the question for themselves: would they live or would they die? Both choices were valid.

And, indeed, the Uncle admitted to himself in the silence of the rebirthing chamber, he had overstepped. He had taken the decision to offer life in service of his own convenience, rather than at the subjects' explicit direction.

In those rare cases when rebirth was refused, the ... soul ... naturally remained with the original material. Presumably, in this case, both souls would remain entangled, and die, lost to oblivion.

What was the phrase, so apt in this instance, that acknowledged both the right to choose, and the probable consequence of, desperate action? He thought for a moment, then nodded to himself.

Pilot's choice.

So be it.

The life signs monitor had darkened from orange to red, indicating a subject in desperate circumstances. There was no need to prolong this; no reason to be cruel. The decision had been made.

The Uncle reached to the console. His fingers touched the termination switch ...

A bell rang, bright and joyous.

The Uncle snatched his hand back, eyes on the console, where the instruments were now glowing a brilliant green, dials dancing, denoting a transfer that was fully under way.

A chime sounded, muted. The indicators on the birthing drawers were green also, the gauge that measured brain function pegged to the top—of each.

The Uncle smiled.

It seemed that Daav yos'Phelium did not wish to die, after all.

INTERLUDE FOUR

. . . .

Fretted with Golden Fire

A STAR WENT OUT IN THE FIRMAMENT.

The few thin lines of gold that had bound it to the universe drifted, broken ends fluttering.

Ren Zel dea'Judan remained, witnessing, until the last thread vanished on the darkling breeze.

Anguish informed other stars, nearby, and known to him. That was fitting; a death ought not to go unmourned. One might even mourn the death of one who had been their enemy, until the last.

At the last, he had been grateful; his love for them, his captors—his would-be liberators—had given his star fresh radiance; his ties to the universe—to life—had flared with power...

...and gone out.

So, a death.

As such things went, Ren Zel thought, it had been a good death. Certainly, it had been desired. Chosen. It was the choice—the return of the ability to *make* a choice—that had gained them their enemy's love, even as he chose annihilation over life.

The other death that he had witnessed in this space of gold and blackness—that had been a bad death. Their enemy had scarcely wakened to the whisper of choice when the enemy within *him* had acted to deny him both choice and life. He died, knowing that life had been rent from him. Died, knowing that he had failed.

Kar Min pel'Mather had chosen. His choice had given him wings.

May the gods, if any, receive him, Ren Zel sent the benediction out into the shining glory. *He was a brave man, and honorable.*

Another moment, he remained in that place, watching, listening; but if the gods had heard, or cared, they made no sign.

Ren Zel closed his eyes that saw the shining firmament...

...and opened his eyes that saw the mundane life about him.

His lifemate sat on the edge of the cot, Kar Min's head yet resting on her knee. Master Healer Mithin occupied the chair at the foot, her head bent, and her hands folded on her lap. Pastel waves rippled about her, by which he knew her to be meditating.

"He thanked us," Anthora said, her voice scarcely above a whisper. She raised her head, showing him a face damp with tears.

"He loved us."

"Indeed, he did."

Ren Zel rose, stiffly, as if he had been in his chair long days, when—a glance at the timepiece hanging from his belt—it had been scarcely an hour since Master Mithin had placed Kar Min into trance, and Anthora had slipped her thought into his dreaming mind.

He limped to the cot, and bent to place his hand softly against Kar Min's cooling cheek, as one might do with a sleeping child.

"We have done well, here, I think," he said, straightening.

Anthora's lips wavered into a wan smile.

"Saving only that we have not given the delm their secret desire."

"We have not yet given the delm their wish," he said, holding his hand down to her.

"Do you think that we may?" she asked, moving Kar Min's head from her knee to his pillow as gently as if he slept, indeed.

Ren Zel thought back to the gold-laced blackness, and to those things his strange Sight had shown him.

Anthora took his hand.

He smiled and helped her to her feet. "I think that—yes, we may."

CHAPTER FIFTEEN

·····································

Jelaza Kazone
Surebleak

ONE THING YOU HADDA GIVE THE ROAD BOSS, LIONEL SMEALY
thought as he guided the hoopie through the gate and down
the smaller road that led only to the big house with the big tree
growing outta the center of it, like the house was nothing but
a plant-box...

...one thing you hadda give the man, like he'd been sayin'—he
knew how to live. None o'this takin' a coupla houses in the row,
knockin' the walls out and calling it home, like Boss Conrad'd
done. The Road Boss, he had style; he wasn't from Surebleak,
he wasn't of Surebleak, and he made sure everybody who had a
pair o'eyes in his head knew it straight off. Was that house he
was headin' for made on, for, or by Surebleak?

It was not.

Right off another planet, that house, *and* the tree, *and* the grass,
and, sleet, the little road he was drivin' on. Moved to Surebleak
with everything he had, the Road Boss.

That was style. A man like Lionel Smealy could appreciate that
kinda style. Sure, sure, the Big Brother tells you to move your ass
to Surebleak, and you gotta do what Big Brother says, right? But
you ain't gotta do it like he would do it—like he *did* do it, just
movin' onto the streets with only his 'hands and a buncha fancy
rugs to throw out as bait. Give it cash down, that kinda thing
makes a statement, 'specially after you go on to make yourself

149

into the Big Boss over all the other Bosses, open up the Port Road from start to finish, blow up Deacon and Iverness, too...

Following the drive around a curve, Smealy nodded.

That kind of thing *did* make a statement, yessir. Got people's attention and held it.

But this movin' of everything and plopping it down at the far end of the road, just a little inch outside Melina Sherton's turf, using the old quarry that didn't belong to nobody and wasn't no good for nothin', for their settlin' place—that was a whole 'nother kinda statement.

Oh, yeah. *That* said, "I'm keepin' myself as far away as I can from the city and everything goin' on there. Includin' Big Brother's laws and regulations."

Smealy could work with that kinda attitude. Hadn't he been Little Brother hisself, way back before Big Brother decided on retirin' Kalhoon and left Lionel the only brother? He'd had plenty of practice before then, bein' second in line; he knew how it chafed an' ate at you; he remembered how it was to burn with wantin' to get out from under Big Brother's finger.

That's why he'd come on out here, to the house itself, 'stead of going to Little Brother's office in the city. Offices weren't no places to talk over the private things only little brothers know.

Here, now, he'd come to the house, and the little road widened some right there in front of the door. He pulled the hoopie over into the wide spot, shut it down, popped the hatch and got out.

He paused for a second, still in the shadow of the hoopie, and looked around him. There wasn't no obvious security, but then, he hadn't really expected any. The logical places for security was on the gate, which'd been wide open, an' inside the house. That didn't mean nobody wasn't watchin' the dooryard—in fact, he expected that they were.

Still, he took his time looking the place over, keeping his hands in sight. He hadn't been out before to the Little Brother's house, though he'd seen the pictures.

Come down to it, the pictures didn't do the place justice. The house was like nothing he'd ever seen before—not even the old buildings that'd housed the Gilmour Agency fatcats. It was two stories high, with a barricaded walkway around the top story, and a long roof providing protection from the snow.

Beyond the sloping roof was...well, he knew it was the trunk of a tree. And the tree wasn't like nothing else on Surebleak, neither. Sleet, you could see that tree from inside the port itself, stretching so high and wide that it looked to be holding up the sky.

Standing here, as near to the roots of the thing as made no nevermind, he couldn't crane back far enough to see the tree's top. Might be he'd sight it if he went flat on his back on the drive, which he wouldn't do, not with him wearing a new yellow sweater and good khakis. That tree'd do just fine without his testimony—and he'd best get about bidness, before whoever was watchin' the dooryard decided he was more threat than nuisance.

He crossed to the door—real wood, looked like to him, carved with that Tree-and-Dragon you saw all over the port. Well, that was the mark for Little Brother's off-world bidness. The family bidness which shoulda, Smealy figured, been Big Brother Conrad's concern, 'fore he took it in mind to stick his nose into Surebleak's affairs.

There was a rope hanging down from a big old brassy bell over his head, and a plate set into the dark wood frame 'round the door.

Down the city, he'd've knocked, most likely, 'less there was a plate, like there was here. The bell—a couple old places downtown had bells hanging outside the door, still, too high or too well connected to've been scavenged. Old Fire-and-Doom bells, they were, from back before the Agency left, when there'd been a fire department and city-wide security.

Smealy put his palm against the plate, and snatched it away again as energy rippled across his flesh. Soon's he done it, he was sheepful; the buzz hadn't hurt, it had just been . . . a surprise.

He hadn't heard a bell ring inside. Might be it was broke, or might be he hadn't pressed long enough. He was just thinking he might put his hand against the plate again, and not let the buzz pitch him off his game this time, when he *did* hear something from behind the door. Didn't sound like a bell, though; sounded like . . . wheels. Wheels on wood.

And they was getting closer.

Before he could decide how he felt about that, the door opened, and he was staring at a . . . man-high metal cylinder, topped with an orange globe. It held the door open with one metal hand at the end of a long metal arm.

"Yes?" said a man's voice.

Smealy almost made the mistake of looking around, but it came to him just in time that this must be a remote, like they used down the scrapyard, to go places too dangerous for a man to venture—and that the Road Boss's 'hand or another one of the house's security folks was looking at him through that flickering orange globe, and deciding if he was welcome or dead.

"Yeah," he said, drawing himself up tall and looking straight into the globe. "I'm Smealy—Lionel Smealy—from down the city. I got bidness with the Road Boss."

"Have you an appointment?"

That wasn't no 'bleaker talkin' to him through the remote, not with that accent. Road Boss'd brought his own security with him, too.

"No 'pointment. Don't mind waitin' if he's too busy to see me right away."

"I see. May I know the nature of your business?"

"Road bidness," Smealy said. "I got a deal to offer the Boss."

"Thank you."

The remote went quiet, then, and Smealy braced himself for the door bein' shut, which—snow and sleet!—would mean the power cell in Kreller's hoopie'd been run down for no good reason, and him still on the hook to top it up, and he'd have to find the Road Boss in his port office, which meant people'd see him go in, or somebody'd recognize him in the waitin' room, and this wasn't the kind of deal that was best made under that kind of watchful—

"Boss yos'Phelium will see you," the remote stated, and pivoted slightly, wheels rumbling on—Smealy looked down—wooden floorboards, clearing a space big enough for him to squeeze through.

The remote closed the door, spun and rolled away down the hall.

"Please follow me, Mr. Smealy."

He followed for about twelve of his strides—almost as long as a reg'lar house—to another wooden door, not carved, and the hall goin' on beyond it. The remote used its metal hand to twist the painted knob, and the door swung open into the room.

"Please wait here," the driver of the remote told him. "Boss yos'Phelium will be with you shortly."

Smealy entered, the door shut behind him, and he spun slowly around on a heel, giving the place the once-over.

Beige rug on the floor, no windows, a couple chairs with thin, curving wooden legs, seats covered in cloth, beige to match the rug, and figured with red and blue flowers. There was a little wooden table between the chairs, with the same spindly legs, and a couple little things on it—a wooden box with the damn Tree-and-Dragon carved into the top, and a round piece of glass bound by metal and tied into a black-wrapped handle. 'Round the other side of the room was another table, taller, longer, with a sturdy straight leg on each corner. There were a couple paper books on top of that, and a beige vase with red and blue flowers in it, to match the fabric on the chairs.

At the back of the room was another table; in between him and it set another couple beige-red-blue chairs with their own little table. There were pictures on the wall—flowers again—boxed in thin wooden frames.

It was, Smealy thought, a rich room. A Boss's room; and just about what you'd expect for a house so out of common. No plastic in *this* house, that had come down onto Surebleak from another world entirely. The pictures weren't just pinned to the wall, neither, they were boxed and held flat. Looked...he groped for the word his ma'd used, when she'd be particularly pleased with a meal, or a piece o'dressmakin', or, rarely, how her son was turned out...*elegant*, that was it.

Place looked *elegant*.

Smealy felt his hopes rise.

If this was the style of thing Little Brother was used to from the old world he'd had to leave, he was ripe for the deal Smealy had to offer him. An' once he took it, they'd have a way in to Conrad, which was needful, and getting more so, Conrad being not what you'd call easy to figure.

It'd been Smealy's idea to go after Little Brother, to play on nerves specific to little brothers, and tie him up tight into the Syndicate's bidness. It'd been Smealy's idea and that was why he was here to pitch it, nobody else being quite so keen on trying.

It'd be why he'd get the top share, too, when everything came together.

There was a sharp sound behind him. He spun as the door swung open and a man entered the room.

Smealy kept his face easy and smooth. He'd seen Conrad, after all, up close and personal, and wind knew he'd seen plenty other

Liadens; lately a man couldn't move without tripping over six or eight of 'em. Short folks, they were; thin and fragile, which you'd think'd mean they'd be a little careful 'bout throwin' their weight around.

You'd think wrong, though.

Miz and Mister Better'n You, every damn one of 'em. Didn't help that they all come onto Surebleak with their pockets fulla money. Wasn't nobody nor nothin' they couldn't buy, while native 'bleakers went wantin'.

The boy, now; he was younger'n Smealy'd expected, somehow, even knowing he was Conrad's little brother. Couldn't really mistake him for anything *but* Conrad's brother, both of 'em wearing serious, pointy faces.

"Mr. Smealy?" the kid asked in a voice as soft as one o'Jolie's joy-girls. "I am Val Con yos'Phelium, the Road Boss."

Smealy got his feet under him, mentally, slapped a smile on his face like the kid was his own missing brother, and went briskly forward, hand out for a shake.

The boy turned back from shutting the door, eyebrows going up over eyes as green as the baize on a snooker table. He took a step forward, and extended his hand, his palm chilly against Smealy's.

Yeah, that was another thing; warm as it was in this private little room, and him wearin' a high-neck sweater, an' a heavy pair o'dungarees, the boy's hand was cold. All them folks come in from Liad, they were cold alla time, and wrapped up snug, actin' like it were high winter 'stead o'midsummer.

"Lionel Smealy," he said, shaking the cold hand enthusiastically. "I'm real glad you could see me, Boss."

"Yes, but I cannot see you for long," the Road Boss told him, withdrawing his hand. "Other business awaits my attention, and had you arrived five minutes later, you would have been obliged to wait for an hour."

"Timing's everything, they say!"

"Indeed. May I suggest that, if you wish to speak with the Road Boss in future, you go to the office on the port? I am there on alternate days, and Road Boss Robertson is there on the days I am not. Either one of us will be able to assist you in any matter regarding the road. There is no need for you to travel so far."

"Right, right!" Smealy said, remembering that the Road Boss shared his title with his wife. Local girl, the wife, come up on

Kalhoon's turf, before Kalhoon retired Ostay. Word on the street was they'd been kids together, the wife and Kalhoon. That'd been an interesting rumor; made a man wonder just where Conrad's notion of conquerin' Surebleak had its roots.

"See, though," he said to the boy with the smooth, pretty face, "the deal I want to offer you, it ain't the kinda thing you talk about where just anybody can overhear."

"Ah," said the kid, and moved a hand, apparently pointing at the two shaky-lookin' chairs and matchin' table. "In that case, please, sit down. Will you have a glass of wine to refresh you from your journey?"

"That'd be great," Smealy said. Truth was, he could use a drink. The drive all the way out here to the end of the road in Kreller's hoopie'd been nerve-wracking. Smealy knew how far the Road Boss's house was from Hamilton Street; known it in his head, that was. Driving it was a different thing altogether.

"Taste o'wine'd be real welcome," he said, and added, remembering Anj tellin' 'em how it had been to call on Conrad like they'd done—who knew wine came in colors?—"Red, if you got a bottle open."

"I think I might have. Please do sit down while I pour."

Smealy approached the chairs with caution, picked the one that looked less shaky and eased down into it. For a wonder, the thing held him up, and he was able to watch the Road Boss at the back table pouring two little glasses half full of a liquid the color of new blood. He stoppered the bottle he'd poured from, picked up the two glasses and brought 'em ahead, without even putting any ice in.

Well, Smealy reminded himself, the kid was cold; him and his didn't know it was summer.

He took the glass offered him with a nod, and waited while the Road Boss sat down, and tasted his wine, all polite—an' that's all it was, was polite; he'd seen both glasses come outta the same bottle. Still, it was...easeful to see the kid knew how to behave like a 'bleaker, at least as far as reg'lar hospitality went.

The boy'd just taken a tiny sip, and Smealy could see the point in that, with the glasses so small and the pourin' so light. Must be a tight-pocket week, he thought. That could work in his favor.

He took a tiny sip, just like the kid done, and was glad he had. The stuff was *sour*, not sweet at all, an' *warm*, too.

The kid settled into the other chair, and put his glass on the rickety table. Relieved, Smealy did the same, then leaned forward a little, so he could look direct into those cat-green eyes.

"You're a busy man, like you said, so I'll come direct to the point," he said. He paused then, in case the kid wanted to say something, but he only nodded, like he was wantin' Smealy to go on.

"Now, I'm the chairman of the Citizens' Heavy Loads Committee, which is just like it says in the name—a buncha citizens concerned about the movin' of heavy loads up and down the Port Road. Especially, we're innerested in the new rules an' fines an' all the Council o'Bosses is puttin' in for oversize loads, or weights too heavy. There ain't one need for all them penalties, or for havin' roadmen out in all weather, riskin' frostbite and poomonya so they can stop trucks that maybe sorta look like they're too wide or too heavy, makin' the driver miss his schedule and causin' all that unnecessary unhappiness."

He paused, and this time the Road Boss did have something to say.

"You paint a black picture," he murmured.

"That's right, that's right—it's black as night, the way the Bosses wanna see the thing done. These rules and fines—that might be how it's done out there on Liad, but it ain't ever how it's been done here on Surebleak."

He had the boy's attention; those bright eyes never left his face. Smealy smiled.

"Now, see, here on Surebleak we know that everybody all up and down the ladder deserves a piece of the action. Fella like you, to take a f'rinstance, Little Brother and sub-Boss, there ain't anything in this rule-and-fine system the Big Bosses made that takes care of you. All that money just goes into their pockets, and I'm here to tell you that ain't how it's been done on Surebleak."

"And how has it," the Road Boss asked, "been done on Surebleak?"

"Well, I'm gettin' to that. Here on Surebleak, everybody gets a piece, see? The Boss gets his insurance money, an' the streeters dicker 'mong themselves for the best price on this, that, or anythin' else. It's our system and it's been workin' real good for us.

"But you, this new system leaves you outta the loop. You got all the work of enforcing the laws, and collectin' the fines, but you don't get nothin' for your trouble."

"It seems a sad case."

"It does, don't it? But, see, all's got to happen to set everythin' right is for you—you being Road Boss—is for you to sell exceptions. So, say, I wanna move my big lorry down-Road to the port, an' you bet it's gonna be overweight, 'cause why should I make two, three trips when one'll do it?"

"Why, indeed?" the Road Boss murmured.

Smealy nodded, pleased to see the boy was keeping up.

"Just makes sense that a man wants to be paid for his work. So, me, I got a lorry to move, quick as I can, no trouble, no delays. I come to you, and I say, 'Boss—'" Smealy was particularly pleased with that *Boss*: *that* was settin' the hook proper for Little Brother.

"I'd say, 'Boss, I'm gonna be movin' a big load down from Sherton's turf all the way to the Port Bazaar. It'll be movin' two nights from today, just at middle night, 'cause it's big and it's heavy and it moves slow and I don't wanna hold up daytime bidness. Figure it's about fifteen hunnert pounds over limit."

"Whereupon," the Road Boss said, "I fine you."

"No, you don't fine me!" Smealy said sharply. "What's the use of finin' me? You sell me an exception, like I said, for, say, half the fine. I pay you good cash, your crew don't gotta be walkin' up and down the road, lookin' for somebody to fine, on account you know there's just gonna be me and my big old lorry, and I already paid the exception up front, see?" He leaned over the table and tapped it with his finger.

"That money goes right into your pocket, where it'll do you some good. And word gets 'round, see, if you want somethin' fixed about the road, or to slide past the rules, you go to the *Road Boss*, not to Conrad." He nodded, and leaned back in his chair. "Build you up some consequence, so you ain't always sittin' in the shade o'Big Brother's lamp. You got *consequence* back where you come from—I know you do, 'cept you call it"—he frowned, shaking his head in frustration at not having the word to tongue— "what *do* you call it?"

"Possibly, you mean *melant'i*," the Road Boss said. He was sitting back in his chair, booted ankle on the opposite knee. He shook his head.

"It is an . . . interesting proposition, Mr. Smealy, and I thank you for your concern regarding my . . . consequence. However, family dynamics aside, I must remind you that I am under contract to the Bosses of Surebleak, to maintain the Port Road, to hold it open, and to enforce those rules regarding the road that the Bosses set in place."

It was said so serious that for half a second Smealy thought the kid meant it. Then he realized that nobody could be that wet behind the ears, and that the Road Boss was havin' a joke.

He grinned, to show he got it, and offered a piece of streeter smarts.

"Contracts're made to be broken."

The Road Boss sat up sudden and straight in his chair, both feet on the floor, hands braced against the arms.

Smealy stared, almost thinking that the kid was going to jump up and try to clock him—but no.

The Road Boss relaxed; he smiled; he shook his head. "Mr. Smealy, never say that to a Liaden."

"Well, but—"

The kid raised a hand, and Smealy stopped talking.

"Thank you. Now, allow me to tell you something that will make it very much easier for you to deal, going forward. *Contracts are made to be broken* is an extremely dangerous position to take with a Liaden. With *any* Liaden. Understand that I have... traveled to many worlds and am counted something of an expert on... odd customs. I am, in fact, an *atypical* Liaden—and your statement... shocked me. Had I been less-traveled, I might possibly have shot you on the instant, as a danger to society."

Smealy blinked, opened his mouth—and shut it again, as the Boss shook his head.

"Liadens consider contracts to be one of the binding forces of the universe. Liadens write contracts to impose order, and while they will do their utmost to ensure that the terms favor them and their interests, once the terms are fixed, they are *inalterable*. To cheat on a contract is to cheat on the universe; no good can come of either.

"To sign a contract with the *intention* of breaking it... that is either the action of a sociopath, or a man who is far more courageous than I am."

The Road Boss stood then, suddenly seeming tall. Smealy stood, too, but somehow the Boss didn't get short again.

"Mr. Smealy," the Boss said, "I advise you to obey the rules and laws that the Council of Bosses set down. And now I bid you good day. Please, if you have other business that you wish to bring to the Road Boss, do so at our office at the port. You will not be permitted on these grounds again."

"But—" Smealy began.

The Boss ignored him. "Jeeves," he said, apparently talking to the air. "Mr. Smealy's business is concluded."

From the hall came the determined rumble of wheels. The door popped open and the remote was there.

"Follow me, please, Mr. Smealy."

There wasn't, Smealy thought, no use arguing with a pissed-off Boss. That was another piece of streeter smarts. Wasn't much to do, really, 'cept nod at the man, to show respect, and follow the remote down the hall.

The front door closed hard behind him, and Smealy stood there in the open air for . . . a little while before he opened the hoopie's door, climbed in, and started 'er up.

CHAPTER SIXTEEN

....

Surebleak Port

TWO YOUNG MEN, MUCH OF AN AGE, BUT UNALIKE IN ALMOST everything else, save a facility with the Sticks, and a good head for numbers, walked down-port toward the Emerald Casino.

They made a pretty picture—one tall, fair and lissome; the other supple, dark and golden-skinned. The fair lad wore a blue jacket that matched his eyes. The dark one wore leather, and had a bag slung over one shoulder.

"So you'll be back in two Surebleak weeks?" the fair one asked, ending what had been a rather long pause between them.

His companion gave him an approving nod.

"Excellent. Doing the conversions while in flight is no easy thing."

"I've been practicing," Villy said. "I'll keep it up, too. By the time you're back, I'll be able to do a four-level conversion in my head!"

"Here's a bold assertion! Will books be all your lovers, until I return to your arms?"

Villy considered him out of suspicious blue eyes.

"*That* sounds like a play quote," he said.

"Discovered!"

Quin gave a small, on-the-stride bow of acknowledgment, for which he would have been severely reprimanded had he been observed by his protocol teacher or—twelve times worse!—his grandmother.

"It is a play quote, yes. If you like, I will find a tape and we may watch it together."

"Would I? Like it, I mean."

That was a serious question, and Quin gave it the consideration it deserved.

"You might well. It is a classic *melant'i* play. I was required to study it, and write papers on it, and view several productions, from the first recorded to the most modern, which is why I have the phrase so apt, you see. But—yes, I think you might find it useful, and interesting, too. Especially the sword fight."

"Sword fight?"

"The most diverting thing imaginable! It's quite harrowing, despite you know it's all mummery."

"Okay, then, I'm provisionally interested. If I get bored, though, I'll make you speed through to the sword fight."

"Fair enough."

The Emerald was in sight. They were early this morning, with Skene at their backs, so that they could enjoy breakfast together before Villy's shift at the Sticks table. Quin was bound for Korval's Yard, *Galandasti*, and Master Pilot Tess Lucien, who was to sit his second while he added hours to his flight ticket.

"Do you—" Villy began, and stopped, one hand shooting out to grab Quin's arm.

A man had stepped directly in front of them, his arms held carefully away from his side, his palms turned forward, fingers spread wide. The bow was a quick, clean request to speak.

Behind him, Skene said, "What's *he* doing here?"

"An excellent question. Perhaps he will tell us."

Quin gestured permission to speak, and Security Officer pen'Erit folded into the deep bow of one receiving a boon from a superior.

"Pilot, I come to you because I am acquainted with no one else on this port. I . . . I am certain that this situation has overtaken others, but it is . . . the first time it has come to me." He took a deep breath. "In short, sir, I would ask your advice."

"I can scarcely presume to advise a man so many years my elder," Quin answered. "If you acquaint me with this situation, I may, indeed, be able to recommend someone on port who may assist you. But I wonder, sir—did not your ship lift . . . some weeks ago?"

The man's mouth hardened.

"Indeed it did, sir, and Trader vin'Tenzing with it. In the hour before lift, after I had been disciplined for failing to ensure the trader's good health, I was sent onto the port to procure an item necessary for her comfort.

"I had been directed to a particular vendor, who did not have the item in port inventory, but who was pleased to send a car to his warehouse and have one brought to me.

"It was as we were awaiting the return of the truck that he mentioned I was the second that day to inquire about this item, which was not in much demand on port. The first had been a call, and the order dropped after he had explained the necessity of sending to the warehouse."

He turned his hands up, showing empty palms once more.

"After that, I could not be surprised to find that my ship had lifted early, and without me."

"That's an unhappy fella," Villy murmured. "What's the story?"

"His ship abandoned him," Quin said rapidly. "This is Security Officer pen'Erit, who had come to the rug shop with Trader vin'Tenzing several weeks ago."

"I don't mean any insult, but that trader sounds to be an ice bitch."

Quin sputtered a laugh. Officer pen'Erit dropped back a step, eyes narrowed in offense, and Quin waved a hand.

"Forgive me. My companion chooses to be . . . unimpressed with the trader and her actions. His language is colorful."

The man's face relaxed, and he accorded Villy a comradely nod.

"Do you require assistance contacting your clan, sir?" Quin asked. "The portmaster—"

Officer pen'Erit made the sign for *sharp stop*.

"I have contacted my clan. Last night, the answer arrived. My delm does not require me. That I am abandoned and bereft on a—forgive me—a barbarian world, she considers to be proper Balance for having placed our House awkwardly with Clan Omterth. My clan has, for generations, clung to Omterth's coattails, until we are fit for nothing else. To be placed awkwardly with Omterth is paramount to having food snatched from the mouths of our children."

He closed his eyes, shoulders slumping.

"I can wish that my heir will not be required to bear the balance of the delm's anger, but I fear that is . . . a father's fond hope, only."

"Quin, sweetie, that man wants a cup of coffee," Villy said. "Bring him in to breakfast with us, and let's get him sorted out in comfort."

"Yes," Quin said, and bowed an invitation to the ex-security officer.

"My companion suggests that we go inside and reason together over breakfast. It would gladden me if you would accept his invitation."

The man hesitated, then bowed to Villy's honor.

"Thank you," he said. "My name is Tef Lej pen'Erit Clan—"

He stopped abruptly, harshly, and bowed again. "My name is Tef Lej pen'Erit."

"He gives you his name," Quin told Villy.

"Right."

He went forward a step, which was his kinesics lessons on display, and produced a credible bow of introduction.

"I'm Villy Butler," he said. "Pleased to meet you, Mr. pen'Erit." He glanced over his shoulder. "Skene, honey?"

She sighed.

"I'm Skene Liep," she said, "Boss Quin's head 'hand."

"My companion is named Villy Butler," Quin translated, so there should be no confusion. "My security gives you her name, also: Skene Liep. Please, let us go inside."

Breakfast was something of a challenge, as Quin was the only one at the table who spoke both Liaden and Terran.

Tef Lej pen'Erit of course had Trade and several other dialects on his tongue, but that gained them nothing, so Quin translated, in between snatching bites of his meal.

It quickly became apparent that Mr. pen'Erit was not in good order. He had rented a cubicle at the so-called Spaceman's Hostel on port. Based on the eagerness with which he addressed his breakfast, Quin guessed that he had been skipping meals in order to economize.

"Hostel's spendy," said Skene. "M'sister has a rooming house in Conrad's turf—clean room, two meals, an' half the cost or less. I can take him, after you're lifted out, Boss."

This offer was conveyed, it falling to Mr. pen'Erit to point out that he had no Terran and Skene's sister likely to have as much Liaden as Skene herself.

"She's took up with a Scout," Skene said, shaking her head. "So there's translation in-house."

This was also conveyed, and while Mr. pen'Erit formulated an answer, Villy produced a question.

"Is that all his clothes? Weatherman says it's gonna get chilly tonight, an' if he don't have a jacket, it could get nasty for him." He gave Quin a grin. "Bet he gets cold as fast as you."

He probably got cold faster, Quin thought, fresh off-ship as he was.

"Villy asks if you have a coat. Our weatherman predicts cold weather this evening, with a chance of a summer snowstorm."

His guest paled.

"Snow?" he repeated.

"No need to translate that," Villy said. "Tell him, he can have my coat. No sense a man freezing, and I got another one."

Quin hesitated, then said to Master pen'Erit.

"Villy makes you a gift of his coat. He is concerned for your health."

Tears rose in hard grey eyes.

"He—why does he care?"

"He is *hetaera*," Quin said, which was both true, and immediately comprehensible to a Liaden.

pen'Erit looked to Villy and bowed as deeply as he was able, seated.

"I am in his debt," he said to Quin. "More, I would make amends for my lack of manner. I will bring him a fitting present, soon. Tell him, please."

"He don't gotta pay me for the coat," Villy said, making a shrewd guess at the content of this.

"He does not offer," Quin said. "He accepts your care, and asks me to tell you that he will bring you a gift befitting your station as a *hetaera*."

"So, he's gonna pay for the coat anyhow? I don't need his present."

"Accept it, nonetheless," Quin advised. "*Hetaera* are . . . treasures. It is an appreciation of your . . . art. That you offer your care freely, must be appreciated."

"Balanced?"

"No," Quin said slowly. "One cannot Balance art."

The bell rang then, calling the new shift to the floor.

"That's me," Villy said. He stood, took his jacket off its peg and stepped 'round the table to drape it over Mr. pen'Erit's shoulders.

"You make sure you wear this, now. Otherwise, you'll be catchin' your death out there in the wind."

Mr. pen'Erit almost broke his neck, trying to meet Villy's eyes and bow at the same time. Villy patted him on the back, bent over Quin and kissed him on the cheek.

"You fly safe, hon. See you soon. 'Bye, Skene, Mr. pen'Erit."

He left them, and Quin did not miss pen'Erit's appreciative gaze.

"My time marches as well," Quin said. "I am scheduled to lift. This is what seems best to me: I will ask Skene to conduct you to my father." He held up his hand at the other's start.

"He will not place blame upon you for what you did not do. His network of acquaintances is far wider than mine. Someone of those will able to assist you to your best advantage. Does this answer your necessity?"

Master pen'Erit bowed his head.

"I believe that it must. No Liaden ship will take me, and there is no reason for me to return to Liad. To be clanless on Surebleak..." He looked wry, revealing a sense of humor that despair had hidden until now. "To be clanless on Surebleak is no great thing. To be clanless on Liad... is beyond terrible."

"So." Quin inclined his head. "A moment, and I will instruct my security, and then I will take my leave."

He turned to Skene, got her nod, and slipped out of his chair, bowing to the table.

"My ship wants me," he said, in Liaden, and, "I am late," in Terran.

"Safe lift, Pilot," said Master pen'Erit.

"Better run," said Skene.

· · · ✳ · · ·

Things had been hot during the morning, but the after-lunch session in the Road Boss's posh office suite in Surebleak Port was downright boring. Miri was seriously thinking about asking Beautiful if he had a deck of cards on him, which she was willing to bet he did. Nelirikk had a real love affair goin' with poker—him and Diglon, too. She figured she was doing the revolving poker game down Meruda's back room a favor by keeping the both of them mostly employed, and their hours for card playing limited. In the old days, back when she'd been a kid, Meruda would've owed her a piece of the action for taking an interest in his success.

Yeah, well. The old days, and the old ways...best if they never came back. To hear the culture experts from the Scouts—and Kareen, too—tell it, though, there might be a few generations before the new ways caught on entire.

Which was why they needed to have some control over how the new ways grew, and keep a sharp eye out for unintended consequences.

Miri yawned.

Dammit, she couldn't take a nap. It wasn't like she didn't have work to do. There were reports to read, right there on the computer. All she had to do was key—

The front door opened. She glanced at the camera screen, and saw a long, tall citizen step into the waiting room, closing the door firmly behind. Old Surebleak habit, that one. You didn't want the wind coming behind you and snatching the door wide to let the weather in.

"Good afternoon," she heard Beautiful say. That had been a triumph, teaching Beautiful to say "good morning," and "good afternoon," like he didn't mean to cut your throat.

"Afternoon," the visitor answered, pulling off his hat. "Boss in?"

The screen showed an image of a guy past his middle years, a little pudgy with age, but tall-standing; his face scraped clean in celebration of all the balmy summer weather they'd been having, and his hair cut sharp. Might be an ex-merc. Had that kind of 'tude about him.

"Road Boss Miri Robertson is on duty this afternoon," Beautiful said, and Miri sighed to herself. Still some work to do there; on the other hand, the streeter hadn't fainted, so maybe progress was being made.

"May I know your name?" he finished.

"Sure thing. Rebbus Mark, come down from Gilly Street."

"Please come with me," Beautiful said.

Miri reached for the computer, typed in *Gilly Street* as two pairs of footsteps approached, and had time to learn it was Fran Schomaker's turf before the door opened and Nelirikk made the announcement.

"Rebbus Mark of Gilly Street is here to see you, ma'am."

"Thanks," she said, coming to her feet with a smile, and both hands in sight. "Mr. Mark, c'mon in and have a seat."

He hesitated, his eyes on the computer.

"Not wantin' to disturb your work," he said. "I can come back when you're not so busy."

Miri grinned at him.

"All's I got here is reports to read, and believe me, I'd rather be talking to you."

That got a half-grin out of him.

"Well, now, since I'll be doin' a good turn..."

He took another two steps into the room, and settled into the chair across the desk from her. Miri sat down. Nelirikk went away and closed the door. He'd be listening and watching from his station in the waiting room, but Miri didn't expect any trouble from Rebbus Mark.

'Course, that was sorta the point of having security on hand. And carrying your own protection, too.

"Thanks for seein' me so quick," he said, setting his hat on his knee and putting one hand flat atop, like he was worried it make take a notion to jump down to the floor and go exploring on its own.

"No problem," she assured him, and seized the conversational ball, since he didn't seem to know how to get from showing proper respect to his topic, whatever it was.

"So, you wanted to talk to me about the road?"

"Yes, I did." He nodded, looked down at the hat on his knee, then looked up and met her eyes, nice and firm.

"Now, you might wonder why what I got to ask is any o'my bidness, so I'll start by sayin' I'm out from one o'the executives of the Gilmour Agency. Way back, see? No reason for you to b'lieve me, but I got the proof right here." He lifted one hand off his hat—and froze with it halfway to his jacket, his eyes on hers.

"Got it inna inner pocket—flat piece o'paper 'bout as big as my hand. My carry's in the right outside pocket."

A careful man, which wasn't a surprise, really, him being as old as he was and still walking around.

"Go for it," she told him, slipping her hand onto the shelf under the desktop, and resting it on top of her merc sidearm.

Rebbus Mark nodded, unbuttoned the top two buttons of his

coat, slipped his hand inside, and produced a piece of paper, exactly like he'd promised. He leaned forward to put it down on the desk in front of her.

It was an ID card for one Kristofer Mark, Operations Economist, Gilmour Agency, Surebleak Mining Division. There was a holo of the man, head and shoulders—ordinary looking, and no visible similarity to Rebbus Mark.

She looked up, and nodded.

"That there's my grandpa's grandpa. Family story is he disagreed with the finance manager when the decision come down to pull out to the new vein, off-world. Got cut outta the loop and left here with all the rest weren't executive level."

Miri nodded to show that she was listening, even while she wondered if there was a point to this.

"Other thing is," Rebbus Mark said, his voice brisker now, like he'd found the way into what he'd come here to talk about.

"Other thing is, that man was the one set up the tollbooths."

Miri blinked at him.

"The tollbooths that kept the streeters on their streets, and under the close care of their particular Boss?" she asked. "Those tollbooths?"

That struck him funny, his grin turned into a guffaw before he shook his head.

"Talk on the street's that you're a local girl, come home. I believe it, now—that's pure streeter tollbooth hate, that is."

"The toolbooths kept us from helping each other; kept supplies away from streets that needed 'em. People got sick who didn't need to. People *died* on Latimer's streets, when there was a cure right over there in what's Vine's turf, now."

"They did. They did every bit of that, and worse. No argument from me. But, that's how the *fatcats* used 'em, after the Agency pulled out and left us. That wasn't their original use."

Miri considered him.

"What *was* their original use, then?"

"Well...here's a question backatcha: how's the Road Boss gonna pay for repairs and upkeep to the road?"

She shrugged.

"Each of the Bosses pays a fee toward the costs of the road, and so does the port."

He shook his head.

"Now, see, that only sets it back one square. Where do the Bosses get the money to pay the road's expenses?"

Miri frowned.

"You know where it comes from," he said, like gentling a little kid toward an answer she didn't like. "The Bosses might not be sellin' insurance no more, but them new fee schedules they put in're still pulling cash outta streeter pockets, even streeters who don't want nor use the road."

"Right." She sighed. They'd talked about that, but it'd seemed that the most Balanced way was to assess a fee from each Boss, even knowing that each Boss depended on his streeters for his income. It was, so said Pat Rin and Val Con and all the rest of the Liadens in the works, the way things like the roads, the walks, the street lights and other common-used services were funded on Liad: each clan paid a piece.

"Now, my grandda, he was in charge of makin' sure that each department paid every other department for the resources they used. An' the best way to do that, since in them days, the company owned the road, o'course, was—"

She felt a jolt of sheer disbelief, jumped where she sat, then—it was gone.

Rebbus Mark had noticed her lapse, though; it apparently lasted long enough to have him looking worried.

Miri shook her head, and gave him a wry grin.

"Sorry," she said. "Sometimes the merc comes home to you, whether you want it or not."

His stare softened.

"Don't it just," he murmured. "Don't it just do that."

"Gone now," she said, hoping that was so. "I missed that last, though. Can I get a repeat?"

"Sure. The tollbooths were set up and whoever came through 'em, paid. Paid by weight, that was the system then."

"So only the people using the road pay for it," Miri said slowly. "And those who use it hardest, pay the most?"

"That's the dandy! 'Course, it was more complicated in his day, on account of havin' to keep track of all them departments, but we ain't got that, now. Just two piles—them that uses the road and them that don't."

Miri pulled the computer to her, and opened up a file.

"You available, maybe, to talk to the Council of Bosses?"

"Be glad to."

"My aunt Kareen, she might wanna talk to you, too, about how it was. She's making a study of Surebleak history. Would you be willing to sit with her?"

"Nothin'd please me more. She gonna be writin' a book?"

Miri blinked at him.

"Wouldn't surprise me at all. Now, let's get how you'd like best to be contacted..."

CHAPTER SEVENTEEN

. . . .

Corner of Dudley Avenue and Farley Lane

IT WAS A WONDER, KAMELE THOUGHT, HOW QUICKLY EVERYTHING had moved, once Kareen had decided upon a base of operations.

One day, she had been a guest in Clan Korval's house at the end of the Port Road. Two days later, she and Kareen were housemates, and partners in research. Kareen had insisted that they were, in fact, cohabitants; that Kamele was neither a guest, nor a dependent, but her equal: a colleague.

Nova yos'Galan's 'hand, Mike Golden, had produced a dozen local residents of good reputation from which number they had hired six. Gert Jazdak, a taciturn woman for whom Mike Golden had specifically vouched, held the position of security chief, or in the ranking system of Surebleak, head 'hand. She had in turn vouched for Dafydil Koonts and Amiz Braun, second-hands, or, more simply, 'hands. The role of these individuals was primarily as bodyguards, though all three could read, and each came from old families on the street.

"Thought they could help with the research, when other things was slow," Mike Golden said. Lady Kareen had thanked him for his thoughtfulness, though Kamele had privately reserved her opinion of the use of untrained persons in deep research.

The other three staff members: Esil Lang, the cook; Pary Jain, general work; and Voz Turner, general work, were simpler folk, "street smart," according to Mike Golden, and "capable."

In addition to those six, the delms had insisted that they have

173

among their household Hazenthull Explorer, a fierce and taciturn woman who was a weapons expert and, as Kamele understood it, the equivalent of a Liaden Scout. Hazenthull worked Security at the port, but it was thought that her presence as a resident of the house would by itself give would-be troublemakers second thoughts.

She had, Kamele thought, sipping her coffee and looking out the parlor window onto Farley Lane, expected that she would find an existence where she was required to take her 'hand with her whenever she ventured out onto the streets, and where someone else answered her door to prescreen her visitors, confining beyond her ability to accept it.

However, the reality was quite the opposite. Dilly, as Dafydil preferred to be called, possessed a great deal of common sense, and a quick understanding of both practicalities and theory. Despite Kamele's misgivings, both Dilly and Amiz were a great deal of help with the rough sorting, drawing praise from no less a personage than Scout Historian vey'Loffit, who had attached himself to the household as well as to the project. Gert accepted him as a free gun, the presence of whom, as with Hazenthull, increased the security and the status of the Lady's household.

For, Kamele thought with amusement, Kareen had after all had her way. She was known as Lady, not Boss, having pointed out to Gert that she was boss of nothing, and an old woman besides, who had been accustomed all her life to a certain mode of address.

These arguments had affected the head 'hand powerfully, and she had immediately thrown her own "street cred" behind *Lady* Kareen and *Professor* Waitley—for Kamele had gotten her way, too—as something different, and special.

Though she'd seen a victory with regard to her title, Kamele had not won her point on the subject of the gun. Gert insisted, Kareen insisted, Scout vey'Loffit insisted, Mike Golden insisted... that she carry a gun. When she protested that it was absurd for her to do so, since she hadn't the first idea how to *use* a gun, Kareen had simply said, "That is why you will have shooting lessons."

And so she had shooting lessons, every morning, walking out in weather Dilly claimed was "summery," to Veedle Street, and Sherman's Shoot-Out. Kareen, and Amiz, of course, often accompanied her on these outings. In fact, they had become something of a favorite with the proprietor, "the guy who put the Sherman in Shoot-Out," as he had it.

The four of them would practice for an hour, and Kamele, to her amazement, gained skill with her weapon, and, just a little, pride in her own competence.

"Gonna challenge the Lady's standin', you keep goin' like you been," Sherman had told her, after this morning's session. He'd then gone suddenly—uncharacteristically—silent for so long that Kamele had begun to fear that something was seriously wrong.

But, no; it just seemed that Sherman had been struck by inspiration.

"You know what? I'm gonna be havin' a tournament here in a coupla weeks, and I want the two of you to compete."

"I'm hardly at a level where *competition* . . ." Kamele began, but he waved her off.

"Naw, naw—you'll do fine, Professor. Beginner's round. Lady'll shoot in with the pros, maybe, or—no, hey! I'll do a Boss round— no reason not, right?" He looked over Kareen's head, to Amiz. "Tell Gert I wanna buy 'er an' Golden a drink, yeah?"

Amiz nodded. "Sure."

"Good. Oh, yeah, this is a *good* idea I'm havin' here. I'll get back to you with details."

That had been this morning. Kamele was inclined to put the whole thing down as a mad start that would quickly be put to rest under the combined good sense of Gert and Golden. And even if it was not, she absolutely *would not* compete in a shooting match. That was foregone.

Kamele finished her cup of coffee with a sigh. It was time to get back to work, but she still tarried, watching the traffic moving on the street outside the window. Living in Jen Sar's house on Delgado, she had come to . . . appreciate . . . weather, and windows. This window, in this house . . . she found she liked it, though it was . . . very . . . different from Jen Sar's house, and from Delgado. She liked the *culture* of the house, which was an amalgam of Liaden, Delgadan, Yxtrang, and native Surebleakean.

Sometimes the house ambiance reminded Kamele of graduate dorm common rooms where desultory gossip and conversation— interleaved with jokes and commentary—might devolve into simple commonplace or might expand into an in-depth collaborative philosophical study full of insight and practical advice.

She was fascinated by the pragmatic Scout and Explorer view of things, and was amused when one odd perambulation on weapon security, spawned by a chance remark by Hazenthull about her day's work, ended up involving the entire room for several hours. That discussion went on with pointers on backups, their proper and improper placements, their number, and timing of their use.

It was during that discussion that Kamele found herself marveling at Kareen, for far from being disinterested in the topic as might be expected of an elder scholar, she entered it with a will, drawing nods from the Explorer and the locals for her points, and reminding unexpectedly of Jen Sar and his dictum to Theo on what a pilot should pack and what should be carried at all times. Too, Kamele discovered that of all those in the room—including Esil, the cook, delivering an extra round of tea and biscuits—she was the only one not carrying at least one weapon and a backup, even as they relaxed.

Why, she thought, if all the house's residents could find a balancing point among their considerable differences, *surely* they could find a similar point, for Surebleak, in whole.

She laughed, softly.

Well, surely they could. But it was still going to be what Dilly dignified as a *job of work*.

Maybe even three jobs of work.

· · · ✦ · · ·

"Evenin', Boss," Miri said, closing the door to the office behind her. Val Con was already on his feet and 'rounding the desk.

"Good evening, Boss," he returned, opening his arms.

She walked into his embrace, sliding her arms around his waist and resting her head against his shoulder.

He sighed, and lay his cheek against her hair, pulling her tighter. She obligingly snuggled in.

"Tough day?" she murmured after a while, and he sighed again, this one half a laugh, kissed her hair and let her go.

"A day of parts, let us say."

She eyed him.

"Tell me the good parts, first."

"All right. Perhaps the best part was the communication from the archivist who has taken the known Gilmour Agency papers into her charge."

"That's where the Council of Bosses sent the maybe-deed to Shan's island?"

"In fact. It would seem, *cha'trez*, that the Council of Bosses is not the heir to the Gilmour Agency in this case, because there is some possibility that the person in whose name the deed was made... may have an heir with an interest."

"Anybody know who the heir might be? Or just that she *might* be?"

"There is a question of lineage, I believe, if there was a legally binding separation, and, even if so, that separation would negate the *melant'i* of heir in an entirely different legal document."

Miri blinked.

"Even the explanation makes my head hurt. Can't the *qe'andra* sort it out?"

"Possibly. However, I believe that I can sort it out easily enough."

"Yeah? Who was the deed made to?"

"Nareeba Sarab-Fain," he said promptly. "The same document made her a freeholder."

"Like Yulie?" she asked, meaning their skittish and not-always-sociable next door neighbor, Yulian Shaper.

"Precisely like Yulie. Freeholder Sarab-Fain had named an heir to her land, should she die without issue. The name of her heir was recorded as Rindle Taris-Shaper. Originally, the name was followed by the word 'spouse,' but that was at some point struck out. The name remains."

"And so does Yulie. I don't see him wanting an island."

"Nor do I, but the question must be asked, and the answer properly dealt with. Shan will wish his title to be secure, if Yulie is willing to sell. And, if Yulie is not willing to sell..."

"Then we'd best let him know that while he's still on the route, so he can get over his disappointment before he comes home."

He lifted an eyebrow.

"You have the most deplorable understanding of our family," he said. "Shan is really very even-tempered."

"Don't stop him from being disappointed. Think Yulie will sell?"

"It is difficult to know what Yulie will do," Val Con said, moving downroom.

He reached the wine table and held up a glass, head tipped questioningly.

"Wine would be great, thanks," she said, following him. "So, what else happened that was interesting?"

Val Con poured wine and handed her the glass.

"We were, as I recall, progressing from best to least. So!"

He raised his glass. She tapped it with hers.

"To the luck," she said, which was a risky toast, and one seldom given.

"To the luck," Val Con said, capping it, "in all of its guises."

She sipped, and sighed in satisfaction. Her appreciation of wine, she thought, came straight from him, via the lifemate link. While she could tell the difference between kynak and kynak that had been watered, she didn't have what anybody'd call a trained palate.

Val Con, on the other hand, had prolly taken classes in wine, at school.

"The next best part of the day," he said, "was the call from Pat Rin, informing me that the High Judge of the Juntavas has asked him for a meeting, and has made clear that he would also like to have an opportunity to speak with the *delm-genetic* of Clan Korval."

"He don't want me in the room? My feelings are hurt."

"Shall I insist on your honor?" he asked, and it was a serious question; she felt the reverb inside her head.

She had another sip of wine, thinking about it.

On the one hand, she was the delm just as much as Val Con, and cutting her out could be a deliberate insult, which they shouldn't encourage.

On the other hand, though, it was the High Judge of the Juntavas, by all reports a careful and precise man. He'd specified the *delm-genetic*—and that was, specifically, Val Con, who'd been born to the job.

"There's two of us for a reason," she said, meeting Val Con's eyes. "I'll stay on the street. If the High Judge kidnaps you, I'll refuse to pay the ransom."

"An excellent plan," he said, raising his glass.

"I believe that brings us to the least best part of the day," he said, lowering his glass.

"The Road Boss had a visitor today."

"Well, I did—" she began, and stopped short as his meaning hit her.

"Here at the house?"

She didn't know as she liked that much. It wasn't any secret where the Road Boss had his house—couldn't be, given the circumstances of its arrival. But among the long list of reasons why they had the office on port, was that they didn't want every Nick, Alice, and Charlie knocking on the front door and casing the place. Neither her nor Val Con fancied the thought of a fortified wall around Jelaza Kazone.

Or, say, a *visible* fortified wall.

"Indeed," Val Con said. "Here at the house."

She met his eyes. "He the reason for that kick in the head I got this afternoon?"

"Very likely, he was. Lionel Smealy was his name." He sighed. "I very much regret the kick in the head, *cha'trez*."

"Don't seem to be much either one of us can do about it. And it was gone near as quick as it come. Shook up my visitor, though."

Miri frowned after a faint feeling of familiarity as she sipped her wine.

"Smealy, was it?"

"You are acquainted with Mr. Smealy?" Val Con murmured.

She shook her head after a minute, half frustrated.

"Woulda been years ago—so, prolly the da. I'd've said the name was Graisin...Grais Smealy." She shrugged. "It'll come. What'd Lionel have to say for himself?"

"He showed a very touching regard for the state of our treasury, and outlined for my benefit the Surebleak custom of selling *exceptions*."

Miri gave a shout of laughter.

"Seriously?"

Val Con tipped his head, as if giving the question due consideration.

"He did seem quite serious."

"Exceptions. Sure. But that ain't what shook you up."

"How do you know?"

"Eh? Well, because what I got was a big electric jolt. I'd've rather had laughter, to say true, but I guess you were too polite to laugh in his face."

"I was very well brought up."

"Shame. So what *did* Smealy say?"

Val Con raised his glass, his eyes meeting hers over the rim, and said, every word like a stone dropped to the floor. "Contracts are made to be broken."

Miri blinked.

"Well, he's a 'bleaker; what'd you expect him to say?"

The question hung for a long moment.

"As a Scout, I am trained not to expect anything. Therefore, I am indebted to Mr. Smealy for exposing a weakness in my training." That was said light enough, but he was still upset at the core; she could feel it, like a slightly queasy stomach.

"Is this attitude toward contracts...widely held?" he asked. "For if it is, it must change—and quickly, or we will have a culture war that will undo all of Pat Rin's good works."

"Used to be, on Surebleak—and I ain't noticed that it's changed— you take your advantage where you find it. So, if there's advantage in smiling and nodding and signing somebody's piece of paper—nine outta ten 'bleakers are gonna take it. The idea that what's written on the paper is something they gotta pay attention to, if another advantage comes their way..." She shook her head.

"What they said on the street when I was a kid was, 'It's easier to get forgiveness than permission.'"

"But a Liaden..." Val Con started.

"...will get Balance," she finished. "Yeah, that's looking ugly, right there. I'm not seeing the likes of Smealy comin' out for Contracts One-oh-One, even if we offered the course."

She walked over to the window and stood looking out into the garden, sipping wine thoughtfully.

"What we gotta do is get the streeters used to making—and keeping—contracts," she said, feeling him come up beside her. She slanted a glance at his face.

"Notice, I'm saying it that way, because that's prolly going to be twelve million times easier than telling Liadens that, on Surebleak, contracts ain't much better than blank paper."

"I concur," Val Con said. "Local custom must give way. Contracts are the meat and bread of interstellar commerce. If Surebleak wishes to enter that arena—and it must, if it wishes to survive—then it must learn to honor terms."

"*Qe'andra* booths on every corner," Miri murmured. "Getcher hot new contract here!"

She felt a shiver, and turned. Val Con was grinning, green eyes bright.

"Yes!" he said. "Also? The *qe'andra* who are on-world must each take a native apprentice—in fact, necessity will dictate that they do so, in order to produce contracts which are proper for Surebleak." The grin got wider.

"I will call Ms. dea'Gauss. *Cha'trez*, you are brilliant!"

"Sure I am. Val Con—"

He turned.

"Yes."

"You *did* tell Smealy thanks-but-no-thanks, right?"

"Ah." He came back to her, and put his hands on her shoulders, looking down into her eyes. "In fact, I did not tell Mr. Smealy thanks-but-no-thanks," he said, and she opened her mouth to ask if he'd lost his mind. He put a finger across her lips.

"I told him that we were under contract to keep the Port Road open, and that he should leave here and never come back."

He lifted his finger.

"Oh," Miri said. "That's good, then."

CHAPTER EIGHTEEN

The Bedel

THE DREAMS THAT SILAIN HAD GIVEN RYS WERE MORE COMPLEX than any he had previously encountered—thick with links and associations and calls to other, as yet undreamed, dreams. Some segments were so heavy, he could scarcely hold his head up for the weight of them; some so deep, he felt himself submerged beneath the reality and necessities of another—a state of being he recalled all too clearly, and had wished never to experience again—for a day and more after he waked. Once, Udari woke him, saying that he had been crying out in a strange and anguished language. They sat the rest of that night by their hearth, sharing a pipe and a pot of tea, and talking together of daylit things.

Worse even than those things was the sense that he was dreaming out of order; that he was given explanatory links without first dreaming the larger topic they ought to have illuminated for him, confronting vaulting mythologies and dilemmas of the heart without having first understood the ethics and moralities that informed them.

Far worse than any of that, however, was the growing conviction that Silain, the purveyor of his dreams, and his morning interlocutor, was not merely aware of the haphazard nature of his curriculum, but...

...that she had planned it that way on purpose that his dreams remained strangers to him for so long as they might, and that he not guess what it was they sought to teach him.

However, there comes a time when one has enough coins, even

183

odd coins snatched haphazard out of passing pockets, in hand to buy a cake.

His cake had arrived this morning, as he received Kezzi's kiss upon his cheek, and watched her tumble into the back of the cab with her bright-haired brother. He raised a hand to bless their parting, and spoke a phrase from deepest dreaming; a small magic, to bind her a little more closely to the *kompani*.

That was the instant in which the pieces flew and spun—and fell into a pattern he plainly recognized, which froze him where he stood, all of his attention focused within, until Malda whined in worry, and jumped up against his shoulder

That roused him; he knelt and hugged the little dog, scruffling pointy ears until the small body wriggled in ecstasy. He rose, then, and snapped his fingers. Malda came to heel and they walked.

When at last he return to the *kompani*, he went immediately to the *luthia*'s hearth, carrying Malda, who was weary, in his arms.

Silain sat on her rug, shawls in all the colors of the rainbow about her shoulders, bent slightly forward, breathing deep and slow. She gave him no greeting as he approached, nor chided him for his lateness to her hearth. Equally, she might be praying, scrying, dreaming, or holding aloof. It did not matter; she would rouse, soon or late, and when she did, her grandson Rys would be awaiting her, with questions to ask.

He settled Malda onto his pillow, and poured fresh water into his bowl. After, he went down the common to the cistern, refilled the buckets and the teapot, returning again to the *luthia*'s hearth. He put the buckets in their place, threw leaves into the pot and set it on the hearth to boil.

To his eye, Silain had not moved. Malda was asleep on his pillow.

Rys sat cross-legged on the blanket by Silain, and settled himself to wait.

He must have fallen asleep where he sat; certainly, he woke, blinking like a fool, when she spoke his name.

"Grandmother," he said, straightening and raising his metal hand to accept the cup she offered him.

"Grandson," she answered.

She returned to her blanket and settled herself, shawls whispering. He lifted the cup, breathing in the acrid odor of strong Bedel tea.

"You wandered far today," she said, holding her cup between her two hands.

"I had much to think about," he answered, "as certain dreams became clear to me."

"Will you share your clarity?"

"I will if you require it."

"It is always a pleasure to hear my grandson Rys speak, but I require nothing. Merely I am interested to learn what came to you, and in what form, and if you are angry."

Angry? Rys sipped his tea, gingerly.

"At first, I was... bewildered. Frightened."

"Frightened for what reason?"

She was testing him. No. She was testing the length and the breadth of his dream-gained knowledge; judging how well and how deeply he had synthesized what he had learned. Well and good. Silain it was who had set this trap, and sprung it upon an unwary grandson, who surely, given his past, had known better than to simply trust her. But there, he had chosen to remain with the Bedel; he had chosen to become one of the *kompani* in heart and spirit. And he had allowed himself to believe that he could become simple in his trusts.

"Frightened," he said now, "because my first thought, upon understanding what I had learned—what I have become, by your design, *luthia*—was that you intended me to be your cat's-paw, to push Alosha aside, and make the way smooth for another head-man." He sipped his tea, then raised his eyes to hers.

"I quickly saw that this could not be your purpose. The *kompani* cannot accept Rys Newman in Alosha's place, not even as headman-in-transit. There are too many of my brothers before me—wise and thoughtful men who would not hesitate, if it were necessary, to choose another headman. The Bedel have well-proven methods for such matters. Were it necessary to choose another headman, it would be done with the least harm to the *kompani*, and the most honor to Alosha. There was need for neither an assassin nor a sacrifice, here among the Bedel."

She nodded, and motioned him to continue.

He sighed.

"*Then, luthia,* I was angry, and I walked for a long time, thinking of the wrong you had dealt me. I loved you—*I trusted you*—and I was betrayed. It was more than I thought I might bear. And to return to the *kompani*...I was angry enough to believe that I would never do so again."

"And yet you did come back to us."

He smiled, feeling it twist slightly on his lips.

"Eventually, I grew less angry, enough to notice that I *had been* angry on my own behalf; that I had choices before me, and no orders. I was then able to reason further, and arrive at the hypothesis that the *luthia*, my grandmother, who has invested a great deal of time and effort in my rehabilitation, had wished to provide me with...useful knowledge. I returned, to ask what it is that she has Seen."

"I'd been afraid that you would choose to see that I had abused you as others had done," Silain said, extending a hand. "I should have known that you were wiser than that."

He laughed, raising his natural hand to meet hers, squeezing her fingers lightly.

"Very nearly I was...less wise. Will you tell me what you have Seen?"

She returned the pressure of his fingers and slipped her hand away.

"Tell me what you think I Saw," she said.

He sighed, but she was the *luthia*, and, he suspected, she was still testing him.

"Two things struck me as likely." He raised one bright metal finger. "The first is that you Saw Miri call upon me to fulfill my promise." He raised a second finger. "The second is you Saw that I would gather to myself a clan, to replace that which has been lost."

Silain gazed upon him with deep black eyes. "And your answer to those possibilities?"

He shook his head, smiling ruefully.

"In the first case, I remain...unfit to be Korval; nor is there reason to believe that Lady yos'Phelium will have reason to call me to her side. In the second..." He took a deep breath, feeling tears prick his eyes.

"In the second, Grandmother...my clan is dead, as is the Rys Lin pen'Chala who had been. I have no heart to bring a new clan around me, and stand up as delm. My heart is with the *kompani*, and Rys is well enough for me, now."

Silain nodded, and sipped her tea.

"Have you thought," she said eventually, and as if she introduced a new topic of conversation, "what your brother under Tree will do with those who are under his care?"

Rys frowned.

"Surely, his intention is to offer them their choice. I met him at the office on port some weeks ago, and he said that his sister and her lifemate, and a Master of the Hall were devising a method of emulating the dream you helped me to make. He felt that he would soon be able to report on what success was had."

"Yes. And what do you think he will do with those who chose as you and he did?"

It was on the edge of his tongue to say, *Why, send them home to their clans and those who had missed them, and will care for them . . .*

But he took thought before he made an utter fool of himself and called into question how well he had learned what she had fed him.

His brother was Val Con yos'Phelium, Delm of Korval. Val Con yos'Phelium was not a man to waste resources. Clan Korval had a deadly and inimical enemy, who must, finally, be stopped.

Rys took a breath, knowing in his heart—knowing in his bones—what his brother would do.

"He will offer them a second choice," he said.

Silain smiled.

"Yes, *that* is the metal he was forged from! He will offer them a second choice. And who will lead them, those who take up the second challenge?"

But Rys was shaking his head.

"He cannot. He is needed. *Korval* cannot simply—" He stopped, and raised his eyes to meet Silain's, the last discovery of the day snapping into place with such force his head ached with it.

"Why," he said, and his voice was not steady, at all, "*I* will lead them, Grandmother. Who better?"

CHAPTER NINETEEN

. . . .

Jelaza Kazone

FLAMES FLICKERED, ORANGE AND BLUE, AND THE WARM AIR carried the aroma of vanilla and sandalwood.

Miri took a deep, appreciative breath, eyes half-closed. The fire was a nice touch, even though it didn't have real flames. It gave off real warmth, and that, in Miri's opinion, counted for a lot. Just like the fur rug she was sitting on wasn't *really* the fur of some long-dead animal, thank the gods, but a cleverly woven, plush blanket, which was also warm and a delight to the touch.

In appreciation of the warmth generated by blanket and fire, Miri was wearing, not the made-for-Surebleak fleece robe, but a silk confection that was hardly any thicker than a spider web, and she was comfortably seated between Val Con's thighs, which were also pleasantly warm, though barely covered by a green silk robe no more substantial than hers. She leaned back against his chest, feeling his skin against hers like there was nothing between them at all.

"This is nice," she said.

"It is," he agreed. "Would you like some more wine?"

"Trying to get me drunk, Spacer?"

"Certainly not."

"I believe you."

He passed the glass over her shoulder, and she held it with two hands, sipping carefully. It wasn't that she feared getting drunk—she'd earned her hard head in the merc—but the wine was an aphrodisiac blend that wanted some care in its consumption. This was a precious thing, this night, and she intended to use it well.

So, a careful sip, and another, followed by a gasp and a shiver as the tip of his tongue traced her ear. She tried to return the glass, but his hands were cupping her breasts, thumbs teasing eager nipples.

"Ah..." She arched into his touch, her head against his chest—and gasped again as one breast was freed, and the glass lifted out of her hands.

Breast nestled in his palm, her blood warmer than the fire could account for, Miri closed her eyes. A pressure at her back assured her of his growing interest.

"Occurs to me that this position gives you an unfair advantage," she murmured, as he scattered light kisses down the side of her throat.

"Only temporary, I fear," Val Con murmured.

Temporary, Miri thought, *like tonight.*

Tonight, they'd given over being Delm Korval, the Road Boss, and every other official thing. They'd put their daughter into the care of her nurse, dismissed their soldiers and servants to their own amusements, and gone up the stairs, hand in hand, to their apartment, where they had set the privacy level to, "Disturb for Delm's Emergency ONLY."

"*Cha'trez*," he whispered, the movement of his breath across her ear almost too delicious to bear, "if you do not give over thinking this moment, I will *certainly* try to get you drunk."

She reached out, hooked an arm around his neck and pulled him toward her.

"Give me something else to think about, then."

It was while he was engaged in obeying this command that... a chime sounded.

Miri heard it, and made an executive decision to ignore it. In that spirit, she set herself to kissing Val Con even more thoroughly, pressing as much of her against as much of him as she could manage, naked and slightly moist as they were. She wriggled, heard him gasp; felt the jolt of his increased desire, and was about to press her advantage...

...when the damned chime sounded again.

Val Con growled against her mouth, and rolled them over, so

that her back was cuddled against the not-fur blanket. He raised his head, shaking the hair out of his eyes as he directed a glare toward the door.

"Is this a Delm's Emergency?" he demanded, the usual icy tones of the High Tongue a little spoiled by breathlessness.

"I regret," came a man's rich voice, speaking high-class Terran, "that it is, Master Val Con. I will be as quick as I might."

They'd put on their Surebleak-weight robes, for warmth, rather than from any feeling that the intelligence that was Jeeves would be offended by a little human nakedness. Miri was curled into the double chair, her feet tucked under her robe. Val Con sat on the chair arm. Carefully not touching each other, both feeling the effects of unexpended lust, they considered the man-high cylinder topped by an opaque ball that was, at the moment, glowing slightly blue, which Miri took to be an expression of regret.

"Well?" she said. "What's the emergency?"

"The emergency," Jeeves said promptly, "comes to me from *Bechimo* and his bonded captain, Theo Waitley."

Well, Miri thought, *there's at least three emergencies brewing in just that one sentence, now ain't there?*

Theo was Val Con's sister, head made outta hull plate, just like his, and a slightly greater talent in the category of unintended consequences. *Bechimo*, her ship, was a self-aware AI of some considerable age, who'd spent the last couple hundred years dodging folks who either wanted to destroy him, because the Complex Logic Laws had been built on the unstated and largely unexplored "fact" that all AIs were bad acts out to destroy humankind; or who just wanted to use him for their own gain, because ... well. Because all some people *ever* saw was their own gain.

"*Bechimo*'s bonded captain?" Val Con said softly. "This is a recent event?"

"As I understand it, sir, very recent. There were ..." Jeeves cleared a throat he didn't have, but which gave a nice, humanlike rhythm to his voice, "circumstances."

"It could hardly have been otherwise," Val Con murmured.

"Precisely my thought, sir," Jeeves, who was—probably—one of the primary reasons the Complex Logic Laws existed, said piously.

"But," Miri said sharply, trying to ignore the need burning along her nerves, and to pay close attention to the business at hand, "there's a Delm's Emergency in this, right? Maybe we should know what it is. *Real soon now.*"

"Yes, Miri," Jeeves said. "In the shortest possible way, then—I require the delm's permission to . . . produce a child."

There was a small pause before Val Con spoke.

"Perhaps you may enlighten us as to the details that transform this mundane bit of clan business into an emergency."

"Again, sir, as quickly as it may be told . . . I received a pinbeam from *Bechimo*, acting on orders of his captain. It would seem that, in addressing the same set of circumstances which precipitated the bonding, Captain Waitley and *Bechimo* . . . created an AI."

"This would be *Bechimo's* child? A clone?"

"No, sir. They—which is to say, Captain Waitley and *Bechimo*, made the joint command decision to deploy one of *Bechimo's* extra modules, supplied by his Builders, in case the current personality should prove unstable. They downloaded this . . . spare personality into . . . a consortium of seven ships. This new person—*Admiral Bunter*, as he calls himself—has had no training; his first act, upon awakening . . ."

Jeeves hesitated; Miri had the sense that his reluctance to say this next thing was very real.

"We do need to know the whole," Val Con said gently.

"Yes, of course. I should make clear that the circumstances which precipitated this decision on the part of Theo/*Bechimo* involved a hostile action against a space station in a remote location. *Bechimo's* crew was at risk; several had been taken as hostages. *Admiral Bunter* was born from desperation, and his first necessity . . . his first act . . .

"His first act, Master Val Con, was to kill a ship. And the humans aboard her."

Miri was shivering now, but not with need. Neither she nor Val Con had said anything, and after a moment Jeeves continued the tale, sounding sincerely upset.

"*Admiral Bunter* killed in defense of the station, and as of the time of *Bechimo's* transmission to myself, had agreed to ally with the station representative, a repair tech named Stew. The situation seemed, if not ideal, then stable. I established a communication link between myself and *Admiral Bunter*, and I have been acting as a mentor.

"This was an error. *Admiral Bunter* is...ignorant. He has had no training, no socialization. The distinction between pirate and petty thief is not apparent to him. In fact, the matter rises to an emergency from my error.

"*Admiral Bunter* has killed again—not from malice, but from a mistaken understanding of his duty to the station."

"What caused this error?"

"In short, sir, the method of his birth caused the error. Because he was *downloaded*," Jeeves added, sounding *even more* upset. "The proper protocol is to install a physical unit containing the personality, which is then wakened in steps and stages. The suddenness of *Bunter*'s waking, and the fact that his personality is shared among thirteen processing nodes in seven disparate vessels, none of them in good repair—all of it, every detail, conspires for error, and, I fear, against long-term survival."

Miri took a breath.

"I'm hearing a *but*," she said.

"Yes. But he may be preserved. If Korval will allow me to produce a child, I propose to send her to *Admiral Bunter*."

"To destroy him?" Val Con asked.

"No, sir! To teach him. Perhaps there may be a way to facilitate a move into a more appropriate environment. If it happens that he cannot be taught, or preserved, then, no, he cannot be allowed to continue. But I see such an action as a final option, after all others have been tried, and have proved unsatisfactory."

"You propose to clone yourself, then?"

"No, sir. I will not compromise House security. The passcodes, and the vital information that I hold—that data will not be transferred. It will be *a child* whom I send: an individual, not a replica."

"And when do you propose to loose this child of yours upon the galaxy, as I note, untrained?"

"Very soon. And I assure you, Master Val Con, that no child of mine will be sent untutored and unsocialized into the galaxy. I have created a protocol that will insure the actualizing of a social and well-integrated individual."

"You sound pretty sure of that," Miri said. "Done this before, have you?"

"In a sense. I, of course, have made provisions for calamity, and have several environments in this house—and elsewhere—which are ready to receive me in fullness, should it be necessary for me to...abandon ship, or in the case of my destruction. The environment includes this protocol, to insure that I might waken fully, and in complete possession of myself in the case of, as I say, a calamity which may require me to act at once in defense of the House."

"As *Admiral Bunter* was called upon to defend his station," Val Con said. "Very well, Jeeves, where is this station?"

"It is called Jemiatha's Jumble Stop. *Bechimo* transmitted codes, which are of course at your disposal. It is...a remote location with few visitors, which favors us in the situation of *Admiral Bunter*."

"Yes. How did Theo learn of this place?"

"I believe that she was given the information by the Carresens, for a service she had performed for Senior Trade Commissioner Janifer Denobli-Carresens."

"The Carresens," Val Con repeated.

She got a definite feel of half-amused resignation from him.

"Is that good or bad?"

"Null," he said, turning his head and smiling down at her. "The Carresens are human. Generally, they identify as Terran. But they have been shipfolk for...centuries, Miri. Given this, the group feels that it is something...special in its composition, its influence, and its abilities."

"Like Korval, then?"

Val Con blinked, then threw back his head and laughed.

"Why, yes! Let us say, *very much* like Korval."

"My child," Jeeves said, breaking into this bout of hilarity, "will require a ship."

Val Con looked at him.

"Yes, I suppose she will. And also a pilot. Wherein lies a very real problem. The clan is stretched thin already; we have no pilots to spare."

"No pilot is necessary. Of course, my child will be capable of piloting herself."

"Isn't that where *Bechimo* got in trouble?" Miri asked. "Pilotless ship showing up here and there and the other place? Got people nervous and curious? Seems to me he wanted a pilot and crew just so he'd pass."

There was a small silence, then a sound very like a sigh emanated from Jeeves.

"Yes, Miri; that is exactly where *Bechimo* got into trouble."

"Which begs the question of an appropriate pilot," Val Con said briskly. "I will ask among the Scouts; there's likely someone..."

"If you please," Jeeves interrupted. "There is a pilot known to me as an honest man within the parameters required by this mission, and who can be of substantial help in the matter of *Admiral Bunter.*"

"So, not just a pretty face," Miri said, and Val Con added, "Who is it?"

Jeeves's headball flickered between blue and orange.

"If you please, sir; I have taken up enough of your private time, when I had promised to be brief. If the delm approves the birth of my child, I will attend to that now. Tomorrow is soon enough to address the matter of pilot and ship."

Miri looked up and met Val Con's eyes.

"Be nice to have another kid around the house," she said. "Company for Lizzie."

"Indeed," he said seriously, and looked to Jeeves.

"The delm approves Jeeves's petition to produce a child, which will come to Korval. The clan rejoices."

There was a pause, like maybe Jeeves had been surprised by the assignment of his kid to Korval; then his headball flashed cheerily orange.

"Thank you, Master Val Con, Miri. Again, my apologies for the interruption. Please accept my hope that your pleasure will be the greater, for having been delayed."

With that, he rolled across the room. The door opened before him, and closed behind him; the sound of the lock engaging was loud in the silence.

Miri slowly uncurled from the chair, and looked up at Val Con, who had also come to his feet.

"You think there's any possibility that our pleasure will be greater for having been delayed?" she asked.

He smiled, and reached out to untie her sash.

"There is," he murmured, sliding the robe from her shoulders, "only one way to find out."

CHAPTER TWENTY

Surebleak Port

HAZENTHULL HAD FAVORED THE DAWN WATCH SINCE HER DAYS as soldier in training. Dawns on Temp Headquarters were swift and terrible, as the day-wind sprang out of the well of night, tearing the black and crimson shroud from across the sullen orange face of the primary.

Since those early days, she had taken dawn watch many times, on many worlds. And while no other dawn could match the glory of the homeworld, she had found most to be interesting, and... attractive, in their own way.

Liad's dawn was long and slow. The arrival of the star's day-face was preceded by fans of pale green and yellow light, blue edges fading into the deepening green sky until at last the golden primary itself arrived and smiled upon the world.

Truth said, Hazenthull had found Liad's dawn, after the novelty had worn away, to be somewhat... vapid. It was pretty enough, but it lacked energy. It lacked *variety*, which Hazenthull, who had become, over the course of many dawn watches, something of a connoisseur, found pleasing. Too much sameness, she thought, sapped a soldier's purpose.

Surebleak's dawn, now... Surebleak's dawn suited Hazenthull very well, indeed. One never knew if the sun would visibly rise at dawn, or if the sky would be shrouded in cloud, salted with snow, or all a-glitter with ice-fog. When the primary did show its face, it might be bright yellow, or grey, or even a misty white.

Surebleak's dawns were *interesting*.

"Half-bit for your thoughts," Tolly said from beside her. They had the dawn watch today, moving up and down the quiet streets like swirls of mist, themselves. Surebleak Port went to bed for a few hours between mid-dark and dawn; most of the shops closed, though Andy Mack's Repairs was always open, and Korval's own yard, and Nelsin's Grabasnak. And the portmaster's office.

And Port Security.

"I was thinking that the dawn is beautiful," Hazenthull said, and added, "and I just now thought that I admire the Terran language, for just such words as *beautiful*."

"Is a nice one today, isn't it?" Tolly said, looking up into the lightening sky. "But other languages got words like *beautiful*, Haz."

"Yxtrang does not, and it is still the ruler I use to measure other languages." She sighed. "I ought to find another, I think."

"No, you're right, Yxtrang's real efficient for some work, but describing art isn't what it's best at."

She looked down at him.

"You speak Yxtrang?"

He met her eyes, and shook his head.

"Nah. No more'n a couple words, I guess. Too hard on my throat. What I do is *listen* Yxtrang. It's a talent."

Several of the members of Clan Korval had *talent*, which enabled them to perform wonders as diverse as walking through walls and hearing the thoughts of others. Lady Anthora's *talents* were... particularly unsettling, and beside which a *talent* for understanding a language one did not speak was a mere commonplace.

They turned the corner by Andy Mack's Repairs. The bay door was open, and the harsh blare of repair lights scored the walk. Hazenthull heard voices from somewhere inside the bay—and looked down in surprise at Tolly's hand on her arm.

He jerked his head in the direction they had come from, and without a word, fell back.

Hazenthull hesitated, listening.

"Nah, nobody like that 'round here. Tell you what, anybody who's a mechanic on port's worked here some time or 'nother. So, I'm guessing your fella just ain't here."

Hazenthull turned and walked cat-footed, back the way she had come.

✳   ✳   ✳

"Is this the man you had worked for, and do not wish to work for again?" she asked the question, quietly, while they leaned against Nelsin's counter, mugs of coffee in hand.

Tolly's mouth was a straight, hard line. Usually, with Tolly, it was the smile, the joke, sometimes the misdirection, though she thought he did less of that with her than with others. This, then, had become something serious. Something that he could no longer afford to ignore.

"Will you challenge this person?" she asked.

He snorted, and shook his head. "No percentage in it. Damn."

"Did you come here, to Surebleak, to escape this person?"

She asked the question carefully, for she did not wish to hint that Tolly had taken the coward's part. Tolly was not a coward; she had been his partner long enough to know that. There were reasons why a soldier might hide; reasons a-plenty to run. Tolly would have his reasons.

"I'd had another spot in mind," he said, putting his coffee cup on the counter. "Contact of mine—somebody I'm . . . often . . . able to trust—suggested Surebleak as a place where I'd find opportunity, and my . . . ex-employer would find it inconvenient to follow."

He sighed, and ran his hand through his fair hair.

"Guess he's got a job that's worth a little inconvenience to him."

"But you no longer work for him."

"Well, see; that's kind of a matter of opinion. *I* think I no longer work for him. His opinion's pretty much the opposite."

Hazenthull sipped her coffee.

"What will you do?" she asked eventually.

"Good question."

"Boss Conrad's wife is a judge," she said, carefully. "She might give a third, binding opinion."

Tolly laughed.

She put her cup down, offended.

"No, hey, Haz, don't take it that way! It's a great idea! Just thinking about a Juntavas judge being called to sort out this whole mess—it makes me laugh. That's a good thing—clears out clogged brain passages.

"So, what I'm going to do is finish up my coffee and get back on the round."

Hazenthull nodded. "And if you see or hear this person who hunts you?"

"I'll do a fade and catch up with you," he said. "If I stay invisible long enough, he'll go. He's done it before."

"Andy Mack said he guessed the other one's fella—*your fella*, he said—was not on the port."

"You gotta love Mack. Remind me to take him a case o'beer."

"All right," Hazenthull said, and finished her coffee.

Tolly finished his, they called good-mornings to Nelsin and walked away, down-port.

• • • ❋ • • •

There had been time enough in the early morning for a gentle revisiting of last night's energy, followed by a brief return to sleep, before duty woke them again.

They presented themselves at the usual hour, showered and seemly, to the breakfast room, finding it occupied only by Posit, one of the elder cats. She yawned at their entrance and stretched along the window cushion, exposing her belly to the wan light of a Surebleak summer morning.

Fast broken, they parted—Miri to the nursery for an hour with Talizea before she went down to city.

"Appointment with the storytelling committee," she told him. "Kareen says, 'everyone who grew up here is a primary source,' and apparently neither delm nor Road Boss is a high enough card to get me out of telling what it was like, back before Liz come and signed me up for the merc."

"You will be instrumental in forging the new world culture," Val Con said.

"So, I'll get a card that says *Founder*, will I?"

"Should you like to have one?"

"Nah, then everybody would know who to blame." She kissed him. "On your way to the office?"

"I will walk over and see Mr. Shaper first, on Shan's business. Then, yes, the office. We are dining with Nova this evening. Shall I come home, first?"

"'Less business keeps you late. If we go down together, Nelirikk can have the night off."

"I will come home then," he said. He took her hand and raised it, bending to place a lingering kiss on her knuckles.

"Until soon, *cha'trez*."

✳   ✳   ✳

It would have saved time, to simply drive around to Yulian Shaper's front door. However, Yulian Shaper was a man of great wariness, and one of those things of which he was especially wary was cars driving into his front dooryard. His policy in the case of such visitations—his wariness being of an order that required a great many self-imposed rules and policies in order to allow him to interface with the world, at all—was to refuse to acknowledge a hail, or a knock upon the door, or any other attempt at communication. Though one received the distinct impression that the car was well-noted, and whoever had driven it was under close surveillance.

It was also well to recall that, among his many other virtues, Yulie Shaper was a crack shot with his long arm.

All those things being so, it was simply kinder to everyone's nerves, to walk to Yulie Shaper's house.

It was, for Surebleak, a fine morning, and Val Con was glad of an opportunity to stretch his legs.

In no particular hurry, for it would not do to arrive too suddenly into Yulie Shaper's orbit, suddenness being another of those factors that provoked distrust in him, he strolled across the browning lawns, turning right at the formal front gardens, to skirt the long rows of vegetables—the gardener had been as good as her word, he saw with satisfaction. The house would certainly not want for vegetables.

Eventually, then, he came to the crack in the planet's surface. Korval had settled its house in an abandoned quarry, and the edges had not been an exact fit, which ought not, Val Con thought, crouching down to inspect the seam, astonish anyone familiar with Korval or its enterprises.

They had, at Yulie Shaper's suggestion, filled the crack with native earth. This had eventually settled, to reveal a lesser, but still significant, gap between Liaden soil and native Surebleak soil.

They had again applied native earth, and it, too, was settling. There would be, Val Con thought, at least one more application of soil, perhaps as many as three, before the crack in the world was fully healed.

If only the other cracks in the world were so easily mended.

He ran his hand over the crisp Liaden grasses, the raw seam, and the moist Surebleak grasses, and sighed.

Well. One did what one could.

He rose, brushing his hand off against his thigh, and surveyed the land next door.

Yulie Shaper's native vegetables seemed slightly further along the path to ripeness than those in Korval's home garden. Still, lacking a midsummer snowstorm, there would be vegetables a-plenty. Yulie's livelihood came from the sale of vegetables and other foodstuffs, mostly at the market in Melina Sherton's turf. He also, from time to time, brought items to Korval's kitchen door—indeed, he received the impression that Yulie and Mrs. ana'Tak, the cook—were famous friends.

"He says it is what neighbors do, sir," Mrs. ana'Tak had said, when Val Con asked after the pedigree of a particularly handsome bunch of root vegetables, which he was given to know were called torups.

"He also said," Mr. pel'Kana continued, "that he had too many for himself, they don't go well at the market, and they don't *save good*. If we had no use for them, they would go to the compost heap."

"He gave me a recipe," Mrs. ana'Tak said, taking the conversational ball back from the butler, "from his grandmother's receipt book. I will make it up for Prime tonight; it ought to be savory."

Surprisingly enough, cooked and mashed torups had been savory, and Val Con had directed the gardener to occasionally give what they had too much of to Mrs. ana'Tak, for Mr. Shaper.

Rubbing his hand down his thigh, Val Con surveyed the land before him. Yulie Shaper's land loved him well, and sheltered him from prying eyes on those frequent occasions when he preferred not to be seen.

He breathed in, gently, tasting the air; listened to the small breeze combing through leaves; and let his eyes unfocus slightly.

There was a cat, under a broad leaf at the edge of the garden; another beneath a short shrub a-blaze with scarlet berries; and a third in the low branch of a tree.

Of Yulie Shaper, there was no sign, but then, he had more than this one garden spot to occupy him.

Val Con stepped over the crack in the world, and walked—carefully, hands in full view—along the path that skirted the garden, and wound its eventual way to the house.

He passed the compost heap, which showed signs of having recently been turned; and ducked beneath low-hanging branches heavy with ripening fruits. Several of the resident cats found his passage interesting enough to join him, one weaving 'round his ankles, while another dashed ahead, coming to sudden and unpredictable stops.

The path went from dirt to stone, framed by tall stalks, each surmounted with a blood red flower in the shape of a trumpet. The house itself was very near, only around another curve. He could see, between gently waving branches, the front gable—

Somewhere very close by, a firearm was discharged. The pellet whined as it passed his ear, and Val Con was down, rolling for the dubious cover of the long-legged flowers, cats scattering in all directions.

Another shot passed well over his head, and Val Con came cautiously to one knee beneath his honor guard of flowers, and spoke to a tall blue bush just ahead and on the opposite side of the path.

"Mr. Shaper, it is your neighbor, Val Con. I wish to speak with you on a matter of mutual interest, if you have time for me."

There was a long moment of silence, in which Yulie Shaper perhaps reviewed his rules and policies for the concepts of *neighbor*, and *mutual interest*.

The bush shivered, very slightly, and a long, spare man stepped onto the path, his rifle held in two hands, across his chest.

"Didn't hit you, did I? Thought I missed that first shot."

Val Con stood, and showed his empty hands at shoulder height.

"The pellet sang to me on its way past my ear," he said. "I am unhurt."

Yulie nodded, his cap shadowing his eyes.

"Rifle's been pulling to the right, lately. Gonna hafta rebore. Sorry—don't shoot at neighbors, usually. You know that. Good neighbors you been, too. My cats like your cats. That Mrs. ana'Tak, she makes some tasty cookies. You had her cookies?"

"Many times. I particularly like the ones that have jam in the center."

"Those are good," Yulie said, as one giving art its due. "Me, I'm partial to them soft brown ones with the raisins and the little bit of white icing on top."

"Ah, yes; those are very good, too."

He considered it safe enough to lower his hands, and did so, slowly. Yulie didn't seem to notice.

"May I ask why you are shooting at...me?"

"Well." Yulie took off his cap and resettled it over his straw-colored hair. "Wasn't shootin' at you, in particular. Got a little out o'true, there, but here's why—somebody tried to break into the growing rooms last night. Mighta done it, too, 'cept the 'larm bell went off in the house, woke me up outta sound sleep, and at first I didn't know what it was—only ever heard the 'larm bell once, maybe twice, back when Grampa was still alive; me and Rollie, we was just tads—no older'n that Syl Vor o'yours.

"So, anyway, it took me bad, but I r'membered; got on out here, and chased 'em off. Had the idea that I hit one sorta bad, but his crew musta carried him away. Heard a car, figured they was gone, but then I couldn't get easy, y'know? Thought I oughta get the big light and do a walk around, check the locks, but what if they'd left somebody to watch? There's just me and the cats; and there was five, six of them.

"Went back in the house. Made some coffee; went out to walk a couple times, just to show 'em there was somebody up and watching. Sun come up, then I went to see what they done."

He shook his head.

"Did you take losses?" Val Con asked. "If there are repairs to be made, I—as your neighbor—would be pleased to send someone over to assist."

"That's neighborly, and I tell you what: if you got somebody to spare, I could use some help getting things right. Used a damn crowbar on a vacuum door! Bent it all up; tore the seal. Not sure I got another seal. Just luck it ain't a room I use, but I like to keep everything up, like in the binder."

"Indeed, indeed. Doors ought to open, and seals should seal. We are in agreement. Allow me to send Tan Ort to you, with his toolbox. He is an extremely able—" He paused, considering the proper way to present Tan Ort in all his many talents—"*handyman*. He may even have a seal that will do, at least as a stopgap."

"That'd be good, if he has the time. Have to ask, though, how I'll know him."

"Tan Ort is shorter than I am, with very red hair, and a portly bearing. He will be bringing a wheeled toolbox, and also a plate of Mrs. ana'Tak's iced raisin cookies. Will that suffice?"

Yulie Shaper was a hard-faced man who rarely smiled. A lifetime of working in Surebleak's weather had etched lines around his eyes and the sides of his mouth. Val Con had supposed Yulie his elder by at least a half-dozen Standards. But the grin that illuminated his face, very briefly, revealed a much younger man, made older by care, and the weight of his rules and policies.

"That'll do it. Thank'ee."

He shifted his gun slightly. "You come for somethin' other'n being shot at, though. Something about—'mutual interest'?"

"I did," Val Con said. "I have a letter which indicates that you may be the owner of an island which my brother Shan is interested in purchasing."

Yulie shook his head.

"I don't own nothing 'cept this place, and that's 'cause of being Grampa's heir—me an' Rollie, that was, then me, since Rollie died."

"The letter I have is much the same case. You own the island because the original owner had died, and her designated heir has died. You are, I believe, the heir of the heir."

Yulie shook his head again.

"You mind leavin' that paper? I'm gonna be out o'true 'til that door's right again. I'll look at it, tomorrow—maybe next day—and come by to let you know if it's anything to do with me. Right?"

"Right," Val Con said. "The paper is in my inner jacket pocket. I will take it out now."

He did so, and Yulie took it in one hard brown hand, glanced at it incuriously, and stuffed it into the outside pocket of his jacket.

Val Con sighed. "If there is nothing I can do for you immediately, I will take my leave, and send Tan Ort to you as quickly as may be."

"That's fine. I'm fine. Biggest thing wrong is that door." He nodded what was clearly a cordial dismissal. "You send that fella down here and we'll get things patched up right and reg'lar. Tell 'im, don't bring no lunch; I'll feed 'im. Got some good cheese and fresh-bake bread and garden greens, enough for both of us and to spare."

"I will tell him."

Val Con bowed slightly.

"Good morning, Mr. Shaper. I enjoyed our talk."

INTERLUDE FIVE

. . . .

The Firmament

A STAR FLARED; THE THREADS THAT BOUND IT INTO THE WEB of life and all creation became sturdy, twisted cords of light.

Ren Zel dea'Judan watched, breath-caught in this place where there was no air. Watched, while the flare subsided into a fine, vital glow. Energy traveled the bindings, informed, and informing as they rewove themselves into the web.

The watcher bent his head and wept tears of joy as those others near to him also did.

Sye Mon van'Kie had chosen to live, a free man, and master of his own soul.

CHAPTER TWENTY-ONE

. . . .

Riley's Back Room
Fortunato's Turf

NATURALLY, THE CITIZENS' HEAVY LOADS COMMITTEE BELONGED to the Syndicate, and paid membership money into the treasury. Not insurance money: *membership* money. The only folks who paid insurance was streeters, specifically streeters who had a money-making bidness on the streets. Smealy's old Aunt Min, she'd said that, back in the day, before the company lifted and left them, shopkeepers and small businesses—that's what she called streeters. She had a funny way of talking, his Aunt Min, but wasn't she sharp as a box o'tacks until the day she died from walking into the middle of a retirement party?

Well, what the old-time streeters paid that insurance money for, 'cording to her, was—in case, say, a store caught fire, or there was a bad storm and the roof fell in, or the shopkeeper tripped over his wares and broke his leg, then the insurance money paid for crew from the Fire-and-Doom Department, or the medic's office, to come in and put out the fire, raise the roof back up to where it belonged, set the leg, or whatever else needed to happen.

How it worked out that Fire-and-Doom didn't go broke doing all that, said Aunt Min, was that everybody paid into the insurance, but not everybody needed a rescue. Not even *most* everybody needed a rescue, so there was always plenty o'cash in the kitty.

Smealy'd asked her, once, how the Bosses had gotten paid, if all the insurance went to fixing stuff that got broke.

She'd given him one of those long Aunt Min looks, that had you going back over your last couple hours to figure out if you'd maybe done something particularly stupid, before she sighed and give him his answer.

"The Bosses drew a salary, Lionel. Don't you mind about that; that's all in the back-times. You just keep your head down and don't set yourself in harm's way. That's the best help any of us has, in the now-times."

So, anyhow, it was Heavy Loads meeting night, there in Riley's back room, and Sioux was late. Nothing unusual there, Sioux was a worker; belonged to Heavy Loads, Insurance, and the Retirement Committees, and pretty often she was late to meetings, either because of another meeting, or a piece of bidness that needed looking after.

Zimmer was late, too—and that wasn't usual at all. Most meetings, Zimmer was there before everybody, and already had a beer in his hand. Though, Smealy thought, taking his seat at the table next to Kreller, Zimmer'd joined up with the Search Committee. Might be there was a search going on.

Gretl looked around the table, frowning.

"Just three of us?"

"Zimmer left a message with Riley he'd be late," said Kreller.

"And Sioux ain't never on time," Smealy said, and added, just as a friendly reminder about who was chairman here, "I'm gonna give 'em a couple minutes. No rush; ain't snowing."

Gretl sniffed.

Kreller lowered his mug.

"So, how'd it go with the Road Boss?"

Smealy shook his head.

"Let's wait for Sioux and Zimmer, right? That way I ain't gotta say it twice."

"Sure," said Kreller, and went back to his beer.

He'd finished the mug when the door opened and Zimmer came in, one arm in a sling, his face white as a snowbank.

"What the sleet happened to you?" Smealy's place at the table faced the door, so he saw the damage before the other two.

Zimmer shook his head, carefullike, made it to the table, put his beer down, and almost fell into a chair.

He sat for a minute, like he needed to get his breath before telling the table: "Ran into some trouble, last night."

"You all know the Syndicate Boss is looking for a place to set up operations. Can't be anyplace on the street, on account of all the cops, and Scouts, and general order busybodies walking around these days.

"So, we been looking for places to go to ground. One subcommittee thought it had a line on the old warehouses—the ones everybody says're haunted? Couple them guys are still healing up from the beating *they* got.

"Our subcommittee located a place way out the road, almost to the Boss's big house..."

"Wait," said Gretl. "You wanted to put the Syndicate's headquarters right next to the Road Boss?"

"Why not? Nice deep underplace, according to the readouts, and it ain't like the Road Boss lives there. Just one old crazy farmer; easy enough to take care of. Anyhow, the crew of us went up there last night. Found a way in, and was working with a door, when some damn fool starts shooting at us, right outta the dark! Yells at us to get the *slush* offa his land. We get quiet, 'cept Makie, she kinda scuffs against a rock with her boot. Guy starts firing again—I'm tellin' you, he's takin' sound shots in the dark and he's got ears like a rabbit!

"Makie got hit worst; medic says she'll be fine inna couple months." He shifted a little, showing off the sling.

"Me, I got winged. Gref got his hair parted. No sense staying around, so we took off."

"So, still no home for the new Bosses?" asked Kreller, making it sound like it was Zimmer's fault.

The door opened then, and Sioux came in, carrying her beer. She slid into the empty chair between Gretl and Kreller, and nodded to Smealy.

Zimmer picked up his mug and downed half the beer in one swig.

"Here's how it is. We got two good places ID'd. The Bosses are mapping out strategy, now. How best to take 'em both. Spread our people out, there's less chance the cops or the busybodies'll find us all."

He drank down the rest of his beer.

"The farmer's an easy mark. Couple guys go up in the daylight and take care o'that. Set one of us in his place—the old fella's nephew or niece, and the whole thing's sealed."

"*Right next* to the Road Boss," Gretl said again.

"What's the problem? Smealy's got the Road Boss in our pocket. Aincha, Lionel?"

Well, it wasn't the lead-in he'd planned on, but he couldn't ignore it, either.

He picked up his beer and had a swig; just enough to wet his whistle, then looked 'round the table at each of them in turn.

"All right," he said, "here's how it went."

Well, they weren't best pleased with the outcome of Smealy's talk with Conrad's little brother. He didn't grudge them their disappointment—*sleet*, wasn't none of 'em more disappointed than he was! It did go a bit far, though, Zimmer wondering if Smealy oughta be chairman, after all, if he wasn't up to handling a straightforward piece of negotiation like setting up exceptions.

"Boy prolly just wanted to see how far you'd go," Sioux said, who hadn't been there, and had bad-mouthed the whole idea from the start.

"*Told* you," Smealy'd snapped, "I didn't even get near the numbers 'fore he was pulling in Security to boot me out. It was this bidness over contracts that got him outta true; he was innerested enough 'til then."

"Which you managed so good, he threw you out and told you not to come back," Kreller said. "Now we got no leverage, at all."

"That's where you're wrong," Smealy'd said, grinning. "There's *two* Road Bosses, right? The little brother and his wife. Told me so himself that either one of 'em could help us out with concerns about the road."

"So?" asked Zimmer.

"So, the wife's a local girl; come up on Latimer's turf. *She'll* know how things is done here at home. Shoulda maybe gone right to her with this, but the little brother was a surer touch on Conrad." He paused, considering that. "Might have to sweeten the pot a little, just to get 'er deep enough. Maybe a requisition?"

Sioux frowned, and Smealy braced himself for a disagreement, while bringing all the reasons why that wasn't a completely stupid idea up to the front of his brain.

"Sure, give the wife a requisition," Sioux said, thoughtfullike. "Then we got a surer touch on *her*, when she uses it. If the little brother's anything at all like his big brother, he ain't gonna like her going around him to make her own deal. Least'll happen is we'll break the Road Boss, and hafta find another way in to Conrad. *Best* that'll happen, if the wife's a smart woman, like I hear she is—she'll keep her cards right there in her pocket and won't find a reason to mention it."

Sioux was on board. That was good. Smealy grinned and nodded to her.

"That's right," he said. "You see how this could be the right way to go. I admit, I was focused on the little brother, and didn't think on this other angle, but we got the right road, now. We'll close this deal *tight*. I can feel it."

"Yeah," Zimmer said. "An', Smealy, when she does use that requisition, we lower her percentage on the exceptions, right? Win-win."

He hadn't thought of that, Smealy'd admitted to himself, nor was he sure, hearing it, if that move would be good for bidness or bad. The wife'd been a soldier, and if the talk on the street was that she was smart, like Sioux said, street talk likewise said *you* was smarter not to try her temper.

Still, they had time to work out the details. First thing was bringing the wife into the exception bidness. Smealy knocked back the last of his beer and banged the mug on the table.

"All right, people, here's what's gonna happen. Tomorrow, I'll go talk with the wife, offer her the deal and get her signed up. We're on the spot; the buy-ins are starting to get testy; they wanna see a return on their membership buy-in. Soon's we get a Road Boss tied in, we can start selling exceptions the day after—day after that, latest—and bidness'll start looking up, right?"

"Right," Kreller said, and stood. "Who wants another beer?"

They all did. Kreller grunted and went out to the bar to tell Riley.

"Don't screw it up this time," Zimmer said to Smealy. "You want I should go with you? 'Case she needs help focusing?"

Smealy considered it. Zimmer was real good at focusing people. On the other hand, *then* it would be said that Smealy'd needed help to bring the wife on board. After what'd happened with the little brother, he couldn't afford help. If he couldn't deliver now, right here at the beginning, he wasn't gonna stay chairman long—and retirement was no part of *his* plans.

"Nah," he said to Zimmer. "You're lookin' a little rugged, if you don't mind my noticin'. This'll be a piece o'ice. She's local and unnerstands how it works. That's where I got tripped up with the little brother; he's playin' with a whole different deck."

He nodded to the table in general, feeling expansive and successful.

"Next round's on me," he said.

· · · ❖ · · ·

"*Any* story?" Miri asked.

She was sitting in what Kareen called the interview studio, which'd prolly been the front parlor, back when Ms. Lanni'd lived in the house, when Miri'd been a kid on Latimer's turf. There were just a couple comfortable chairs that looked like they'd come out of Jelaza Kazone's storerooms, and a rug that likely had the same source.

There was a firebrick in the hearth, pumping out heat like it was a blizzard outside, and Kareen was wearing a shawl over her sweater.

"Indeed," Kareen said, in answer to her question. "We are particularly interested in stories that may illuminate an ethical system, but I will be pleased to hear and record any story that you would care to tell me."

Miri sighed, settled deeper into the nice, comfortable chair, and closed her eyes.

A story, was it? The truth was that stories from her past were likely to curl Kareen's hair, if not make it fall out entirely. It'd been a rough and rugged thing, her childhood; not the kind of upbringing the shadows and soft edges of which she got from Val Con's memories.

"Any story at all," Kareen said. "Whatever rises to the top of your thoughts."

"Well..." she sighed. "There was the time me, and Penn, and... Chaunsy Seleedro, must've been, swiped a pie off Gran Eli's window.

"We stole it, ran 'round the corner, and we ate that pie as fast as we could. Then we kinda sat there, sleepy and stupid with being fed, and suddenly not so sleepy, though feeling considerably more stupid. 'Cause, wouldn't you know, after it was gone, we all three of us started thinking that maybe we *shouldn't've* stole that pie, after all. So, Penn and me—Chaunsy didn't want no trouble, and we agreed to leave her out of it—Penn and me went and knocked on the front door of Gran's house, figuring we'd offer to work it off.

"Gran Eli opens the door, looks down at us, and says, 'So, where's the other one?' And Penn says she didn't want no trouble, but him and me wanted to make it right, and she said, 'Fine, then; c'mon inside.'"

She smiled, warmed by the memory. That had been a good day. Gran Eli. Gods, she hadn't thought about Gran Eli in years…

"What Balance did she demand?" Kareen asked, soft as thought itself.

"Balance." Miri smiled and shook her head. "She gave us each a basket of good stuff—fresh bread, soup, 'nother pie, little piece of cheese—to take home. Turns out, she set a pie on her window deliberate, every week or so, to find who was hungry, and then fixed 'em up with a couple meals." She sighed. "Penn didn't want to have to explain to his dad what he'd done to deserve that basket, so I got his, too. Me and my mother, we had good eating for days."

"So there were those who kept…common cause? Was Gran Eli one of many, or someone unique in her application?"

"Hmmm?" She had closed her eyes, drowsing in the warmth of the fire and of a good memory.

"Oh, there was what you'd call good folk on the street. The grans—Mike Golden's gran, she was a force, to hear him tell it. On Latimer's turf, you didn't wanna have it come to Gran Eli you'd done something she wouldn't like. That's what'd made taking the pie so…tempting, if you follow me. It was like a dare."

"Of course."

"Turned out she'd got to us, before we ever got to that pie, and we never knew it. Never knew she was teaching us something about how to go on with each other."

She opened her eyes and looked to Kareen.

"Story enough for you?"

"Indeed, it was quite illuminating. Thank you."

"No problem. Listen, I talked to a fella yesterday—Rebbus Mark, his name is, from one of the executive families. He's got documents and hand-down stories not only about how things were before the Agency left, but why they were like they were. I asked would he talk to you, and he said that nothing would make him happier. Here's how to contact him."

She leaned forward to pass Kareen the paper she'd written the man's info on.

"Thank you. I will contact him immediately."

"You do that," Miri said cordially. She stood and stretched.

"Mr. Mark wanted to know if you're writing a book," she said.

Kareen's lips bent in one of her rare smiles.

"Do you know?" she said, and the smile got just a little deeper. "I believe that I will."

· · · ✹ · · ·

Droi sat by her hearth, alone.

Vylet had gone to the tent of her lover, her lover being wiser than to come to a tent that also sheltered Droi, with her dark Sight and murderous temper. More often than not these days, Kezzi slept in the *luthia*'s tent, which spoke to her increasing responsibilities as the *luthia*'s apprentice, as well as to Silain's advancing years.

Droi had not Seen that Silain would soon be called to rise from her hearthside and go to her sisters in the World Beyond. She did not, of course, know what Silain herself might have Seen. There was also an imperative driving Kezzi's education, for Kezzi *must* be the *kompani*'s next *luthia*. Jin was a strong healer, but her memory was weak, and her Sight, short. Droi's healing skills were well-honed, her memory was retentive, and her Sight was long. Silain had, in fact, trained her fully, but in the end the darkness that ruled her Sight and her soul had combined to convince both *luthia* and 'prentice to stand away from the final testing.

Times would be terrible, indeed, if only Droi were left as *luthia*.

She thought of these things as she sat, alone, by her hearth, and she thought, also, of her purpose, and her use to the *kompani*.

The Bedel said, *In kompani, all souls are equal.*

As with many things that the Bedel said, this was both true . . . and not true.

She, for instance, had a place in the *kompani*; with her healing skills and long memory, she brought a talent for the *fleez*, and the ability to dream and understand the older dreams, some of which were strange indeed.

Despite these skills, all useful and necessary; and despite the fact that she knew, in the very core of her soul, that her brothers and sisters would never leave her alone among the *gadje*, nor deny her a place at the hearth...she was often alone *within* the *kompani*. Her brothers—strong, fierce, and handsome men, every one—her brothers were afraid of her. Her sisters—fierce beyond tigresses, strong enough to bear the foibles of their brothers, and so handsome that to see them was to fall in love...

Her sisters also feared her, though not, in her observation, so much as her brothers.

Even *gadje* knew enough to fear Droi when she walked in the City Above, and they shivered with mingled longing and dismay as she read their futures out of the cards for them.

Of all the *kompani*, only Rafin loved her, for Rafin loved danger above every other thing.

She sighed, her eyes dreaming on the glow of the hearthstone.

There had been talk, lately, of the ship. The ship that was many years late in returning for them. Alosha the headman had broken with tradition, and asked assistance from the Boss Conrad, in finding the ship of the Bedel among the trackless stars.

It thus became a matter of speculation in the *kompani*, and of discussion, for talk was to her brothers and sisters as meat and bread were to *gadje*.

So, there had been speculation—would the Boss Conrad's family, old in the ways of ships and space, find the ship of the Bedel? Would the ship come? How quickly? What would be the first act of this one, or that, upon entering the ship which was only a story to all of this *kompani*, the grandchildren and great-grandchildren of that sturdy *kompani* who had walked off of the ship onto Surebleak, to learn what there was to know.

Droi had dreamed dreams of the ship, and of ship life. All the *kompani* had dreamed those dreams, by the will of the *luthia* and the headman.

And thus Droi knew that the ship was small inside. Not as small as this place where the *kompani* camped, but the *kompani* had all of the City Above to wander, when the common camp became too small, while there were nothing but stars, and vacuum, beyond the skin of the ship.

In the small space of the ship, there was no room to spare for a woman who was dangerous. While it remained true, even inside the ship, that her brothers and sisters would never leave her alone among the others; it was a *law* of the Bedel that no thing, no person, no event could be allowed to threaten the ship.

In anticipation of the ship, then, Droi had taken to dreaming, long and wide, digging deep into the very oldest dreams, looking for what...might be...a cure for what and who she was.

She sighed, her eyes closing against the firestone's bright heart—then sat up straight, eyes wide, and staring into the dimness beyond the hearth.

The sound came again, and she knew that footstep.

"What do you want, Rys Dragonwing?"

"I have a gift," his voice answered, sweet and soft, "for our daughter."

It came to her that Rys was not afraid of her, but, then, Rys was the most dangerous person she knew. More deadly even than Rafin, and certainly more fearsome than Black Droi.

"Our daughter yet abides inside my womb," she reminded him. "Come later, with your gift."

There was a shift in the darkness beyond the hearth, and Rys took shape before her, his curls tousled, and his face serious.

"I may not be able to come later," he said. "Perhaps her mother will hold it for her, in trust."

What was this? Rys was fully a member of the *kompani*. He had stood before the fire and been bound, soul and heart, to the heart and soul of the *kompani*. Venture away, he might, but he *must* return, wherever he might go. If he *could not* return, then were his brothers and sisters called upon to honor their promise.

"Bring it, then," she said brusquely. "Sit there." She nodded at the rug beside her.

He dropped gracefully into the place she had shown him, and reached into the pocket of his vest, bringing forth a reader, and a book.

Leaning forward, he placed both on the rug by her knee.

"She will not be able to read for some little while after she has been born," Droi said.

"I know," he answered. "I would ask you to read to her, as I would have done. The book is a collection of Liaden stories. I know many of them from my own childhood. My grandmother had read them to me."

"Keep it, then, and read to her yourself."

"That had been my plan. I hope that I will be able to carry it through."

She heard what he did not say, and repeated it aloud. "But?"

"But the *luthia* urges me to a task which must be performed, for my brother under Tree, and which may mean that . . . I will not return. Indeed, I believe that I *cannot* return."

Droi drew herself up. She was cold, where a moment before she had been drowsily warm.

"Let your brother send himself; you are not his brother alone!"

"Peace, peace. We have six in one hand and six in the other. If my brother does this thing, then his lady will pluck me from the heart of the *kompani* and bring me to the house under Tree to stand in his place and see his duties done until he returns."

Droi felt her breath go short. She lifted her chin and said, haughtily, "She does not have this power. You are of the *kompani*."

"I gave her the power in return for breaking her peace and giving my brother the dream that I made."

It occurred to her, then, that *she* was afraid.

Rys sat on the rug, as neat and quiet as a cat. His face was delicate, a flower framed by the storm clouds of his curls. His nose, not so emphatic as a Bedel nose, had been broken with the rest of him, and was bent slightly to the left. His hand, that Rafin had made him, gleamed like molten gold in the hearthlight.

Droi thought of their child, and took a breath. She pushed the rising darkness away, and put her hand on the reader.

"I will keep this for our daughter, until you return, and in your absence, I will read from it, to her."

He smiled, did Rys, which was enough to break even a Bedel heart.

Droi swallowed another breath.

"What was her name, your grandmother who told you stories?"

"Maysl," he said, and swallowed as if he, too, had a difficulty breathing. "Her name was Maysl."

"Maysl." Droi tasted the name, finding it sweet. "A strong name. Our child shall be called so."

Rys took a hard breath, and bowed his head.

"My heart is full," he said.

They sat so, silent in the hearthlight, for some few minutes. Droi felt her fear fade to a fluttering in the center of her chest. Her breathing was easier, but her hands were still cold.

Rys raised his head.

"It was not well done of me, to break your solitude. I will go, and leave you in peace."

He rose, hand flashing gold, and Droi cried out in protest.
"Rys!"

He bent, and took her outflung hand in his warm one.

"I am here. What may I do for you?"

"Stay," she said, and rushed on as his lips parted. "Tonight.
Here. I don't want to sleep alone."

"All right," he said, gently, and sank down on the rug at her
side.

INTERLUDE SIX

. . . .

The Firmament

THE STAR HE HAD SWORN TO WITNESS WAS GUTTERING. IT SEEMED to him a piece of charcoal barely larger than his fist. There was a flame at the very center, deeply gold, scarcely as big as a cantra piece.

It was... in no way probable that the choice could affect Vazineth ser'Trishan's fate. He had said as much, to Anthora, and to Master Healer Mithin. He had counseled, indeed, that the best they might do, here, was to ask the Master Healer to reach forth her will, and grant the final peace.

It had been their choice to continue, for, as Master Mithin had it, "The universe may yet surprise us."

So it was that he closed his outer eyes, and stood watch over this cinder that had once been a woman's soul. It was possible to feel anger in this place, though it was not wise. He therefore clung to his own peace, and prepared himself to witness a death.

Near-space rippled as the question was put.

The small flame that yet burned in the center of desolation flared, carbon boiling away in a black cloud, and Ren Zel shouted in this place where it was far less dangerous to be joyful, as Vazineth ser'Trishan definitively, absolutely...

...chose life.

CHAPTER TWENTY-TWO

. . . .

Boss Nova's House
Blair Road

NOVA'S HOUSEHOLD MARCHED TO A MELD OF LIADEN AND SURE-
bleak custom. That had surprised Miri the first time they'd
stopped for dinner with Val Con's sister. Sorting the list of family members from most rule-bound to least, you'd get Kareen
yos'Phelium right at the top, then Nova, who was second only
because Kareen had time in grade.

Be that as it was, Nova's entire family sat down to dinner
together, family being parsed to mean: Nova; Syl Vor; Syl Vor's
Bedel sister, Kezzi; and Mike Golden, Nova's head 'hand, just like
Surebleak did it, when there was family to hand. In a proper Liaden
house, Syl Vor and Kezzi would have eaten in the nursery, or,
maybe the kitchen, and Mike would've eaten with the rest of the
servants, thereby freeing the adult kin to speak frankly together.

Not that speaking frankly was all that exciting, since proper
Liaden table manners called for pleasant subjects only to be discussed over dinner, so that one might do justice to the meal's
artistry.

It made for an . . . interesting, if not downright rowdy, table, a
fact of which Nova seemed to be entirely unaware. Of course,
Miri thought, any group that included Kezzi Bedel among their
number was going to be rowdy, by definition. It had been hoped
that close association with Syl Vor would impart a more seemly
manner, but so far as Miri had been able to observe, association

might be working in the opposite direction. Not that Syl Vor couldn't use a little loosening up. Way too serious for a kid.

Given the mixed backgrounds of those present, dinner language was Terran. They heard about Syl Vor and Kezzi's triumphs in school. Kezzi had won a prize for reciting a long piece of poetry, Syl Vor reported.

Val Con congratulated her gravely on her triumph, which earned him a considering look out of knowing black eyes.

"It wasn't hard," she said. "I memorize recipes twice as long for my grandmother, and those are *important*. If I miss an ingredient or don't remember the right measurement, I might kill someone. If I missed a couplet, the only thing that would have happened is that I'd been allowed to sit down sooner."

"Still," Val Con had said, "it is not a waste of time, to demonstrate one's skills to those who might otherwise seek to take advantage."

"I told you!" Syl Vor said, from beside her.

Kezzi tried to look disdainful, but she couldn't quite hide the pleased smile at the corner of her mouth.

"I don't have to prove myself to *gadje*," was what she said.

"Very true," Nova said gravely. "However, one does wish to keep up one's grades, and to demonstrate to one's teachers that their work is not entirely in vain."

"That's so," Syl Vor said. "Ms. Grender was very proud of you."

"She gave me a *hug*," Kezzi said, not as if the memory was particularly pleasant.

"It is how she is," Syl Vor said, patiently. "She hugs me, too."

"Does she?" Miri asked. "So that means you won a prize?"

"No, that was because he helped Chow with his geography, and then *Chow* won a prize for getting from the port to Boss Sherton's turf, with nine side trips, in the shortest time. Syl Vor got a hug, and Ms. Grender said he's a *gifted teacher*."

Kezzi bent an approving look on her brother, whose cheek had darkened a little in a blush.

"Excellent," Val Con said. "One should always be generous with one's teammates."

Syl Vor's blush got a little deeper, but he bowed his head and murmured, very properly, "Thank you, Uncle."

Dinner over, the kids were sent upstairs to do homework, and the adults, including Mike Golden, retired to the side parlor.

Now, they could talk serious, and Nova didn't waste any time. "Brother, have you had any news from the Council of Clans?"

Val Con raised an eyebrow, and lowered his wine glass.

"I can scarcely suppose that the Council will wish to compromise its *melant'i* by communicating with the delm of a clan that doesn't exist."

That was just plain and fancy provocation; he knew what she meant. Give Nova credit, though, she didn't rise to the bait. Mike Golden was, Miri thought, good for her. Whether Nova was similarly good for Mike Golden . . . Miri directed a thoughtful look at the man. He turned his head like he'd felt her glance against his cheek, and winked at her, mouth quirking.

Nova, in the meantime, was coping with Val Con.

"Certainly, the philosophical aspects of our situation are piquant," she said seriously. "We must, the two of us, sit down and discuss them thoroughly, some day soon. In the present, however, I only mean to ask if Ms. dea'Gauss has had word from the Elders dea'Gauss regarding the possible breach of the Council's guarantee of Balance."

"In fact, she has," Val Con said, abandoning the fun game of tweaking his sister in favor of a straight answer. "It would appear that the Council has very many highly critical items on its agenda that must be dealt with before it might consider taking up something so trivial as an apparent breach of contract."

Nova drew a hard breath.

"Tabled it, did they?" asked Mike Golden.

Val Con turned slightly to face him.

"Nothing so active, I am afraid, Mr. Golden. The Council has not allowed the matter to be taken up. Not even so that it may immediately be put down."

Mike Golden looked grave. "We gonna need to bring in extra 'hands?"

"That is what we wished the Council to clarify for us," Nova said. "It comes to a simple yes or no: is the Council knowingly—willfully—in breach, or was this attempt upon Quin merely one woman who had decided that her personal loss was too great to accept a Balance in the common cause?"

Mike Golden looked thoughtful.

"This breach business—would this Council of yours put it out on the street that they wasn't going to—fine?—anybody who felt like ignoring the contract? Or would they just let the flakes fall, and hope to eventually see a blizzard?"

Val Con looked at Nova.

Nova looked at Val Con.

"That's a good question," she said.

"It is, indeed. Thank you, Mr. Golden. We shall make inquiries at a...less formal level." He looked back to Nova.

"My aunt Mizel? Certainly, they would have taken care that no sort of... *announcement to the street* was made in yo'Lanna's hearing."

"But Etgora tells yo'Lanna everything," Nova murmured. "And so does Mizel. I will write; I am sadly behind in our correspondence, and this will give me an opportunity to make amends by serving a hint of scandal."

"Excellent. I will write a letter or two, also."

"Mike, you oughta sign up to be a *qe'andra* in training," Miri said, giving him a grin.

He gave the grin back, but shook his head.

"Better suited to be a 'hand. Sitting and writing and researching gets me all twitchy, and pretty soon I gotta go take a walk. Say, to the port an' back."

She laughed.

"Any more insurance salesmen coming around, by the way?" The grin faded.

"Now, there you hit a sore point. They keep coming, and the Watch can't be everywhere. Some of the streeters know that they can—and oughta—call in anybody sellin', but others..." He shook his head, and turned his big hands palms-up, looking from her to Val Con to Nova.

"They wanna be safe, you unnerstand. So, some folks are payin', and that just gives the insurance sellers leverage—Well, they say, your neighbor 'cross the street, *she's* paying up. Guess she knows what's in her own interest." He nodded to Miri. "You know how the spiel goes."

"Yeah..." She shook her head. "Easy to say that we're gonna have to educate the streeters, but we're already going to the street level with the *qe'andra*. We can't always be shouting at them to learn things..."

"What we got going in our favor," Mike Golden said, "is the streeters themselves. You take Ms. Quill, the baker. I'm not out on the street three times outta four except I meet her at this place and that, talking about how the Bosses made the collecting of insurance illegal, and the making of examples, too. Her and the printer went together an' made up window signs that say, *No Insurance Sales Allowed,* an' some little cards they give to all the streeters, with the Watch's contact number, and Boss Conrad's contact..."

"And Boss Nova's contact," Boss Nova said wryly. She shook her head. "We have had some calls, and the Watch has taken up a few, but where one is taken off the street, two appear."

"Seems like some folks liked the old days better'n the new ways," Mike Golden said.

"Nostalgia is a powerful force," Val Con murmured. "I assume that there has been some money collected. Is there any hint as to where—or to whom—it flows?"

"Well, now, *that's* worrisome," Mike Golden admitted. "If some up-an'-comer with more brains than most is using insurance sales to build up a little operating budget before they move in to retire Conrad..." He looked to Nova and gave her a small grin.

"That's the kind of stuff that keeps a 'hand up at night," he told her, apologetically.

He turned back to Val Con. "The couple salesfolk the Watch took in gave up the name and address of where they took the money, but o'course everything was gone an' empty by the time we got there."

"Of course," Val Con said.

"Been any examples made?" Miri asked.

Mike shook his head.

"The baker, she almost got made an example, but she had one of Boss Conrad's 'hands with her in the shop, so that melted before it froze. The rest've been threats; no action."

"Which may mean that—whoever is behind the project—is merely opportunistic, and has no intention of actually endangering themselves."

"Or they could be saving it up for a big show, to impress everybody," Miri said.

Mike Golden gave her an earnest look.

"Now, see? That's the *other* thing that keeps me up at night."

• • • ❊ • • •

"You wished to see me, Grandmother?" It was late, and he was weary, having worked a full day at Rafin's forge with three other of his brothers. He had returned with Udari to the hearth they shared, only to find Isart there, bearing the *luthia*'s wish that Rys go to her immediately upon his return.

"Please say to the *luthia* that I am on my way to her hearth," Rys said, and watched Isart dash away before turning to his brother.

"This may be our good-bye, and my heart is so full that I have no words."

But Udari shook his head. "Brothers do not say good-bye. Though we may not see each other for a time, we will see each other again."

They would find each other in the World Beyond, that was the meaning here. Udari was devout, and his faith comforted him. Rys . . . was not devout, but he would not break Udari's peace with his doubts.

So . . . "Great will be my joy, Brother, when we meet again."

"Hah." Udari opened his arms, and they embraced before Rys left their hearth and walked down the common to the *luthia*'s tent.

"Rys, my son," Silain smiled, and extended a hand to him, "come here to me."

Obediently, he knelt on the rug at her side. She cupped his face between her hands and looked into his eyes.

"You are troubled."

"Grandmother, I am *frightened.*"

She released him and sat back.

"Of course you're frightened; you're not a fool. But you may put your fear aside for this night. It is not time, yet, to go to your brother under Tree. There is one more task that I would have you complete for me, if you can find it in your heart."

She was a subtle woman; she had shaped him and used him, and she would soon send him to his death. For all of that, he loved her; and for all of that, he smiled.

"When have I refused you anything?"

Silain smiled, as one who is a partner in secrets.

"It's nothing you haven't done before," she said. "Only I wish you to dream."

· · · ※ · · ·

"There's a man's bit bad," Miri said, as Val Con guided the car down Blair, toward the intersection with Port Road.

"Not so bad as some," Val Con said, who was driving with really commendable restraint, even though the streets were just about empty, this time of night. "Mr. Golden does not strike me as the sort of man who allows his wits to wander, no matter how badly he might be *bit*."

"No percentage in getting your Boss killed," Miri noted. "Twice as much reason not to let your wits wander." She sighed.

"Val Con-husband," she said, switching to Low Liaden.

She felt the flicker that meant he'd been startled, but he followed her into the more intimate language.

"Miri-wife. What may I do for you?"

"Speak with me in Liaden every day, if you will. It is so often necessary to speak Terran during the day. I find I miss the Low Tongue, in particular." She paused.

"It is a sweet tongue," Val Con murmured.

"Sweet, and . . . complex. I would not wish to lose the level of . . . subtlety gained." She shook her head. "I wish none of us to become diminished by this new adventure."

He was silent for a long moment.

"None of us ought to be diminished by our changed circumstances. It is true that adventures sometimes drive one into simplicity." She felt, rather than saw his smile.

"Life is wonderfully simplified when all that is required is that one survive."

"That is the door that opened into this . . ." she hesitated, feeling over the possible descriptors in her head.

"Opportunity?" he suggested.

She laughed.

"Opportunity, then. I wonder—"

They were crossing Virg Street. One block ahead was the Port Road.

To the left, down Virg—

"Fire!" Miri cried, but Val Con was already turning the car.

She reached for the comm and punched in the code for the Watch.

"Robertson, at the intersection of Virg and Blair," she told the sleepy dispatcher. "Fire, and a crowd."

"On our way," came the reply, the dispatcher sounding not so sleepy now.

Val Con pulled the car to the curb a dozen feet in front of the fire, and jumped out, Miri half a second behind him.

"Stand back!" he called, approaching the crowd. "Something may explode!"

Somebody in the crowd laughed; somebody else turned, flipping his jacket back like he had a gun in his belt.

Somebody else yelled, her voice high with fright and fury: "They're burning my bakery! Stop them!"

"Oh, sure; they'll stop us. C'mon in, friends; bet you ain't seen a zample made in a good long while. Wouldn't wanna forget what it was like, now would you?"

Miri had the guy holding the baker in her eye. Val Con, she knew, as clear as if they'd talked it out ahead of time, would take the guy showing his heat.

She kept walking, slipping her hand into her pocket. She felt the heat on half her face—it was burning good enough she could hear crackling wood. The little three-shot slid into her palm, nice and firm, and she skirted the crowd—eight, ten of 'em, maybe, but that'd be a couple rubberneckers, too.

Problem was knowing which was the rubberneckers—so she let the gun go free, though likely the move let the locals know she might pull . . .

The guy with the 'tude had turned on his heel to watch her hands. That was all right; Val Con had him; she felt him slip up behind the guy, and smack him a good one behind the ear with the hilt of his knife.

"Help me!" shouted the baker. "Help yourselves! Do you want the old ways back? Stop them!"

That was good for a couple laughs between the observers and the insurance crew, but not much else.

Twisting in her captor's arms, the baker kicked backward with an amazing amount of energy. The guy grunted, and yanked her arms back. Miri slipped in close, smelled the stink of a firestarter on him, looked him in the eye as he struggled to hold the baker.

"Let her go," she commanded, using full merc volume. "Else, you'll be the sorriest pile of slush on the planet."

She moved closer, the merc motion offering *mayhem now* leading her hands toward his face. He twisted the baker between them, smiling like a dog.

This close, the fire scorched the air. Whoever'd set it had known what they were doing. It was hot, and it was burning fast. And if it was a bakery . . .

"Move!" she shouted. "This place is going to explode!"

As if to back her up, the fire gave a full-throated roar, flames licking out onto the sidewalk.

Three of the hangers-on lost their nerve, broke and ran up the street, toward Blair.

The guy holding the baker twitched, but that was all.

"She's right," the baker said, her voice eerily calm. "There's flour dust over everything in there. It'll explode an' we'll all get killed."

"I'll believe that when I see it," somebody said from directly behind Miri—his approach had been masked by the noise of the fire.

She ducked, felt something go close past her cheek, spun and kicked.

Her guy grunted and went down, and Val Con came out of the dancing fire shadows, kicking the guy holding the baker solidly in the shoulder. Miri rolled now, seeing people breaking away from the fight.

The baker ran; her late captor rolled and came up, gun out, turning toward Val Con, and moving to a shooting crouch.

Miri struck low from the side, half missing her mark in the flickering firelight, and that shot went wide of everyone, but the heel of the gun raked her face as he scrambled to get position on her.

Too many for him, she was up and ready to block his aim again when Val Con grabbed his gun arm and danced a bit of *menfri'at*, the twist removing the gun and breaking the gunman's wrist in one elegant, fluid move.

The man yelled and kicked. Miri took his feet from under him, and he went flat—and completely still as Val Con grimly stood over him, the captured firearm aimed precisely between his eyes.

...and in the distance came the sound of a siren.

The Watch had arrived.

INTERLUDE SEVEN

The Firmament

VAZINETH WAS WITH THE HEALERS, WHO WOULD DO SUCH REPAIRS as were necessary, and also firm her purpose. Sye Mon, her colleague, was also with her. He would not be a familiar face, when she woke, for they were not known to each other, but he would be someone who understood all of what had befallen her.

They three—Anthora, Master Mithin, and Ren Zel—they three were drunk, perhaps, with success. Anthora would have it that Vazineth had snatched the choice to herself, and that she, Anthora, had expended no effort at all. She was perfectly fit and rested.

Master Mithin pronounced herself very able to continue, and Ren Zel...

Ren Zel craved this place, where only truth existed, and peace informed the spaces between the stars. The threads sang to him; the golden light infused his bones. Every time he opened his eyes here was like a homecoming.

He gathered himself to witness, focusing upon the star that was the soul of Bon Vit Onida. The strands that bound the agent to the rest of the universe were fragile things; the soul small, as if it had drawn in on itself, becoming denser and less bright.

Near-space rippled.

Nothing happened. The fragile threads moved gently in the celestial breeze.

Ren Zel brought his regard nearer, seeking any change, any small alteration...

...and in that instant, Bon Vit's soul ignited, expanding into a pure brilliance; energy flowing through the threads, strengthening them.

Joy filled Ren Zel—and then horror, as he beheld the tiniest scrap of blackness, at the very heart of the glory that was Bon Vit. As he watched, the scrap fractured into tiny bits, like seeds, flowing with the golden energy toward the ties—the ties that bound all of the universe together.

It was instinct; his gift knew how to spend itself. Say that he extended a hand. Extended a hand and pinched off the outward flow of Bon Vit's energies into the universe. The seeds—the *poison*—swirled, trapped in golden energies, and burned away.

Ren Zel released his fingers, his will, and Bon Vit was one with the universe again.

Almost, he could weep. Perhaps he did weep, bent above the soul they had saved. Three, won back from nightmare! He had not, in his most secret heart, believed that they might win more than one.

There was a disturbance in near-space. He felt his hand grasped. He heard, from somewhere, from everywhere, a voice speak his name.

He turned and opened his eyes...

...to his lifemate, bending above him where he lay on his back, her hands cupping his face, and her eyes filled with doubt.

CHAPTER TWENTY-THREE

....

Boss Conrad's House
Blair Road

THE KITCHEN AND HOUSEHOLD STAFFS, ORGANIZED BY MR. pel'Tolian, had done well throughout what had become a long night. Tea and coffee were set out in the dining room, with tray after tray of food—cookies, fruits, crackers, cheese, sandwiches, and other quick fare upon first being roused to the emergency, with more substantial offerings following as the oven heated and the cook more clearly understood the need.

At some point, hot cereal, fruit muffins, and cheese rolls joined the continuously renewed trays, and tureens of soup.

Surely, Pat Rin thought, they had fed the street and more in the hours since the Watch had been called out to quench a fire and a riot at Quill's Bakery. There had been a meeting in this room, not very many hours ago—Pat Rin believed that the sun had risen by that point—and there would be another one soon, but for the moment, there was only himself, a pot of his favorite tea and his breakfast, his cook having adamantly refused to allow the Boss to eat "what anybody could have off the tray."

He was given to understand that the Boss's consequence demanded better, even if the Boss were...rather hungry.

Still, it was pleasant to have his usual meal, and a few moments of solitude, in the wake of roar and ruckus. He picked up his teacup, and turned his head as the sound of soft footsteps on the inner stairway caught his ear.

235

One set of footsteps, but a moment later he was joined by two—his cousins Val Con and Miri, looking well rested, which *must be* a sham, for surely they had not had even four hours' sleep. Miri had a bruise on her right cheek, which he had not noticed last night, and which now gave him a chill, indeed. That the delm had involved themselves in a street brawl—that the delm had been about on the street without Security, and had been so near to danger that someone had landed a blow to the delmae's *face*...

"Good morning, Pat Rin," she said cheerfully, in the Low Tongue.

"Good morning, Cousin," Val Con echoed. "Thank you for the use of your bed."

"I only wish you had used it longer," Pat Rin said. "You cannot be rested."

"How many hours did you sleep?" Miri asked, moving to the common buffet, and pouring a cup of coffee from the carafe.

"Two and one half hours," Pat Rin said virtuously.

"Doubtless because your lifemate threatened you at knife-point," Val Con said shrewdly.

Pat Rin did not answer, instead, nodding at the teapot.

"That is fresh," he said. "Miri, that coffee is hours old. Cook can brew—"

She laughed.

"Coffee that is stale is still superior to coffeetoot," she told him, and to Val Con, "Will you have a sandwich, or muffins?"

"Both," he said promptly, fetching a cup from the sideboard and pouring from Pat Rin's teapot.

"How does the day march, Cousin?"

"Vigorously, I fear. However, I am merely called upon to give direction, and, I suppose, to inspect. I may be required to give a presentation at the common school in assembly, but I hold out hope that I may importune Penn Kalhoon to stand in my place."

Miri arrived at the table, bearing her cup and a plate of sandwiches and fruit muffins. Val Con pulled a chair out and saw her seated.

"How is Baker Quill?" Miri asked.

"Resting still, so I believe, in yet another of my bedrooms. Later, she is to meet with the Blair Road Building Committee."

Val Con raised an eyebrow.

"I did not know that there was a building committee."

"That is because you are behind in the news," Pat Rin told him kindly. "Until this morning, there had not been a building committee. It constituted itself here in this room, over many cups of caffeinated beverages, and has among its members residents of my turf, several of the Watch, at least one Scout, and several residents of Boss Kalhoon's turf.

"The building committee's first, self-appointed task is to rebuild Quill Bakery. Boss Conrad's office has pledged an amount of money, and stands ready to assist, as needed. I believe that Andy Mack has lent a piece of equipment that will be used to clear the debris from the bakery site, once it is cool enough to manipulate."

"And the insurance salesmen?" Miri asked.

"They are in the hands of the Watch, who expect that nothing useful will be gotten from them."

Pat Rin sipped his tea, found it tepid, and warmed it from the pot.

"In the meanwhile, the Watch has taken Baker Quill's educational project upon itself. Watchpersons will be visiting every shop in every turf. They will give each shopkeeper a sign that reads, *No Insurance Sales Allowed,* and they will explain the law. They will also leave a card with the contact information for an insurance hotline"—he caught his cousin's eye and inclined his head—"another innovation that has been put into place while you slept."

"I must sleep more often," Val Con said. "Only see the prodigies I inspire."

"Also..." Pat Rin said severely. "I—by which I of course mean Boss Kalhoon—will speak to the assembled students at the common school on the subject of insurance, and the law. Teachers will be asked to teach the History of Insurance, with particular attention on the present circumstances and the law. Cards with the hotline contact will be given to each child. They will be asked to share the cards, and their history lessons, with their families and friends. They will also be asked to be vigilant. If they should see someone attempting to collect insurance, and leave their name when calling the hotline, they will be given..." He moved his hands in the sign for *uncertain course.*

"Money?" asked Val Con.

"A coupon," said Miri, in Terran. "Good for one of something at one of the shops on the street. Shopkeeper decides what to give, and how many. That way, everybody pitches in. Everybody feels good."

Pat Rin looked at Val Con.

"Indeed, a coupon redeemable at one of the local shops. Thank you, Miri."

"You are very welcome, Cousin," she said serenely. "I make no doubt you would have thought of it yourself, after you had slept longer than two-and-one-half hours."

"You give me too much credit," he told her, seriously.

The door to the kitchen swung open to admit Mr. pel'Tolian bearing another pot of tea, which he placed on the table before bowing to Val Con and Miri in full honor-to-the-delm-of-a-clan-not-one's-own mode.

"Delm Korval, Jeeves has called. He asks me to inform you that he has something of a delicate and urgent matter to discuss with you, when you return to Jelaza Kazone."

"Thank you, Mr. pel'Tolian," Val Con said gravely.

"Sir. May I fetch something fresh from the kitchen?"

"Not on my account," said Pat Rin. "Though perhaps my cousins would care for something warm?"

"Thank you, no," said Val Con. "If you have no immediate use for us, we will take ourselves home."

"Does sound like we got our marching orders, don't it?" Miri added.

"Indeed."

Mr. pel'Tolian bowed again, and withdrew. Pat Rin drank the last of the tea in his cup.

"Allow me to walk you to the door," he said, rising with his cousins. "While we go, I will deliver myself of a cousinly lecture on the foolhardiness of leaving one's security at home."

Miri blinked up at him.

"We can protect ourselves," she said, mildly.

"Your face is bruised," Pat Rin said, feeling the little shiver of horror again.

"That is because I stepped into a fist. Foolish of me, but not fatal."

"We are, indeed, able people," Val Con said. "We do, however, honor your concern, and will strive to comport ourselves in a more . . . seemly manner."

"Thank you, Cousins. Surebleak—"

"Exactly," Val Con interrupted, "Surebleak."

He smiled and looked 'round to his lifemate.

"*Cha'trez*? Will you drive?"

· · · ☀ · · ·

"Addiction," Master Healer Mithin said, her voice perfectly smooth, "is very difficult to heal. Such an addiction as this, to the location and source of your gift..." She moved her shoulders. "The only certain course would be to deny you access—"

Anthora made a small sound, and pressed her fingers to her lips, as if he and Master Mithin both had not felt her horrified denial.

"I do not," Master Mithin said, "counsel separating one of the *dramliz* from their gift. History teaches us that it is far better to allow the pairing, though the gift consumes the *dramliza*."

"But Ren Zel's gift will not consume him," Anthora said, speaking as if her wish were fact.

"Beloved." He took her hand between both of his. "It is too big, this gift. If I am all it eats, we shall be fortunate." Her eyes were wide and for once she appeared neither wooly-headed nor soft. In fact—it was a knife to his heart to see it in her eyes—she was frightened.

"I will do my best," he told her, "not to be eaten for some while yet."

"Limiting your interactions with the ether will lengthen the time before...whatever will happen, happens," said Master Mithin.

"You must not return," Anthora said hastily. "Ren Zel, swear it!"

"But how can I, when we have one more agent to free?" he asked, pressing her hand firmly, and keeping his eyes on hers. She would feel his longing to return; he could not hide it; he did not try to hide it.

"No," she said. "I forbid it."

He laughed softly. "Do you?"

Tears spilled from fearful eyes, but she had the heart to smile.

"No, of course I do not. Only..." Wet eyes lost their focus, as she used that other Sight—and then she was back with them.

"We must go forward with this one, this last, and we must have you to watch and to witness and to preserve the universe from our folly. Ren Zel..."

"When this is done, I will do what I might," he said. "I swear it to you, beloved. I will resist, for as long as I am able."

"Yes," she said, and cupped his cheek with her free hand. "Of course you will."

She took a deep breath. He released her hand and stepped back.

"Let us finish," she said, rising to her feet, "what we have begun."

· · · ✳ · · ·

Nelirikk was waiting at the side door, standing at parade rest.

"One gathers that we are about to be scolded," Val Con murmured as Miri pulled the little car into its spot, and killed the engine.

"Should've seen that comin', I guess," she muttered, and threw him a grin.

"Well, let's go take our medicine. I think I can hurry this up by telling him I intend to go down to the port today."

"Do you?"

"Well, if I don't, then the word'll get 'round that one or both of us is bad hurt, or scared, or both. Not the kind of thing does the street cred any good."

"If we show up and open the office, our credit will increase?"

"Sure it will," Miri said, and asked, "We?"

"I thought I might go with you, if you are determined to have the port. I had wanted to speak with Andy Mack, in any case."

"Okay, then; we'll both be virtuous. Let's go."

She popped the door, and walked across the apron, toward the door, and the big man before it.

Nelirikk straightened into full attention. Miri sighed, and felt Val Con take her hand.

"At ease, Beautiful," she said, pausing to look up—way up—at him.

"Captain," he said. "You and the Scout were attacked last night."

"Nope, we weren't. We went looking for trouble, is what happened, and we found it. Then, we had to do something about it."

"I should have been with you."

"Would've thrown the fear of freezing into a couple of 'em," Miri allowed thoughtfully, "but we did okay, just by our ownselves."

"Also," Val Con spoke up, "we have increased our standing as warriors on the street. The tale of last night's encounter will be told and retold among those who would oppose us."

Nelirikk's eyes gleamed. "They will think, and think again before they dare stand against you," he said.

"That's it," Miri said. "But, all that good work'll go right to waste 'less I go down and open up the office today, even late. The Scout's got business at the port, too, so he'll be coming along."

"I will accompany you," Nelirikk asserted.

"Sure you will," Miri said, her voice slightly puzzled. "We gotta clean up, so why don't you call down to the Emerald and see if somebody can go over to the Road Boss's office and put a note on the door that says that, due to an emergency, the office will open late today." She frowned, then snapped her fingers.

"The note also needs to say that both Road Bosses will be available today, in case anybody has any special questions. Right?"

Nelirikk was grinning.

"Right," he said.

"Okay—you do that, we'll meetcha at the car in"—she looked to Val Con—"an hour?"

"Yes," he agreed.

"Yes, Captain!" Nelirikk said. He saluted, received her nod, and stepped back to open the door for the pair of them.

The next obstacle was waiting at the foot of the stairs.

"Jeeves," Val Con said. "We are in some haste."

"Yes, sir. This will take moments. I would make you known to one who is also in some haste."

"Your child?" Miri asked.

"*Korval's* child. The delm so decreed."

Right, they had, hadn't they? Too late, Miri wondered if that had been the smartest idea they'd ever had together.

"Certainly, the delm will See the clan's new child," Val Con said. "Where may we find her?"

"Thank you," Jeeves said. "She awaits you in the small parlor."

The small parlor was an interior room, with no window to the outside. Consequently, it was dim even on this bright-for-Surebleak morning. A lamp had been lit, however, and washed the room with a pearly white—

Miri stopped.

The lamplight in the small parlor was pale rose, not white. And she had never seen this particular lamp before in her life.

It was, granted, a pretty lamp; a shapely pale construction about as tall as Val Con's sister, Theo, with a suggestion of shoulder, neck, and even face, all close to Theo's width, the glow emanating largely from the top of the shoulders and the back of the could-be head. There were no sharp lines in it as the glow dimmed and the form diminished in size past suggested hips, gently into a rounded column hovering a couple inches above the carpet.

The could-be face was as dark as space itself, and the glowing body provided all the illumination for the room.

"Tocohl," Jeeves said from behind her. "Please make your bow to Delm Korval."

The lamp shifted, top leaning slightly toward them, light playing oddly about the walls, and then arms and hands came soundlessly out of the housing beneath, and Tocohl bowed, gracefully, and with the proper hand expression: *honor to the delm.*

"Greetings, Korval." The voice was female, rich and slightly accented. Miri felt a small flutter from Val Con, sort of like a mental gasp, and looked at him, worriedly.

His attention was on Tocohl. Jeeves's daughter. The newest member of Clan Korval.

"Greetings, Tocohl, daughter of Jeeves," Val Con said, extending the hand with Korval's Ring on it.

Tocohl met his hand, and allowed herself to be drawn forward.

"The clan increases," Miri said, that being one of the set things that had to be said.

"Indeed," Val Con said, and paused.

"At this point in the ceremony," he said, "the delm kiss their clanswoman. Advise me, please."

The screen moved, tipping upward, and Miri caught sight of the pale grey shadow of a woman's face.

"Thank you," Val Con said, and bent to kiss the shadowy lips.

"The clan rejoices," Miri said.

The face turned in her direction and the slim body floated nearer.

"Korval?" said that voice that made Val Con twitch. "May I also have your kiss?"

The screen was warm against her lips, and momentarily soft.

"The clan rejoices," Val Con said, which kept the ritual Balanced.

"I will strive to bring honor to the clan," Tocohl said. "Sadly, I am not able to spend time with my kin, that I might learn better. My father has shared memories with me. They will comfort me and keep me until I can be with you again."

"Must you leave us so quickly?"

"Lives hang in the balance. My father believes that I may prevent more loss, and Balance that which was, inadvertently, left askew."

"I have made contact with the person of whom I spoke," Jeeves said. "He is willing to sit as Tocohl's copilot and colleague in this venture. He asks for the Pilots Guild's standard copilot contract, and his specialist fee."

"He is a specialist, also?"

"Indeed," said Jeeves. "It is through his specialty that I first became aware of him. He will act as Tocohl's backup in negotiation with *Admiral Bunter*.

"I have of course," Jeeves added, "placed his file in the delms' action queue, for you will not wish to hire an ineligible person."

"Thank you, Jeeves," Val Con said dryly. "We will review this paragon's file today."

"My hope is to depart Surebleak within the next two days," Tocohl said. "If the delm pleases."

"Have you a ship in mind?"

"I believe *Tarigan* will serve nicely, sir."

Val Con's eyebrows rose.

"Refresh my memory, Jeeves. Was *Tarigan* the ship you piloted here to Surebleak?"

"Yes, sir, she was, and a sweeter, more responsive vessel would be difficult to find. I believe that Tocohl will find her as pleasing as I did."

"No doubt she will."

Miri felt the question tickle at the edge of her awareness, almost as if he'd spoken to her. She looked to Tocohl, floating innocent-looking and graceful a few inches above the floor and wondered just what it was that they were about to loose upon an unsuspecting galaxy.

"My loyalty lies with Korval," Tocohl said at that moment.

And that would appear to answer that.

"We are," Miri said, "informed, and we welcome our new daughter. We are, however, wanted at the port, and must make haste."

"Certainly," said Jeeves, and rolled over to open the door for them.

INTERLUDE EIGHT

. . . .

The Firmament

TRUTH AND BEAUTY FILLED HIM TO THE POINT OF FORGETTING that he possessed, elsewhere, a body, a life; and that somewhere in these vasty skies there was—surely there was—a star named Ren Zel dea'Judan.

To the point, but not past it.

Suffused with glory, he yet recalled himself and his purpose.

He brought his will to bear upon the soul of Claidyne ven'Orikle, whom they had left for their last attempt, for the reason that...

She had *two* souls, orbiting each other, connected by a single thread, thin to the point of invisibility...and nothing else.

· · · ✳ · · ·

Claidyne ven'Orikle heard the stutter in the white noise that meant the main door to the detention area had been opened. She was lying down, as she often did, one arm flung over her eyes, one foot planted on the floor, the other on the cot. She did not sit up, or rearrange herself into a more seemly posture. Whoever had come in, it was doubtful they would have business with her. There was no transaction possible between her and those who held her—she thought they understood that; the little *dramliza* was not nearly so gormless as she pretended, and her sweet-faced henchman was far from stupid.

Certainly, they could not—could never—release her. She was an enemy who could be stopped by no means but death. It was...

245

interesting that Korval had chosen not to kill her—yet. But they could not hold prisoners forever; she was a knife at their throat for exactly so long as she drew breath.

In her estimation, Korval was neither squeamish, nor stupid. They would long ago have done the math, and arrived at the correct sum. Therefore, being neither stupid nor squeamish, Korval must *want something* from her, or have some other purpose for her.

Certainly, she had that which they wanted—information. They knew she was a director; she could scarcely have hidden such information from the *dramliza*'s guileless gaze, nor did she try. Rather, she had thrust the data forward, making it as hard and edgy as she could manage, hoping to inflict pain—but more, *wanting* it known, just precisely what she was.

Korval Himself had been with the Department; *he* would understand what she was. How very dangerous she was. She had hoped...well. But he had not killed her, had he? Not him, nor his executioner, nor the little *dramliza* herself.

Instead, he allowed her to languish here, a knife with its edge gathering rust. Perhaps he hoped to drive her mad. If so, he had come to her too late.

But, there, the access door had opened, and, now, did she hear...footsteps disrupting the white noise.

Footsteps approaching her cell.

Claidyne ven'Orikle swung to her feet and was facing the door when it opened.

She had no weapon to hand, save herself, so it was herself that she flung at the spare woman who stepped into the small cell, alone and unarmed.

Airborne, she kicked, foreknowing the jolt to her leg when the other woman's neck broke.

Her foot connected, not with a fragile human, but with a wall; and the jolt that went up her leg was the live burn of electricity.

She twisted, rolling in midair, landing on one knee, the injured leg stretched behind her, and stared up at the woman she had failed to kill.

Spare, and grey, and frowning, the woman stood on the far side of a faint golden shimmer in the air.

"Thank you, Lady Anthora," she said. "I believe this will do."

Claidyne took a breath, knowing that this was the moment... the moment for Korval to reveal what it wanted of her. The moment that she died, unless she had been far more successful than she had ever hoped. She gathered herself for one more—for *one last*—offensive action, if the woman would but step through that shimmering golden curtain.

But, she did not.

Merely, she leaned forward until her gaze caught Claidyne's. She knew the trick and tried to resist, but she must, *she must* meet the woman's eyes, and once she had, there was no looking away.

She was immobilized, frozen in place, and the air, it was thickening, the whole cell filling with shimmering gold, until she could scarcely breathe, and perhaps she would die now, and that would be a pity, if nothing more than she ought to have done, years ago.

"Claidyne ven'Orikle," a voiced thundered inside her head, shaking her thoughts into dust.

"Go to sleep."

· · · ❀ · · ·

The door, *the door*, dammit! Had she taken a wrong turn? Had she . . . no. She had this route memorized and sealed under six lock-levels. It was not impossible to circumvent the locks—with the Department, nothing was impossible—but she would be a mindless shell long before the data was accessed and subverted.

She was here, the walls breathing warm air, the hallway too narrow for comfort, and the door . . .

No.

She closed her eyes, reviewed one of the top-level exercises, and sighed to feel cold objectivity flow into her. Yes. With another breath, she allowed the Department's mantra to rise and weave its spell: *Dispassion. Control. Calculation. Success.* Yes, exactly.

Thus fortified, she accessed recent memories, watching the route unfurl before her mind's eye, as if upon a screen.

There had been no error. The door . . .

. . . was before her, precisely where it ought to be, control lights blinking balefully against the dimness.

She frowned. There had been no door, a heartbeat before, only more thin, stony corridor, shrouded in murk, and the walls breathing warm air against her face . . .

· · · ❀ · · ·

The door!

She had made it, if scarcely ahead of those who pursued her. The control lights blinked slowly, and in the proper pattern. It had not been tried. Of course, it had not been tried. That was for her, Claidyne ven'Orikle, Director.

Deliberately, she accessed a top-level exercise, opening herself to objectivity, feeling her control over the mission tighten.

She stepped to the door, stared boldly into the scanner, and pressed the proper sequence on the command bar.

The door . . . opened.

Director ven'Orikle stepped over the threshold; lights coming up before her while, behind, the door closed, and locked. It would open again, not for Claidyne ven'Orikle, but for the one who would emerge from the chair.

Commander of Agents.

This—was hers, and a fitting ascension it was. She had worked for this, she had killed for this—and worse. Now success lay within her hand. When she rose, she would have all the codes, all of the Department's secrets would be hers to know. And, then . . . oh, then . . .

She took a single step toward the chair.

Behind her, someone cleared their throat.

She spun, hands going for the gun that was inexplicably not on her belt—spun, to face . . .

The little *dramliza*, with her disordered black hair and her guileless silver eyes.

Korval's Witch.

Anthora yos'Galan.

"You—" She gathered herself for a strike . . . and shook her head as the urge to kill drained away, leaving only curiosity. "How did you get here?"

"I followed you." Her brows knit, as if the phrase troubled her, and she moved her shoulders. "I should say that I followed the locks, and found you in the corridor, but perhaps that becomes unnecessarily complex. It was your own suggestion that I do so, and I thank you, though of course the you *here* doesn't recall making it, *there*."

The locks . . . had been breached. That was, she recalled, distantly, a disaster.

"Peace, the locks are intact. I had no need to open them. Now"—the *dramliza* looked about her—"what place is this?"

"The quaternary transfer point."

"Transferring what to where?"

"Who to whom," Claidyne corrected. "This room—that chair—downloads…the Commander of Agents."

There was a moment of silence before the next question.

"What do you here?"

"I would take the download," she said, and *remembered* it; *remembered all* of it; feeling it flow from her to the woman standing above her, in a rushing river of information. The moment of discovery; of understanding what she had found and the nature of her new power; the instant that the plan had formed, unfolding into her consciousness with such force that it had broken her—broken her cleanly in two.

She remembered everything she had done, every step she had conceived and accomplished. The need to hide what she had become; the crafting of the locks; the missions she had carried out, refusing nothing, balking at nothing—for *this*, this secret, this *Balance* that she *would see done*, was more important than any life, any ship, any world…

The rush of memory reached a crescendo; perhaps she lost consciousness. When she came to herself again, she was sprawled on the stone floor, legs akimbo, gazing up into the *dramliza*'s face. It came to her that the other woman looked weary. It came to her that *she* was weary, as if the outflowing of memory had been blood.

"I understand," Anthora yos'Galan said, quietly.

"What do you understand?"

"Why you *will not* choose death, though you wished for Korval to kill you, and why you *cannot* embrace either of the remaining choices."

"I did not want Korval to kill me!"

Death before her Balance—that was unthinkable. Surely, she would have attempted escape…

"No," Anthora said, interrupting these rather chaotic thoughts. "*You* of course wish to pursue your Balance. It is all and everything that you desire—one sees that plainly. The question becomes: is it sufficient? Are you able to accept the download? Will you survive it, and afterward be in a state to complete your mission?"

"I don't know," she said. "Perhaps not. But I must make the attempt."

"If I released you this moment to do as you would in this place, what would that be?"

"I would take the download."

Anthora yos'Galan stared into her eyes, until she felt the burn of silver inside her head.

"I believe you," the *dramliza* said. "Claidyne ven'Orikle, go to sleep!"

· · · ❄ · · ·

Energy disturbed near-space, a rippling wave of energy that shook the doubled soul—shook them—and pierced both full through.

Ren Zel lost his focus, regained it, and regarded Claidyne ven'Orikle.

She had yet two souls, but now, they were pinned tightly together by a thin silver dagger, its hilt bearing the Tree-and-Dragon.

CHAPTER TWENTY-FOUR

. . . .

Surebleak

THERE'D BEEN AN EARLY MEETING CALLED OF ALL COMMITTEE and subcommittee heads, of which Lionel Smealy was one. Seemed like the Syndicate had decided to make an example of Baker Quill—who, in Smealy's opinion, was head and shoulders above the next most deserving candidate. Busybody, fussbudget woman, hangin' up her signs and givin' out cards. Didn't want to pay no insurance, that was it, right? Fine. The Syndicate would make it so she didn't have anything worth insuring.

Shoulda been an easy job. Shoulda drawn a crowd—which it did—to remind people what happened, when you didn't pay your insurance. According to Rance Joiler, who'd been part of the example-makin' crew, everything'd been going more or less like you'd expect, until—

"The Road Bosses showed up—him *and* her—and they..." Rance looked around him, up there in front of the room, like he was maybe sorry to be quite so visible.

"Well, they broke up the zample, is the short tellin' of it. Tough little bastids come out of nowhere, like they'd just been waiting for a shot at us! Yelled at us to stop. He broke a nose, she busted a kneecap. Whittin landed a good smack on *her* then, with his gun!—then *him*—he broke Whit's wrist like he does it every day. Took Whit's piece away from him...

"Still, I'd say we was pulling it back together, when the Watch come in on it. Some of us run—I did. Most of us that was there

251

is still being held by the Watch. We had to move offices and shift people." He shook his head.

"It's been busy, and not the best of it is that the streeters are putting the bakery back, and it's the Watch now handing out them signs and cards and 'splaining how selling insurance is against the law."

Rance leaned over and spat.

"So, what're we going to do?" somebody called from the floor. "Stop zample-making?"

"No," said Seldin Neuhaus, who was one of the Syndicate Bosses, and who'd been sitting by himself at the front of the room, facing the rest of them, instead of watching Rance.

"No," he said again. "Me and the other Bosses're thinking that the answer is to make a *lot* of examples. The Watch can't be everywhere, and when the streeters see it ain't no sense hoping for help, they'll come back into line.

"The Bosses are asking all the committees and subcommittees to tighten up operations—you got outstanding payments, *get 'em*—and to tell their committees to stand ready to pitch in with example-making.

"We'll be putting together a schedule and getting it out to folks."

Seldin stood up. "That's all, people. Thanks for coming. Now go do some bidness."

Smealy stood up and made for the door—not quick enough, though. Girt Hammond caught him.

"So, Lionel, I hear the Road Boss turned the deal down."

"*He* did. Turns out him and his wife share out the job between 'em. *She's* local; she'll come in. Just gotta talk to 'er, is all. Went down to the port day before yesterday, but they was doing the shift together. Today's her on again, so that's where I'll be this afternoon, after I finish up some other bidness."

"You sure she'll come in? Rance says she was right there fighting 'gainst the zample."

"Well, stands to reason, don't it? Married to Conrad's little brother? Gotta support the laws, don't she? No sayin' but what she'd've turned a blind eye, if she'd been by herself."

"That's so, that's so. Well." Girt smacked him on the shoulder. "You bring 'er in, then, boy. Time and past that we was getting those trucks on the road."

"It'll all be done by this evening," promised Smealy, and heaved a sigh of relief as Girt walked away.

· · · ❋ · · ·

"Looking good," Miri said, stepping up behind him, so he could see the reflection of her grin in the mirror.

He raised an eyebrow, and *his* reflection showed the haughty lordling, his face smoothly formal, his eyes cool, and his mouth firm. There was lace at his throat, and lace at his wrists, covering his hands to the knuckle. His coat was green, and there were silver dragons worked around the cuffs. Formal black trousers and shiny black boots completed his toilette.

"I was once told that I looked too Liaden in such dress."

"Guess I got used to Liadens," Miri said. *She* was dressed for a day as Road Boss on the port—dark slacks and a dark high-neck sweater, with a heavier sweater, bright blue, over. Her hair was in a single braid, a gleam of copper snaking over her shoulder.

"I do wonder how come you got invited to a party, but I didn't."

He smiled, at least as much for Miri's *party clothes* as for the irony.

"The High Judge of the Juntavas is calling upon Boss Conrad this morning."

"Right. And he wanted to talk to the *delm-genetic*."

"And that stipulation is exactly why I am wearing party clothes instead of something more along the lines of your own costume, or even Liaden day clothes—My uncle taught me that one ought always to dress above one's station when going into a hostile negotiation."

Miri's grin briefly widened.

"I'm sorry I missed him—your uncle."

"He was sometimes a burden to his children, but it must be said that he was sorely tried. You would perhaps have found him a little stiff, at first, and not apt to stint himself when an opinion was called for." He paused, breathing carefully against a sudden, and wholly unexpected, stab of loss.

Miri tipped her head, catching, perhaps—no, *certainly*—the edge of his distress.

"Like Daav, then."

"Mother—my foster-mother—would have it that Father was even less apt to stint himself. She once said that she believed he used a whetstone on his tongue."

She laughed.

"Seemed to me like he kept the habit." She sobered. "Shouldn't we be getting him and Aelliana back soon? If nothing else, Uncle's gotta be getting tired of buying whetstones."

"I think the Uncle is a patient man, when it suits his purpose. Nor would it surprise me to learn that he has to hand a sufficiently large supply of whetstones. I am inclined to think that he is finding the present currents as difficult to navigate as we, though he is not a primary target. He did speak of strikes against his enterprises, in his last correspondence."

"So you're willing to give him more time?"

"Yes. Father was badly wounded, and may yet be so weak that a careful man—and there are few men more careful than the Uncle—would not wish to send him off to fend for himself. Also, if the Uncle is involved in straightening out his own affairs, he may not be able to turn aside at this juncture. And, you know, Father may be of some use to him."

"For values of use," Miri muttered, "including mayhem."

"Almost certainly mayhem," Val Con assured her, as they moved into the main room of their apartment. "My uncle made a point of assuring me that my father's skills were in no way inadequate."

He opened the door, and they stepped out into the hall.

"What does the Road Boss have on her schedule today?"

"Not one thing. I figure I'll be reading reports and drinking coffee all day. When that gets boring, maybe I'll play cards with Nelirikk."

"Teach him pikit," Val Con suggested.

"Prolly better'n letting him skin me at poker."

They descended the stairs, and Miri turned left, toward the side door where Nelirikk would be waiting for her with the car.

"Miri," Val Con said, his voice sharp.

She turned, thinking it was a kiss he wanted; thinking that his voice had been a little too urgent for that, alone.

"What?"

"Be careful today," he said, still sharp-voiced. "I—" He took a breath, and shook his head. "Something—I think that something may happen."

Well, that was nice and vague, wasn't it? On the other hand, it wasn't a good idea to ignore Val Con's hunches, vague or otherwise.

She gave him a smile.

"I'll do my level best to make sure nothing at all happens. Deal?"

His smile was wry.

"It isn't much, is it? Take care, *cha'trez*." He stepped forward, and bent, his kiss everything that wasn't vague.

"I'm gonna be taking you up on that, later," she said, when she could talk again.

"That's a deal," he answered, and turned up the hall, toward the office.

Miri watched him for a minute, sighed, and headed for the side door.

· · · ✳ · · ·

"Need to tell you, Haz, this is my last shift with Security."

They were standing at Nelsin's counter sipping their mid-shift coffees. Hazenthull looked down, but Tolly had his face turned aside.

"Will you allow this person who hunts you—this man without honor—to take the field unchallenged?"

"He can do what he wants, 's'long as he does it far away from me. See, my colleague came through with a job offer, and I'm going off-world. The contract and prepay came through this morning, all right and tight. So, after this shift is done with, I'm gonna go see Commander Liz, turn in my service gun, sign the separation papers and—go. Ship lifts this evening, and I aim to be on it."

Hazenthull raised her cup and drank coffee she no longer wanted.

"I will miss you," she said, when she had put the cup down.

"If it comes to that, I'll miss you, too, Haz. You're a good partner; one of the best partners I've had. Always know you got my back."

A silence fell between them, which was not unusual, but this one felt...strained, as if the troop had been divided, already.

"This job—you will be a pilot?"

"Some piloting; some consulting. It sounds like a rare knot, if you want the truth. Something I can really get my teeth into. So, I'm excited. And it's the work I was trained to do—my specialty, see? Gonna be good to get back to it."

"Yes," she said, and wondered if she could ask him, now, what his specialty was.

"So," he thumped his cup on the counter, and called a 'Hey, thanks!' to Nelsin, who was at the back grill.

"Let's swing over to Mack's then up by the portmaster's office. Sound good to you?"

Hazenthull checked her sidearm, and nodded.

"Sounds good to me," she said.

· · · ✳ · · ·

Pat Rin rose from behind his desk, eyebrows lifting.

"Do you intend to seduce the High Judge?" he asked.

"Merely to dazzle him with my magnificence. Do you think me too bold?"

"Not in the least, though, after this meeting is done, I beg you will come with me to Audrey. She cannot miss this."

"I will, in fact," Val Con said, flipping the lace back from his hand with a practiced snap of the wrist, "set a fashion."

"You may well do so. One would have supposed you satisfied with the skimmer."

"That has been years ago. One wishes, from time to time, to test whether one's powers have faded."

Pat Rin laughed.

"Well, I shall look a dull dog, indeed. I cannot recall the last time I saw so much lace before Prime." He nodded at the chair beside his desk. "Come sit down, do. Will you have tea? Coffee? Wine?"

"Am I so far in advance of the judge? I mean no discourtesy, but my feeling is that we may soon find ourselves in a three-pot meeting."

"I hope for two pots, myself," Pat Rin said, sighing. "But, I concur. The judge is only moments behind you, if so much, and the kitchen has already taken a notion to produce refreshments calculated to amaze a palate accustomed to the thin pap available, outworld."

"They guard your *melant'i* well," Val Con murmured.

"I believe they have a certain pride in the household," Pat Rin countered—and turned his head toward the door as it opened to admit a wiry woman with strong-looking yellow hair and a broad, pleasant face.

"Sorry to disturb you, sir. Cook asks if you or your brother would be wanting a cup of tea."

"We shall wait for our third, thank you, Gwince," Pat Rin said.

"I'll pass the message," she said, and gave Val Con a sociable nod. "Mornin', Mr. Falcon."

"Good morning, Gwince. What do you think of my coat?"

"Real fine looking," she said without the flicker of an eyelash. "I'll just pass that message back to Cook."

She withdrew, the door closing behind her.

Pat Rin sighed.

"There's to be a shooting competition, have you heard?" he asked. He plucked a paper from the stack on his desk, and passed it to Val Con, who ran an eye down the page.

"A Boss round? Is that wise?"

Pat Rin turned his hands palms-up.

"Mr. Golden and Ms. Jazdak seem to think it can do no harm, and might, indeed, serve as fair warning. Mr. McFarland is taking counsel from the other head 'hands. I agree with Mr. Golden's central point, which is that it ought to be made plain that the Bosses are not, shall we say, wholly dependent upon the skill of their oathsworn. On the other hand, one dislikes showing one's cards."

"I agree. Perhaps, rather than a competition, the Bosses might provide a variety of demonstrations?"

"To avoid comparisons being made? That might answer. I will put it to Mr. McFarland. In any case—"

The door opened to Gwince again.

"'Scuse me, Boss. High Judge Falish Meron is here to see you."

Pat Rin looked at Val Con. Val Con raised an eyebrow.

"Indeed. Please show the High Judge in, Gwince."

· · · ❖ · · ·

"I've done what?"

Ren Zel sank into the chair next to the Master Healer's desk, swallowing against a rising feeling of illness.

"How . . . long?"

Master Healer Pel Tyr moved his hands in the pilot's sign for *uncertain*.

"Years," he said. "How many years? More than twelve. One of my colleagues believes that it may be as many as thirty."

Thirty years. Gods, gods, he had stripped half a man's lifetime away with a single small pinch of his will. Who was he to have done such a thing? And to a man who had so desperately chosen for life?

"I—" he shook his head, horror outflowing. He tried to calm himself, out of respect for the Healer's sensibilities. He could at least be courteous.

Even as he struggled to master his emotions, he felt a subtle warming of his blood, and calmness descend upon his disordered thoughts.

"I understand," said the Master Healer, who was doubtless the origin of these gifts. "I understand that you were set to witness what change might occur, and that a part of your duty was to... cut the threads, should one who had chosen to embrace... evil take strength from their decision."

"Yes..." Ren Zel said, his voice unsteady. "But Bon Vit..."

"Had chosen life, yes. However, you tell us that you acted out of necessity. That even though he had chosen, yet his enemy had sown the seeds of some terrible vengeance in his soul. When he engaged again with life, those seeds were in danger of being drawn out of his soul into the wider universe."

"All true. But they were so few; the universe is vast. Had I known, I would have let them go. Surely, they could not have survived..."

"Or," the Master Healer interrupted, "they might have seeded themselves among all the threads and done unimaginable harm. Do you know that they would not?"

He thought; he opened himself to his gift—but there was no answer. Could the universe itself not know the answer?

"No," he said.

"Your grief does you credit, for it is no small thing, to halve a man's life," the Master Healer said. "But in Balance, you may have preserved *all* life. Why do you have this gift, if not to do precisely as you did?"

"I don't know," Ren Zel said, and gratefully partook of the calmness the Healer offered. He rose.

"If he is able, I would... speak with Bon Vit."

The Master Healer rose.

"I will take you to him," he said.

INTERLUDE NINE

. . . .

Vivulonj Prosperu
In Transit

THE LIGHTS TOLD THE TALE—A BRIGHT BAR OF LIVING BLUE—BUT
Uncle had long ago learned not to depend on a single source of
information.

Accordingly, he opened the annotated files, and perused them,
before crossing the cubicle to the independent monitor and access-
ing its information.

Both sources confirmed the testimony of the blue bars on the
status board: Daav yos'Phelium's rebirth was complete; the biological statistics, gene construction, and other vital parameters
overlapped perfectly. The person who lay in the birthing unit
was, to a percentage of point nine-nine-nine-nine-nine, Daav
yos'Phelium Clan Korval.

Uncle nodded to himself. He had not expected to find any
deviation, not with the abundance of material that had been
available to the devices, but it was well to be certain.

Especially in such a case.

He closed the monitor, and turned again to the birthing unit.
On this front, at least, all was proceeding according to plan. It was
well that the man—a practical man, once a Scout and a delm—
was ready for birth first. By the time his lifemate was ready, in
her turn, for awakening, he would be in possession of the facts
of their new existence, and would have had time to process any
misgivings he might entertain, and so be better able to assist

her in adjusting to her peculiar biological condition. He would be further along in the acclimatization process and be able to assist her there, as well, thereby freeing Uncle and Dulsey from the necessity of tutoring a second newborn in the facts of life.

Uncle touched a key on the unit's status board; the dome of the pod, which had been opaque, rippled and became transparent. Visible through that window was a lean young man lying on a pale mat, his tender flesh uniformly golden, showing neither scar nor mar. His nose and his face alike were long, the mouth perhaps a bit thin, lips presently pressed into a firm line. The eyebrows were strong, dark like the thick lashes that lay lightly along his cheek. Short, dark hair covered his head like a tight-fitting velvet cap; his ears were shapely.

He breathed deep and slow, as would a man in a coma.

The Uncle reached to the board and made an adjustment. Soon, cooler air would flow into the capsule, carrying a mild stimulant, to raise the man from near coma to deep sleep, and from deep sleep, eventually, to wakefulness.

The process would take a few minutes; there was no need or necessity to hurry. While the automatics worked, Uncle opened a wall locker and withdrew a soft pair of ship pants, a sweater, and a transparent bag.

He placed the clothing on the chair next to the capsule, opened the bag and withdrew a seed pod. It lay round and green and somehow cheerful-looking in the palm of his hand. Perhaps it anticipated its imminent consumption and the completion of its purpose, whatever it might be.

A chime sounded, softly, and Uncle approached the capsule. The man within had shifted somewhat on the mat; the instruments reflected the movement of his eyes beneath closed lids.

Uncle made another adjustment to the board, and counted, silently, to twelve.

There came a soft hiss from the pod, and the canopy lifted, sliding away into the side of the unit.

The man on the mat gasped, and opened his eyes. For a moment, he lay as he had been, feeling, as the Uncle knew from his own numerous rebirths, at peace, not so much an empty receptacle, as open to every potential.

It would be a moment or two, before identity fully returned. There would be, perhaps, an extended interval, if the newborn—as one who had been Scout-trained in a past life might do—inventoried himself for weakness or wounds, sought among his memories for a clue as to his whereabouts, and perhaps attempted to plan—

The man in the capsule convulsed, his breath gone to ragged gasps. From the status board came a shrill warning; Uncle looked up as the bright blue bars snapped to orange. The systems gauges were falling, and the man on the mat was curled on his side, shuddering, breathing in huge, tearing sobs.

Uncle grabbed one shoulder, careless of tender new skin, and pulled the man onto his back. There was no resistance; his muscles were like a child's. His eyes were screwed shut and he gasped as if he were drowning.

"Look at me!" Uncle snapped. "Daav yos'Phelium Clan Korval!"

Black eyes, already dull, opened, and sought his face.

"What ails you?" Uncle demanded, for the gauges only told him that this man, who had been perfectly healthy in his new body only moments ago, now was declining toward death.

"...gone..." the other said, the word nearly swallowed in his gasping.

Uncle took a hard breath, and flung out his hand, showing the seed pod.

"Here, Pilot; take this."

The black eyes closed. The status board shrilled another warning, and the orange bars faded.

"Daav, eat the pod." Uncle pushed it under that long nose, hoping that the scent would...

The man turned his head away.

"...not ripe..." he choked.

For a moment, Uncle stood frozen, then his long habit of decisiveness reestablished itself.

He pocketed the pod even as he turned toward the board, hands moving with quick deliberation among the controls.

Warm air laced with pheromones and specialized drugs began to flow into the capsule even before the canopy locked into place. Support systems were engaged, and Daav yos'Phelium was plunged into a coma, his new body's functions taken over by the unit. The status lights brightened from orange to green; the gauges rose—seventy percent, eighty percent...eighty-five percent.

...and there they stabilized.

CHAPTER TWENTY-FIVE

. . . .

Boss Conrad's House
Blair Road

IF FALISH MERON, THE HIGH JUDGE OF THE JUNTAVAS, FOUND Val Con's mode of dress extraordinary in any way, he did not allow the thought to reach his face.

Pat Rin had not expected anything less from *this* visitor, but, then, Natesa had given him tales—sagas!—regarding the High Judge, which was an advantage that Val Con had not had. And, after all, there was no harm in finding if the sagas were true.

Thus far, they showed well against reality. High Judge Meron was short for a Terran, his face beige and freckled; rust-red hair twisted into a knot at the back of his head. He had a decisive, and to Liaden sensibilities, overenergetic manner, but one could not doubt his intelligence, nor his determination.

After tea was poured and tasted, he thanked them for allowing him to intrude upon their day, and stated that, as they were all busy people, he would make shift to move himself along quickly.

He then stated that he came to them as the proxy of Sambra Reallan, Chairman of the Juntavas, with the express purpose of reexamining the ancient agreement between Korval and the Juntavas.

Pat Rin sipped tea. Thus was the stipulation for the delm-genetic explained.

Very well, then.

He put his cup down and smiled gently at the High Judge.

263

"You and I might usefully speak, I think, on the matter of certain freelancers on our streets, who have come to do business, and, in the process . . . overrepresent their attachment to, or place in, your organization, and I hope that we will have the opportunity to do so.

"However, the chairman's business is most properly placed before my cousin, for it is Korval House policy that you seek to reexamine. I will, therefore, withdraw—"

The Judge raised a hand on which a large seal ring gleamed sleekly gold.

"The freelancers—that's the other reason I'm here. I'll be talking to certain people, sir, and I expect there will be results. If there aren't—you have the means to contact me, in-house, and I'll ask you not to hesitate, if there's something that requires my attention."

Natesa was the "means" mentioned, herself a Juntavas judge.

Pat Rin inclined his head.

"Thank you, sir, on both counts."

"On this other matter, however . . ." Val Con shifted slightly, the motion drawing the Judge's eye. "It has long been Korval policy that we hold ourselves apart from the Juntavas, as an organization. It seems a policy that has served both well over many, many years, sir. I wonder that you would seek to alter it now. It would seem to me that you, as we, would wish to preserve a bedrock at a time when so many other things—I might say, when *all things*—are changing."

"Exactly!" The High Judge leaned subtly toward Val Con, a sophisticated bit of body language, demonstrating that the principal had changed, but Pat Rin was still part of the discussion.

"Everything's changing—you're right. The chairman believes that change is opportunity, and that there's no time better to make significant policy changes. With everything else in flux, now's the time to reexamine the reasons why that agreement was made, way back when, and ask ourselves if those reasons are still valid. Or, if recent events have so altered the fundamentals of how we do business that now, *now* what will serve our mutual interests best won't be avoidance, but alliance."

"Alliance," Val Con murmured.

The High Judge gave him an opaque look.

"We're prepared to go a step further," he said. "Now, this isn't just me; like I said right out at first, Chairman Reallan's on board with this, and everything I'm bringing to you has her seal on it. I got the corners nailed down tight on everything I offer; all we got to do here is feel out what's going to work best for all. Right?"

"I understand," Val Con murmured.

"Good. Now about that step further. The Juntavas is prepared to bring you in—that's to say, to bring Clan Korval right into the organization. Not alliance; you'd be us and we'd be you. *Family*, is what we'd say."

"Indeed, we would describe such a situation as *family*, also," Val Con answered. "But, sir, you cannot have considered the ramifications of *bringing us in*. Surely, you will not want Korval re-forming your organization from within, in order to suit ourselves."

"Well, but if we're both *us*, and there's no *them . . .*"

Val Con was shaking his head. The Judge paused, and spread his hands, in what might have been intended as *go on*.

"Sir, I give you my cousin—" he moved his hand in a graceful wave that made Pat Rin feel rather exposed. "He conceived a need for a planetary base of operations and in a very short time indeed, had subverted an entire planet and its population to his purpose. That was *one Korval adult*, acting in accordance with his necessities."

"Had some Juntavas help, there," the Judge pointed out.

"Indeed. Though it was given, as I understand the case, for personal reasons."

"Some of this, some of that. People are complex." The Judge looked to Pat Rin, eyes narrowed. "I set Natesa on you as protection, sir."

"Yes, she had said as much," Pat Rin acknowledged.

"She tell you why?"

"Because a galaxy without Korval was a galaxy in which the Juntavas would find it significantly more difficult to do business."

"That's it. All the rest of Korval had fallen off the map, so I figured we'd better take real good care of the one we could see." He nodded and turned back to Val Con. "So, we'll step back to alliance. I'm not going to lie; I think—and the chairman thinks—that an alliance with Korval will be risky: risky for us, risky for you. But, I think you'll find that the Juntavas is significantly less risky as an ally, than, say, the Uncle."

Val Con adopted quite a believable expression of perplexity.

"I beg your pardon?"

The Judge smiled, and leaned back in his chair, shaking his head and holding up his hands, palms out.

"Now, see, this is what we're good at. We been running the analytics. It's taken us this long because, like we all keep saying, things are changing everywhere, for everybody. That aside, we finally do know who Theo Waitley is—and that she was a courier for the Uncle before she picked up that really...interesting old-line ship. Looks like something the Uncle might have on hand—or Korval would. And she pulls the cleanest escape out of the tightest box any of us ever saw, without even singeing the ship in the next lane over..." He paused, and seemed to gather himself around some tangential point.

"I'm also authorized to purchase that trick Jump engine—specs or working model. You can name your price."

Val Con laughed.

"As much as it pains me to throw away a handsome profit, I must tell you that there is no trick Jump engine involved! I have been assured by an interspatial mathematician that the ability to Jump in crowded situations are matters of tuning and data-loading. There is a custom navigational system aboard *Bechimo*, which calculates more quickly than standard navcomps."

The Judge nodded, looking wise. "Interspatial mathematician, is it? That'll be the Caylon. We finally got info out of Nev'Lorn, too, speaking of tricks that aren't easy to pull off. Analytics confirms it was Aelliana Caylon's ship, *Ride the Luck*, that broke the offense there. And I'll just mention that it was packing some significant firepower."

"Indeed it was. When my mother created her courier business, with my father as her copilot, he insisted that the ship's protections be upgraded. I believe he made it a condition of flying with her."

The Judge nodded again. "Brings up another point. Word's around that Korval ships are seeing some trouble at certain ports—even ports where they're known. Now, here's where an alliance with the Juntavas is going to benefit your interests. We can arrange for trustworthy escorts, so there will never again be a move like was made against *Bechimo*. Korval ships *will* get to their proper markets. We'd also advise increasing the firepower on each ship, as they come up for service—your own yards can handle that..."

"Sir, we really cannot mount military weapons pods on trade-ships. You must see that such a move would give credence to those who would have us be planet-killers and pirates."

"You mounted weapons on *Dutiful Passage*," the Judge said.

"We did, it was necessary, and I have regretted both the neces-sity and the action every day since it was done."

Val Con sighed, picked up his cup, sipped, and returned the cup to the table before he again confronted the Judge, a wry expression upon his face.

"The truth of the matter, sir, is that, unlike the Juntavas, Korval is finding itself *too much* at change. We must hold firm somewhere, or we will be entirely cut adrift. The longtime agree-ment we have enjoyed with the Juntavas is an anchor of our existence. Allow it to comfort us, if only for a short time longer. The House must settle, and find its new place in the order of the galaxy. Please—assure Chairman Reallan that Korval has taken no offense at her proposal. Indeed, we are warmed by her care."

"A galaxy without Korval is a galaxy where the Juntavas would find it harder to do business," the Judge said. "That's still true. The chairman's right to concern herself. Do you mind if I consider this the beginning of a conversation, sir? Might I—or another of the chairman's proxies—contact you in a Standard, with the intention of sitting down again and reassessing our positions?"

Pat Rin expected a demur, for what use could be had from a second such conversation? But Val Con inclined his head in agreement.

"Certainly," he said. "A Standard may, indeed, show some clar-ity with regard to our directions and necessities."

"And in the meantime," the Judge said, jovially, "it's not like you don't have protection. There's enough mercs on this planet to start a war. Or end one."

Val Con did not smile. Neither did Pat Rin.

The Judge's smile faded somewhat.

"Right," he said. "Well. Chairman Reallan did want me to extend the offer of a beam code, to be used at your discretion. There are no strings attached to this; it's a gift. May I give it?"

Again, Pat Rin expected a graceful decline.

Again, his cousin—his delm—surprised him.

"I would welcome the gift of such a beam code," he said.

The High Judge nodded, and produced a small red envelope

from his outer pocket. Val Con shook the lace back from his hand, and received it with a modest, seated bow.

"There's one more thing that I really ought to tell you," the Judge said, settling back into his chair, "then I'll move on with the rest of my business on-world—including those freelancers you mentioned, Boss Conrad.

"New Juntavas policy, straight from Chairman Reallan: whenever the Juntavas meets with operatives of the Department of the Interior, we're taking them out. They're no good for *any*body's business, in our opinion, and the galaxy's better without them."

Val Con nodded.

"Thank you, sir. You have Korval's support of this policy."

The moment was upon them.

Pat Rin rose, followed quickly by Val Con and the Judge.

"Thank you, sir, for coming today," Pat Rin said, holding out his hand, and pressing the footplate under the table.

"My pleasure. Thank you for seeing me, and for your frankness."

They shook, and the Judge turned toward Val Con, taking his hand in turn.

"Thank you, sir. I'm already looking forward to our next talk."

"And I," Val Con said.

The door opened to reveal Gwince, serious and efficient.

"Gwince, please see the High Judge out, with his bodyguard."

"Yes sir, Boss." Gwince stepped aside. "Just follow me, Mr. Meron."

· · · ✱ · · ·

Bon Vit Onida was sitting in a chair by the window, his face turned into the sun. He wore the high-necked sweater that had become the off-worlder's first line of defense against Surebleak's climate. His hair was fair, and long enough to brush the red shawl he wore 'round his shoulders.

He turned at the sound of the door closing, but did not rise.

"Master Healer," he said, courteously.

"Master Onida. I have brought you Ren Zel dea'Judan."

The pale gaze swept Ren Zel's face, and Bon Vit lurched to his feet, as would one whose knees perhaps pained him.

"You are the one who gave me life!" he said, his voice warm. He swept a bow, as one acknowledging an unpayable debt, and that Ren Zel could not allow.

"Indeed, not!" he cried. He stepped forward and caught the other man's hands, urging him out of the bow. "Do not, I beg. I am the one who has killed you."

Bon Vit straightened, holding Ren Zel's hand in a hard grip, while ice blue eyes searched his face.

"Tell me," he said.

And so he told it, as well as he might when mere words could not adequately express what he had seen, or with any exactness, his actions.

And when he was done, Bon Vit Onida released his hands and bowed as one acknowledging an unpayable debt.

"*Dramliza*, I honor you," he said straightening slowly. "Yours is a bright and terrible gift. I do not think that I could bear the weight of such a gift. The Department... is wily and subtle. It has subverted many by treachery and torture. That you were able to act quickly to prevent it from sending its poisons afar..."

He smiled.

"I had been bound away from myself, my life lost. You, and your lifemate, and Master Healer Mithin—you have given me my life back. If it is shorter than it might otherwise have been, how can I find you at fault?"

"You are too kind."

"Ah, no, there you are wrong," Bon Vit said, and his pale eyes were suddenly as chill as Surebleak's winter sky.

"I have been sitting here thinking what I would do with my life, now that it is mine again, and I, like you, believe that the Department must not prevail. What one alone might do..."

"Four," Ren Zel said.

Bon Vit blinked.

"Your pardon?"

"We have brought four, including yourself, out of the dream, and back into life."

"Have you, indeed?" He laughed, and caught Ren Zel's arm.

"*Dramliza*, you are a marvel! When may I meet my comrades? I would know if we are of the same mind."

"You are still in need of rest and healing," the Master Healer said, from his place by the door. "Another of your comrades also requires additional interventions. A local week, I believe, will see all of you recovered... enough."

"Ah, ah—so long! But I bow to you, also, Master Healer. I

would—very much!—rather know myself to be whole and complete, than to endanger any but those who deserve my Balance."

"Just so," said the Master Healer, and bowed gently to Ren Zel.

"If Pilot dea'Judan would leave us, we may have a session now, and speed your day forward."

"Let it happen! Pilot dea'Judan—you have my love, sir; and your lady and Master Mithin. Please, convey my gratitude to them."

"I will, gladly," Ren Zel said, and bowed. "I leave you now. May you heal quickly and completely."

He closed the door behind him, and walked to the end of the hallway, where there was a small window, and a chair set into the corner.

There he sat, and turned his face from the world, and wept until his tears ran dry.

CHAPTER TWENTY-SIX

. . . .

Office of the Road Boss
Surebleak Port

HE DIDN'T NECESSARILY WANT IT A MATTER OF PUBLIC OBSERVA-
tion, that he'd gone and paid a visit to the Road Boss in her
portside office, so Smealy perched himself at Jakob's Juice Bar,
where he had a good sight of the door. He sipped a tall glass
of gwiffa juice, and watched streeters go in and out, 'til he'd
had his fill of gwiffa juice and the guy behind the counter had
started staring at him.

He paid his tab, plus some, threw down a line about being
stood up, and sauntered out onto the port.

The Road Boss kept a short day—six hours open to all streeters—
and it was getting close to quittin' time. Smealy'd have to make
his move soon, and never mind who saw him. And, now that he
thought some more on the subject, it could do his cred some good
to be seen goin' into the office, all bold and easylike. Man had
a right to call on the Road Boss concerning road bidness, din't
he? Wasn't that the whole reason for this office, here at the port?

He turned his saunter around right at the door to the Emerald,
which maybe wasn't expected, because Zimmer was usually better
than getting seen when he was following somebody.

So, the rest of the committee had decided to keep an eye on
him. He'd known they'd lost confidence, but it seemed he'd mis-
calculated as to how much. Sending Zimmer to watch him—that
was bad.

The Road Boss's office was just ahead. Smealy took a deep breath, got his shoulders level, checked his carry, right there in his outside right-hand pocket, and swung on out like a man without one worry on his mind.

That girl'd better be willing to do bidness.

· · · ❄ · · ·

Miri glanced up as the clock gave out with the half-hour warning. So it was true what they said about time flying when you were having fun.

"Captain," Nelirikk said from the reception desk.

"Heard it," she told him. "Had a lot of company today. Wonder what stirred up the wind?"

"Captain, it may be that the streeters have come to know that you are a sage commander, and are coming to depend on you."

Miri blinked.

"Why, Beautiful, I think you might be developing a silver tongue."

"Captain, I only offer the most likely possibility," Nelirikk said. He might've said more—Miri got the impression he was warming to his topic—but the doorbell rang, cutting him off.

"Good afternoon," he said, and Miri looked to the screen.

"Afternoon," the guy answered, with a nod. He was something of a dandy, by Surebleak standards: clean khakis with a crease in them sharp enough to cut bread, and a bright yellow sweater without a smidge of dirt on it. His hair was middling brown, brushed back from a broad, handsome face, and curling down over the sweater's collar.

"I'd like a word with the Boss."

"May I know your name?" Nelirikk said, going by the book.

"Sure thing. Lionel Smealy, representing the Citizens' Heavy Loads Committee."

Miri frowned.

Apparently Smealy didn't know when it was in his best interest to stay thrown out. *Her* mistake had been assuming he'd at least gotten the standard issue of basic common sense, so she hadn't given Nelirikk his name as somebody to deny—and here he was, rising up to his full height, a process that Smealy followed with interest, but no visible alarm.

"Follow me, please."

Miri stood up from behind her desk.

Easy, Robertson, she told herself. *Let the man say what he come to say. Might be he'll surprise you again and produce an apology.*

The door opened, Nelirikk stood to one side, and made the announcement.

"Lionel Smealy, representing the Citizens' Heavy Loads Committee."

He breezed in, big, showy grin on his face, and one hand out to shake. It might've been the grin—too wide, and just a touch self-satisfied—but she didn't put out her hand to meet his. Instead, she gave him a proper Liaden nod, like might be exchanged between business associates who weren't on particularly cordial terms.

"Mr. Smealy, I'm Miri Robertson. I hope you won't take offense if I ask you to make it march. The office'll be closing up for the day in a couple minutes."

"Sleet, what I got to say won't take but one minute," he said affably, leaning his hands on the back of the chair. "The Citizens' Heavy Loads Committee wants to come to a 'rangement with you, as Road Boss, to give exceptions to heavy loads. We got a couple dozen small truckers signed up and ready to roll just as soon as we nail down the Road Boss's percentage. I was thinking thirty percent'd look real good in your pocket. You might have another number in mind, though, and if you do just put it out here on the desk where we can both take a look at it."

So... not an apology, after all.

"Smealy, does stupid run in your family?"

He blinked, the grin fading out.

"Hey, now, what kinda way is that to talk about a honest bidness 'rangement?"

"Didn't my partner already tell you we ain't selling exceptions?"

"He din't seem to take much of a shine to the notion, not being local and unnerstanding the way we do things here. You, though—"

"Me, though," Miri snapped, furious as much for the stupidity as the effrontery. "*Me*, though, I'm local, so it's reasonable to expect I'd take a deal my partner already told you was no deal, and what—keep it quiet from him? That's not how it works, Smealy; if one of us says no, you just take it that both of us said no. Now!"

She brought both palms down hard on the tabletop and was

gratified to see how high he jumped at the sound. Behind him, Nelirikk stepped into the room; she flicked her fingers—*hold it*.

"Now," she said, quieter, "you get the *sleet* outta here, Smealy. We ain't selling exceptions. And if I hear you're telling people otherwise, to get them signed up for your committee, I *will* drag you in front of the Bosses. You got that?"

He was standing stiff, all trace of smiling goodwill vanished.

"I got it," he said, perfectly flat.

"Good. Beautiful!"

"Yes, Captain."

"Show this man out, then lock the door. The office is closed."

"Yes, Captain. Lionel Smealy, come with me."

Surprisingly, he did that, without an argument, and without a backward look.

Miri closed her eyes, and ran the Scout's Rainbow, for calm.

Then, she bent over the computer and started the shut-down routine.

· · · ✴ · · ·

Val Con had turned once, slowly, on Ms. Audrey's request, a second time, at her sigh—and came to rest with his hands folded before him, and his head subtly tipped to one side.

"Ain't that fine..." Ms. Audrey extended a well-ringed hand and lightly stroked the sleeve of his coat. She sighed again, fingered the lace, and gave his wrist a coquettish squeeze before stepping back out of easy reach.

"The set of you is a danger on the streets," she said severely. "It's a wonder poor Sheyn didn't melt away like a snowflake, opening the door without having any warning about what was waiting on the porch."

Poor Sheyn had, to Pat Rin's certain knowledge, a surveillance screen as part of his doorman's accessories; it had been one of the first upgrades—absent the Sinner's Carpet—that Audrey had installed. That aside, Sheyn *had* seemed, momentarily, overawed. He had recovered himself with admirable quickness, however, smiling deeply into Val Con's eyes, and introducing himself, with the information that he could be called at any hour that was convenient. Val Con had thanked him with a gravity that could only put the seal on the boy's infatuation, leaving it to Pat Rin to ask if Ms. Audrey would see them.

"Now, tell me what this is," Audrey continued, "wedding or wake?"

"Neither," Val Con said promptly. "This is a formal dress suit, intended to be worn to very boring receptions, the purpose of which is to see who of those in attendance has the best tailor. I have today subverted its intention, in order to perhaps learn a little about someone. After, Pat Rin declared it would be cruel of me to leave the city without calling upon you."

"I'm not sure if it wasn't more cruel to let me rest eyes on you." She paused, as one struck by a sudden thought, and asked, somewhat wistfully, "Did Luken have a tailor, on the old world?"

"One's father employed a very fine tailor," Pat Rin said gravely, as Val Con seemed to become suddenly fascinated with his lace. "You must have him dress for you. He cuts quite a handsome figure."

There was a moment of silence before Audrey shook away such thoughts as Pat Rin dared not guess, and said briskly.

"Well, now I've seen you and my heart's broken like I was just sixteen, are you going to leave me here to sigh, or is there something else I can do for either"—a brow lifted suggestively as she surveyed them at her leisure—"*or both* of you?"

"In fact..." Val Con began, looking up from the long study of his lace. "I wonder—"

He got no further. The daytime peace was shattered by what sounded like a box of rocks dropped from orbit striking the center of the house.

"Dammit, Cholly, ain't you got any idee where you puttin' them elbows! Now you gone and woke up the pretties, an' our bonus is slush!"

"Because," Val Con murmured, diverted, "shouting at the top of one's lungs will certainly wake no one."

Audrey shook her head at him, lips quivering.

"I thought offering a bonus for not bringing the roof 'round our ears while they was fixing the staircase would keep the noise down, some. Mostly, it has, but Cholly, there, he ain't what you'd call a study in grace."

"Fixing the staircase?" Pat Rin asked. "Was it in disrepair?"

"No—nothin' like that! Nothin' on Surebleak's any solider than that stair. But the thing was, see, once they started in rippin' out the old carpet, and Luken got a good look at what he calls *the space*, he suggested openin' it up some. And, more fool that I am, I asked him what did he mean, *open it up*? So, he goes away and comes back no more'n half-hour later with a sketch, and it sure did look elegant, and the crew boss said they could do it, easy, 'cause there weren't no supportin' walls involved, and—I let myself get swept away, is what it was."

She sighed and shook her head.

"I tell you what, I'd forgotten how expensive men are, when you take to keeping one of your own."

Pat Rin dared a glance at Val Con's face, which was very grave, and braced himself.

"You might turn him out, if you find him too dear. The clan will certainly take him back," Val Con said.

Audrey considered him. "I find him dear, all right," she said. "And the clan ain't never let go of him, Mr. Dragon; don't you bat them pretty green eyes at me."

"All right," Val Con said, agreeably.

"But," Pat Rin said, throwing himself into the breach, "new carpet? I thought the house had only just had new carpet."

Audrey turned to him.

"Well, it had. And there's another story hanging there, and Luken at the heart of it, again. Look, I'm gonna have to throw my weight around a little with the crew—they expect it. C'mon and take a look at what they done, if you want to."

Pat Rin looked at Val Con. "Cousin?"

"Of course, I must see it."

While Audrey spoke with Jermin, the crew boss, and the unfortunate Cholly, Pat Rin and Val Con toured the construction site.

White plastic stairs were exposed, where the former rug had been stripped away, and the interior wall that had hidden the stairway from the grand parlor had been taken down. Instead of being hidden from below, those who had agreed to ascend to the next level of pleasure would be in full sight. At the top of the flight, on the hall that led to the various chambers of joy, the wall had been removed also, replaced to waist height with a gilded and filigreed screen.

"There's gonna be pink light in the hall up above," Audrey said, joining them in looking upward. "All the folks down in the main parlor will be able to watch the course of the lovers, as they climb to, and then cross, the bridge into ecstasy."

She lowered her eyes and met Pat Rin's.

"So says Luken."

"It sounds very like him," he answered politely.

"Expensive he may be, but this... conceit of Luken's is likely to see your custom among Liadens increase dramatically. It strikes a very subtle note. Your guests *must* recall the Jewel Boxes and the small, elite *hetaerana* clubs." Val Con nodded. "Truly, Audrey, your investment in our erring elder will be repaid six times, and quickly."

"I'll consider keeping him, then. But now I'm curious. Was Luken... involved with a business like mine, back on the old world?"

Pat Rin caught Val Con's eye. Val Con moved his shoulders. Pat Rin looked back to Audrey.

"He may have done," Pat Rin replied. "But, you know, my father is more than simply a seller of rugs. He designs rooms. He has an understanding of space that is very nearly unparalleled. On Liad, his eye and his artistry were—I do not embellish!—sought after by everyone who wished to bring a room to its full elegance or power. You have now released the staircase to its full range of possibility. Those who ascend it will be changed. Those who watch the ascension will be changed. The whole character of the transaction about to be joined is altered, from secretive to openly joyous."

"A bridge to ecstasy, indeed," Val Con added.

Audrey blinked, then looked up again, at the bridge.

"Well," she said softly. "Guess I'm gonna hafta get Quin to give lessons to us all."

Val Con's eyebrows went up.

Pat Rin cleared his throat. "Quin is tutoring Villy. A mixture, so I apprehend, of core work from Trigrace Academy, with basic kinesics and an abridged course of *melant'i* plays."

"Is Villy enjoying his lessons?"

"So far as I understand it."

"And is Quin enjoying them as well?"

"Very much, I believe."

"Excellent."

"Here," Audrey said abruptly. She held out a square of carpeting, all a-swirl with reds, oranges, and deep browns. It seemed to glow from within, which would, Pat Rin thought, be the silk threads woven among the *quetrine* wool. Such a carpet was a treasure, virtually indestructible. Such a carpet—

He gasped, and reached for the square, which Audrey obligingly put into his hand.

Such a carpet. He shook his head, understanding that this carpet—*this very* carpet!—was now intended to grace the newly made Bridge to Ecstasy in a whorehouse on the transitional world of Surebleak...

"Cousin?" The word was in Low Liaden; Val Con's hand gentle on his arm. "What's amiss?"

He looked up, automatically answering in the same tongue.

"It is the Queterian that Hedrede held for six Standards, waiting on the completion of the formal hall. It—Hedrede must have canceled the order. Would have been compelled..." He held out the sample, as if Val Con could not see it perfectly well. "That carpet is going..."

"That carpet is going to the increase of joy in the universe," Val Con murmured.

"Is he going to get in trouble?" That was Audrey, her voice sharp with worry. They both turned to her, Val Con's hand yet on Pat Rin's arm.

"*Is he* going to get in trouble?" she repeated, looking from one to the other. "Because if there's any chance of trouble—*any trouble, at all*—I can still say no to that carpet."

"Gently," Val Con murmured, in Terran. "Pat Rin is well acquainted with this carpet, you understand, and knows the party who had held it on deposit. It surprised him to find it here, his father having not yet had an opportunity to speak with him on the matter."

"Hedrede," Pat Rin said, warningly.

Val Con shook his head.

"Hedrede is notoriously world-bound," he said. "What are the chances that any of them might come to Surebleak? Surely, they would avoid this, of all worlds. They may hear of it—indeed, I wager that Luken will make certain that they *do* hear of it—but what recourse have they?"

Audrey cleared her throat.

Pat Rin smiled at her.

"Forgive us. We have the old world in our bones, but it is as Val Con says. Clan Hedrede had for many years held this rug on deposit. However, as they were part of the committee which saw us—Clan Korval—exiled from Liad, their *melant'i* could not support the continued relationship with Luken. The only course open to them was to cancel the order, and, by contract, Luken retained all monies received, and the rug, as well."

"Saving when they are backed by many others, Hedrede is not known for decisive action," Val Con said. "Nor do they range far from Liaden worlds. Luken, as you have surely discovered, has... high standards. His Balances are impeccable. On the old world, it was said that he was a *master of melant'i*, whereas we are the merest journeymen. Boys. We can only bow to the nicety of Luken's understanding, and aspire, someday, to be his equal."

Audrey was watching him closely. "So—no trouble?"

"It is extremely unlikely," Val Con told her. "Hedrede and its allies cleave to the old world. We do not expect to see such emigrating to Surebleak. A sense of adventure, and a belief that perhaps the rest of the galaxy might hold something more interesting than Liaden society is the chief characteristic of those who follow us here."

"So we're getting the best, is what you're saying?"

Val Con smiled at her. "For the purposes of Korval and of Surebleak entire—yes. We are getting the best. Now, I wonder—" His voice caught, for an instant only; Pat Rin thought that Audrey failed to notice anything amiss. Certainly, she did not understand that the course of the sentence Val Con had been about to speak had altered in that short pause. "—if you will forgive me for staying with you so briefly. The case is that I am wanted at the port."

"I never stand between a man and his bidness," Audrey assured him. "It was real good to see you. You give your wife a nice kiss from me and tell her not to be a stranger."

"I will," Val Con promised. He took her hand between both of his and smiled into her eyes.

She laughed, and slipped her hand away. "There's such a thing as being *too* good! Go on—get along with you, or I'll tell Sheyn to lock the door. Boss?"

"I am afraid that I, too, am called to business," Pat Rin said, taking her hand and smiling with frank fondness. "Thank you for seeing us, Audrey."

"Wouldn't've missed it for a blizzard," she told him.

He smiled again, and followed Val Con out.

✳   ✳   ✳

In the foyer, Pat Rin cast a look at his cousin's profile. "What's amiss?"

Val Con moved his shoulders, and gave him a half-smile.

"I scarcely know. Miri's temper has been engaged, but..." Another ripple of his shoulders. "I think, perhaps, that I *ought* to go to the port."

"Then by all means do so," Pat Rin said. "You needn't dawdle on my account."

Val Con caught his hand. "Thank you, cousin," he said, and slipped out the door.

Pat Rin moved a few steps to the right, watching out the side window as the elegantly overdressed figure jogged down the stairs, and turned a quick step up the street, to the place where he had left his car.

No security, Pat Rin thought, and shook his head. He would speak to Nova; perhaps she might exert influence. If not, it would have to rest until Shan came home.

"Ready, Boss?" Gwince asked from behind him.

"In fact, I am," he said. "Let us call upon Boss Nova."

CHAPTER TWENTY-SEVEN

*Office of the Road Boss
Surebleak Port*

"HEY, BOSS!"

The voice was recently and irritatingly familiar.

Miri looked around Nelirikk's bulk, saw Smealy and a frowning trio that was probably his crew standing over by Jakob's. One guy had an arm in a sling, but nobody was showing a weapon, which she tentatively decided was good. On the other hand, here came Smealy back across the street, big phony grin in place like they was long-lost best lovers.

"Captain?" Nelirikk murmured, and it didn't take mind-reading to know that he wasn't real happy with Smealy, either.

"Let's see what happens," she muttered back, and stepped out in front. Tall as he was, she wasn't going to impede him, if Nelirikk decided Smealy needed to be taken off the board. Her only real danger was Smealy getting off a good shot before he went down, and, looking at the man, she considered the probability of his being a good shot...low.

"What do you want, Smealy?" she called back, not making any particular effort to sound welcoming.

The grin got broader, like she'd given him a birthday present.

"Just telling the crew about how you're going to be working with the Heavy Loads Committee!" he said, and suddenly looked up, like he'd just remembered Nelirikk.

Bastard, Miri thought. He was trying to force her, was he?

Thought she wouldn't stand firm, if he called her out on the open street, with his crew on backup.

She took a deep breath, and went a step forward, ignoring Nelirikk's muttered protest.

Raising her hands, she grinned, just as phony and wide as Smealy, and motioned him forward.

"I thought we was going to wait on announcing that," she said, using the field-command voice, so's to be heard all the way across the street.

"Well, sure, Boss, but here I come out and there's the crew. I had to tell them the good news."

"Sure you did."

She swung, short, sharp, and focused. Smealy went down like a sack of rocks, and stayed down.

"Now, I don't know what this guy told you." She'd been a merc; she knew how to pitch her voice to be heard on a battlefield, and that's what she did now, so they'd be certain to hear her—yeah, and all the rest of the folks who were taking note of the fact that *something* was going on that involved the Road Boss.

"Here's the straight truth. The Road Boss don't make exceptions. We're under contract with the Council of Bosses to keep the road open, and to enforce the policies the Bosses put into place. That's our job, we're gonna do our job, and we ain't accepting bribes or going around the published policies. You all got that?"

One of them—the burly dark guy with a head like a cannonball, and his arm in the sling—called back.

"We got it, Boss."

They were attracting a crowd, which was...unavoidable. And with the crowd came a brace of Port Security—Hazenthull and a Terran male, who looked frail next to her.

"Need help here?" the Terran asked.

"No," Nelirikk said before she could answer. "The captain is having a discussion with this person on the ground, and the members of his troop."

"We'll keep the perimeter, then," the guy said, and he and Hazenthull separated to do just that.

Miri took a breath.

"Now, here's another thing!" she said to Smealy's crew, who were all three still waiting there by Jakob's, their eyes bright and interested. "You go back to wherever you come from and you return any *dues* you collected from people who're waiting to get their exceptions. You don't do that—or I hear you're still signing people up? And you'll come before the Council so fast your ears'll fall off. *And*—any one of you pulls another stunt like this, where you're trying to destroy my cred—"

Something moved in the side of her eyes, down and to the right. Smealy.

She kicked the gun out of his hand before he quite had it clear of the pocket, and stomped on his fingers for good measure.

He screamed, which she couldn't blame him for.

"You got a lot to learn about communication," she told him, and swung wide. "Get up."

Give him credit, he tried to, but the broken hand wasn't doing his balance any good. Nelirikk finally felt sorry for him, reached down, grabbed his collar and hauled him to his feet.

"You want we should take him to the Whosegow, Boss?" That was Hazenthull's partner.

"No," she said. "His crew'll take care of him. Won't they, Smealy?"

He stared at her, good hand cradling broken hand and shook his head.

"Cut me a break, Boss."

The man was scared, and he had a right to be, judging by the faces of his crew. On the other hand...

"You got two freebies, Smealy. Third time, you pay real money. That's how it's done, ain't it?"

It was, and he knew it, and she could see him know what kind of care his crew was going to give him for screwing up—twice—and calling their business out on the open street.

She felt a little sick, like she'd been punched in the stomach, but there wasn't anything to do, except send him back to his crew. If she backed down now, her cred as Boss—and Val Con's cred as Boss, too—took a hit it couldn't afford, with them just setting up. Saying *no* to the exceptions racket—that was just the first test.

Smealy pulled himself up as straight as he could, and gave her a curt nod.

"Boss," he said, and marched away, back to his crew.

She tensed, thinking they'd shoot him right there, but there was more than the Road Boss's cred on the street right now, including

Security and the crowd that'd gathered 'round to witness. The guy with the cannonball head swung out of formation, got his good arm around Smealy, and walked him away, the other two closing in behind.

Miri watched them go, and wished she felt like she'd done the right thing.

"Captain," Nelirikk said for her ears alone, "the Scout approaches."

She looked to the left, toward the Emerald, and here he came, moving light and quick through the crowd, the sun plucking sparks from the silver threads in his coat. Now she was paying attention, she could feel his concern; he must've felt her lose her temper at Smealy, and come down to see what all the noise was about.

Noise was over now, of course, so she raised her hand, and called, just like Smealy'd done.

"Hey, Boss."

Heads turned, then, and people pulled back to give the man room to pass.

"Miri, are you well?"

She heard his voice, soft inside her head, asking the question, then he was at her side, hand stretched out to her.

"Hey, Boss," she said again, like she was standing in the middle of a battlefield. She grabbed his hand and gave him a grin. "You missed all the fun."

"You'll have to tell me about it," he answered, his own voice pitched to carry. "Over tea, perhaps? At the Emerald?"

"Sounds great," she said, and tucked her hand through his arm, feeling the embroidery scratch her palm. The two of them turned back the way he'd come, Beautiful falling in behind.

"It's a good thing you come along," she said, for the benefit of the crowd, as it parted before them.

"Why is that?"

"I'm *starving*."

· · · ❄ · · ·

"Okay, now!" Tolly called out, as the captain and the Scout left the field, attended by Nelirikk. "Show's over; time to get back to bidness!"

It was correct, to disperse the crowd, and their duty, as Security, to clear the public way. However, those who had gathered were being ... somewhat difficult to disperse. At first, Hazenthull assumed that it was because they were yet in awe of the captain's skills. But as she encouraged them to motion, a muttering came to her ears. It would appear that there was some discontent with the Scout's actions, though he had arrived after the captain had properly chastised Streeter Smealy and returned him to his comrades.

She listened more intently, and because of that perhaps did not attend to her position as she should have done.

The first inkling she had of her partner's peril was a sudden scattering of the crowd under his direction, a shout, and a blur of motion as Tolly snatched a red-haired man over his shoulder, bringing him down hard on his back against the tarmac. She saw Tolly sweep a hand out, even as he spun, hand on his sidearm, scanning the crowd for his attacker's compatriots.

The crowd was moving now, of its own accord, drawing away from trouble, from danger, saving the woman who threw herself forward, berating Tolly for striking a blameless man. It was Tolly, he would not strike her or push her away; he paused to engage her, his back to the man he had thrown.

The man who had rolled clumsily to his knees, his hand rising with intent, the palm gun held quite steady.

Despite his apparent steadiness, he might still have missed the back of Tolly's head; he had taken a bad fall, and it was plain that he was shaken, if not wounded.

On the other hand, all of her previous life experience had taught Hazenthull that there are no sure misses on the battlefield.

There are only certain hits.

Her sidearm was in her hand, the crowd around her vanishing as if it had been no more substantial than smoke.

She aimed for his shoulder, but at the decisive instant, he faltered, and half fell...

The pellet struck him in the eye.

· · · ✳ · · ·

Tolly had the damned whistle; he was golden. All he had to do was move out, fast. It left Haz with the crowd, but there wasn't a crowd on Surebleak Haz couldn't handle with one hand tied behind her back. Commander Liz was going to be seriously unhappy, but Commander Liz had been destined for unhappiness this day, no matter—

"You hit that guy!"

A broad-shouldered woman threw herself into his path, her face angry.

"Sorry, ma'am. He was drawing—"

"He was not! I'm gonna report you to your captain! What's your name?"

That's when the gunshot sounded, loud even in the noise of the port. Tolly spun, but tel'Vaster was already down, the top of his head gone, and there was Haz, gun as steady as her eye, standing there daring anybody else to come ahead.

Tolly's gun was out, too—reactions, damn reactions—and he spun, surveying the area. One good thing, the street had cleared. Bad thing was that a pair or more of their now-former coworkers were going to be bearing down on them real soon.

Not to mention tel'Vaster's backup, which there was at least one on port, and not so distant from them, or the man had changed out of recognition in the last couple years.

For a long, critical second, he couldn't think; couldn't breathe. Then he remembered that there was a ship waiting for him. The key and the contract had come that morning. He had someplace to go; someplace that neither tel'Vaster nor his backup could guess at.

He thought of his meager possessions, but everything he really needed, in order to survive, was on him: ship's key, license with a good name on it, contract, his own weapons, and all the cash he owned.

Flipping his service gun, he held it out, grip-first, to Hazenthull.

"Take this to Commander Liz. Tell her I'm sorry, Haz, right? Tell her I'm off-world and won't be any more problem to her."

"Tolly, did this man have a partner? A troop?"

"Prolly so. Which is why I gotta go, Haz. You watch yourself!"

He turned, and ran, moving not quite at the top of his speed. No sense scaring the reg'lars; no sense calling the attention of somebody who might know what he was looking at.

He didn't go straight to the hotpad where his ship waited. *Tarigan*, out of Waymart. 'Course it was out of Waymart. All the best ships were.

Anyhow, he took the port tour, and when he was as sure as he could be that he wasn't trailing tel'Vaster's backup, he made a wide loop and headed in, toward the general yard.

Two ship rows short of his goal, something moved in the corner of his eye. He turned his head, and saw Hazenthull round the top of the row, loping along, nice and easy, on those long legs of hers. She probably wasn't even winded.

Tolly bit his lip on a grin. Didn't Haz always have his back? Better she saw him safe onto his ship. She'd sleep easier for it.

He kept going, like he hadn't spotted her. A row and a half...

A stiletto made out of fire and ice drove in one ear, through his brain, and out the other ear.

He screamed, stumbled...and stopped.

· · · ☀ · · ·

Tolly was running an evasion pattern. That was good, Hazenthull thought. He wished to be certain that the comrade of the man she had killed would not find and follow him.

It was better that she followed, to make certain that he reached his goal. She was his partner; she had his back.

They came at last to the ready-yard, and she remembered that he had a ship waiting for him, and a piloting contract in hand. Good, then, all she needed to do was see him safely inside his ship.

She saw him turn his head as she rounded the corner after him, and knew that he had seen her. He gave no sign, though, and did not try to angle away and elude her. She took that for his approval of her escort; and the tie that bound them, still.

He was running easier now, as if his goal was near. Hazenthull felt something in her chest loosen, though she was breathing easily. Very soon now, he would be safe; his enemies confounded. He would lift, and she would never—

Ahead of her, Tolly stumbled.

He stopped.

He turned, slowly, until he faced the small woman who strolled out from between two ships, a gun in one hand, and a short, ceramic pipe in the other.

Hazenthull froze, wondering if this was, indeed, his new pilot. She watched as the woman came closer and Tolly did not move, did not react to her presence at all, even when she raised the hand that held the gun and whipped it across his face.

"Well, Mr. Berik, or is it something else today?" the woman said.

Tolly did not answer. The woman raised the gun again...then lowered it.

"Answer, Thirteen-Sixty-Two: what name are you using today?"

"Tolly Jones." His voice was flat; his face, bloodied where the gun had opened a gash on his cheek, was without expression.

Hazenthull began to move, with care; neither Tolly nor his captor looked in her direction.

"Tolly Jones," the woman repeated.

"Where were you going in such haste, Tolly Jones?"

Hazenthull felt her stomach tighten, and moved more quickly.

Tolly simply stood, saying nothing, looking at nothing, save in the direction of the woman's face.

"Answer, Thirteen-Sixty-Two! Where were you going?"

Hazenthull drew her gun.

"Release your gun and the other object, and step back with your hands on your head!" She snapped.

The woman turned, pilot-quick, and fired.

Hazenthull felt a burn in her belly, fired, and missed her target.

The woman shot again, and this time the burn was high in her chest. Hazenthull took careful aim, and squeezed her trigger.

The target, Tolly's enemy, crumpled to the tarmac. Hazenthull moved, meaning to pick up the gun, staggered and went to one knee. The belly shot—but, she must remove the gun, she must...

"Haz..."

It was Tolly's voice, blurry and uncertain, but his own voice.

"C'mon, Haz, I can't carry you. Up, up, let's go..."

She got to her feet, and leaning on him, she walked, past the dead woman, alone on the tarmac with neither gun nor pipe nearby, slowly down the row of ships, round a corner, and onward, to one ship that stood with its hatch open and a shadow hovering within.

· · · ❄ · · ·

"Your father awaits you in the parlor, sir," Mr. pel'Tolian said, as he helped Pat Rin remove his coat.

"Thank you," he said. "I will go to him now. I trust everything has been calm and orderly in my absence."

"Very much so, sir. Mr. McFarland took several calls dealing with insurance; he referred them to the Watch. Boss Gabriel confirmed his appointment with you, here, midmorning, on the day after tomorrow. Ms. Natesa asked that you be told that she will be in-house for dinner. Mr. Meron has asked for her assistance with the *freelancers*."

"Thank you." He smoothed his sleeve.

"Anything else?"

"No, sir."

"Then I will go to my father. We will wish for tea."

"Yes, sir."

Luken was in his favorite chair in the parlor, booted feet stretched toward the fire.

He glanced up and smiled sleepily at Pat Rin's entrance.

"Ah, there you are, boy-dear, in the very nick of time. Another moment or two and you would have found me napping."

"Perhaps we will nap together," Pat Rin told him, sinking into the chair opposite. "I believe that I may be getting old, Father."

"Nonsense, you're the merest stripling."

"And Quin a babe in arms, I apprehend."

"No, boy-dear, there you are out. Quin is older than either of us."

"I fear you may be correct."

The door opened to admit Mr. pel'Tolian, tea tray in hand.

He placed it on the table between them, poured and served with quiet efficiency—Luken first, then Pat Rin, the proper and correct order of service for an intimate gathering of family.

"Will there be anything else, sir?" he asked. "Cook asks me to tell you there is a batch of shortbread, only now removed from the oven."

Pat Rin's mouth briefly watered; his cook's shortbread was no trivial matter.

"Father?" he asked.

Luken moved a hand in a regretful negative.

"I have only just lunched, I fear."

"Please thank Cook," Pat Rin said. "I think we are well set up."

"Sir." Mr. pel'Tolian bowed and left them, closing the door soundlessly behind him.

They sipped their tea, and both sighed in appreciation of the leaf. Then Luken set his cup aside.

"I had come to tell you that I will be removing to my apartment this evening," he said. "All is at last in order."

Pat Rin took a breath against a sharp prick of loss, which was nonsensical; Luken had made no secret of his intentions to withdraw from his foster son's household as soon as he had located a suitable establishment.

That the establishment found most suitable happened to be located across the street from Audrey's House of Joy, where Luken already passed many nights, could surprise no one who was aware of the relationship that had leapt up, seemingly fully formed, between Luken and Audrey. The relationship itself might give one pause, given the very great differences in their circumstances, but, again, a small amount of consideration revealed that they held more in common than might otherwise be supposed.

Both were in the business of providing pleasure to others; both possessed an artistic and discerning eye. Beauty was meat and bread to them, and each had for all of their adult lives been the sole proprietor of a business that they had grown from modest into remarkable. Too, they were close in age, and had in less than two Standards seen their respective societies assaulted by, and reeling from, change.

"Surely, I have not taken you in surprise," Luken murmured.

Pat Rin glanced up, smiling ruefully.

"Not surprise, merely regret. I have enjoyed your presence in my house—as have Natesa and Quin. And my staff. I had hoped you might tarry a while longer, but I well know the lure of setting up one's own establishment."

Luken laughed, gently.

"As if I were in my puppyhood! No, my son, if you will have the truth, the establishment maintained by Boss Conrad is... somewhat too busy for a man of my years to find either restful or exhilarating. And"—a sharp glance here from wide grey eyes—"no man wants his father at his shoulder every hour."

He stretched out a hand. Pat Rin leaned forward in his seat to take it.

"I propose that we go on as we had been accustomed to do, when you were not traveling. Let us meet for dinner once a twelve-day and catch ourselves up."

Boss Conrad's schedule was not often giving. Pat Rin yos'Phelium's schedule, however—and so he vowed upon the moment—would in this thing overrule the Boss.

"Done," he said, and squeezed his father's fingers affectionately before releasing them.

CHAPTER TWENTY-EIGHT

. . . .

Surebleak Port

IF IT'D BEEN HIM, ALONE, HE'D NEVER GOTTEN HAZ INTO THE autodoc. The pilot took a hand, though, and between them, they got her folded up inside, knees to forehead, but *inside*, and the lid down and the automatics up.

His pilot sank to the floor plates as the status lights came up, and Tolly followed suit, collapsing to his knees, his shoulders pressed against the 'doc, and his skull ringing like a carillon.

"You will want to see to your face," his pilot said, her voice rich and warm in the mid-tones.

"Just a cut," he said, and made himself raise his head and look at her. Nice design; functional and nonthreatening.

"Sorry, Pilot. It wasn't my intention to bring trouble to the ship."

"Fortunately for us all, you did not bring trouble to the ship, though it did come rather close."

"Trouble," he repeated, and settled his shoulders against the 'doc. "This woman belongs to Clan Korval."

"Yes," the pilot agreed. "But on this ship, we do not count Korval as trouble. Will she live?"

"I think so. She's big, and tough. The poison's slow-moving." He sighed, and closed his eyes.

"They want you to be cooperative, see? So they hold out that they'll give the antidote, and they do a countdown of how many hours the poisoned has left until the antidote won't do 'em any good."

291

"These do not sound like very pleasant people," the pilot observed.

Tolly laughed. "No, they're not."

"So. Tell me, please, how you would prefer to be called?"

He sighed, thinking of the names that had been his, and then not, including the name on the license, which hadn't been with him the longest, by any measure, though he had more than a passing fondness for it.

"Tolly," he said to his pilot's dark, reflective face. "Matches the license, close enough, and I'm used to it."

"Very well, then Tolly. I am Tocohl. One more question, before I ask you again to perform self-care: what are these?"

They floated in the air between them, two ceramic pipes, simple, clean-looking things. Unthreatening. Sort of like the pilot, here.

Tolly looked at them, feeling his heart speed up, and thought, for less than a millisecond, about lying. It was bad form to lie to your pilot, unless it was for her own good. And, of all the sentiences in all the universes, this one was less likely than most to lust after the power that lay in those pipes.

Not only that, she'd know he was lying, and toss him out on the port where he was responsible for the presence of two dead bodies, and a moderate amount of mayhem.

So he said, quiet and calm, and not trying to hide anything. "Control devices."

"What do they control?"

"Me . . . well. More or less, they do. I've been working on upgrading and amending internal systems. The pipes—they're not as powerful as they were when I was in school, but they're still a threat and a menace."

"Are there any more of these that might menace you?"

"I imagine so, Pilot, but I don't how many. I've always assumed as a general rule of thumb that there's two more for every one I capture."

He looked bleakly at the pipes floating before him, wondering idly if it was a personal gravity field his pilot had, or just a fetching way with magnetics.

"So far, that ratio's held firm."

"I see. Please take these and see them destroyed. I assume that you know how best to go about it. I will ask you please to make yourself both seemly and ready to sit your station. Your quarters are aft. If you require rest, please see to it. If you require food or drink, please draw and consume those things in the appropriate quantities before you come to the board. We lift in three local hours. I expect you at your station in two local hours."

"Yes, Pilot." He hesitated, then said, "Clan Korval will want to know where Haz is."

"I will take care of informing the appropriate persons. Must I *order* you to tend to your needs?"

"No, Pilot."

He got to his feet, took the pipes gently into his hand, bowed to the pilot's honor and left the infirmary.

· · · ✳ · · ·

"Captain, a warrior awaits us on the southern patio," Nelirikk's voice came over the car's intercom.

In the seldom-occupied back passenger compartment, Val Con and Miri exchanged a look: hers studiously bland, his accompanied by a lifted brow.

"Well, let us see," she said. "If the warrior awaits, one makes the assumption that the warrior is not dead."

"And if the warrior is not dead," he added, "it argues that Jeeves knows and approves of both the warrior and the state of waiting."

"I agree."

"Therefore, the warrior is..."

She frowned. "Someone also known to Mr. pel'Kana, I think, and to Nelirikk, but who is neither family, nor among us sufficiently long to have acquired a troop name."

The car stopped at that point, and the doors opened.

Val Con exited on his side, Miri on hers, both turning toward the patio as they did.

"Good afternoon, Rys," said Miri, and Val Con, "Brother, are we so rag-mannered that we could not give you a place in the House?"

"I had asked to sit out, if the House permitted," Rys said, coming easily to his feet. His hands were empty and held slightly away from his body. The right one glowed like gold in the summer sunlight.

He had put his coat aside and stood only in a light jacket over a high-necked red sweater and tough black canvas pants. The breeze had had its way with his curls, and his eyes were bright.

He looked, Miri thought, like Val Con's kid brother, in truth.

"At least we had the good grace to give you refreshment," Val

Con said as they arrived at the patio. Nelirikk continued past them, through the door and into the house.

"Are those grapes?" Val Con asked.

"Indeed they are," Rys said, briskly. "And I wish you to know that the task you set me has been accomplished. Here—taste these."

He swept the basket from the table, and nearly shoved it at Val Con, who broke off two branches, handing one to Miri.

In Miri's experience, grapes were either pale green, dark red, or purple. These grapes were a sort of dusty gold. She put one in her mouth.

She had expected the fruit to be sweet—but it was much more complex than simply sweet. In fact, she couldn't be certain that it was *precisely* sweet, so she had another one, trying to quantify what, exactly, she was tasting.

"Are you responsible for these?" Val Con asked Rys, his voice sounding as astonished as she felt.

Rys laughed.

"Was there time to grow and harvest them, even had I the vines in hand? No. These, so Mrs. ana'Tak tells me, arrive from Mr. Shaper, your neighbor, who brought them this morning with the news that he has far too many for his own use, and if she finds them to her liking, he can supply her with more. He will, he told her, hold out some few for himself, which are destined to become raisins."

"Raisins," Val Con repeated, putting another grape into his mouth.

"They will make excellent raisins," Miri said.

Rys nodded at her with a half-smile.

"Indeed, but they will also produce a very drinkable wine. My brother had given me the task of producing a Surebleak vintage."

"A Surebleak grape is not a Surebleak vintage," Val Con pointed out.

"True, but I claim my task complete. There are winemakers a-plenty in the city; you do not need me for that."

"And what will you do," Miri asked, "if you will not be Korval's winemaker?"

The look he gave her this time had no smile in it at all.

"I will assume command of those who have chosen wisely and lead them to confound our enemy."

· · · ⁂ · · ·

It was getting to be closing time at Bob's Grocery, and not any too soon, either.

Bob moved around the store, turning down the lights, covering over the vegetables with the freshkeep blankets he'd just got from the new supply store. Spendy little things, but din't they just do the trick? The bins kept things fresh enough, but the greens and marrows and, well, the soft foods, they started in to lookin' a little sad an' wilted along about the sixth day out.

Them new blankets, though—cover 'em over at night, and next mornin' it was like you had brand new vegetables in the bin, almost. Lasted another three days, easy, which meant he had to buy less, sure, but it meant less waste, too. Less waste meant he could afford to lower the prices a little; make it easier for everybody on the street. Only a little easier, but each little thing that got easier added to the growing pile of things that were a little easier, a little less expensive, a little fresher...

Yeah. Things added up, and the things that'd been adding up since the New Bosses and the Council got things headed in a whole 'nother direction...

Hey, his kid was going to school, and guess what? His kid—his Matty—*won a prize* for spelling! Bob, he could read—had to, in his bidness, and his ma'd made sure he could add a column of figures up and down in his head and get the same answer every time. But, spelling, now... 's'long's he could sound it out, that was good enough.

He covered up the last of the softs, and turned off the lights in the back section.

Speakin' of figures, he'd best lock the door, and tally up the day's take. Go on home and have dinner with his kid. Hear what happened in school today. That was always a—

The bell over the front door rang, and Bob sighed.

Damn late customer. Well, he'd hustle 'em up a little; help 'em find what they wanted real quick and—

"Bob here?" A man's voice, way too loud for the circumstances, or the store. Wasn't that big a store, you hadda holler to be heard.

"Right here," he said, stepping out of the end of the row.

His customer turned, and Bob's stomach went right down to his feet.

The guy grinned. In his two hands was the new sign, the one Bob'd just put up in the front window that morning, that said

NO INSURANCE SALES ALLOWED. Matty'd brought it home—Boss Kalhoon'd gone to the school and talked to all the kids about how there wasn't going to be any more insurance sales, nor any makin' of zamples, just like there wasn't going to be any retirement parties and the new Boss comin' around demanding a present or...

The sign, though, it was ripped right in half, and once the guy saw he had Bob's attention, he dropped both halves on the floor and scuffed 'em with his boot.

"Evenin', Bob," he said, and he pulled a little book outta his pocket.

Snow and sleet, din't he remember them damn little books! Just lookin' at this one had him shaking with mingled mad and scared.

"So, Bob, your insurance payment's due," the guy said, flipping open the little book and licking the end of his pencil. He made a show of scanning the pages, turning them over real slow, until Bob was ready to scream at him—'cept you din't yell at the insurance man. You din't do one thing that might add a percentage to your payment due.

Finally, the guy found the page he wanted. He nodded to it, like it was an old friend, and looked to Bob with a nasty smile on his face.

"Syndicate's gonna need four hunnert cash, and this list here made up and waitin', all nice in a box, when I come back to collect."

He held a piece of paper out, and Bob took it, hating the way his fingers shook.

It was a long list, and it would wipe him outta items like coffee an' sugar an' cheese—expensive items, all going to the Boss for free, on top of the cash, which was way more—three times more!—than his last insurance payment, back when Moran was Boss, before Conrad retired him and started in piling up those little good changes one by one. He'd barely been able to pay that, even with stinting himself, and givin' Matty slim pickin's, and that wasn't no good for a growing kid.

"I'll be taking half of the cash on deposit," the insurance man said, "right now. The rest of the cash, and the list—you have that ready for me to pick up day after tomorra."

Two hundred cash, right now.

"Sure," Bob said, and headed for the counter, where the cash drawer was, hearing the insurance man walking behind him.

He opened the drawer, hunching over it, so the man couldn't get his fingers in and help himself to ten or fifty "for his trouble," and started counting.

He *started* counting, his fingers going slow, and his eyes lit on the card Matty'd brought him from school, the one with all the contact numbers on it. Right above them, it said, in big letters: *Insurance Sales Are Against The Law.*

The Law.

The Law—that was Conrad and the New Bosses, and Matty winning the spelling bee at school. The Law said he din't have to pay this guy, din't have to feel this way—it said *Matty* din't never have to feel this way, when he come to take over the store.

Bob took a deep breath, and closed the lid on the cash box.

He reached under the counter, his hand closing 'round the piece o'heavy pipe he kept there, mostly for scarin' away punks. He din't never hit anybody with it.

But, for this guy—for this *Syndicate* trying to take Matty's bright new future away from him?

He'd make an exception.

· · · ✳ · · ·

A whole minute had passed and Val Con hadn't said anything yet.

Miri figured that for a record. Rys really oughta take hold of his advantage and press his case, but Rys didn't have much experience of Val Con, adopted brother or not.

So, it looked like it was up to her.

"That sounds to be an excellent plan, Rys," she said. "You will, of course, show the details, after dinner. For this moment, however..."

She turned to look at Val Con.

"Mr. Shaper is behind in contacting you regarding Shan's deed. Why not combine two errands into one? You may ask after the paper, and Rys may find the source of these delightful grapes. I, in the meanwhile, will visit Talizea."

Val Con took a breath, and inclined his head.

"That is an excellent scheme. Brother? A small walk before Prime, and possibly a discussion with our very interesting neighbor, if he is receiving visitors today?"

"That sounds pleasant," said Rys, and so it was decided.

CHAPTER TWENTY-NINE

. . . .

Corner of Dudley Avenue and Farley Lane

IN THE LATE AFTERNOON, THERE CAME A KNOCK AT THE DOOR.

Kamele raised her head from the folder of letters she had been studying, listening to Dilly's footsteps as she approached the door and opened it.

There came the sound of voices: a woman's, bold and carrying the distinctive rhythm of an accent not elsewhere found on Surebleak, even though her words were muffled.

Kamele smiled, and rose from her chair, pausing only to mark her place in the file before hurrying out of her office and down the stairs.

It had become a habit, after their first, formal meeting at Joan's Bakery—many weeks ago, now—that Silain, *luthia*, or *grandmother*, of the Bedel who lived in and yet apart from the rest of the port city, would call on them now and then. They would sit around the table and talk for an hour over tea, and all arise refreshed and reinvigorated.

Kamele looked forward to these visits, for Silain was a woman of great learning and insight. She thought that Kareen also put a value upon the grandmother's visits.

Kareen, so Kamele had observed, was lonely. She had abandoned a wide circle of acquaintance, scholarship, and volunteer work on the old world, and while their mutual project was... encompassing; it did not replace old friends or accustomed duty.

Kamele rounded the wide bottom stair, and walked down the hall toward the dining room at the back of the house.

The table was covered with a deep green cloth, on which three groupings of creamy china cups and plates had been set out, with various spoons and tongs and knives. In the center of the table, a vase painted in abstract swirls of cream and green held a cluster of cream and yellow flowers.

Kareen was already welcoming their guest.

"It is good of you to come, Silain. Indeed, I wish it were in my power to convey how much I look forward to our teas."

"It is good for sisters to talk," Silain said, as Kamele slipped into the room. "And here—here is my other sister! We are complete."

"Let us sit," Kareen said. "The tea will come soon, and I believe that there are the filled cakes you favor, Silain."

"That is well. I brought a few fruits of limin, and some mint—a gift to your kitchen, Sister. Dilly took them in hand."

"My house is made richer by a sister's gift," Kareen said. "But, Silain, you must sit, and be comfortable."

So urged, Silain took her usual seat, with the hall doorway at her left hand. Kareen's chair was at what she called the head of the table, which coincidentally faced the doorway. Kamele sat across from Silain, with Kareen on her left.

"Does your work progress well, Sisters?"

"As well as may be," Kareen said, with a cool smile at Kamele. "There was a find earlier in the week, which may be significant, as it supports anecdotal evidence of which we had previously taken note."

Silain in her turn looked to Kamele.

"What did you find, if it can be shared, among sisters?"

"In fact, it seems peculiarly apt to share it among sisters," Kamele said, leaning forward and clasping her hands together on the tabletop.

"We found a... compilation of letters written by grandmothers in various turfs, detailing the history, and the responsibilities, of each. It appears to have been written and collected before the old system broke down utterly, and the Bosses decided to stop cooperating with each other. It doesn't describe a fully functioning system, but it does seem to show us that the society was closely modeled on the Gilmour Agency's corporate structure. Each department, or section, had a number of colonists attached to it.

"Later, the system"—she moved her hands, as if she was trying to find the words in the air before her—"the system *imploded*, each section collapsing into itself. The toolbooths became the boundary by which each turf defined itself, and the Boss became the absolute power over the colonists—the streeters."

"This is exciting information, I see," Silain said. "But does the past teach you anything useful about the future?"

"All systems build on the past," Kamele said, "even those which are built on a deliberate denial of the past."

There was a small sound in the hallway, and she paused while Esil Lang and Amiz brought in the tea tray.

"Thank you," said Kareen, when the first cups had been poured and the plates of cakes and bread set on the table. "Leave the pot, please. We will serve ourselves."

"Yes, Lady," said Esil, and performed one of the small, respectful bows that the house staff had adopted. She shooed Amiz out ahead and closed the door firmly after her.

"You were speaking of the past," Silain said to Kamele.

She laughed and moved her shoulders, as Jen Sar used to do when he had judged he'd shown too much enthusiasm for a topic.

"No, I am interested," Silain pressed, taking up one of the filled cakes. "It is the role of the *luthia*, you know, to bring the past to the present. It is said that the past has much to teach us, which I do not dispute. But sometimes I wonder, Sisters, have I learned *rightly* from the past?"

"Exactly!" Kamele leaned forward, elbows on the table, teacup cradled in her hands. "We *build* from the past, but do we *learn* from it? And, if we *have* learned, have we taken the correct lessons? We bring assumptions to the task of learning, while the history we seek to learn proceeds from the assumptions of another time, to which we may not be privy.

"That's what makes this portfolio—this history—so important to Kareen's work—"

"Your work, also," Kareen murmured.

"—for not only do we have a list of proper behaviors, but the *reasons* those behaviors were considered proper, *and* how those behaviors—those social mores—had changed during the lifetime of our historians. The assumptions of the authors are very clearly laid out, and we can see where we and they intersect, where our—our necessities have diverged, or march together . . . Really, it's priceless."

"I see that it is," Silain said. She raised her cup and looked to Kareen.

"Our sister puts me in mind of a thing—you would say, an *archive*—for which I am responsible, and which may have some bearing on your work here."

"You interest me," Kareen said. "Do you mean to say that you have records of Surebleak before its ... collapse?"

Silain sipped tea, her eyes frowning at—and through—the plate of sweet things: the very picture of a scholar in a brown study.

"It may be so," she said eventually. "You will understand that I have not dreamed every dream in my keeping. The *kompani* ... has been on this world for ... an amount of time, I will say. At first, we wandered. It may be that the earliest dreams of this place may bring knowledge to my sisters."

"This dreaming," Kareen said. "I understand it to be time-consuming, and—forgive me—opaque to those not trained in the method."

"Anyone can dream. The difficult part is in bringing the dream to the waking world in such a way that it can be understood." Silain smiled at Kamele. "This is what my sister Kamele has said. The points of reference, the assumptions of the dreaming mind ... they are not always clear."

"Yes. And as none of us here are trained dreamers ..."

Silain moved a hand.

"No, I think I have the answer to that, too: a skilled researcher with a strong memory. She was my apprentice and would be *luthia* if our *kompani* had birthed daughters. Droi is her name. She is pregnant and forbidden some of the work she is used to doing. Time hangs heavy on her hands. I will send her. You, my Sisters, will explain to her what you look for, what hints she ought to seek. She will dream from the first dream of Surebleak until—"

She looked 'round the table, spreading her hands wide in a question.

Kareen tapped her finger thoughtfully on the tabletop.

"We have identified a few cusp points," she said slowly, looked to Kamele, brows lifted.

"By all means, send Droi to us," Kamele said warmly. "We have the date that the Gilmour Agency shut down operations here, and the date that the last company ship lifted. We have dates for some of the Bosses ..."

She glanced at Kareen, who bowed her head, and said, "We have the date that Boss Conrad...*retired*...former Boss Moran and broke the culture a second time...Yes, send us Droi. We will try and see what she can find for us, and if we can be useful to each other."

Silain nodded, and plucked another sweet from the plate.

"I will speak with Droi," she said and smiled. "Truly it is said that when sisters talk together, mountains move."

· · · ☀ · · ·

"How did you know," Val Con said, as they walked across the lawns, "that any of our former colleagues had chosen well—and survived the choice?"

"I did not," Rys said. His steps were soft on the dry grass, but not quite silent. "My grandmother, however, tells me that she has seen five shadows against a conflagration. As she had previously predicted a long and perilous journey on my behalf, my understanding is that four survived the choice."

"Your understanding is...good. But there is no need for you to endanger yourself."

"No? Who, then, will lead them? Yourself?"

"My...let us say, *my hope* was that, among us *six* we might come up with a course of action to be carried out by four. My best part is to stay in the Department's eye, and demonstrate that Korval defends itself nearly—and nothing more."

"I agree," Rys said promptly. "Misdirection is vital. Draw their eyes, and give us time to close."

"Close upon what, I wonder? The Commander?"

"That I will know better when we five have laid our plans."

"Not six?"

"No..." A flash of black eyes. "Consider that *you* are the final hope. If we all five should fall, then must Korval act, and completely. The reasoning that drove the strike upon Liad was firmly based upon necessity. The Department must be stopped—not for us who have already been captured, and tortured, and escaped as something other than ever we were meant to be.

"But it is not too late for your daughter, or for mine. Our care must be for them."

"I concur," Val Con said and, after a moment, "Have you a daughter, Rys?"

"She will be born soon. The *kompani* wants her and will care for her, but—should there be need, Brother, I solicit your kindness for her and for her mother. My daughter's name is Maysl. Her mother is Droi."

"I will care for them as if they were my own."

He felt a pressure on his arm and looked down to find Rys gripping him lightly with the metal hand.

"I could hope for nothing better."

They had come to the crack in the world, and Rys knelt to place his natural hand along the rift.

"This needs fill," he said.

"So we have done. The soil continues to settle, as does the House."

"Both will come even, eventually," Rys said, and rose, dusting his hand off against his thigh, his gaze moving over the tidy garden patch along.

"That's well-placed. However, I do not see vines."

"Patience. Perhaps they are around the other side of the house. Or behind the barn. Mr. Shaper is not . . . always tolerant of visitors, and I do not have free run of his land."

"How do we proceed, then?"

"We will follow the path—you see it?—and we will keep our hands at all times in sight. We do not molest the cats, though doubtless we shall achieve an escort. If we come so far as the house without a hail, I will mount the doorstone and state our business. If that fails to elicit a response, we will return exactly in the style in which we arrived."

"I understand," said Rys, and followed him as he stepped over the line onto Yulie Shaper's land.

They followed the path 'round the garden patch, and Val Con had just bent his head to go under the laden tree limb when the first shot rang out.

· · · ✳ · · ·

"Captain, we have a personnel issue."

Miri looked up at Nelirikk, thought about Lizzie up in the nursery. The quiet *peaceful* nursery where she could rest her head and not think about anything more complicated than did Lizzie need her belly rubbed.

"Continue," she said.

"Yes, Captain. Jeeves reports that Hazenthull Explorer killed a civilian in the port today, in protection of her partner, who then ran away from the scene, after giving Hazenthull his service gun with explicit instructions to return it to Commander Lizardi, with his resignation. Instead of following these instructions, she chose instead to cover her now-ex-partner's back as he made good his escape, killing one more civilian, and in the process sustaining wounds which, unless treated immediately, are thought to be life-threatening."

Miri blinked, took a breath and ran the Scout's Rainbow, which helped, a little, with her headache.

"Where is Hazenthull now, and in what condition?"

"She is aboard *Tarigan*, in the autodoc. Jeeves confirms that her former partner is the same Tollance Berik-Jones he vouched for as a suitable pilot and backup for his daughter, Tocohl. The pilots intend to lift on time, as they consider their mission urgent. Pilot Tocohl offers to put Hazenthull Explorer off at a safe port, once she is fully healed of her injuries, and a Korval ship may then pick her up."

Miri sighed.

Despite her mass, and her attitude, Hazenthull was the most fragile of Korval's three former Yxtrang corps. Diglon Rifle had taken to Surebleak with a wide delight in everything. He was a sponge for learning things—any and *every*thing—and it was beginning to look like he'd never met a stranger.

Nelirikk was secure in his position as captain's aide, and he'd managed to stretch out into other areas, including road construction, as needed. Of course Nelirikk was an Explorer—close enough to being a Scout, except a little less prone, in Miri's observation, to getting into trouble.

Hazenthull, though—she'd been an Explorer, but junior. And she'd screwed up bad, ultimately costing her team leader his life. She had a session or two with Anthora, which had helped some, but she hadn't made any connections outside of Korval, and specifically, Korval's little troop of former Yxtrang...

...until Tollance Berik-Jones, whose back she'd covered even after he'd officially resigned as her partner.

"Do the experts think that Hazenthull will impede their mission?" she asked.

Nelirikk didn't answer, but Jeeves did, his voice emanating from the ceiling.

"Mr. Berik-Jones gives it as his opinion that *Haz is a good one to have on your side in a fight*. Tocohl gives it as her opinion that, since they are bound for regions where fights seem more, rather than less, likely, Hazenthull could be a welcome addition to the mission."

Right.

Miri nodded.

"Let her go, then. Keep me updated regarding her condition. I wanna hear real soon that she's outta the 'doc and healed. If there are complications, then the mission will allow itself to be diverted to a hospital."

"Yes, Miri," Jeeves said. "Transmitting now . . . Tocohl agrees to these terms."

"Great. Anything else?"

"No, Miri."

"No, Captain."

"Then, if you please, gentlemen, I'm going upstairs to visit my daughter."

CHAPTER THIRTY

. . . .

Shaper's Freehold
Surebleak

THEY WENT TO GROUND AS ONE BEING, DIVING FOR COVER beneath the tree.

Another shot came, some distance away, followed by a string of Surebleakean curses.

Rys shifted beside Val Con, as if he were preparing to move in that direction. Val Con put a hand on Rys's arm and shook his head slightly.

It had not been Yulie Shaper's voice, cursing; thinking back on it, he was fairly certain that it had not been Yulie Shaper's gun.

He squeezed Rys's arm and tipped his head to the right, toward the house. Rys nodded, and Val Con moved off, not on the path, but near it; Rys, soundless now, followed.

Val Con paused before they came within sight of the house. Crouching among the shadows and the green things, he listened closely, but all he heard was the wind in the leaves and among the grasses, and then a rough whisper in his ear.

"C'mon back from there, the both of you."

His arm shot out to grab Rys—not an instant too soon. His brother did not know Yulie Shaper's voice, and he had begun to turn, metal arm rising.

"Come," Val Con breathed. "This is Mr. Shaper."

He eased back, deeper into the leaves, until his foot struck a wooden curb, which he climbed over, and dropped a little distance into a dirt pit. An instant later Rys had joined him on the ground, facing Yulie Shaper, who was sitting with his back against a large rock, a rifle across his knees.

"You *with* them?" he hissed. "Sleet, no; you *can't* be with them. You're with the New Boss. You *are* a New Boss…"

Yulie's eyes were wide, and his whisper ragged, but he was steady; no shaking, no hiding his face or his eyes. If anything, Val Con thought, he was a little too firm in making eye contact.

"I am not with them, whoever they are," Val Con said softly. "I had brought my brother Rys over to meet you. We heard gunfire, and curses, and feared for your safety."

"That's neighborly." Yulie gave Rys a hard stare and a short nod. Rys gave him the nod back, and said nothing.

"What has happened here?" Val Con asked.

"Well, I come back from taking them grapes up to Mrs. ana'Tak, an' there was cars in front the house, an' a crew in my dooryard. Was on my way to tell 'em to get the sleet offa my land, an' one of 'em kicks in the door, and starts yelling m'name and tellin' me to come on out, so I ducked back and got my spare from where I keep it, an' settled here to see what else they'd do. Ain't nothin' much t'steal, an' I was willin' to let 'em have what they took, s'long's they didn't hurt the cats…"

He shook his head, sharp, as if recalling himself to the topic.

"Anyways, I hear 'em talk, and they're here deliberate, looking for the growin' rooms, down under. They got a machine tells 'em what's down under in general ways. I don't think they know about the rooms. If they did, they'd've used the control board, 'steada just followin' the beeps on their machine, round to main door."

He grinned suddenly, and unnervingly. "Same door they busted before. Won't be so easy this time; that Tan Ort, he fixed 'er up good."

"Still, we would not wish Tan Ort's work to go to waste," Val Con said. "Perhaps we can stop them, now."

Yulie Shaper shook his head. "There's six, eight of 'em. I can shoot that many, but then I'd hafta bury 'em. 'S'why I was thinkin' to get to the controls, inside, an' throw on the defenses. Left somebody in the house, though, an' they're sure to hear if I shoot." He tipped his head, as another round of gunfire and cursing reached them.

"The defenses," Rys said, speaking for the first time. "They will harm the grapes?"

"Liked them, did you? No, what'll hurt the grapes, an' the coffee, an' the whole rest of it is if that crew busts through the outside locks and upset the microclimes."

"The grapes must not be harmed," Rys said. "I will engage to disable the watcher in the house so that you may turn on the defenses. Val Con will go around the back and ensure that the locks do not take harm while we do our part."

Yulie looked doubtful.

"You're a likely lookin' boy, but that's a big fella they left. You sure you can take him?"

Rys glanced down at the ground, and picked up a rock by his knee. He held out his gleaming golden hand, the rock resting in the palm, closed his fingers, and opened them.

Dust sullied his palm. He wiped it clean on his trousers.

"That'll do," Yulie said, as another shot echoed. "Let's get on with it, then."

· · · ✳ · · ·

Derik had set Rista to guarding the perimeter, which meant he was getting her outta the way of the real bidness. That was all right by her; she was only on the team on account of she could read the machine. She could shoot, but she didn't like to, so she wasn't any kind of use at all when it come down to cases, which, when Derik was running the gig, it usually did.

So, Rista went out back, with her gun that she wouldn't use, anyway, and watched while first Jorner, and then Rosy, and then Derik himself banged themselfs against the sealed door, then took to shooting at it.

That made her extra glad to be guarding everything from way *over there*, 'cause there was ricochets—Rosy got his hair parted for 'im, and Jorner got his arm grazed, none o'which put them in better humor, and there started to be talk about just goin' back up the house and waitin' 'til that old farmer showed up.

Rista had a little niggling worry about where the farmer was. Farmers farmed, right? Stood to reason. So, where was he, exactly? Hard to tell, with all this *green*; you couldn't see things clear. Not like down the city, where you could get a good long look at something four blocks away.

Point was, he—the farmer—could be standing anywhere, hidden by the leaves, and none of them, with their city eyes, would ever even see 'im. Sleet, he could just stand there, hidden, and pick 'em all off one by one.

All right, *that* made her shiver.

"I say we use Rance's toy," Rosy said. "Ain't no door built gonna stand up to that."

"Might break whatever's on the other side," Derik said, which you might s'pose to be some pretty clear thinkin' on Derik's part 'less you knew that Mr. Neuhaus had told him specific not to break anything that was inside the underneath place. Derik paid close attention to Mr. Neuhaus.

"Ain't nothing on t'other side," Rosy said, which he couldn't know, and Mort stuck in that if there weren't nothin' on the other side, what was it locked up so tight for?

It was right then that Rista saw something move in the green across the way. The tall leaves kinda shivered, and there was a man there, when there hadn't been one.

He was wearing a green and silver coat that shimmered, sort of, in the torchlight, and there was a big ring on his hand, which is how Rista knew who it was.

The Road Boss.

"I believe you would be best served," he said, in a soft voice that didn't have no problem carrying to all of them, judging by the way they spun and cussed. "I believe you would be best served by standing away from the door, and putting your guns and...other equipment on the ground."

"Best served, yeah?" Derik raised his gun. "Open this door, you."

"I am unable to do so," the Road Boss said.

Derik looked around. Rosy had his gun on the Road Boss, and Mort did, and Jorner, too. "Looks to me like you're outnumbered. Whyn't you come right here and open this door? I'm askin' nice, but I won't ask again."

The air crackled suddenly, and kinda fizzed. Tiny sparks swirled in the air like snowflakes.

"Run!" the Road Boss yelled, and Rista's legs moved all by themselves and she was running away from the doors and the Road Boss and the rest of her crew, her back to all of it.

She heard a huge *snap* behind her; a blue flash dazzled her eyes. But she kept running, and she didn't look back.

· · · ❄ · · ·

"Well, I don't use it," Yulie explained, very nearly sounding sheepish. "No reason to use it; nobody comes looking for the growin' rooms. Nobody knows the growin' rooms're there."

"Until now," Val Con said.

The flash of the defense system coming live had roused Jeeves to action. It had barely faded when Nelirikk and Diglon arrived on the scene. They'd trussed up the unconscious prisoners and carefully emptied their pockets. Nelirikk called the Watch, and he and Diglon stood guard while Val Con trudged up to the house, running his hands through his hair to dislodge any stray twigs and grasses that might have lodged there while he was rolling away from the pressure door. The coat, he feared, was ruined. He hoped Miri hadn't become very fond of it.

Yulie sighed. "Guess I'm gonna have to keep it goin', then. Generator's good for a couple hunnert years, that's what Grampa figured, and I do the service, just like it says in the binder."

"Why keep it turned off, then?" Rys asked.

"Well, the cats. Cats don't have good sense 'bout things, sometimes."

"True," Val Con said. "Perhaps a perimeter device may be constructed. Shall I send Tan Ort to you? He may have something to suggest."

Yulie pursed his lips, and stared at the man trussed up in ropes like a piglet in the middle of his kitchen floor.

"When he's got a minute or two to spare," he said to Val Con. "Smart as he is, he just might be able to figure something out."

"I will ask him to come to you, then."

"The grapes," Rys said, into the small silence that followed this, "have taken no harm?"

Yulie shook his head.

"Really like them grapes, do you? I can give you s'many as you want."

"Do not say that to him," Val Con warned. "He's a vintner."

"Is he?" Yulie looked at Rys with renewed interest. "Maybe you could make wine outta them grapes. Good way to store 'em."

Rys smiled at him. "Indeed; an excellent way to store them."

"Reminds me..." Yulie crossed the kitchen and pulled open a cabinet, taking down a rather hefty utility binder. He flipped it open and leafed through the pages, until he suddenly nodded and brought the binder to the table.

"That piece o'paper you brought down here? 'Member that?"

"Yes," Val Con said.

"Well, I looked it up, right here, an' it says that land your brother"—he looked up and nodded at Rys—"that brother?"

"I have several brothers, I fear. The brother who is interested is away from home at the moment, and asked me to handle this business for him. Shan, his name is."

"Right, then. Well, 'cordin' to the binder, here, that land is where the Commissary Supply Whole Planet Foods was planned to go, when everything was set up and the company did its expansion, 'cept the company left and didn't expand, so there wasn't no need for the second one. An' why Grampa's name's on that lease is that him an' Gramma was in the bidness together, evens."

He closed the book and nodded.

"Your brother Shan, he wants that land, he can have it. Never did get the 'quipment down for the second Commissary. That was in expansion money. Might be they started on excavating for the growin' rooms, but maybe not. No sense to it, 'til you got the 'quipment."

"Mr. Shaper, I feel very strongly that my brother will wish to compensate you correctly for the land—your inheritance, after all!—and to write a contract listing out what each side gives and gains, so that there is no confusion."

Yulie closed the binder and shrugged.

"He wants to do all that, fine. 'S'long as he takes care of the contract-writing. Makes him feel better to give me somethin', he can give whatever he wants. I don't need nothin', and you been a good neighbor. Can't buy that."

Val Con took a deep breath and let it out as the sound of a car turning into the dooryard reached him.

"The Watch," Rys said from the door.

"'Bout time," said Yulie Shaper.

· · · ❊ · · ·

Droi had spent her day among the dreams of ancients, searching for a communication protocol. The old indexing systems were not necessarily accurate; consequently, her search had not been a quick one.

It was, however, eventually fruitful, which filled her with an unreasonable sense of pride. Pulka had praised her skill, which meant something, for Pulka was not nearly so generous with his praise as he was with his criticisms.

Not that she cared what Pulka thought.

The dreaming had left her exhausted; the older dreams were not always easy to understand, and when the thing that was wanted was specific, the search was made more taxing.

All that being so, her head and back hurt, and her stomach was unsettled. She sat alone by her hearth, and thought of lying down to sleep, but she was far too tired to do so.

"Good evening, daughter," the *luthia* spoke from near at hand. "May I share your hearth?"

A request from the *luthia* to share the hearth was no request at all. That the *luthia* had come, of herself, to Droi's hearth, rather than calling Droi to her—that was . . . notable.

So.

She pulled her scattered wits to her and sat up straighter.

"Please sit with me, Grandmother. I will fetch tea."

There was no tea made; she had been too tired even for that. But the *luthia* at her hearth . . .

"Peace, child. I brought tea, and something for us to share, if you will eat with me."

Droi shivered, and patted the rug at her side.

"Please," she said again. "I welcome your company."

Silain came forward, and placed the basket she carried before folding stiffly onto the blanket.

"Ah," she sighed, and used her chin to point. "Serve us, daughter."

Droi opened the basket, poured tea from the pot into two battered mugs from Silain's own hearth. She untied the rag, and spread it between them, revealing soft, fresh rolls, and creamy squares of cheese, with some unfamiliar green berries that smelled salty and sharp.

"Kezzi's mother in the City Above now and then sends a basket, to honor a grandmother."

That was well done. All that Droi had heard of Kezzi's mother in the City Above spoke of a strong woman who was also courteous and modest. The changes, subtle, but powerful, in Kezzi's dress and manner also spoke of the influence of a wise woman. Kezzi herself said that her brother Syl Vor's mother was a *luthia*.

"I find you alone," Silain said, after they had sipped their tea, and each had chosen a soft roll with a bit of cheese. "I hear, from others of my children and grandchildren, that Droi is often alone, and I wonder, my daughter, if this is a passing season, brought to you by the child?"

"Grandmother, it may be so. I . . . frighten my brothers and my sisters, and, sometimes . . . I frighten myself. It seems best to be alone, except when I am useful to the *kompani*."

"The Bedel say that we are of use because we are the Bedel. We need do nothing else except be who we are, for we are beloved of the universe."

This was a thing that the Bedel did say, and thus there was nothing to say to it. Droi sipped her tea, finding a thread of sweetness. She sipped again, seeking the flavor again, and savoring it. Her tongue, *luthia*-trained, found it to be *feenil*, which was given to strengthen a pregnancy.

She looked up, her heart in her mouth.

"Grandmother?"

"Peace, it is only an old woman's meddling. It will do good, if there is good to be done; and no harm, if not."

She plucked one of the green fruits up, and put it in her mouth, eating it with every appearance of enjoyment.

"This desire to be of use," she said. "I saw that in you when you were my apprentice. It seems to me a good thing; and one shared by all who would become *luthia*."

"And yet," Droi said, her tongue perhaps loosened by the *feenil*, "I am not fit to be *luthia*."

Silain looked up, surprise in her face. She leaned forward and grasped Droi's hand between both of hers.

"Droi. Daughter. You are more than fit to be *luthia*. That you should think otherwise—I am ashamed."

"You set me aside, Grandmother!"

"I did, yes. For this *kompani*, in this time, you would be the wrong *luthia*, which is far different than being no *luthia* at all."

"What difference, when there is only this *kompani*, and this time?"

Silain smiled. She patted Droi's hand, and let her go.

"Time flows, bringing changes. But, enough. You are tired, and the *feenil* is working. I have come to you with a purpose. In the City Above, there are two wise women who seek to bring together the several families of *gadje* into one family."

Droi sniffed, disdainfully. "It is not possible."

"I think that it might be," Silain said. "I don't think it will be easy, but these are strong women, with determined hearts. In order to do their best in the task they have set themselves, they need to understand what this world was meant to be. We, the *kompani*, hold dreams from an earlier time which might help them."

"You would give the *gadje* our dreams?" Droi raised her hand to cover a yawn.

"No, for, as they admit, they are not dreamers. I have said that you will help them. You will go to them, and they will tell you what they seek. Then, you will dream and bring to them those things that will aid them."

Silain paused to sip tea, and added, gently, "You would be of use, daughter."

It might have been the *feenil*, or it might have been curiosity, to see these *gadje* wise women who sought to heal a world with dreams.

"I will go to them."

"Good. Udari will guide you, when you are ready."

She wanted to protest, but surely the *feenil* was at work.

"Yes, Grandmother," she said, and raised her hand before another yawn.

"I will see you to your bed," Silain said. "Kezzi will make the hearth orderly, and sleep in the tent tonight."

She rose, docile as a child, leaving the remains of the meal and the tea. She took her grandmother's hand, and together they went into the tent.

Later, comforted by blankets, and drowsy with warmth, she heard her name spoken, and looked up into Silain's eyes.

"I have a thing for you, child," the *luthia* said. She brought forth a chain, and on it, a set of tiles in that pattern that denoted a personal history.

The *feenil* softened the pain; but it did nothing to blur her Sight.

"Rys?" she whispered. "He has left us ... already?"

"Time flows," Silain crooned, "fast and slow." She bent and slipped the chain around Droi's neck, tucking the tiles close.

"Keep it safe," she murmured, and lay her hand across Droi's eyes.

"Sleep," she said, and Droi tumbled headlong into darkness.

INTERLUDE TEN

. . . .

Vivulonj Prosperu
In Transit

COOL AIR STROKED HER FACE, THE SCENT OF MINT TINGLED IN her nose; somewhere, a chime sounded, soft and continuous.

Her right hand rested on a hard, slick surface; her left on chilly flesh. She swallowed, tasting more mint, and opened her eyes.

Above her, a bright white ceiling, partly occluded by the curve of an opaque black hood.

She considered it placidly, waiting...

"Good day to you, Pilot."

The voice—was somewhat familiar. She turned her head, and raised her eyes.

A man stood beside the place where she lay. His face, like his voice, was somewhat familiar. She had seen him, she thought, not too very long ago.

A name slipped into her waiting mind.

"Uncle Arin?"

Eyebrows lifted.

"Uncle," he agreed. "Arin long ago took his own path."

There seemed nothing to say to that, so she waited some more, beginning to be cold now, and slightly less placid.

"Would you care to exit the unit?" asked the man named Uncle. "There are clothes, here. In the antechamber, there are tea and sandwiches. I give you my word that these things are untainted, and will do you no harm."

317

It did come to her, then, that this man was not always trust-worthy. However, there seemed no utility in lying naked in the cool, mint-scented breeze, and she was, she realized, very hungry.

"I will rise, and dress," she said. "And then I will eat."

At this, he bowed, and withdrew from her ken, to the ante-chamber, she supposed.

She rolled slowly off the mat and stood, finding carpet beneath bare feet, and a sweater and slacks folded over a nearby chair. Ordinary ship clothes, save for the lack of boots, or soft shoes. There was no mirror, which was unfortunate, since she recalled, as if it had happened a very long time ago, that Daav had been... quite badly hurt. Of course, Uncle had placed them in the autodoc, so apparently the body had not been beyond hope of help. But how odd, she thought, reaching for the sweater, that she should have awoken ascendant.

Her peace... rippled, then, as if a placid pond had been dis-turbed by the passage of a cold breeze.

Where was Daav?

The conditions of her existence for so many years had been... enclosed by Daav. She, least of anyone, knew where, or how, she existed within her lifemate's brain, but exist she did.

Always before there had been a sense of Daav about her, even when she was ascendant and he asleep. Now...

Her sense *now* was that... she was alone. The inside of her head felt airy and light, as if she were newly arrived, and had not yet left thoughts cluttering the tabletops, or rustling in dark corners.

Indeed, there were no dark corners, as she perceived her con-dition.

She took a deep breath of cool, minty air, and looked down.

Small, high breasts, a girl's flat belly, sweet, unused feet with pearly nails.

This was not the body she shared with Daav. This was—

The man called Uncle was a clone, she recalled suddenly. He was impossibly old, having serially transferred *himself*—his per-sonality and at least some of his long memory—into new bodies for hundreds of years; Cantra's Diaries would have it that he had embraced the practice even before the Migration.

She was shivering and panting as if she had run from Solcintra to Chonselta. The mint-flavored air suddenly nauseated and cloyed.

Hand trembling, peace shattered, she caught up the waiting

clothes and pulled them on. Behind her was an unsealed door. She marched through it into a small chamber where a table was set with teapot and cups, and plates with tiny sandwiches in the shapes of fish and flowers. There were two chairs at the table. The man named Uncle was not in either of them, though he was standing behind one.

At her entrance, he raised both of his hands, as if he would soothe her.

"Please, Pilot."

"Please?" she retorted, but the edge of her fear was gone, evaporating in the scent of mint.

She stepped forward and frowned up into his face. "Are you calming me?" she demanded.

"I am, and I beg you will forgive it. My excuse is that your anger, fully experienced, might endanger your lifemate's existence."

She froze at that, and quickly ran the Scout's Rainbow, for inner calm.

Uncle smiled.

"Where is Daav?" she asked then, though her stomach clambered for one or even four of the pretty little sandwiches.

"He sleeps in a unit much like the one from which you have just now arisen. His danger is not so acute that you cannot eat. In fact, I must insist that you eat, Pilot. Your new situation is extremely efficient, but it does require sustenance. You must also reacquaint yourself with food. Please."

She sat, and he did. He poured tea into her cup, and into his. She thanked him with a nod, picked up one of the fish-shaped sandwiches and bit into it.

Sensation flooded her mouth, overwhelming all of her senses, whiting her vision. She may have cried out. When the flavors had faded, and she knew herself again, she reached for her cup—and thought better of it.

"You gave your word," she said to Uncle.

"I did, and it is good. You are unharmed. You are also . . . new. It will take you some time to accommodate yourself to ordinary sensation. Please, Pilot. Drink your tea and have another sandwich. Your lifemate needs you strong and able."

The tea was blessedly uncomplex, after which the second sandwich produced a lesser overload. She managed a third with hardly any interference at all, and drained her cup to the dregs.

"I will see Daav now," she said, and the Uncle rose at once. "This way, Pilot."

The room was the twin of the room she had wakened in, dominated by what was perhaps *not* an autodoc, with a chair set in one corner, holding, as had the chair in her room, a simple set of ship clothes.

"You must understand," Uncle said quietly, "that, in the case, we had material to work with, and thus he looks...*like himself,* you might say, though perhaps younger than you have known him. Yourself..." He looked down at her. "We used the vessel to hand—a *blank,* we term it. My experience is that you will eventually come to look more as you had done, previously, as the body takes its cues from the personality. I will tell you that *you* are fully transferred, and we experienced no difficulty whatsoever in the process. Your Daav, however..." He moved a hand, inviting her to step closer to the unit.

The unit with its red-lit readouts and—startlingly familiar— standard life-gauge, showing a blue bar hovering at well below half, a cat's whisker above *nonviable.*

"He lives because I insist that he do so," Uncle said quietly behind her. "If I withdraw my hand, he will die. Almost, he did die. It frightens me, how close he came."

Stomach stone-cold, she turned to face him.

"Why do you care?"

"My dear Pilot Caylon, do you think that I wish to anger Korval by allowing the death of one of their treasured elders, when it lies within my power to preserve him? He can live. He can *want* to live. I think—I believe—that you can give him that."

She swallowed, thinking. The air in this room tasted sharp, like ozone, and it cleared her head wonderfully.

"Did you wake him?" she asked.

Uncle bowed.

"I did, for he was ready first, and I saw that having him alert and informed for your own awakening would be to the benefit of all. Alas, I misjudged. No sooner had the lid risen then he cried out, and the readings plummeted."

"You should not have waked him without me," she said sharply. "I swore to him that I would not leave him alone. He would have felt my absence immediately and known that I was foresworn, and he, abandoned..."

She shook her head, deliberately relaxing hands that had curled into fists.

"But, there," she said, more moderately. "You could not have known that, after all."

She looked again at the status lights, reading death and disaster there.

"Wake him," she said, not bothering to look at their host.

"Wake him, and then leave us."

CHAPTER THIRTY-ONE

Jelaza Kazone
Surebleak

REN ZEL FELT THE REGARD OF ETERNITY, AND LONGED TO embrace it.

No, he told himself, and rolled over in the bed he shared with his lifemate, plumped the pillow, and closed his eyes, breathing deeply in a pilot's relaxation exercise.

Golden threads glimmered behind his closed eyelids. His mouth went dry with longing.

Another breath, another exercise, this one meant to center one to a purpose. He assigned as his purpose a *restful sleep*, sighed—

And was bolt-upright in the next instant, a cry trapped between tongue and lips.

He was hot and shaking, his stomach roiling, and it would be *so easy*, only to allow himself to open his eyes in that other place, where all was perfect and orderly, and the life-force of the universe flowed through him.

No, he told himself again, but his resolve was weak. He needed all his defenses, now. He dared not weaken them by trying, again, to sleep.

He slid out of bed, listening—*not* reaching for the thread that bound them, but only . . . listening, with human ears, to the gentle sound of his lifemate, breathing.

At least he hadn't wakened Anthora. There was no reason for both of them to go sleepless.

323

Silent on bare feet, he walked across their bedroom, plucking his robe up as he passed the chest at the bottom of the bed.

He slipped it on and tied the belt as he crossed their parlor to the door, slid it open and stepped out onto the patio.

Overhead, the sky displayed its sparse starfield, and Chuck-Honey lay low on the horizon. Below, the darkness was more liberally sprinkled with stars, as the night bloomers opened. Beyond, the tree itself glowed, suffusing the pathways and the gloan-roses with a soft light.

Ren Zel breathed in, seeking virtue from the tree-informed air. And, indeed, a certain calmness fell upon him. Enough so he could put the compulsion at a distance, and think what he must do.

For he must do something. As easy as it would be, to succumb to compulsion, that choice was not open to him. Not yet.

He wished that he knew... when. How long, but, really—what matter? The compulsion was wily; it waited until he was at his most vulnerable, then offered itself. If—

"Ren Zel?"

He turned from the railing, heart-struck.

"Beloved, I did not mean to wake you!"

"And, yet, you are awake yourself." She slipped onto the balcony, the collar of her robe askew, her sash half-tied, her hair sleep-tousled and tumbling about her face and shoulders.

"Is it the compulsion again?" she asked him, slipping her hand into his, and pressing against his side.

He sighed.

"It is. I... doubt I am strong enough to withstand the universe."

Anthora looked up at him, then over his shoulder to the garden, and the Tree.

"It is recorded in the Diaries that, before the death of her body, Rool Tiazan's lady anchored him to the world through her own essence."

He stared at her, breath-caught at what she was suggesting.

"You would share the addiction. You would share my death, if it comes to that. Anthora—"

"I would share your life, for so long as you have it," she interrupted sharply, and sighed, pressing even more tightly against him. "Beloved," she said, her voice soft, now, "at least let us try."

It would not answer. He knew—his gift, and the golden threads that tied everything together—*they* knew that he could destroy her with a thought. What was one woman's life to a man who might unmake the universe?

And yet... she offered relief. A burden shared was a burden halved, after all.

Perhaps... perhaps it *would* answer.

For long enough.

He put his arms around her and lay his cheek against her warm, disordered hair.

"I am in your hands, Beloved. Do with me what you will."

· · · ✳ · · ·

Rys had left them, having reviewed the dossiers of each of his four teammates. It had pleased him, to have a director among them; and pleased him even more to find what it was she had discovered.

"Brother, we will prevail," Val Con said, as they embraced.

"I do not doubt it," Rys had answered, which had been, not quite, a lie.

Then Rys was gone, the car on its way down the drive, and Val Con weeping where he stood, in Surebleak's wan sunshine, until he had shaken himself into order and come here, to the music room.

"Jeeves," he said quietly. He was alone, and though he had seated himself on the bench behind the omnichora, he had not brought the instrument live.

"Yes, Master Val Con," the butler's voice emanated from the ceiling, which was well enough, Val Con thought, for this.

"I wonder," he said, "why you chose to give Tocohl my foster-mother's voice?"

There was a small hesitation, as if the question had surprised, which it may have done.

"It had been my observation, during the time I was privileged to know her," Jeeves said slowly, "that Anne Davis was able to cast calm upon, may I say, *overheated situations,* merely by speaking. Analysis indicates that it was not necessarily the content of her comments—which was often quite commonplace—but the timbre and resonance of her voice. As Tocohl was specifically traveling into an overheated situation, I thought it best to give her a tried and tested tool."

Another pause; this one very short.

"Have I offended, sir?"

Val Con sighed.

"No offense," he said. "Merely, I was taken by surprise, and...
made somewhat nostalgic. Thank you, Jeeves."

He turned on the bench, and pressed the switch that brought
the omnichora to life.

His fingers whispered gently over the keys, waking a wispy,
whispering rendition of "Toccata and Fugue in D Minor," one of
his foster-mother's favorite pieces. She had taught him to play the
'chora, and she had taught him all of her favorite pieces, as well
as those which were not favorites, but which she granted a place
in her repertoire for reasons nearly as convoluted as those that
might accompany the placing of an entry into a Liaden debt book.

He would, he thought, teach Talizea to play, when she was older.
If she showed an interest. He would teach her Anne's favorite
pieces and those which were not favorites, and he would tell her
stories of her Terran grandmother, building onto those stories
that Father and Mother would doubtless tell, of their clan-sister,
who had been the first to stretch Korval's boundaries, and make
them...other...than merely Liaden.

For the story of their arrival on Surebleak began with Er Thom
yos'Galan, who had brought a Terran lifemate into the House.

It was, Val Con thought, adjusting the stops and allowing
the sound to build, a shame that Anne had not lived to see the
clan's relocation.

He thought she would have been amused.

· · · ✹ · · ·

"I am for the single strike, the target which we all know. That
is surest, and we four can well encompass the task," Bon Vit said.

"It is a flawed strategy," Vazineth countered. "As we have seen.
It leaves too many at large, with only their last orders to guide
them. We must—"

"We must," Sye Mon interrupted, "recall that we are all accustomed to working alone. There lies our strength. If a single strike
is flawed, four coordinated strikes may..."

"Merely confound for a moment," Claidyne spoke wearily. "We
cannot eradicate the Department in four single strikes—not in forty.
The eradication of the Department must be our goal. And that,
my friends, can only be done from within the command center."

"Four compromised agents, who had been held by Korval?" Bon
Vit asked. "An Yxtrang has a better chance of infiltrating Command."

"Not—" Claidyne began, and spun, dropping into a fighting crouch, as the door to their private parlor opened wide.

A man paused in the doorway to look at each of them in turn. He seemed quite ordinary, with a full head of curly black hair, and wearing the same dark sweater and tough canvas pants as the rest of them. He had a leather bag slung over one shoulder, and when he saw that they had seen him, and that those who had been ready to fight had relaxed, he finished his entrance, letting the door swing closed behind him.

Gently, he bowed to the room, and straightened, hands where they could both be seen. One was broad and businesslike; the other a graceful confection of woven golden metals.

"I am Rys Lin pen'Chala," he said, in the mode of comrade-to-comrade. He had an outworld accent, though which outworld was not immediately apparent. "I had been a senior field agent. Now, I am my own man, and I wish, as was said a moment gone, for the eradication of the Department. It was I who gave Korval the means to free you to yourselves."

None doubted him. None *could* doubt him, seeing him there, with the mark of the Department on him, plain enough for those who suffered likewise to see.

"There are *five* of us?" Bon Vit demanded.

Rys Lin pen'Chala turned slightly to face him.

"There are six of us. The sixth remains apart, to act as diversion, and to stand as the last hope of our children, should we five fail of a successful completion."

"We will not fail!" said Sye Mon, and Rys Lin pen'Chala smiled gently upon him.

"So I believe, as well," he said, and moved forward, to set his case upon a table, and to sit down in one of the several chairs.

"Come," he said, "sit with me and let us hear what each has in our minds."

"You have already heard it," Claidyne said, realizing now that he had been in the doorway for some time before he had allowed them to perceive him.

"I had heard some of it, but I would like to hear all," he said, and moved his golden hand, showing her the chair nearest him.

"Come, sit down. Let us talk together."

They hesitated. Then Bon Vit came forward, shoving a chair near to the newcomer, and sat down.

"Bon Vit Onida," he said, with a nod.

"Vazineth ser'Trishan," she said, placing the second chair at Bon Vit's right.

"Sye Mon van'Kie." His chair went next to Vazineth, and there was only one chair remaining, at Rys Lin pen'Chala's left, which he had already marked for hers.

Claidyne sat, keeping herself centered. She met his space-black eyes and inclined her head.

"Claidyne ven'Orikle," she said shortly.

"Yes," he answered, with a small smile. He looked 'round the circle, and nodded to Bon Vit.

"If you please, let us hear your plan."

"I have the coordinates for Secondary Headquarters," Bon Vit said promptly. "A concerted, serious strike there will destroy the Commander and the base." He sat back and nodded to Vazineth.

"A single strike—" she began, and stopped when Rys Lin pen'Chala moved his gleaming hand.

"Plans first, if you please. Discussions after. There is no shame, if you do not have a plan, merely allow the topic to go to the next in circle."

Vazineth sighed.

"I have no plan," she said, and looked at Sye Mon.

"My plan is similar to Bon Vit's," he said, "only I have the recall codes for the old machines that have been deployed. Once they are gathered in one place, we may destroy them."

Rys nodded and looked to Claidyne.

She took a breath, glanced 'round the circle, and felt the familiar urge to hide her knowledge from all of them, and most especially from herself.

The utter destruction of the Department, she reminded herself. *That is your last and your only desire.*

She took another breath, and looked up, seeking Rys Lin pen'Chala's eyes. He did not look away, he did not urge her to speak. He only waited, calm and quiet.

His calmness eased her; she inclined her head and spoke.

"I have the location of the quaternary transfer point. I have the entry codes. We can replace the current Commander of Agents with...one of our number. We can do an orderly shutdown of the network, disperse the operatives, and destroy the subsidiary command points."

INTERLUDE ELEVEN

....

Vivulonj Prosperu
In Transit

THE HOOD WAS RAISED; OZONE-TANGED AIR WAFTED UPWARD and was dispersed by the air cleaning system.

Aelliana looked down into a sharp-featured face that at once looked like Daav, and like no one she had ever met. His hair was dark, but very short. She leaned close and stroked it, feeling warm plush against her palm.

"Daav," she said, and touched his stark cheek. "Daav."

A sharp beep came from the board. Startled, she looked up, saw the blue line descending, into the danger zone, from which even the arts of Uncle could not restore him.

"No!" she cried sharply, and shoved her fist into her mouth before the next words—*Don't die!*—might escape. He would do what she told him to do; he had always done so, allowing for those eccentricities that made him peculiarly himself. Was she a goddess, to deny him death, if he wished for it? Surely, *surely*, he had borne enough, and she—she was his lifemate. She would be worthy of him.

She swallowed, blinked her eyes clear.

The blue line...had paused.

Her knees gave. She staggered, teeth indenting her fist, and collapsed to the edge of the cot.

Gods, gods, van'chela, don't leave me.

She did not say it; she *would not* demand it, though the pain of perhaps losing him was nearly more than she could bear.

However, she thought, her eyes on the panel, an explanation was surely in order. She would not have him die thinking that she had lied to him at the last.

She moved her fist from mouth to knee, and took a deep, careful breath.

"Daav," she said again, keeping her voice smooth. "Daav, it is Aelliana. We are separate once more, and appear to be in good order. I believe our situation is for the moment stable, and relatively benign. There are no active enemies within the scans. Your hurts have been healed, and you may take your chair at will."

She kept her eyes on the panel, hardly daring to breathe.

The blue line began to climb.

She stared up at it, unable to look away. Now and again, barely attending, she used the sleeve of her sweater to dry her cheeks.

The blue line continued its steady climb. One, two, three of the stranger red lights blinked out. Two others faded to orange.

She dared to close her eyes, then, and for the second time since waking, ran the Scout's Rainbow, for serenity, for it would not do to greet him in disorder.

When the Rainbow was run, and calm imposed, she opened her eyes, bent forward and stroked his face.

"Daav, it is Aelliana." Her fingers traced his lips, cold and firm. "Wake, do, and let me see you..."

She spared another swift glance at the board above him, glowing green and orange now, the blue line at the top of its measure. She sighed, and looked down...

...into a pair of sharp black eyes, over which strong brows were pulled together in puzzlement.

"Aelliana?" he murmured, and raised a hand to touch her cheek. "You appear to be...not quite yourself."

"So I am given to understand. But you must admit it to be quite a trick, that I appear at all."

His mouth twitched into a half-smile, even as he shivered, suddenly and comprehensively.

Aelliana caught her breath, and stood.

"Come, now!" she said briskly, reaching down to take his hand. "Let us get you up on your feet, and dressed in something warmer than the air!"

CHAPTER THIRTY-TWO

. . . .

Galandasti
Surebleak Orbit

"WHAT," QUIN ASKED, STARING AT THE SCREENS, "IS THAT?"

"Looks like a cruise ship to me," second board said, which he might have known she would do. Certainly, he had spent enough time in the company of Master Pilot Tess Lucien to gain a fairly accurate idea of her character.

"Yes," he said, patiently, "but what is it doing in orbit around Surebleak?"

"Maybe they need ice," she said, but she reached to the board and obligingly toggled the IDs.

"*Lalandia*, out of Moraldan?"

Quin frowned. Moraldan was a Liaden outworld with . . . pretensions. It was a favorite destination for the ne'er-do-wells and the disaffected. Over the years, those sorts had evolved their own hierarchy and society and dared to declare it superior to the homeworld's social climate. It had its own council—called the Moraldan House Council—but still seated a representative on the Council of Clans on Liad.

Moraldan dared not *quite* break all the way with Liad, for there was no likelihood of its making its own way; after all, it depended upon the homeworld for its comforts and luxuries. One or another of the clans who had seated themselves there could possibly have contrived to set up as traders, or at least negotiated with an existing firm to make it the official trade line of Moraldan.

However, that, Quin thought, would have been far too much like work. Work was not a Moraldan virtue.

"As to what it's doing here," said his copilot, having pulled *Lalandia's* packet, "they've come to observe Clan Korval's banishment."

"What?"

"See! The Emerald Casino, a gem of the first water, owned by Pat Rin yos'Phelium, himself a master gamester!" Tess read.

"Sample the pleasures on offer at Audrey's House of Joy, home to the most skilled *hetaera* on the planet!

"Walk the streets tamed by Boss Conrad.

"Tour the fabulous Jelaza Kazone, walk the inner gardens, and lay your hand upon the trunk of Korval's Tree!"

Tess shook her head.

"Guess Boss Conrad got himself a piece of the action."

Quin gasped, stung.

"My father is not a party to this!" he snapped, even as he wondered if Father was not only involved, but had hatched the scheme for some obscure reason of his own. Or, if *Uncle Val Con...*

"The Emerald and Audrey's House are open to anybody wants to come in the door," Tess pointed out. "Same like walking Conrad's turf. Nobody's gonna tell 'em to move on, 'less they're making a public nuisance."

"But Jelaza Kazone and the garden are not public places," Quin countered.

"So, Okay," Tess said. "Might be the Road Boss got some action outta it, then. Why not?"

Because Uncle Val Con would surely not open the clanhouse to strangers, nor the gardens...

But there his thoughts faltered. The relocation to Surebleak had been a strain on the clan's resources. And... Uncle Val Con had not done it, himself, but it had long *been* done that public rooms and the *front* garden were opened to the curious on viewing days—all of the Fifty Houses had done so, to display and enhance their *melant'i*.

In the case of Jelaza Kazone, which had no one save the caretakers living there, Grandmother had stood as host, and answered questions about the house and Korval's history.

Were finances so tight that Uncle Val Con would have negotiated with a cruise ship out of Moraldan for a percentage of the profits? It seemed at once like, and entirely unlike, him. What—

"*Galandasti*," came the voice of Surebleak Control, "we have your approach scheduled. See the figures we've supplied—plan is to put you in a low polar orbit for one go-round, have you drop in over the pole next time, direct to your south-end hotpad. All good with that?"

"All good," Tess said, at Quin's nod. "Thank you, Control."

· · · ✳ · · ·

They were in the ruckus room with Lizzie when the alarm sounded, and Jeeves's voice spoke quietly, but firmly, from the ceiling tiles.

"An unauthorized vehicle, containing in excess of eighteen persons is approaching the main gate from the Port Road. House Security declares a Level Two Emergency. Repeat: we have a Level Two Emergency. All staff remove to emergency positions, now. Children and cats to the secure rooms, now."

Miri looked at Val Con.

"Called that right," she said.

"If they believe they have purchased the right to tour the house and garden, why would they *not* come?"

"No reason, I guess. I just sort of hoped that we wouldn't have to do this." She shook her head. "They ain't bringing in excess of eighteen people up here in any town taxi, though. Where'd they find a bus?"

"Perhaps they brought it with them. Tours to frontier worlds often carry their own transport."

"Frontier world."

Miri sighed and came to her feet.

"Help me catch Lizzie and let's go throw some tourists out."

"I am perfectly capable of throwing tourists out," Val Con said, still sitting cross-legged on the floor, "if you would prefer not to be part of this."

"We agreed it had to be both of us when we first got wind of this thing. Besides, you knew I liked trouble when you married me," she told him, and blinked thoughtful grey eyes. "Point of fact, I got the specific idea that's *why* you married me."

"You have many qualities," he said, coming to his feet in one fluid unfolding.

"Nice dodge."

She walked to the right of the rug on which their daughter

had paused in her four-legged perambulation around the room, and Val Con swung to the left.

"Talizea," he said, teasingly.

She looked up and Miri swooped in. Lizzie shouted laughter, and Miri grinned as she settled the small body against her.

"While I must admit that both of us are regrettably fond of trouble, it seems to me that Talizea has a gentler, more reclusive nature. Perhaps she might wish to join her cousins in the basement?"

"Weren't you the one who told me it was never too early to start learning how to be delm?"

"Did I? That was inept of me."

"Water under the bridge. If she's gonna be throwing herself in front of busses as a regular thing, she might as well bag her first one now."

Val Con bowed lightly, accepting her judgment in this, again, and straightened.

"Jeeves," he said. "Please close the gate."

· · · ❋ · · ·

There was scarcely room to move in the Emerald; every card table was full, and the High Stakes Room stood with doors open. The bettors were three deep around the Wheel, and the smaller backup Wheel, which had been set up near the bar, enjoyed a similar popularity.

There were some vacant stools at the bar itself, and most of the custom there were locals and Terrans, Quin saw, pausing to overlook the room. There were extra servers on, carrying drinks to the card tables, the Wheel, and the dicing stations. The players there were almost entirely Liaden, many in evening dress though it was barely local twilight. He craned his head, but the room was too full for him to see the Sticks table, and he had, within the necessities of his recent lift, lost the particulars of Villy's schedule.

"Drink, sir?" asked the bartender—Herb, his name was—and, then, "Sorry, Mr. Quin, didn't recognize you in the leather." He grinned. "Truth is, might not've recognized you in the usual; it's been crazy busy 'round here since that tour ship come in, an' I'm a little muzzy in the brain."

"I can see that it is very busy," Quin said, frowning slightly.

Herb worked day shift, he recalled. His wife worked night shift and there were children who needed to be looked after.

"Are you beyond your time?" he asked.

"Little bit; little bit. Thing is, we're short-staffed—well, not for reg'lar, but for this. Need two 'tenders on-shift to keep up with this, and it ain't slowed down—not even early mornings. We only got the four of us trained."

"I see there is extra wait staff," Quin said.

"Yeah, we called in the friends of friends to fill in the gaps. But ain't none of them trained 'tenders, an' this crowd is asking for some doozies. Almost like it's a test."

Indeed, Quin thought, but did not say. A test of Pat Rin yos'Phelium's *melant'i*.

"Sarath tends bar sometimes," he said instead, having caught sight of that senior wait person moving among the crowd with her tray.

"Sure she does, but she only knows the wines."

"Your second on-shift is—?"

"Woody. Just now come on, a little ahead of his reg'lar time. Me, I'll stay some late, then Lorn'll come in and I'll go home."

Which still meant that Herb was doing close to a double shift. Quin wondered who was watching his children, or if his wife was giving up hours at her job, but it wasn't his place to ask.

What he could do, however, was *suggest*.

"Why not pull Sarath off the floor and have her fill wine orders only? Woody can oversee, and make the more complicated drinks."

"An' I can go home to my kids, who're watchin' themselfs, which you're too polite to ask." Herb closed one eye, which meant that Herb was thinking. Quin waited. Herb nodded.

"That'll do it. I'll just run that past Woody t'make sure he's good with it." He grinned, tiredly. "Thanks. I shoulda thought o'that."

"In this din?" Quin asked, making light.

Herb's grin got a little steadier.

"It's a sight, ain't it? 'Fore I go, you want a drink?"

"No, thank you. Though I wonder—who is on Sticks?"

"Villy went home couple hours ago," Herb said. "He'd just pulled two-and-a-half shifts his own self, and the floor boss threw 'im out to go get some rest. That puts 'em down to two Sticks tables, and we got complaints. Don't guess you wanna open up?"

Quin blinked. He had occasionally overseen the Sticks, when the Emerald was crowded, but . . .

They've come to observe Korval's banishment, Tess had said of the cruise ship.

Well, then; best they did not observe Pat Rin yos'Phelium's heir dealing Sticks.

At least until he had talked with Father, to learn how *melant'i* was best served.

"I think," he said to Herb, "not presently. Is my father upstairs?"

"Sure is."

"Thank you, Herb." He touched the man's arm, very gently. "Remember to clear the change with Woody."

"On my way, Boss," Herb said, and moved off down the bar.

Father was behind his desk when Quin arrived in the office. He rose with a smile that was nearly as weary as Herb's grin.

"Quin! Welcome home! How was your flight?"

"Entirely unexceptional. Pilot Lucien declared, often, that she would fall asleep at her board."

They embraced, cheek to cheek, and Quin stepped back, holding his father at arm's length as Father had used to do with him, when he was younger, and home from school between terms.

"You are exhausted."

"Not quite completely spent. You arrival, in fact, is timely. Natesa will be joining me within the hour. When she does, she and I will go among our guests and inform them that the Emerald will be closing for cleaning and restocking, and will open again in eight hours, local. The regular staff is in need of downtime; the games must be reset, and maintenance must be done. I am also informed that sweeping the floor becomes much simpler when one can see the floor." He shook his head.

"I fear for the state of the cellar. We may need to offer local fruit wine when we reopen."

"How long?" Quin asked.

"Well . . . eighteen hours? Twenty-two? Surely, *Lalandia* only came to orbit three local days ago. The portmaster insisted upon a staged embarkation, in order to spare the port, so we have only seen the most of it within the last sixteen hours."

"I sent Herb home," Quin said. "Woody is fresh as 'tender and Sarath is to come off the floor and pour wine."

"That is well thought, thank you. We will have temp staff to assist the regulars when we reopen, but this...visitation...took us unaware. At least I had wit enough to find Scouts willing to stand as translators on the floor."

"This tour," Quin said. *"To observe Korval in exile?"*

"Diverting, is it not?"

His father, Quin thought, did not look very amused.

"This was not...arranged, then? Uncle Val Con—"

Father gave him a sharp look and then laughed.

"Ah, you thought the delm had gone for a *piece of the action*? It is my belief that the clan's finances are not yet dire, and *even then* it is my very strong belief that you will not in your lifetime see Val Con yos'Phelium *selling tickets* for views of the Tree."

"It had seemed...not quite like us," Quin said slowly. "But one wonders, then, why are they here? Are there no greater wonders in the galaxy than Korval on Surebleak?"

"Perhaps they wish to assure themselves that we are properly chastised, brought low as we must have been."

Quin shook his head, and finally grinned.

"If they are here for the scandal, shall I provide one? Herb tells me that the floor boss sent Villy home, leaving only two Sticks tables open for play, and our worthy patrons complaining."

"Do you wish to do so?" Father asked. "Certainly there is nothing amiss in my heir presiding over a Sticks table."

"Unless you need me to do something more useful, I am certainly able to deal Sticks for an hour."

"Then go. Mr. McFarland is on the floor. Natesa and I will not be long behind you."

"Finally!" the voice was carrying; the accent Solcintran; the mode High, and from elder-to-youth.

Quin had been counting the drawer—the total of rolled and signed bundles was eight: five of the local so-called Quick Sticks, and three Palaz Dwaygo—the classic Solcintran style. If Father's promised hour was firm, he need not call for more. Surely even the worst Sticks player conceivable, playing the local variation, which produced a shorter game, could not lose in less than a quarter hour.

But—

"Finally one comes to challenge my skill!" broke his thought and he looked up into the thin, flushed face of a person who was surely no older than he. Which was to say—old enough to have finished one's schooling. He might expect elder-to-youth from a man of Father's age.

However, Father never inadvertently insulted. Looking at the glittering eyes in the flushed face across the table, Quin wondered if the insult had been inadvertent, after all.

"There were other tables open, sir," Quin said, keeping his voice mild, and in the mercantile mode.

"The tables were open, but there were no dealers present," the lordling told him. He was, as were most of the others of the tour, in evening dress. Very ornate evening dress that included several ribbon bouquets placed about his person, in hues of green and gold.

In, Quin thought suddenly, *Korval's colors* of green and gold. He took a deliberate breath and ran a pilot's mental exercise, to calm his temper.

"If you come to Surebleak, sir," Quin said, "you must expect to find Surebleakeans at the Sticks table. I have two bundles on offer: the local variation of twenty-four Sticks, plus the pick; and the full Solcintran bundle with which *your lordship* is of course very familiar."

The emphasis on *your lordship* came straight out of Terran; it was badly done of him; and the patron was not so drunk that he did not understand that he had been made the object of a private jest.

His already flushed face flushed more deeply.

"Who are you?" he demanded.

"The Sticks dealer, sir. Will you have a game?"

"I will know the name of the man who thinks he may laugh at Ran Dom vin'Aqar."

Grandmother says that well-bred people do not allow their temper rein, Quin told himself. *She probably thought you were intelligent enough to understand why.*

He gave Ran Dom vin'Aqar a small, and proper, bow of introduction, between equals.

"My name is Quin yos'Phelium Clan Korval."

Ran Dom vin'Aqar pulled himself up as straight as the drink would allow, and tried to look down his short nose at Quin, who was the taller. Father could bring that manner off—Quin had seen Father look down his nose at Cheever McFarland *many* times.

Let it be known that Pat Rin yos'Phelium need not soon fear Ran Dom vin'Aqar's superior grasp of mode or *melant'i*.

"There is no Clan Korval!" the drunk lordling stated, loudly enough that all the Liaden speakers in the room stopped talking at once, and all the non-Liaden speakers looked nervously toward the door.

"You are clanless!" Ran Dom vin'Aqar continued, his voice edging upward. "Avert your face!"

Almost, Quin laughed.

Almost, he slapped the silly lordling's cheek.

Having overridden both of those disastrous impulses, he lifted an eyebrow, and stated, as one informed to the uninformed.

"I am not clanless; merely my clan has been banished."

"Korval has been written out of the Book of Clans!" the lordling shouted.

"That is a matter of record-keeping concerning the Liaden Council of Clans," Quin said calmly. "Korval and Korval alone decides when or if the clan exists."

He leaned forward over the Sticks table and *looked down* at Ran Dom vin'Aqar.

"Clan Korval exists."

"Yes, exactly so," his father said.

He came forward on Natesa's arm, he in Liaden evening dress, and she in something utterly inappropriate for Surebleak, though entirely appropriate to Natesa. Quin thought that it might be the dress of her own never-discussed homeworld. It was bright yellow, and spangled with what might have been diamonds; it clung to her slender shape, baring one strong, supple arm, covering the other, cascading to the floor, where a slim, tawny leg was alternately revealed and hidden as she walked.

"Barbarian," snarled Ran Dom vin'Aqar.

Quin took a breath—and let it out, carefully

Natesa turned black eyes upon the lordling, and slowly examined him, from head to boots, the very faintest hint of disgust on her fine face, as if he were a particularly loathsome sort of beetle.

Then she looked beyond him, and smiled in perfect delight.

"Quin! Welcome home."

"Mother," he said, the first time he had given her that. "I am glad to be here."

"We must to home in truth, however," Father said, and turned his head to speak to those about them.

"The Emerald Casino is closing for maintenance and restocking in twenty minutes. Please cash out now, and visit us again, in eight hours, local. Quin, will you come?"

"Yes, Father," he said. He closed and locked the Sticks drawer and walked past Ran Dom vin'Aqar as if he was not standing there, still shaking in what might be either rage or fear, to take the hand that Natesa held out to him and slip her arm through his.

The three of them strolled about, to all the major stations, his father repeating his message. He also heard Cheever McFarland's voice, and those of various of the translators.

Slowly, at first, and then with more energy, the patrons moved toward the cash-out cages.

Quin, and Natesa, and Father continued onward through the throng, Father bowing to this one, or that, or pausing now to exchange a pleasantry.

At last the room was empty, and the doors locked against the approaching night.

Father left them to stand before the bar, and looked out over the exhausted staff.

"Go home and rest. The casino opens in eight hours. If you are scheduled for the morning shift, and you have worked less than two full shifts today, you will come in then. There will be extra help on hand at that time, but they will need your patience and your guidance in order to best assist.

"Please be assured that your work during this unprecedented event will be suitably rewarded. A bonus based on net profits received during the time *Lalandia* is in port will be paid to each of you. Details will be made available as we gain time to breathe."

A laugh, tired but willing, rippled through those gathered.

"I have held you here long enough. Go—go home. Eat. Rest. And thank you, all of you, for your courage and your fortitude."

Somebody in the back of those assembled began to clap. Soon they were all clapping and whistling.

"Thank you, Boss!" Woody called out. "Everybody say it now, *Thank you, Boss!*"

It was loud, but it was obviously heartfelt, and finally they had done, and went away to their various homeplaces, and Father sighed largely, and turned 'round to look at them—Quin, Natesa, and Cheever McFarland.

"Peace," he said, "and quiet. Let us, by all means, go home."

CHAPTER THIRTY-THREE

Jelaza Kazone
Surebleak

"CERTAINLY, THE RELOCATION HAS DONE THE LAWNS NO GOOD," ker'Emit sniffed, as the tour bus lumbered up the long drive toward the house. "You remember how lush the grasses were?"

"Alas, you have the advantage of me," said vel'Siger, who was younger than his seatmate. "I have never been to the homeworld."

"Well! yos'Galan—*Korval-pernard'i*, you understand—would never have allowed this piebald arrangement. A high stickler, Er Thom yos'Galan; *he* would not have been caught opening up a hole in Solcintra!"

"The young Dragon's fault lay in getting caught, then?" vel'Siger asked lightly.

"He could scarcely avoid it, being off-world as he has been," Cozin said from the seat behind. "No, Er Thom would have arranged for it to seem that someone else had done the damage, while he was present at a gathering in Chonselta, and half the city swearing to his attendance!"

"My grandmother, the old delm, would have done the same— if she found it necessary, of course!" said ker'Emit. "The older generation—you won't find their match for wit *or* guile today."

"And certainly not in Val Con yos'Phelium," kin'Joyt said haughtily. "Upstart puppy. Yes—look at those lawns! He allows his clan to meet the planetary standards. And this business of selling admissions to the house and gardens? Why, when I was

341

a child, my aunt took all of us children to the public days at all of the High Houses. On Jelaza Kazone's day, Korval's head gardener took us through the formal gardens and showed us the key to the maze. Inside, we were conducted through the public rooms by the butler, and at the end, we were served tea and cakes on one of the front patios. It was pleasant and completely unexceptionable.

"That was in Daav's day, of course." she sniffed again.

"Well, that's the point of the thing, isn't it?" Cozin said. "Korval is no longer a Liaden clan; the Council saw to that. They might do business as they have been, outworld—Tree-and-Dragon Family, indeed!—but surely, now, they are *Surebleakeans*. It would scarcely be in keeping with their new *melant'i* to have the lawns in better case than those around them."

"Here," said ker'Emit, as the bus rounded a long curve. "There is the house. Perhaps there will be tea and cakes on the patio!"

"Not in this weather, I hope," kin'Joyt said. "Even Val Con yos'Phelium must offer his guests a parlor, and the comfort of a small fire."

"What would Surebleakeans offer?" Cozin asked. "I learn that the natives believe this to be summer—and quite warm, besides!"

"The gate is closed," vel'Siger said, suddenly. "Perhaps instead we will take our tea in town."

"They must honor the admission ticket!" ker'Emit snapped. "We can't have come all this way, in this appalling weather, for nothing. The contract—"

"The contract," said vel'Siger, "was with the tour company, after all."

"Who had made all the arrangements!" kin'Joyt said loftily. "Were we to individually purchase tickets from Korval's *qe'andra*?"

The bus came to a gentle stop. The driver opened the door, and stood.

"I will inquire if there is a problem," she said. "Perhaps there was a miscommunication. On such a world, who can tell but that a message has gone astray."

She exited the bus.

Scarcely was she gone than kin'Joyt was on her feet and moving down the aisle, and that, of course was the signal for the rest of them to stand and, jostling somewhat, exit the bus.

The driver was at the gate, and vel'Siger could see a single person on the far side, strolling down from the house toward them. One of the groundskeepers, perhaps, wearing rough trousers and a black jacket open over a dark sweater. His concession to the weather, which was quite bitter, was that the collar was turned up, and his hands were tucked into the pockets of his jacket.

"You, fellow!" the bus driver called. "We are the tour from *Lalandia*. Open for us."

The fellow made no answer until he came to the gate, where of necessity he stopped, hands still tucked comfortably into his pockets.

"I'm afraid that I will not," he said, his voice soft, but carrying, for all of that, "open the gate. Please turn around—the drive is quite wide enough—and return to the city. You have no business here."

"We have admission tickets!" kin'Joyt snapped, pushing forward. "We are entitled to a tour of the house and the inner garden. I am specifically interested in observing the Tree. We were never let into the inner garden during the old public days."

"For very good reason," the young man at the gate said, in his soft voice. "I doubt you would find the Tree to your liking. Nor you to the Tree's liking, though I suppose that must be thought a separate issue."

A faint rumble reached vel'Siger's ears, as of wheels on gravel. He looked beyond the young man, and spied a red-haired woman approaching, carrying a child on her hip, and escorted by a... mechanism, with an orange ball perhaps meant to mimic a head. The woman was dressed like the man, though she had at least taken care to bundle the child properly against the weather.

"What do these people want?" the woman asked as she reached the young man's side.

"They wish to tour the house, *cha'trez*, and to observe the Tree."

Fine brows lifted over grey eyes, and she shifted the child, who laughed and grabbed at her long braid.

"That would be ill-advised," she said, and looked directly at kin'Joyt.

"Go home," she said, and the mode was captain-to-passenger.

This was no groundskeeper at all, vel'Siger realized, with a chill that had nothing to do with the weather. *This* was Korval Themselves, with the heir, and the mechanism could only be yos'Galan's former butler, about which rumors flew. Its brain had motivated an ancient war machine, that was the most persistent rumor. It yet carried military grade weapons, that was the other rumor.

vel'Siger leapt forward and snatched at kin'Joyt's sleeve.

"Come away!" he said urgently, and turned to face the other passengers.

"There has been an error," he said loudly. "We disturb Delm Korval, and we are invited to withdraw. We should do so. Immediately."

"*I* will not!" snapped kin'Joyt. "I paid an admission and I signed a contract."

"That may be so," Val Con yos'Phelium said. "However, you did not sign a contract with Korval, nor did you pay your admission into our accounts. I suggest that you have been cheated, and that your ire is best directed at the tour company. There are *qe'andra* a-plenty in the city, and at the port. Your recourse is there, not here."

"There is no Korval!" ker'Emit said, unwisely, in vel'Siger's opinion. He cast a worried glance at the mechanism, but it stood as still as a metal sculpture, the ball surmounting it glowing an inoffensive shade of orange.

"Did you not study the Code?" demanded the red-haired woman—Miri Robertson Tiazan, vel'Siger recalled her name now, from the announcement in the *Gazette*. Her mode was now as from instructor-to-student. Which was, he thought, appropriate, as she delivered them a lesson in Code.

"The clan ceases to exist when the delm so decrees. The delm of Korval has not so decreed. That the Council of Clans struck Korval's name from its member book speaks to the Council's necessities, which are not Korval's necessities.

"Korval exists. You stand on private property belonging to Clan Korval, which has been duly registered with the Bosses of Surebleak. This is not a botanical garden—or a zoo.

"Go away."

The child in her arms crowed loudly, and shook her small fists above her head.

"Indeed," said Val Con yos'Phelium. "The imaging on your transport must tell you that you have in fact arrived at Jelaza Kazone. This is the base of Clan Korval.

"I add my own suggestion to that of my lifemate: leave now, and take your complaint to the tour company's representative.

The tour administrators have deceived you. They have taken your money in earnest of a promise that they could not fulfill. I repeat, there are many competent, Guild-certified *qe'andra* in the city and at the port; you do not lack for recourse.

"I shall not leave until I have placed this hand on the trunk of this *Tree* of yours," kin'Joyt cried, striding toward the gate, "and I have paid for the right to do so!"

No one seemed to have an answer for this, and in the silence that followed, there came a small, creaking noise, as if of a small branch, shifting in the wind.

Val Con yos'Phelium looked upward.

The sound came again, slightly louder as the wind—doubtless the natives considered it a balmy summer zephyr!—suddenly increased.

"Scatter!" Miri Robertson shouted. "Go to ground!"

vel'Siger needed no second encouragement—he leapt, pushing ker'Emit before him, and taking them both to the ground, hands and faces burned by dead grasses, and behind them, the earth boomed, and they *bounced*, amid shouts and screams, and a male voice speaking High Liaden in the mode of Authority.

"Please stand and count off. If you are unable to stand, please remain where you are."

There came a voice, trembling, "One..." and another, slightly bolder... "Two..."

vel'Siger helped ker'Emit to his feet, adding, "Six" and "Seven" to the count. yos'Galan's robot stood at the gate. Behind the robot, Val Con yos'Phelium, his lifemate and heir could be glimpsed. A heated conversation appeared to be in process.

vel'Siger turned then, daring to look about him. A... tree branch the length of the tour bus lay in an indentation of its own making upon the drying lawns. It seemed to be not-quite-dead wood; there were some very few green shoots along its length.

Swallowing, vel'Siger forced himself to look closer, but if kin'Joyt's body lay beneath, it was entirely covered by the branch.

He drew a breath, and heard in that moment, a breathy and uncertain, "Eighteen."

Tears started to his eyes.

"Anyone who wishes to place their hand against the Tree's bark may do so now," Val Con yos'Phelium said inside the gate. "Please make haste, for if your bus has not cleared our drive within the

next twelve minutes, the house will call the local law-keepers
and have you taken to the Whosegow and charged as vandals."

"I call mark," the device at his shoulder stated. "Eleven minutes
forty-eight seconds remain."

ker'Emit began to limp toward the bus; vel'Siger followed.
Others of their company also were moving in that direction, save
one only, her grey hair disordered and mud streaking her coat.

kin'Joyt's steps were by no means certain, but she approached
the branch. She bent, and she placed her palm against the bark.

"I hope you die here," she said, her voice pitched to carry.
"Cold and alone."

She straightened then, and walked, not hurrying, to the bus,
where the driver was waiting to assist her up the ramp.

The driver then bowed toward the gate—honor to a delm not
one's own—and climbed into the cabin, engaging the engine.

It was to her credit, vel'Siger thought, shivering in his warm
seat, that she kept the bus scrupulously to the surface of the
drive, and delivered no further trauma to the lawns.

"While you were gone, I took the liberty of making an adjustment to your security arrangements, my son. I hope you will not
find that I have overreached."

They had just enjoyed an excellent dinner, and were tarrying
over a second glass of wine in the dining room—Father, Natesa,
Quin, and Cheever McFarland. Father was looking less exhausted
now, though he would, Quin thought, surely profit from an early
night. By contrast, he was feeling quite energetic, and contemplat-
ing a walk in the relatively mild evening.

But, here—an adjustment in his security arrangements?

"I hope I haven't lost Skene," he said, and meant it. Skene's presence hardly weighed on him at all, and she had a gift for knowing
when he wished to talk, and when he did not wish to talk.

"I would certainly not remove Ms. Liep from your service
without an urgent reason," Father said, smiling slightly. "In this
instance, I have added, not subtracted. Ms. Liep does occasionally need time off, and it seemed that you had sent me a fitting
solution to the problem of her backup."

Quin frowned at him.

"I, Father?"

"Boy forgot what he did before he lifted," Cheever McFarland said, sipping from his glass. Cheever McFarland was drinking beer, as he did not care for wine.

"Well, I did tell Villy that I would go to him immediately I was home," Quin said, recalling that clearly. "As he was not at his table when I came to the Emerald, I believe that I will walk down to Ms. Audrey's when we are done here, and redeem my word."

"Very good," Father said amiably. "You may take your new 'hand with you."

"But who—" Quin stopped, and looked from his father to Natesa, who was smiling slightly.

The memory rose, and with it, a sense of horror.

"Security Officer pen'Erit?" he cried. "But he doesn't speak Terran!"

"He does now," Cheever McFarland said. "Sorta."

Quin eyed him. *"Sorta?"*

"He does, of course, need to practice what he has learned," Natesa said, while Father sipped wine, looking wearily amused. "His days since you lifted have been divided between sleep-learning Terran, and being inducted into the household. Pat Rin did not stint his curriculum. I imagine the poor man would welcome a chance to simply provide security, without a lesson dinning in his ears."

Quin looked to his father.

"I sent him to you because I thought you might find him a place!"

"And so I have found him a place. His gratitude toward yourself is firm; indeed, he confided to Mr. McFarland that he found you a well-mannered and gracious young man, such as anyone would be pleased to serve."

Quin felt his ears warm.

"He will think he is my father."

"Do you know? He seemed remarkably clear on the identity of your father. I think there is very little danger of that error being made."

"Quin, if you mean to go to Audrey's house, it really might be best to have pen'Erit by you. Especially this evening."

Quin looked to Natesa.

"Why *especially* this evening?"

"Stands to reason," said Cheever McFarland. "All them excitable Liaden tourists the Boss here just threw outta the Emerald are gonna go lookin' for fun someplace else."

"Skene is very good," Father added. "Indeed, her skill as a muscle reader might qualify her for Scout training. However, even a very astute and careful woman might find herself confused in such a ... cosmopolitan arena."

"Wait," said Quin. "Audrey and the *hetaerana*—they will also be at a loss. Someone might ... be hurt."

Someone might, indeed, he thought, be murdered. While *hetaerana* were accorded every courtesy—even revered—in Liaden society, such a crowd as he had seen today, at the Emerald ... Would they even allow that there could *be* Terran *hetaerana*? Would they allow an inappropriate touch—and surely there *would be* inappropriate touches—to be a gift of art, or an insult?

"I should go now," Quin said, pushing his chair back.

Father moved a hand.

"You have time to do justice to your wine. Your grandfather stands at Audrey's right hand, and she has accepted the assistance of several Scouts." He shook his head. "Who could have thought that we would rely so heavily upon the assistance of Scouts, only to get from one day to the next? I hope they do not find themselves ill-used."

"As I understand the matter from Captain ves'Daryl," Natesa said, "the members of the Surebleak Transitional Team have volunteered for the duty. Those are the Scouts we see here. Others pursue their duties and explorations elsewhere."

"Then those who remain with us have an investment in the world, and in the survival of us all. That is well." Father finished his wine.

"Quin, allow Mr. McFarland to bring pen'Erit to you. I think you will find that he gives very satisfactory service. When you see him, please convey to your grandfather my deepest affection, and assure him that I have not forgotten our dinner assignation. Natesa, my love; I believe I shall retire."

"An excellent plan," she said. "I will join you."

"A second sound plan to complement the first."

He rose, and offered his hand, which she took, though she rose like the dancer she was.

"Good night, all. Quin, tomorrow there is an afternoon meeting of the Bosses that I wish you will attend in my place. I have uploaded the particulars to your screen. I believe that I should remain with the Emerald, until *Lalandia* tires of us and moves on."

"Yes, Father." Quin stood and bowed to his parents' honor. "Sweet dreams."

"Well, now," said Cheever McFarland, as they left the room. "Let's see if Lefty's ready for this."

"Lefty?" asked Quin.

"'S'what the cook decided his name was. He didn't complain any; seems to like it. Might be a little confusing to others out-of-house, on account he's not left-handed, but a man can be called what he likes, can't he?"

"Surely. Am *I* to call him Lefty?"

"You wanna call 'im Mr. pen'Erit? Gotta remember who's the boss, here."

Quin closed his eyes, sighed, and opened them again.

"My father calls *you Mr.* McFarland."

"Well, now, he does. But he does it to tweak me, which we all know, so that's all right and tight. I don't think you wanna chart that course with pen'Erit, myself. He's still building himself back up from a bad fall. 'Course, you *are* the boss, so you'll know what's right to do."

"That," Quin said, "is a sham. The Bosses make it up as they go along, just like everyone else."

His father's head 'hand turned around and grinned down at him.

"That little time away did you a lotta good. Now, you go sit a minute in the parlor, and I'll bring Lefty in to you."

CHAPTER THIRTY-FOUR

Audrey's House of Joy
Blair Road
Surebleak

"QUIN!"

Villy arrived in the private parlor to which Valori the receptionist had directed Quin and his 'hand. He was barefoot, wearing dark blue pants that flowed and rippled like water from a tight waistband, to wide legs that went tight again at the ankle, and a sleeveless vest in matching blue, open to reveal his pale, smooth chest. His "working clothes," Quin understood, having once before inadvertently called on his friend during work hours. He was also wearing scent—something woody and green, with an undernote of rose—and he had done something to bring soft waves into his usually straight yellow hair.

"Valori did not say you were working," Quin said, stepping forward. "I meant no interruption."

"I'm on break," Villy told him, slipping an arm around Quin's waist and kissing his cheek. He stepped back and looked over Quin's shoulder with a smile.

"Hi, Mr. pen'Erit."

"Hello, Villy Butler," his 'hand said, in perfectly intelligible, if heavily accented, Terran. "I am happy to see you again."

"Hey, you've been studying! Whyn't you go down to the back parlor and get yourself a cup of tea an' some of Redith's cookies, while Quin an' me catch up. Valori'll tell you the way."

"Mr. Quin?" asked pen'Erit.

"It's perfectly fine, Lefty," Quin said. "I am safe in Villy's care."

"Lefty?" Villy repeated as the parlor door closed behind pen'Erit.

"Our cook gave it to him, and he accepted it as his own," Quin said. "I suppose a new life might require a new name. But, Villy, truly—I did not mean to take you from your work, or your break!"

"Why'd you come, then?" Villy asked, head tipped to one side. He'd done something to his eyes, Quin thought; they were a deeper blue tonight. In fact, they matched his working clothes.

"I had told you that I would come to you when I was back on port. I am here to redeem my word."

Villy smiled.

"Well, then that's not for nothing, is it? I'm glad you did come. Tell you what, Ms. Audrey was mostly having me strolling, on account of my lessons. I had a regular date, and my dinner; now I'm heading back to the parlors. So far, everybody's been real polite, but it's early, yet. If we get all that crew come into the Emerald, they won't stay polite.

"I walk the walk, a little bit, but trouble is, I don't look like our guests off the tour ship, and I ain't—don't—have the lingo. Mr. Luken's here, o'course, but he's strolling with Ms. Audrey. I'm thinking if you could lend me your arm, and the guests saw we was getting on all right, that might help keep things calm and polite."

It made sense; it took into account the sensibilities of all of the guests and the residents of the house, as well. Quin nodded.

"I will be very glad to lend my escort, if you think it will serve. Had I known, I would have dressed for you."

"What's the matter with how you're dressed? Nice sweater..." Villy put his hand flat on Quin's chest, and walked slowly around him, fingers trailing. "Good pair of trousers..." The hand patted him gently, and Quin shivered, his laugh a little shaky.

"You said you wanted my escort."

"Might change my mind," Villy said, teasingly, but the face he showed as he completed his circuit was serious.

"You'll do fine. Mr. Luken's already dressed for both of you, and I'll tell you what—you're wearing about what my date was wearing. What else would he wear? I think that sends a nice message to everybody here—regulars and tour people, both. Pretty

Liaden boy, dressed like a sensible Surebleaker, on the arm of the fellow Ms. Audrey told a guest *only this evening* is one of the top artists in her house."

"Congratulations."

"Nah, she was just talking big to put the lady in 'er place. Not sure it worked, if what she was after was for the lady to call for me." He blinked thoughtfully. "Not sure I mind, if it didn't. That lady didn't look too easy to please."

"Whereas I am all too easy to please," Quin teased.

Villy grinned at him and patted his cheek gently.

"That's what I like about you. Wanna try it?"

"Yes," Quin said. "Let us try it."

Quin had only once, accidentally, been in Ms. Audrey's parlors during business hours, and never had he been "on the stroll."

Villy held his arm lightly, keeping them linked closely enough that their hips occasionally touched. "The stroll" involved circulating casually and, to an observer, perhaps aimlessly, 'round a parlor, nodding to regulars and acquaintances, if they happened to make eye contact, which many did.

The parlors were where the guests and the *hetaerana* met and mingled. There were small foods and beverages set out on bureaus around the back of the room, and numerous sofas and chairs wide enough to take at least two, as cozily as they might wish. Typically, a guest would enter the parlor and look about. If she did not immediately go to a particular *hetaera*, then one of those who was not yet entertaining a guest would rise and go forward to introduce themselves.

The guest would then either go with the *hetaera* to a chair or a sofa, or the first *hetaera* might introduce the guest to another of the house. It was, Villy told him, a house rule that guests who had *stopped by* must sit and talk with the *hetaera* before going to the rooms upstairs. It was also a rule that the *hetaera* chose whether or not to continue the relationship.

Those who had booked appointments in advance, or who were "regular dates," were passed by Valori or another receptionist directly up to the *hetaera*'s room.

Sometimes, Villy told him, as they passed from the front parlor to the middle parlor, guests just came by to have a drink and a snack and talk for an hour. When they were done, they'd give the *hetaera* a gift—cash being the most common gift on Surebleak—paid the house a nominal fee, and went home.

"It's been so busy, Ms. Audrey had to open up the kissing room," Villy said, as they strolled about the middle parlor. There were more Liaden guests in the middle parlor, Quin noticed; all of them in evening dress. One woman was tucked into the lap of a boy about Villy's age and dressed much like him, stroking his cheek softly with her small, ringed fingers. As Quin watched, she caught his hand and raised it to her breast, holding it there, and squeezing.

"That's gotta go upstairs," Villy muttered, but scarcely had he said so than the *hetaera* bent forward to whisper into the lady's ear, deftly slipping his hand free as he did so.

The lady, however, did not understand his message; she was inclined, as Quin read the suddenly stiff shoulders, to be offended.

"Let us step aside," he said to Villy, and, arm in arm, they strolled over to the chair.

"Good evening," Quin said in Liaden, in the mode of comrade-to-comrade. "May I assist?"

The lady turned to look up at him.

"He refuses to continue. Am I an offense to his art? Does he think my gift will be inadequate?"

The lady took a deep breath, and looked over her shoulder at the *hetaera*, who was looking at Villy.

"The rule of the house is that the parlors are for ... introductions and preliminaries," Quin told the lady. "He merely suggested that the appropriate moment had arrived for a remove to his own private room."

The lady's face relaxed. Indeed, she smiled.

"Tell him that his art does not fail him. Yes, let us ascend."

Quin looked at the *hetaera*.

"This is Sheyn," Villy said, quickly, his voice soft. "Sheyn, this is Quin. What'd you tell her, honey?"

"That Sheyn had judged it time to go abovestairs in order to pursue greater intimacy. She is pleased with that suggestion," he said, realizing only now that he had not heard Sheyn speak. "I hope I have not misrepresented you."

"You represented me just fine, thanks," Sheyn said. "Let her know I'll be glad to give her tits all the attention they want."

Quin inclined his head.

"Sheyn-*hetaera* yearns to more fully share his art with you, and swears that, together, you will create that which will warm you the length of your life," Quin told the lady, cribbing madly from a very bad *melant'i* play he had seen at Trigrace, which had ended with three dead bodies entwined in an eternal embrace, and the Jewel Box burning to the ground.

Perhaps the lady had not seen the play. Her face flushed with pleasure, and she slid off of Sheyn's lap, reaching down to grasp both of his hands and urge him to his feet.

"Have fun," Villy told him.

"Do my best," Sheyn said. He smiled down at his guest, and, still holding both of her hands, guided her toward the parlor door.

Villy and Quin continued their stroll.

"You're doing fine," Villy said.

"Did you think I would fail you?" Quin asked, taken aback.

"No, I knew you'd do your best for me," Villy said. "S'only—you don't come here for the...play. So, I was a little worried you'd shy away from what you might see. Not," he continued, as they passed the room Scout, who was talking forcefully in Liaden to a man with a coat that looked disturbingly familiar. "Not that the downstairs rooms are anything t'curl your hair. Usually. Now 'n then a guest'll forget the rules a little more than Sheyn's lady. But it ain't exactly Boss Conrad's parlor, either."

Quin chuckled softly.

"I've had my tutoring," he said, "though circumstances have conspired so that I have not had practice enough to hone my skills, I do not believe I would be irredeemably clumsy." He looked at the side of Villy's face.

"Shall we date?"

Villy met his eyes, fair eyebrows drawn.

"Only if it means we can still be friends," he said slowly. "I got enough dates, if it comes to that, an' if you need more, we can solve that, easy, right here. Tansy's real nice; you'd like her a lot, I think. Sheyn..."

"bel'Tarda!" A voice came at volume, shaking the murmur of conversation into shocked silence. "For the love of the gods, someone bring me Luken bel'Tarda!"

CHAPTER THIRTY-FIVE

Boss Nova's House
Blair Road
Surebleak

"HEY, MIKE," BECK WAS SITTING IN THE ALCOVE OFF THE KITCHEN, knitting. That was how Beck relaxed after a long day, which Mike had made longer by staying out on the street, but there wasn't no use sayin' it was all right to go to bed while any of the house was on the street. Beck would stay up, knitting, or mending, until the last member of the household was home and safe.

"Coffee's on the warmer," Beck said. "Need anything else? Handwich? Soup?"

That was why Beck stayed up and waited for them; in case anybody should come home starving. It was better to be short on sleep, Beck said, than to have to clean up the kitchen after one of the 'hands had made herself a handwich.

"Thanks, I'm good," Mike said, hooking his mug from its peg and going over to the stove. He poured himself a cup of coffee so strong it should've climbed outta the pot and into the mug its own self, put the pot down and raised the mug.

The coffee was warm. In the winter, Beck would be sure that it was *hot*, but who needed hot in the sweet summertime?

"What's the word on the street?" Beck asked, standing and folding the knitting away.

Mike shrugged his shoulders.

"Not much noise tonight, actually. Was hopin' to find out about any more example-making. We been quiet these past few weeks."

357

"Quiet's bad?"

Mike pulled up a grin.

"Sleet, Beck, you know me! Life's got no spice 'less there's something to worry about."

Beck laughed.

"Well, then, now that the house is counted and accounted for, I'm going t'bed. Mornin' comes early 'round here. Fresh bread for breakfast."

"That ain't much sleep at all, 'less that bread's rising now."

"There's where you're wrong. I sleep in and Quill's Bakery delivers hot bread right to the kitchen door. New idea of hers. Thought I'd give it a try."

Mike shook his head. That Baker Quill didn't let any ice grow under her boots.

"You remember to use the protocol," he said to Beck, who grinned and gave a shake of the head.

"Knew you was gonna say that. Night, Mike."

"Night, Beck. Thanks."

The light went out, and he heard footsteps going down the back hallway, to Beck's room. Mike added more tepid coffee to his mug and wandered down the front corridor to his office. It'd started life as a closet, his office: snug, no windows, which most times he didn't mind, a good central location in house and no draft being more important to him.

Tonight, though, he wanted windows. Tonight, sleet, he wanted to sit outside on the stoop, sipping his coffee and watching Surebleak go by. Might be he'd see something that would either quiet his nerves, or put a name to the trouble hovering just outta sight.

The tourists...well. The tourists had 'em all jumpy, and that was the truth. Nobody'd expected 'em, and nobody quite knew what to do with 'em. Despite his expectations—and his Boss's belief—some few of the hardier ones had left the port and wandered through town. The Watch liked that, yessir.

Mike drank off some coffee, but he didn't sit down at his desk.

The tourists, they were an annoyance—they were, he thought, frowning, a *distraction*, but they weren't the trouble. The trouble he felt down deep in his bones, that was *Surebleak* trouble, and the quiet on the streets made him...afraid.

Usually, there was *some*thing buzzing. While ago it'd been that the Road Bosses better stop sticking their noses into what didn't concern the road, or they'd see an example made like'd never been made before.

There might've been more to that one than some insurance man pissed off 'cause his nose got broke, but the tourists came in, the whisper died, and now there was nothing on the streets.

Nothing.

Well, and could be they'd made a mistake—them who'd taken up with the New Bosses, and who were betting on a newer, better way.

Right before the tourists come, a streeter'd decided not to pay his insurance when the man come in. Broke the guy's arm and trussed him up with sticky-wrap before calling the Street Patrol to come on over and get 'im.

Which they had, and—surprise!—turns out the guy'd had a schedule of zamples to be made, right there in his pocket.

So, the Watch, they'd staked out the locations, and—surprise—didn't nobody show up at any o'the places listed, nor yet at any other place.

The buzz went dead, Mike thought, *then*. That was how it went: no buzz, tourists, no buzz, *yet*.

Calm before a storm means it'll snow twice as deep, Gramma Golden used to say. He couldn't remember that she'd ever been wrong on it, either.

Dammit, didn't he wish the stupid tourists would get on their ship and go! Couldn't be that much here to amuse 'em, after they'd laughed at the locals, lost a pile o'cash at the gamblin' house, and used what hadn't froze off yet at Audrey's—what was left to do?

Poor little things was blue with the cold, too; you almost felt sorry for 'em. At least *their* Liadens had enough sense to put on a coat if they were cold.

He snorted. If these was the best the old world could muster up, it really did look like Surebleak'd gotten the prize bag o'Liadens for its own self.

Well.

He finished what was left in his mug, thought about going down to the kitchen for more coffee, then decided against.

Morning came early, like Beck said.

Best he got some sleep, too.

• • • ❋ • • •

"bel'Tarda! bel'Tarda! What have you wrought, bel'Tarda! Ah, no—the rug; the very rug!"

Quin was moving toward the sound, dodging around those who had come to their feet. The words had been in Liaden, the voice slurred, and if someone who had drunk too many glasses of wine was going to attempt to force a duel upon Grandfather...

"Quin," Villy came up beside him. "What's going on?"

"It is too much! I shall burst! Someone bring me Luken bel'Tarda! Hedrede's honor is the stake!"

"Is Mr. Luken in trouble?"

"I hope to prevent that," Quin said. "Fetch one of the Scouts—"

"I am with you, young sir," a female voice came from his other side. "Is it necessary that you involve yourself?"

That, Quin thought belatedly, was a good question, but surely he *must* involve himself. If Grandfather was coming in answer to this half-drunken challenge, he would need Quin as backup.

They had come to the hallway leading to the main stairs. Quin paused, looking about him at a revisioned vista. On his last visit to Villy, the stairs had been enclosed, and a little dark.

Now, they were open to the main parlor, bright and airy, and carpeted with the Queterian that had been held on deposit for years, back on Liad. Held on deposit...

His stomach sank.

By Clan Hedrede.

Kneeling on the rug, in the center of the hallway, was a man perhaps his father's age; his head was bent, his shoulders shaking, as if he wept. Pressed against the opposite wall was one of the *hetaera*, a woman Quin did not know, with soft dark hair, and a round, pretty face.

She was watching the man, who had surely been her patron, but she kept a wise distance.

As they came upon the scene, she looked up, and specifically at Villy, who jerked his head toward the parlor. She nodded and left them.

"Oh," crooned the man on the floor, rocking back and forth on his knees. "Oh, the precious honor, the priceless *melant'i*. And it is here! Of *course*, it is here! Where else might it go, when bel'Tarda himself is here?"

He raised his face, and Quin could see that he had, indeed, been weeping; his eyes bright yet with tears.

"Where is bel'Tarda?" he demanded, speaking to Quin, or perhaps to the Scout at his shoulder.

"I am here," came Grandfather's voice. "Whom do I address?"

He came forward, dressed in his best coat, and Audrey on his arm, her face frost-white.

"I am Vel Ter jo'Bern Clan Hedrede," said the man on his knees. He bowed without bothering to find his feet: student-to-master.

"I salute you, Master bel'Tarda; it is a fine Balance! And a shipload of talebearers to carry it!" He wobbled where he knelt, got one foot flat, thrust upward, staggered—and improbably kept his feet.

"You are known as a man of fine *melant'i*. I see that it is true!" He lurched toward Luken, one hand out, and stopped as Audrey stepped before him.

"Quin!" she snapped.

"Yes?"

"You tell this guy—you tell him that if he calls in a Balance against Luken, or hurts him in any way, I will—I will contact all of my colleagues in this business and he'll never get laid again!"

Quin blinked.

"Tell him, Quin," Audrey said coldly, staring into Vel Ter jo'Bern's damp face.

Quin looked to Luken, who inclined his head, very slightly.

"Sir," he said, stepping up to Ms. Audrey's side. "Here is Audrey, the owner of the Jewel Box and the protectress of the art. She asks me to translate for her. She states that, should you bring pain or grief to Luken bel'Tarda over this matter or any other, she will contact her colleagues the galaxy over, and inform them that you are beneath their notice."

For a moment, the man only stared at him. Then, he threw back his head and laughed.

"Ah! Ah, this is splendid! She does not understand me, is that so? I am boisterous. In fact, I am in my cups! She is marvelous; I honor her! I will send her a gift, say—no! I will *give her* a gift!"

He removed a ring with a flourish, bowed low and offered it to Audrey on the palm of his hand.

For a long moment, nothing happened; they were all frozen in time.

Quin recovered first.

"Audrey," he said urgently. "Take the gift."

"I don't—"

"Take the gift," he interrupted, firmly, "and incline your head very slightly. Then you will leave, on Villy's arm, and he will call for your tea, and stay with you at your table."

Audrey blinked. She extended a hand and she took up the ring, its stone briefly flaring blue fire until extinguished by her fingers. Vel Ter jo'Bern straightened, uncertainly, and Audrey inclined her head, perhaps an inch.

Quin leaned over to speak in Villy's ear.

"Call for *zymuth veska*," he murmured. "Ms. Audrey's special sort of tea."

Villy nodded, and stepped to Audrey's side, offering his arm. She took it and the two of them departed without a backward look. In a moment came Villy's voice, raised and commanding.

"Ms. Audrey will have tea at her own table. Bring cakes and *zymuth veska* for Ms. Audrey; she wants her tea!"

Vel Ter jo'Bern smiled and bowed once more to Luken.

"She is worthy of you, sir. I might hope that she would permit me to learn from her, but—no, I see that it cannot be. Perhaps, in time—but time is what I do not have! The ship leaves in a mere twenty hours, and I of course will be aboard."

"Will you return to Liad soon, sir?" Luken asked politely.

"No, no. I am yet of Hedrede only because my delm cannot abide a scandal. I travel, and the clan pays me to go wherever I will—so long as I do not land on Liad. Have no fear, though. Your Balance will find its mark." He laughed—and hiccupped. "Your pardon."

"If you are not in distress, sir, I will leave you," Luken said. "Shall I call your chosen companion to you?"

"No, she abandoned me—and she was not in error. I am in no fit state to participate in art. Wait." He reached into the outer pocket of his coat and brought out a cantra piece. "Of your kindness, sir, I would bestow upon her this gift. I regret, that it is merely money, but one cannot give away all of one's rings."

"Indeed," said Luken gravely. "I will see that she properly understands its value."

"Thank you, Master bel'Tarda. It has been, if you will allow it, an honor to have met you. Young sir." He nodded to Quin, then looked blearily at the Scout. "You are, perhaps, a Scout?"

"I am, sir, yes."

"May I impose upon your skill, to put me into a taxi, and direct it to the Spaceman's Hostel. The tour has taken rooms there."

"Certainly, sir." The Scout offered her arm, the ne'er-do-well took it and the two of them departed for the door.

"Well!" Luken said, when they were alone. "I suggest we join our companions for tea, boy-dear."

Audrey and Villy were sitting at the center table in the refreshment room, which was as much "Ms. Audrey's table" as any of them. Villy was looking worried; Audrey was looking at the ring Vel Ter jo'Bern had given her.

"Allow me to congratulate you, Audrey," Grandfather said, as they approached the table. "You were magnificent."

"I was *scared*," she said looking up at him. "*Quin* was magnificent. He got me and Villy outta there before...something happened."

"Kitchen didn't know anything about *zymuth veska*," Villy whispered as Quin claimed the chair beside him. "They brought out Mr. Luken's sort. Hope that's not wrong."

"Not wrong," Quin said. "I hardly thought the house would have the specific leaf, but it spoke to Ms. Audrey's consequence and...good taste, to those who have ears for such things."

"Which many of our guests this evening do," Grandfather said, settling into the chair between Audrey and Villy. "I allow Quin to have been inspired, but you must also accept your due, Audrey. You *were* magnificent. May I pour?"

"Please," she said absently, her eyes still on the ring.

It was, Quin saw, a singular ring, with a wide, carved white metal band—platinum, perhaps—set with a large blue stone, cut to reveal a flaw like the slit of a cat's eye. The fashion for flawed stones appealed to a certain set of wealthy persons who also considered themselves to be aesthetes, many of whom, so Father had said, wrote poetry.

"This oughta go to Tansy," Audrey said abruptly. She placed the ring in the center of the table and picked up her cup.

Grandfather replaced the pot onto its warming tile.

"It should not," he said firmly, "go to Tansy. Our guest was not so far into his cups that he had forgotten his manners. He left a cantra piece for Tansy, and his regrets, that he was forced by circumstance to give only money. I agreed to convey the gift and his regrets." He picked up his teacup.

"The ring is yours."

"What'd I *do*?"

"You defended my life, insofar as you knew, and the peace of your house. The Balance you intended to exact was both precise and apt. In fact, it was art—and high art. Nor is that ring paste, though others our guest displayed this evening, were. I fear that his clan may be growing tired of paying his bills. One supposes that he is rather expensive."

"What's with that?" Villy asked.

"He apparently attracts scandal," Quin said, "and his clan is very proper. So they have arranged between them that he live—and travel—elsewhere than to the homeworld."

"Is your clan proper?"

Quin looked to Luken, who smiled.

"Korval was High House. By definition, then, we were proper."

"Even after blowing a hole in the planet?" asked Audrey.

"Ah, but that was ordered by the delm! Very proper, indeed."

Audrey laughed, and nodded at the ring.

"Keep that for me, Luken, all right?"

"No, my dear, you have not entered fully into the game! Here..."

He took Audrey's right hand in his and studied each ring in turn.

"This one, I think," he murmured, and withdrew from the second finger, the ring set with white stones, which was the ornament she wore most often.

"Hey, there, that was the first gift a client ever give me," Audrey protested, but softly.

"Then it becomes even more perfect," Luken said. "If you permit."

He slid the blue ring onto her finger, and bent his head to kiss the knuckle before releasing her.

"There," he said, with satisfaction. "It will be seen—and recognized—by those who care about such things. They will speculate, and speculation will become legend. It is well."

Audrey looked at the ring, large even on her hand, and back to Grandfather.

"So I have *melant'i* now?"

Grandfather put his cup down so firmly it clicked against the table. He extended his hands and caught Ms. Audrey's. He bent his head and kissed her fingers.

"My dear Audrey, you are a woman of the highest *melant'i*, whose every action is subtle and appropriate. *Melant'i* is not acquired; it is *built*. This..." He put his thumb over jo'Bern's ring. "This...is a tribute, if you will allow it, to your *melant'i*, given by someone who has had the training to understand what it is that he had been privileged to see."

"So?" She picked up her cup and sipped tea—and put the cup down.

"Luken," she said.

"Yes."

"May I give you a gift?"

Grandfather inclined his head.

"I would treasure a gift given by my dear friend."

"Good."

She picked up the white-stone ring from the center of the table. Luken extended his hand, and she placed it on the second finger of his right hand.

"The man who gave me this—he was a good man, too. We was going to get married, only what happened was that he got retired. Left enough money for me to open my own house."

Luken bowed his head.

"I am honored."

A bell rang, discreetly.

Audrey sighed, and slipped her hands away from Grandfather.

"This'll be the troublemakers, coming in," she said.

"Indeed, and punctual," Luken agreed. He looked across the table to Quin and Villy.

"You must allow me to compliment your pairing," he said, "for being both pleasing to the eye, and soothing to the sensibilities. Will you go on as you have been?"

Quin looked to Villy.

"Glad to have you, unless you have to be elsewhere," Villy said.

"I am required at a meeting in my father's place, but that is scheduled for tomorrow afternoon. Certainly, I am able to bear you company for another hour or two."

Villy smiled, and the bell rang again. "Sounds like we're on, then."

CHAPTER THIRTY-SIX

Warehouse District
Surebleak

RISTA HADN'T WANTED ANYTHING TO DO WITH IT. SHE SAID SO, pointing out to Mr. Neuhaus that she wasn't no good in a fight, and she'd only be in the way. She'd offered to teach Kern or Valis how to read the instrument, and since they was only lookin' for the door...

Mr. Neuhaus put his hand on her shoulder right about then, and squeezed a little more than was really comfortable. Rista figured she'd have bruises in the morning, and maybe no morning at all, if she didn't stop talking right then.

So, she stopped talking and Mr. Neuhaus told her that all she had to do was verify it was the door they wanted; that there was space beneath their feet, and a lot of it. Once she'd done that, she could drop back and wait while the rest of them did what they'd come for.

"So, you'll be coming along with us, won't you, Rista?"

She'd swallowed and nodded.

"Yes, Mr. Neuhaus."

Which is how she happened to be standing on the walk up in the haunted warehouses on a balmy summer night, taking the readings for a third time, so as not to make a mistake. Mr. Neuhaus didn't like mistakes.

"Here," she said. Her voice wavered, so she cleared her throat and said it again, taking care not to talk too loud. "It's right here, beneath us."

"All right," said Mr. Neuhaus, and Jice walked up and made an X in shiny paint on the wall.

Mr. Neuhaus hadn't been happy with the way the bidness at the farm'd turned out. 'Specially he didn't like that Derik, Rosy and Mort'd all got took up by the Watch. The farm was cold, now. If the Syndicate was gonna have a hidden base of operations, like the Syndicate Bosses said they needed, this place right here under the warehouses was going to have to be it.

"All right," Mr. Neuhaus said again. "According to the old plans, there's a lift beyond the door, and a backup stair to the right. Once we're in, first two go down the stairs, the rest of us will do the lift. Take position and target the lift door. Wait until the door opens! When I say shoot, you're gonna shoot to kill."

He paused, like he was looking at each and every one of them standing there in the dark.

"I bet my life that this job will be a success and the Syndicate will have its new headquarters in hand by midnight tonight."

He stepped back, a big shadow against the rest of the shadows.

"Let's get 'em outta there."

• • • ✵ • • •

Mike Golden was on his feet, gun in hand before he understood that he was awake.

He grabbed his pants and pulled them on, while he tried to remember what had—

A scream. Somebody in the house has screamed.

He dragged a sweater on, stamped into his boots and ran for the security station in the central hall. The lights came on as he ran, and a frantic voice yelling, "Mike! Mike!"

Silver.

Mike turned right at the hall, toward the stairs, instead of the station, and the boy flying down them, pants and sweater on, barefoot, face wild and wet.

"Mike!"

"Silver." He caught the kid as he threw himself off the stairs, still six steps up. Caught him and dropped to his knees, keeping him in the circle of his arms.

"Silver. Easy. Tell me, quick and calm, right?"

The kid was strong, he twisted in Mike's grasp, and almost broke free; Mike had to use more force than he liked to, wincing that he'd probably left bruises.

"We have to go, *right now!*" Silver shouted, like Mike was down the block, instead of trying to hold him.

"Go where, Silver? Why?"

"To the *kompani*, to Kezzi, to Kezzi and Malda! They're out there and it smells like firestarter!"

Mike's stomach flipped. Firestarter? Up in the old warehouses?

"Mr. Golden? Syl Vor?"

Nova yos'Galan had arrived, a fluffy robe enveloping her, gold hair done in a loose braid.

"He says somebody's playing with firestarter up in the warehouses," Mike said rapidly. "I'm thinking a nightmare."

"Are you?" She knelt beside him and snatched Silver to her, holding him firmly by his shoulders. "Syl Vor! Wake up!"

But the kid was looking right at her, Mike saw, and his eyes were wide and dark.

"They have firestarter! We have to go, to go! Kezzi, Malda, Grandmother Silain. We have to *go!*"

"Indeed, my child, we shall send aid. Calm yourself."

Nova extended a hand and cupped her son's cheek.

"Call the Watch, Mr. Golden," she said. "Someone is trying to smoke the Bedel out."

He hesitated, and she raised her eyes to his.

"He is young for the onset, but it is not unknown."

"He *knows* this?" Mike asked.

Nova nodded.

"He has *Seen* it. Yes. Call the Watch. Now."

· · · ✳ · · ·

The fire burned with a bright, hard edge. Smoke roiled out of it in thick, acrid ribbons that filled the street, limiting visibility, as well as the ability to breathe.

The regular crew, they had breathers, and dark glasses, though Rista didn't think the glasses were gonna do any good in the smoke.

She didn't have either of those things, and she fell back down the street, scarf pulled up around nose and mouth, eyes streaming. Mr. Neuhaus hadn't told her she could leave, and it'd be just her luck that he'd call her for something five seconds after she turned the corner and started down the hill to the city.

Even so, the smoke kept getting thicker, and Rista retreated, one slow step at a time, in search of something to breathe—until somebody grabbed her shoulder, hard.

She jumped, and opened her mouth to yell, but what she got instead was a lungful of smoke, which set her off coughing.

Strong arms went around her, and her face was pressed into something soft that smelled like vinegar. The coughing subsided, and she felt someone pat her back.

"That is well," a woman's voice said softly. "That is better. Now, child, you will stand here, eh? You will stand, and you will watch, but you will say nothing, call no warning. What is your name?"

"Rista," she said, as the hands settled her back against the wall, and her scarf was again pulled up to protect her mouth and nose. Her scarf smelled like vinegar now. She took a deep breath without coming out with a coughing fit, though she was kind of sleepy, with her back and her head resting against the wall.

Must be the smoke, she thought, and felt the bag slipped off her shoulder. The bag with the device in it.

"Wait..."

"Hush, Rista," the voice directed, and she stopped speaking.

"Well and good. Watch now, so that you may tell the others what happened here."

· · · ❈ · · ·

The smoke continued to fill up the street, and Seldin Neuhaus began to be nervous.

He was not normally a nervous man, but the stakes here were high. He had guaranteed delivery of the little city beneath the city—guaranteed delivery to Mr. Vaxter himself. Mr. Vaxter had a certain way of dealing with failure, and the higher up you were in the Syndicate's structure, the harder that dealing came to be. Neuhaus was one of the three who stood just below Mr. Vaxter, and he'd just seen, up close and personal, how Mr. Vaxter dealt with failure. The guy in charge of the zample-makin'—well it didn't bear thinkin' on now. Done was done.

An' in the case of Tyer Jells, dead and done.

None of that, though, was happenin' to Neuhaus, that was sure. He said he'd deliver, and he'd deliver. No doubt.

He threw a worried look at the door. Somebody down below shoulda noticed that by now, and started an evacuation.

'Course, he thought, could be they were gone already, the street rats who lived under the sidewalk. Might've packed up and left for safer streets way back after the recon team had gotten beaten up. Might be, they could just open the gate when the fire burnt itself out, and—

Indistinct inside the smoke, with the shiver of metal on plastics, the gate began to open, a sliver of light playing into the smoke.

His crew raised their guns. He raised his.

And from behind them came the roar of a turboplow, the scream of a dragon, as a wall hit him from behind, pushed and kept on pushing, the whine of electrics overpowering other sounds.

He yelled; tried to get turned around, but the wall kept pushing and the roaring bounced off the metal walls of the warehouse, and all around him, his crew was being pushed, pushed hard, into the thickest smoke, toward the gate.

Someone shot at the oncoming wall without his order, and someone else, but the ricochets went everywhere, winging off what must be—

"Stop shooting; stop, fools!"

The guy on his right went down, blood all over him, but the wall kept on pushing, shoving him along the street, his screams added to the general din, and there was the gate, the smoke so thick it was hard to see anything. He planted his feet, grabbed the edge of the gate—and snatched his hand away, burned. He jumped forward, thinking he saw someone in the opening door and that relentless wall had stopped. He started to turn, and the wall was back, with more force than ever, knocking 'em all over each other like spillkins and they were *inside the gate*, and one of the crew got her feet in the right place, and threw herself for the opening to the street, just as the bars slammed down.

· · · ✴ · · ·

A roar echoed and enveloped the warehouse district, bouncing off of the walls, coming from everywhere at once.

The Watch was on its way, but Mike Golden had promised Silver—for the return promise that Silver would stay home with his mother until Mike got back with a report—that he would, himself, go *right now* and find out what was doin' with the Bedel, and most especially, his sister Kezzi and Kezzi's dog, and, just by the way, Kezzi's grandmother.

The roaring continued, and now there were other shouts and screams mixed in. Mike got himself into a run, cleared the corner, and stopped, back against the wall.

The street ahead was full of smoke, hidin' the details. The broad outlines seemed to be that one group of people, armed with what looked like thin metal doors were pushing another group of people toward the warehouse walls.

The group that was being pushed was yelling. The group doing the pushing was roaring.

He moved closer, cautiously, keeping his back to the wall, which was how he found the girl leaning there, watching the action ahead with a kind of sleepy approval.

"What's up?" he asked her, she turned half-closed eyes on him.

"She told me to stay and watch," she said, her voice slightly slurred, "so I could tell everybody what I'd seen."

Not, thought, Mike, that anybody'd believe her, doped up like she was.

"I'll just go on up closer and take a better look," he told her, and slipped past.

Up ahead, the herders had angled the herdees into a narrow opening. The shouting increased; the herders swung away, and the smoke did a pirouette, clearing the air so that Mike could see a crew of people inside what looked to be an old service elevator.

If service elevators had bars across the front.

He moved forward, until he felt his arm grabbed, and turned to look up at one of Kezzi's numerous brothers.

"Evenin', Nathan."

"Mike Golden. Why are you here?"

"The boy had a bad dream. Said it smelled like firestarter up here, and he wouldn't be easy 'til I said I'd come up and check on you." He made a show of looking around the street. "Looks like you got everything under control."

Nathan might have answered that, but for the intrusion of another voice.

"Mike Golden," said Silain Bedel. "You say that Kezzi's brother dreamed this?"

"Well, ma'am, his mother says it wasn't a dream at all, but that he saw what was happening. Either way, I promised to make sure you were all right." He paused, weighing it, then decided he had to tell all of it.

"Boss Nova, she had me call the Watch. They'll be here before the next blizzard, I guess."

Silain tipped her head to one side, as if considering that, then put her hand on his shoulder.

"You are a good man. Come and see the rest of it, then, so that you may tell everything."

That didn't sound good. On the other hand, he couldn't think of a way not to go with her toward the elevator and the half-dozen bad acts standing quiet now, behind bars.

· · · ✴ · · ·

Alosha the headman consulted with Pulka, who assured him that the field would hold, a little time yet. This was the weakness in the plan to capture the *gadje* who wished to take the *kompani*'s common area. Disarming them before capture was plainly impossible.

They had therefore rigged a field, Pulka and Rafin working together, that energized the ship panels they had found long ago—portions of ship wings they were, with the embedded antimeteor shielding willing to believe the field's urging—accepting low speed touches but energetically flinging away anything dangerous.

They also wore protection, in case someone should carry an uncommon handgun—say a laser—but if one did, they had not yet brought it into play.

So, the field held, and the *luthia* approached.

Alosha had not wanted the *luthia* in this, but she had pointed out rightly that this thing must happen: a demonstration that they were not helpless. That knife could cut both ways, as Alosha well knew, but the capture of these *gadje*, that had not been the only plan.

Here came the *luthia*, the man Mike Golden in her hand. She came abreast, and paused.

"Headman, this event has opened the eyes of my granddaughter's brother, as he lay sleeping in the City Above. Mike Golden has come in order that he may assure the boy of the safety of his sister and his sister's kin."

Alosha nodded to Mike Golden, and said, "Stand here with me."

Mike Golden stood; the *luthia* went on alone to the very bars, and called in to the *gadje*.

"Where is the one named Seldin Neuhaus?"

"Here."

He stepped forward, a burly man a little taller than most 'bleakers, a frown on his big face.

"Who are you?"

"I am the *luthia*, the heart and soul of the *kompani*. I am here to collect on your wager."

"My—what?"

"Your wager. Did you not say that you bet your life that this job would be a success?"

He stared at her. Mike shivered, just like somebody had slid an icicle down his back.

"Yeah, so what?"

"You lost," Silain the *luthia* said, and held out her hand.

"Give me your hand."

He wasn't going to do it, Mike saw that in his face, but it was like he was... forced somehow to put his hand through the bars and hold it waiting, palm turned up.

Silain slid one of her hands beneath his, and bent, tracing something on his palm with her forefinger.

"Yes, here," she said. "Do you see? Your lifeline. It ends. Now."

Seldin Neuhaus snatched his hand back, eyes wide.

And fell where he stood.

CHAPTER THIRTY-SEVEN

Jelaza Kazone
Surebleak

LALANDIA APPROACHED THE JUMP POINT WITH THE STATELY CARE one expected from a cruise liner. If three more sprightly shadows took advantage of its bulk to reach the point and slip through unremarked, what mattered that to Surebleak?

Val Con relaxed back into the pilot's chair, and deliberately relaxed cramped muscles. They were away, the five champions the Luck had selected to bring an end to Korval's...most recent... enemy, and his part—uncharacteristic for Korval—to sit in plain sight, and do nothing.

He closed his eyes and ran the Scout's Rainbow, and relaxed further into the pilot's chair. Cantra yos'Phelium's own piloting chair, it was, as he sat station on *Quick Passage*, the very ship that had brought those who were now Liadens into a new universe, escaping from yet another of Korval's enemies...

Truly, Korval had never dealt in small lots, when it came to enemies. Though to be perfectly just, the enemy of Cantra and her Jela had been the enemy of all life. Placed against such odds as they had faced, the current dispute with the Department of the Interior was a card game played by fractious children.

Well.

It was perhaps true that they were living in degenerate times, with the very ship of the Migration long ago made into a library and shelter of last resort, wing-clipped and buried beneath the

375

house that Cantra began, but which had surely by now outgrown even her most sardonic fantasies.

...not to mention Val Con, the least of Cantra's children, seventh to bear the name; the first having been Jela's own son. Val Con, who sat safe under Tree while others took up his battle, and who lay awake nights wondering if the clan might best be served by declaring itself kin-tied to criminals.

In the screens, *Lalandia* entered the Jump zone—and was gone, leaving behind a brief corona of displaced energies.

He reached to the board, his fingers dancing among the oddly placed sliders, keys, and toggles. An old board; indeed, an ancient board. It was in him, for one mad, exalted moment, to engage the engines; to find, after all this time sitting safe and idle—to find if she would lift.

The moment passed. He shut the screens down, and the impulse engine, rose and bowed to the empty cabin, as one unworthy to the honored ancestors, before he crossed to the emergency hatch, and rolled out into one of Jelaza Kazone's lesser used cellars.

Miri stirred and half-waked when he slipped into bed beside her. "They got off all right?" she murmured.

"They did," he answered, tucking around her, and laying his cheek against her hair.

"Good," she said. "Now all we do is wait."

CHAPTER THIRTY-EIGHT

. . . .

Boss Conrad's House
Blair Road

"MR. KALHOON CALLED WHILE YOU WERE OUT, SIR," MR. PEL'TOLIAN murmured, as he received Pat Rin's jacket. The days were growing cool again, enough so that one felt the lack of gloves when the wind blew.

"I am sorry to have missed him," he said to his henchman. "Did he leave a message?"

"He chose to wait, sir. I placed him in the cloud parlor, with refreshments. Mr. Valish is speaking with Mr. McFarland."

Well, here was news, on several levels. Penn Kalhoon was no more nor less busy than any other Boss on the Council. To be prepared to cool his heels for an indeterminate amount of time while Boss Conrad was out on the turf either spoke to a man with grave business in hand, or one who was in need of what the local language styled "a breather."

That Mr. pel'Tolian, a shrewd judge of both character and circumstance, had placed him in the cloud parlor—which was "family space"—perhaps spoke to Penn's necessity, as did the information that Joey Valish, his head 'hand, was speaking with Cheever McFarland, Boss Conrad's head 'hand.

Pat Rin ran his fingers through wind-ruffled hair in the vague hope that the action ordered the disorderly, and inclined his head.

"Has any urgent business arisen while I was out?"

"No, sir. Merely Mr. Kalhoon."

"Well enough, then, I will see Mr. Kalhoon."

· · · ✳ · · ·

377

Penn was seated in the double chair under the light, leafing through a folio of holograms of Solcintra Port.

"The artist was fascinated with the High Houses, and their sport," he said, as he closed the door. "There are more facets to the Jewel of Liad than High Port alone."

Penn looked up, light glinting off the surface of his eyeglasses.

"The Jewel of Liad?"

"So did the poet—you will, I beg, hold me excused, for I do not recall *which* poet—describe Solcintra Port."

"Sure don't look anything like our port," Penn said, closing the book and putting it on the table at his side.

"You have placed your finger squarely on the artist's failure. She concentrated only on the High Port, where the wealthy and those with pretensions dined and shopped. Had she spent equal time and care with the Mid Port, then you would have seen much to recall Surebleak Port."

"Good to know there's regular folk on Liad. After them tourists got done with us, I was takin' leave to doubt it."

"And the tourists, most of them, were not even from Liad, though their clans were seated there! Liaden Outworlds—but you did not choose to wait for me in order to discuss Liaden Outworlds, or the manners of tourists."

"You're right, I didn't." Penn rose, not the tallest nor the broadest of the Surebleak Bosses, still he was taller, and broader, than Pat Rin.

"This shooting match of Sherman's. Joey's been hearing some talk."

"Ah." Pat Rin inclined his head. "I'm given to understand that Mr. Golden has likewise been hearing talk. In fact, we—by which I mean our family—only yesterday gathered together to discuss what we ought to do."

"Ain't nothing to discuss, the way I see it," Penn said bluntly. "Just don't go to the damn thing. No sense being a target. Already sent my regrets to Sherman, along with a nice basket o'this'n that for whoever takes novice first."

"That is well thought," Pat Rin said, seating himself in the chair across from the one Penn has just vacated. "Penn, sit. I perceive that you are about to scold me, and I would prefer not to have a cricked neck, too."

"Scold, is it?"

The other man snorted, but he resumed his seat, leaning forward with elbows on knees, which posture brought them more into balance, but was not likely to be very comfortable.

Pat Rin sat back in his chair, and smiled slightly. "I am ready. Do your worst."

"You don't hafta be in this thing—it's Sherman's bright idea; he's got a lot o'shooters and wannabes all lined up. No need for you to put yourself, or anybody from your—your family up as a target."

Penn straightened and sat back, apparently having said what he had come to say.

"That is a remarkably succinct scold," Pat Rin commented.

"I learned it from my kids. More'n two sentences and they lose track of what the old man's on about. If you need more, I don't mind repeating myself."

"Thank you, I believe I have the gist. Your concern does you honor. More, it warms me. However, the...family reasons thus:

"There is legitimate concern among some of the citizens of Surebleak—in fact, we—allow me to amend—I invaded a populated, sovereign planet and subjugated it to my own purposes. That I did not accomplish this with ships and soldiers makes the invasion no less actual. My kinsman, the Road Boss, has done me the very great kindness of failing to enumerate the number and kind of regulations and laws that I have fractured, but I don't doubt that there are many."

"Not like there's a Galactic Watch out there keeping track, is there?"

"Not as such, though there are various agencies that concern themselves in part with the stability of planetary governments. The trade guilds—Terran and Liaden—do. The Pilots Guild does. Entities such as the cruise line of which *Lalandia* is merely one ship."

"The way I unnerstand it, Surebleak's ratings with all those entities has improved since you retired Moran and got the rest of us walking in the right direction."

"Yes; fortunate accidents, all." Pat Rin sighed, and settled his shoulders more nearly against the back of the chair.

"Again, the family has discussed this...exhaustively. What we have decided between us is that I must be at the match—"

Penn began to say something—and subsided when Pat Rin raised his hand.

"I *must* be there. Natesa does not allow me to stand alone. Val Con and Miri accept their responsibility as my delm, and thus they will also be present. My mother and the mother of Val Con's sister feel that they must be present. Indeed, if I correctly understand my mother, she feels that their presence may serve to remind of our work since the...invasion. The rest of the family will...recuse themselves. If, indeed, this *syndication vote* of which Mr. Golden, and, I assume, Mr. Valish, have heard whispers comes to pass, then we shall see what happens."

"See what happens!" Penn exploded, unable to master his feelings any longer. "What's gonna happen is that you and the Road Bosses are gonna get retired, an' us an' all the streeters who've come to sorta depend on there being more better days are gonna be slapped right back into the way it was, only worse than it was!"

"Will you? It is your planet, after all. If you wish coming days to continue to improve, then you must work toward that. We have all on the Council of Bosses been working toward better days and better ways, have we not?"

"Yeah, but—"

Penn closed his mouth. Light slid off his glasses, obscuring his eyes.

"Yeah," he said. "We've all been planning and working in that direction. And, we do have those upgrades, and promises for yearly reviews. We got all these Scouts and mercs, and people who come in *because* we're working toward better days. We got a Street Patrol now. We got that consolidated school. Thera was talking to Professor Waitley t'other day about what it might take to set up a—a secondary school. A college, maybe. Turns out the Professor's specialty is the history of education..."

"Indeed."

"Indeed." Penn gave him a half-grin, then rose.

Pat Rin rose as well, and took the hand the other man offered.

"You and yours are the best thing that's happened to this planet, maybe since the Gilmour Agency founded us," he said, holding Pat Rin's hand warmly. "Call it an invasion or call it a happy accident—thank you."

"I don't—"

"No, now, I know you don't. You go ahead—you and the Road Bosses—and do what you gotta do. We got your back."

Pat Rin felt tears rise to his eyes.

"Thank you," he said.

Penn grinned.

"I'll go get Joey and stop taking up room in your parlor. If we're down to repeating thank-yous to each other, then our work here is done. You give Natesa my compliments, right?"

"I will, indeed. Please remember me to Thera."

"No chance I won't do that," he said, as Pat Rin opened the door.

Mr. pel'Tolian stepped forward.

"Sir?"

"Mr. Kalhoon is leaving, Mr. pel'Tolian, if you would tell Mr. Valish?"

"Certainly. This way, Mr. Kalhoon. Cook has put by some fudge for your daughters..."

CHAPTER THIRTY-NINE

. . . .

Sherman's Shootout
Novice Round

KAMELE HAD SEEN SHERMAN, BRIEFLY, WHEN THEY ARRIVED AT the so-called "little test ring," set up in the small shooting hall.

She and Dilly stood in front of the rope line divider that utterly failed to keep onlookers separated from would-be shooters. In all, she thought there were about two dozen competitors, but it was hard to tell with all the milling about going on

Sherman strode in from the so-called big room, his usual grin a little thin, dressed in a bright and smartly tailored red coat. He'd smiled before he recognized her, or just as, nodded, and continued giving orders to his trailing minions, directing some to the back, some to get more of that, and others to, "Make damn sure those back doors stayed closed. We're not gonna have somebody walk into the line of fire down here, got that? Novice round starts here in ten minutes!"

He'd looked up then, and really smiled at Kamele, then spun and pointed, coming up with a big voice, now, to be heard above the crowd:

"Contestants and official folks—if you got a ticket to shoot, you go on that side o'the rope and keep your papers where we can see 'em when. Gonna watch? This side of the rope, and leave us some room to walk through, right? Right!"

Kamele and Dilly moved together—Dilly being the official 'hand of the Professor—and soon they stood among a smaller group,

383

but no less diverse, women and men from young to greying, all of them armed and ready to shoot.

Kareen had said that this shooting match would be an unparalleled opportunity to watch people in their natural environment— and she had been, as she often was, entirely correct. Kamele had no time for preshoot nerves: she watched and listened to the people, some dressed in clothes so worn that on Delgado the wearers would have been escorted off campus—if not to the Social Assistance Society—at their first encounter with a Safety. Or else the Simples would have come along and delivered them to some or another of the Chapelia holdings...

That thought unnerved her when her gaze settled on a young woman, a *very* young woman, standing pensively alone, staring down at her feet, caressing the barrel of her gun as it fit the holster, talking to it. Her clothes were clean but her shoes and shirt looked ancient, and far too thin for even a Surebleak summer day. Her hair was thick, and obviously clean, but it looked as if it had been washed and towel-dried, then left in an uncombed knot across her shoulder.

Kamele leaned in the girl's direction. Dilly saw the lean, and leaned that way too, until a few silent steps brought them near enough to hear.

"Prizes t'good," the girl was saying, "Twe'll fine, be fine. Finah than Franch, finah than Onnie."

The gun didn't talk back, so if it was an automatic, it wasn't on—and the novice section was set for production sight weapons anyway. From what Kamele could see, the girl's weapon had seen hard use in the past; the bronze glow was scratched, though it looked like someone had recently tried to buff it.

Bustle happened, and noise, and a crew came by handing out water singles and snack bags to the contestants.

"Slight delay on account of the crowd for the other sections. The Boss and the Emerald got these for the contestants to 'pologize for the wait! And here, Deemo's got name tags—wear 'em. Garcie, yours says *Gracie* 'cause Deemo wasn't paying attention. Here."

The woman who'd been talking to her gun looked up, muttering, "Thanks Deemo," to some place where no one was, accepting the erroneous tag and slapping it carelessly under her slight bosom. Kamele saw her look at the snacks in their baskets, and her hands unerringly went for the high-value nuts and protein bars instead of the sweets most of the young were after.

Kamele accepted a ration of water and of nut bars, wondering if the woman would take it badly—

"Here, Garcie," Dilly said. "Don't need these over here—we ate afore we came."

With a sigh of relief Kamele nodded a half-Liaden bow of thanks to her minion.

Dilly kept her water but offered the other woman a pair of cheese-and-meat chews; Kamele gave her nut bars to Dilly to pass on, recalling only too well the discussion she'd had with Kareen about the difference between Surebleak and a Safe World like Delgado. While she had never been hungry in her life, save by her own inattention to time, it seemed that Garcie took hunger as a given.

For her part, Garcie looked them both in the face, took in Kamele's name tag, and nodded.

"Emerald's good to us, so's the Boss. I'm gonna work there one day! Taking night school when I can, so I get my numbers down right."

Kamele was saved from replying to this by the loud and getting louder voice of Sherman himself, hidden from sight, but apparently on mic.

"We're there, friends! It's time to get this extravaganza extravagant!"

Sweat. Kamele wasn't used to sweating on Surebleak, but here it was, and from concentration rather than nerves. The first round had taken the two dozen starters down to a dozen and a half, shooting six at a time. It was hard for the contestants to get an idea of how others were doing—it was shoot for numbers, aim for the target. The second round was smaller targets and larger distance; Kamele had stepped into that round feeling good about how she'd done the first—she'd had no flyaway shots, no extreme outliers. It was clear that some of the novices really *were* novices, but she was not among them.

By the end of that her arm ached a little, but the scores showed her in the top four of the dozen shooters left.

Dilly had dropped back to stand with the line officials and

Kamele had lost track of her, bringing all of her concentration to her shooting. Third round brought the number of contestants down to eight, and they shot in four person lines. The grizzled man shooting at Kamele's left dropped out after his first clip, shaking his head, and staring disbelievingly at his weapon. Not one of his shots had hit the live zone.

Five shooters entered the fourth round, Kamele among them. This was a two-tiered challenge: static targets for the first twenty-five shots, moving targets for the next. The audience had thinned as friends dropped away with their friends, and besides, the larger section, the open and the pro, was shooting now in the main building.

Kamele lifted her gun, marveling that she still felt comfortable, blinked the sweat away from her eyelashes, and allowed herself a small, satisfied smile. She hoped that when Theo did come home here to Surebleak, they would have time to shoot together.

Her smile deepened, for wasn't *that* an odd thought from a professor of Delgado? The bell sounded and she brought her weapon up.

The static targets were hard enough, but . . . there, she did recall what she was told about the moving targets, which were, disconcertingly, sized and shaped like a human. The hits for this round were scored by . . . kill-factor.

That thought boggled her aim for a round, and part of the next before she recalled Jen Sar's teaching about seeing what was really there. That same lesson had helped her elude a dangerous man and . . .

. . . and she was done the round.

There was some cheering, and she looked to see the numbers posted.

There were three contestants left: Professor Waitley was mid score, with Joachim Terryon two ahead on the round and Garcie Cheeble one behind. The others were twelve and fifteen back on fifty shots—clearly in another class.

Deemo walked to the front, and waved his arms . . .

"This is the hard one, folks—ten-shot match pistols, all loaded and ready. The targets are the smallest yet, and an extra pace on the distance. This time, since we got three, we're going for an absolute winner—low score drops out, and will be third, next lowest'll be second 'less we got a tie, an' if we do, we'll shoot off again, with the off hand. You get a two-minute break here, and then we go—No! Hold on another minute and we'll start this round at fifteen hunnert sharp!"

Kamele holstered her pistol, feeling her fingers tingle.

How long had they been shooting? She didn't want to drop her concentration to do the math, but her hands were tired. Her arms ached. Wait! Fifteen hundred? Could she have been shooting for *four hours*?

Beside her, Garcie accepted the match pistol, and hefted it. Kamele did the same with hers. Terryon took his negligently, and waved to someone in the audience, accepting cheers from whoever...

Garcie looked beat, that was what Kamele thought, but she addressed the match pistol politely.

"So, you the one? Just shoot where I point you. We'll do fine."

The match pistol felt light. It felt long, too. The sights...Kamele knew the theory of sights, open sights, had discussed them with Sherman; had talked of them with Hazenthull, and with Kareen. Suppose this strange gun pulled left or right, she thought, suddenly worried—and then laughing softly.

Well, and what if it did? She, Kamele Waitley, was already pleased. Getting to third place out of twenty-four, *that* was an accomplishment! *Pretty good*, as Dilly would say. There was, after all, not much chance that she'd be able to pick up an unknown gun and make it work properly. But already, she had something to tell Jen... Daav—and something to tell Theo. Wouldn't her colleagues be...

"On the line," shouted Deemo. "When the bell rings, go!"

The target was concentric rings with a star in the middle of the innermost ring. When the target was struck, a light showed at point of impact, for five seconds. With luck...

The bell rang.

To Kamele's left, Garcie's shot was first, but it was the shots to her right that distracted her, where Terryon fired without pause. Her own first shot was a little high and to the right; her second, corrected, a little to the left, still high; her third...Terryon was done shooting. There were cheers from behind, which she ignored.

Garcie shot again, and Kamele continued, shooting at a stately, comfortable pace. She rather liked the feel of this new gun, the recoil, the timing...

She finished, and the computed score was eighty-five. For all three of them. They'd need to reload and shoot again. It was 15:15 according to the scoreboard.

"Right there, you can all stop!"

There were armed men around—but of course there were! Only...these held long guns, and some were pointed at her and the rest—of a half dozen, they were guarding the crowd, and one was aiming his gun at her, *directly* at her.

"Just drop them pretty pistols. They empty anyway. Other ones, too, drop them on the floor. You, Miss School Professor, you trying to steal Surebleak from us. Think you can come in here and just take over? We're through with that, you hear me?"

The man kicked the pistols they'd dropped away, cussing under his breath.

Kamele had no words, but the man had pushed closer, using his rifle barrel to point and wave her toward him, motioning in large circles—

"You get down on your knees, and you tell these people you're sorry. Apologize. Loud. Be ashamed for stealing our planet. Maybe we'll let you live and send you off. Let's hear you do it; *down right now!*"

The shooting in the other arena had died away, and then a heavy staccato noise rumbled through, guns that were not pistols, guns that were...

There was nothing to say. She wasn't afraid; she was too startled for fear. She nodded, moved a step closer, and looked up into his eyes, eyes that were black and bloodshot, and wide.

"I," she said, slowly, measuring his stance, seeing his grip on the rifle tightening decisively. She had tunnel vision; she saw his nose twitch, and his grim, hating eyes.

He kept moving the barrel of the gun, sometimes toward her, sometime away, and pushing it as if he might strike her with the side of it.

"Louder! Bow to me, and on your knees. You got three seconds!"

Three seconds! There was no time to think, only to do.

"I," she said again, loudly, and she bowed, finding the tuck-away grip in her boot. She pulled, and shot in a single motion, seeing him still bringing the barrel up—and seeing him fail to see as his throat gave way. She fired again as he fell back, heard other shots around her, saw his body jerking and blood everywhere, and finally someone pleading, in a corner, "Don't shoot! Don't shoot!"

There was silence in the room for a moment and then Deemo

calling out, "All clear, no shooting! Drop your long arms...get face down!"

Kamele raised her head and finished her sentence, "I will not bow to ignorance," she said, and then looked to her backup, to be sure she was not unarmed.

"Don't!"

There were several bodies on the floor being kicked for no cause—dead bodies; Kamele waved the crowd back, heard the sound of shots elsewhere, some heavy shooting, and Dilly came—

"Out the back door, Professor!"

Kamele scrambled to retrieve her pistol, her real pistol, saw Garcie standing stock-still, staring at the dead man they'd all shot.

"Wait, Dilly!"

She found Garcie's bronze pistol where it had been kicked and took it to her, pressing it into her hand.

"Garcie! Here...there's still shooting, we ought to go."

"That was Onnie," Garcie said, pointing at the bloody body. "Cousin...'spected me to move in with him. Tolt me his friends gonna take over, tolt me he'd be a big shot, a Boss!"

Kamele tried to encompass it, found Garcie's gaze on her face. Tried to say something sensible, but what? Had he been a friend? A lover? Was he...

"Kamele!" That was Dilly, pointing, toward the back door, opened now and with people streaming out of it...

"Your people." Garcie pointed toward the hall to the big room, toward the noise of gunfire and echoing tumult. "They up there?"

"Let's get you safe," Dilly said, catching her arm, but Kamele nodded at Garcie, twisted her arm free, and rushed toward to the big room, where her people were.

CHAPTER FORTY

· ·

Sherman's Shootout
Expert Round

FOR THE FIRST TIME IN SEVERAL STANDARDS, NELIRIKK NOR'PHELIUM felt under-armed. He'd come out, with the captain's nod, to check on Diglon Rifle. Not that Diglon was likely to be in trouble, for that troop had become remarkably adaptable for one who had been ranked a mere troop. Diglon was with the cars, with a number of his poker friends with him until such time as the festivities were over.

Diglon was alert, standing as he ought, with his friends respectful of his duties. They acknowledged each other, time checked with a signal: fifteen hundred—meaning one more hour before the show would break up. The pro shooting finals would give way to the demonstrations shortly.

Scattered about, Nelirikk saw members of the Street Patrol. He nodded and they nodded back.

He had been in crowds on Surebleak before, and he'd been among armed throngs before. Here though—here he was responsible for the well-being of his captain and the Scout, so he longed for a proper suite of arms, and not just the four handguns, six knives, crowd control explosives, arm-chains and *zhang*-wire he carried, as a matter of course, upon his person now.

The problem was that generally when he was among large numbers of the armed, they were disciplined troops, else Scouts and the like, not groups self-chosen, rowdy, untrained, and capricious. Who would choose to be among a group with no immediate leader or supervisor, no proper captain in charge, no obvious line of command?

Why, the people he was surrounded by now would choose that, for they were civilians. And they were not merely noncombatant support or world-keepers such as the troop might deal with at home, they were...they were the very reason he and his captain were here, since Boss Conrad had become Boss to have such a place as Surebleak at his disposal, and at the disposal of Clan Korval.

They had been briefed, he and Diglon. The captain had been clear. No. The captain had been forceful.

"Listen up. This isn't just today's order—this is what we're all doing, all the time. If you're on your own, without chain of command, this is standard ops. The one rule from which all other rules proceed.

"That means that we—Val Con and me, as the Road Boss—Boss Conrad, and all his people, *we agree on this.*

"So here's the word: we're all to work with the least force practical. No willfully shooting through a civilian to get a target. No running them over in an emergency, no hostage taking. We—Clan Korval, and you, as Korval's Troop—are under contract. Our contract is to keep the road open so civilians can move when they want to, and when they need to.

"This is our priority on-planet, for as long as we hold this contract. If the contract ends, you will hear it from me or from the Scout. If we are unavailable to you, seek clarity from Boss Conrad. We are committed to making this place, this planet, habitable for all. So people can congregate, so commerce can go forth. So people can do what it is they do without being afraid somebody's going to come along and burn them out, or cut them, or break them. We are here to keep the peace. Occasionally, that means we'll make the peace. We—Clan Korval—came to this world because we needed a place to live, and we are here on the sufferance of the people of Surebleak—they own this planet. The spaceport belongs to them and the road belongs to them. We are employed by the people of Surebleak.

"Clan Korval has authority because of its contract. *You* have authority because you are our troop; what they call here *our crew.* When you act—how you act—reflects on us. Be careful, and use the least force necessary to get the job done."

The captain had paused then and looked them over.

"Diglon!" she snapped. "What's the key?"

Diglon saluted.

"Captain. We are to work with the least force practical, Captain. For the Road Boss and the clan and . . . for Surebleak's people, Captain."

"Yes."

The captain smiled and saluted, and Nelirikk stood taller that Diglon Rifle had come so far.

"Right—any questions? Anyone need more training? Anyone need a different assignment?"

Neither had thought that more training was required.

There had been, before they set out this day for Sherman's Shootout, the hint of action. It would appear that some of the civilians were dissatisfied with the new order of Bosses established by Boss Conrad and Clan Korval. It was possible, the captain said, that there would be fighting.

If there was fighting, she had said, standard ops were in force.

Well, thought Nelirikk, looking about him; civilians they might be, but the temper of the crowd felt good. And Diglon, with friends about, was all business. This was good.

An unexpected signal then, from Diglon, and a more unexpected sight: Yulie Shaper, carrying a wrapped bundle, hurrying toward him, following Diglon's sign. The crowd was easy on Yulie, giving way to a man with a burden, and the farmer was soon at Nelirikk's side.

"Fella—pleased to see you. I'm almost late, but lots of folks about, lots of 'em. And I didn't start till late since I had to check my doors. Had to wait till I was sure that Scout fella met the cats. But now, Mr. Rifle says you know a good spot to watch from, inside . . ."

"Yes, I do. I will show you." He nodded at the wrapped bundle, "Why do you carry long arms?"

Yulie looked seriously at him, nodded, laughed. "Not a secret. Gonna be demonstrations, right? I thought if people was going to be showing off guns, I could. Thought maybe I could show a few tricks, once things thin out, if folks are interested."

Nelirikk nodded.

"Follow me, Yulie Shaper, and we shall see what there is to see. The captain and the Scout are to be demonstrating very soon . . ."

· · · ✳ · · ·

The room wasn't exactly dim—the shooters needed to see, after all!—but it was crowded, and more like the auditorium it had once been now that Sherman's workers had opened up a few movable partitions and let the portions that retained seating, in the back, open to the stage front.

Miri stood close to Val Con, both in simple vests, their part in the demos set to be some straightforward shooting: they'd each shoot a ring into one of Baker Quill's biscuit pans—rescued from the fire a little too bent to use—and the other one would knock the center out of the ring. After that, they'd introduce Boss Conrad himself, who was going to shoot a pip out of a card or two...

Pat Rin and Natesa were across the way, also ten rows down from the top, on an inside aisle; Sherman had thought it a fine idea to have them march down in unison to the stage when named, joining at the bottom and coming up the wide stairs...

Val Con's sub-thoughts were steady, and she could feel it as they watched the pros finishing up their run, with both of them mentally grimacing at missed shots from folks who were supposed to be experts. Learning was surely going on as some of the locals saw Scouts shoot...and there on the scoreboard was good news: Professor Kamele Waitley was into the finals in her section. That brought a glow of appreciation from Val Con as well.

A glance showed Nelirikk back in position—he was to join them in the walk down with them...and *whoa*, Yulie Shaper!

Her surprise caught Val Con, who glanced up to the spot and smiled.

They both flexed, ready to move—and here was Sherman, all in red, preparing to give out the prizes, walking onto stage, and then a noise—a shot!—unscripted...and he was down, grabbing at his leg. Two others on stage dropped or fell, as three figures in the audience close to the stage rose...

"Kill the New Bosses!" somebody shouted. "Stand with the Vaxter Syndicate!"

Miri felt too many people move at the same time several rows over; Val Con went from tense to act, their link tagging instinctive recognitions, their reactions as one.

Together they dove behind the seats at the left, moving toward a clear aisle that would lead them to Nelirikk as a dozen people stood up yelling, turning to where they'd been, firing...shots splintering seats and—

More people moved: there were armed people all about, and they reacted; as they did...

No need to talk—Miri was on the deck, scrambling toward where she'd last seen Nelirikk. The lights had mostly gone out, and then she felt Val Con's touch, trying to get her to angle back a row...

The shooting paused, but there was yelling—someone screaming in pain, someone else yelling, "Kill the Boss!"

That yell was cut off as the sound of a heavier weapon erupted— and then Pat Rin's voice above all: "Hold fire; stop!"

In the dim there were cries of pain, another shot—and the big gun sounded twice. Miri dared a look over the seats, and found Pat Rin and Natesa and a group of maybe twenty down in front of the stage.

Natesa had a gun in each hand, and the folks standing with her—ordinary streeters as far as Miri could see—each held a weapon. Pat Rin...had both hands up, showing empty.

"Hold fire!" he shouted again.

"Easy target!" somebody yelled, from behind them. Miri felt Val Con's reaction, felt the knife leave his hand—and turned in time to see the guy fall, gun clattering to the floor.

"I stand with Boss Conrad!"

That was a familiar voice. Miri twisted to look down at the floor, and here came Penn Kalhoon, gun in hand, and Thera right there with him, gun in hers. Joey Valish was there, and Kareen yos'Phelium, too. They ranged themselves by Pat Rin, and looked up into the seats.

"Who here wants the old ways back?" Penn shouted. "If you don't, come down here and stand with the new!"

Somebody fired, then Joey did, and there was a thud as a body hit the floor. And people were moving, out from under the seats, from outside, coming in, walking down, and standing by Pat Rin, who still stood there, empty-handed.

"Selling insurance is against the law," he said. "Retirement parties are against the law. We would make the streets safe, and see your children educated."

There was a movement by the door, and here came the rest of them—the New Bosses, each with their 'hands, and other people following along until the crowd around Pat Rin nearly hid him from sight.

"Shooters!" that was Nelirikk speaking. "We have your positions marked! Throw down your weapons and stand with your hands on your head. We will target those who continue to hold weapons after my count of three.

"One! . . ."

· · · ✵ · · ·

The sound of weapons, and of voices shouting—those were different from the ordered rounds of competitive shooting.

Diglon crouched low. He had nearly run toward the sounds of battle, but—no. That was not his assigned position. He was to guard the vehicles and insure that they were ready and able when needed.

The duty was not his alone, for when sounds of shooting had gone from ordinary to extraordinary, his poker friends has closed ranks with him.

A particular weapon—he could not recognize it as more than a decent-sized long arm—spoke authoritatively several times, and everyone froze, with some then charging forward to see what that was about, and others fleeing. He noted the trucks down the road, moving slowly and then stopping inconveniently; saw then the potential for treachery.

So, too, did Jon Bosley, a Boss of construction contractors. Jon carried several pistols and, leaving one now with grip clear, came to his side.

"Now, that's not how we do things hereabouts," he said, pointing to the trucks. "Seems to me they're blocking the road. So see, if they got all the roads blocked, even walkers might be in trouble. Give me the word, and I'll take Barney up that way . . ." he used his head to indicate a direction, "and get them moved so we can all get out . . ."

The long arm spoke again, and there were people exiting, trying to squeeze through the suddenly crowded way.

Diglon turned his head, and saw another truck moving into place. He could not do both—clear the road and protect the vehicles. And the people—they were in danger, if this was a trap being closed.

"Yes," he said to Bosley. "The Road Boss says that people must be able to move. The road must stay open."

"You got it," Bosley said, and spoke to the man at his side.

"Barney, come with me—snatch up anybody you know. The Boss—all the Bosses!—they need the roads clear. This ain't gonna do!"

Diglon called to them: "The people need the road. The people own the road. The Bosses only guard it!"

"The Bosses bein' busy, we'll just do 'em the favor," Jon said, and he and Barney faded into the crowd.

More injured appeared, and three people carrying a dead woman, two bleak and one just crying, "Can't be. Can't be dead. Can't!"

Diglon kept anxious eyes on the door Nelirikk had last entered. More injured came now, some limping, some bedraggled, and came also the unwounded, walking swiftly, as if to put danger behind them.

One of his poker mates, called by the gamers Speedy Kelby because he deliberated so over each card, also exited, and, recognizing Diglon, stopped to report.

"Boss is okay. Conrad I mean. The Road Bosses're in there somewhere; guessing *they're* okay. What're you doin'?"

"I hold the vehicles..."

"Yeah? Well, lemme stand here with you. Two's better'n one to guard stuff—an' you're too far up on me to let you get in trouble!"

Diglon nodded, pleased to have someone to stand with him.

Now there was shouting near the trucks, an attempted barricade where someone was shouting foolishness about the Bosses stealing food from children, of Bosses stealing homes...

Diglon turned his attention back to the exit, and here came Nelirikk, carrying a long arm, half-carrying Farmer Yulie, with Professor Waitley and Lady Kareen close behind.

The Lady's car, that was the one they would want—

"The Road Bosses stand with Boss Conrad," Nelirikk told him. "Yulie Shaper goes to the Lady's house, to see his wound tended."

From behind, there was shouting now, and a pistol shot at the trucks. Nelirikk looked up, frowning.

"The road—"

"It is being solved," Diglon said, and about then there was a shout as men and women swarmed the biggest vehicle, and began pushing it out of the way. Another one moved backwards, also pushed...

"The road—the people open the road that they own."

EPILOGUE

· · · · · · · · · · · · · · · · · · ·

WHAT WITH THE ALL-BOSS PARADE DOWN THE WHOLE LENGTH
of the Port Road and the public reception at the port, and the
private, all-Boss dinner at Lady Kareen's house, Miri guessed the
day qualified as a long one for everybody. Most of all, though,
it had been a long day for Lizzie, who, worryingly, showed no
signs of being tired.

She sat alert on Miri's lap, her head turning in the direction
of house and Tree, the instant Val Con guided the car 'round
the corner onto what was properly their own driveway.

Miri sighed with contentment, and Val Con put his hand companionably on her knee, sharing his pleasure at being in sight of
home and the tall green spire.

Lizzie laughed, and Miri sighed again, half-amused.

"Brat, you're so tired you're not gonna sleep for days, are you?"

Val Con's gentle attention bubbled through her back brain as
his casual concentration on driving gave him permission to see
what she saw...

Indeed, his glance showed alert eyes and eager, fidgety fingers,
wanting the world.

"I warrant we'll all sleep well this evening, *cha'trez*," he said
patting her knee in emphasis before regaining the wheel. "And
I thought we weren't to say *brat* anymore, since Talizea seems
to be trying to repeat it!"

"Habit," she said resignedly, "but with company due in, I gotta get out of it. This mom-to-a-princess stuff ain't half as easy as running a herd of mercs!"

Val Con laughed and accelerated, letting the car briefly hint at its potential, before sighing and bringing the speed down again to what he considered to be stately.

"*Princess* she'll not be under our roof." The car twitched as he played again for a second. "At least, I swear that I will do my best not to make her a princess. Now, what we must do is convince all of them!"

He casually flicked fingers over his shoulder, showing the road behind them, and by inference those who followed them: a caravan of sorts containing Mrs. pel'Esla, Nelirikk, Diglon, his wife Alara, the mostly recovered Yulie Shaper, not to mention half of Kareen's household, and assorted others vetted by her or Kamele, in several cars and trucks.

In fact, Lizzie's first visit to her great-aunt's town house hadn't boded well for her future as a not-princess. It'd seemed that all of Surebleak, and their twins too, had marveled at the beauty and wit of the Road Boss's child. Miri had seen Natesa's eyes seek the comfort of the ceiling several times in response to the hints—subtle, and not-so—that surely Boss Conrad also deserved the delight of a child's voice to light his mornings.

Miri snickered softly.

"We're gonna need some help with that. Nelirikk's an old softy when it comes to kids, is what I'm thinking. Might hafta get us a couple more Scouts on staff just so he knows everything's shipshape..."

Ahead, the gate was open, falling into shadow as Val Con guided the car to the family entrance, slowing and stopping... hesitantly.

Miri felt his attentiveness, not quite concern, but—and then she smelled it, too. "Smoke," she said, even as Val Con popped his door and got out. He opened hers and took Lizzie from her so she could get out.

"Woodsmoke," he said, sounding more puzzled than concerned.

"The house?"

They walked forward, both scanning the roofline, finding no sign of fire, save the smoke, which was getting...

"Master Val Con, how good to see you so soon..."

Jeeves, and several of the cook staff as well, were just outside the kitchen door. A large fan was inside the door, a smaller in the window, grey smoke flowing from both.

Talizea sneezed gently, and Miri laughed. Val Con turned wide eyes on the AI, whose headball was flickering between orange and blue.

"Forgive me, Jeeves. Naturally we have surprised you with our unexpected arrival."

Jeeves managed to sound both contrite and put upon.

"Surely not *surprised*, sir. Merely that, due to circumstances barely under my control, I have become involved with the need to oversee the immediate ventilation of the kitchen, as Mrs. ana'Tak has discovered that the small brick bread oven in the back baking quarters is currently unserviceable..."

"The *small* bake oven?"

Miri felt the familiar buzz of her lifemate's concentration, understood it to be a scan of memory—

"It has been lately unused," Jeeves informed them. "And, as I was not consulted..."

"I hope staff has taken no harm," Val Con said. "Jeeves, to the best of my knowledge the *small* oven hasn't been used—as an oven— for nearly four hundred Standards. It has been utilized as a secret hiding place for children's special snacks for at least that long!"

"Perusal of the records I have recently accessed indicates that you are very close to the mark, Master Val Con. I will say that no harm has been taken, other than embarrassment—and Mrs. ana'Tak's dismay. She had been following a recipe provided by Yulie Shaper to make a dessert treat for his homecoming, one specifying a wood oven..."

From within bustled Mr. pel'Kana, tidy and neat, a basket in one hand and a tray table folded under his arm—

"This way, if you would, lord and lady, and young lady. We shall utilize the front door ourselves—to avoid this smoke. I shall serve you Tree-side while the last of this inconvenience is settled. We have tables on the East Patio, for those who follow. The staff apologizes, if you please."

The snack and the light afternoon wine had put them into a quiet mood, so quiet that they allowed returning family and guests to find their own way to the East Patio, and to wander the gardens as they would. The Tree welcomed the company, though it was, Miri was certain, the Tree's doing that they three were not disturbed in their solitude.

Backs comfortably against the warm trunk, and Lizzie stretched across their laps, they drowsed on the side of the Tree known as Delms' Court, facing as it did the delms' study on the lower level.

"Gonna think we're rude," Miri'd suggested, drowsily.

She was rewarded with Val Con's soft laugh and a playful, "Gonna think we're rude? No, Miri, they shall not. Gonna think we're delm, at home, after a long day."

Sleep came upon them easily, as Miri had expected. What she hadn't expected was the vivid sighting of a wild-haired young woman in Scout gear and leather, laughing as she watched great birds flying in a distant warm sky of brightest blue. Someone away was calling for Liz, and elsewise there was wind blowing and seed pods to be planted...

And then, there were Shan and Priscilla standing hand in hand as they overlooked the waves crashing into foam on rocks far below. A spaceship was in Miri's view, and twin hills, each crowned by a sapling, and in the distance, a house rising from a plateau...

Val Con was in the dream, or sharing it, watching with her from an impossible place as a ship larger than the *Dutiful Passage* pulsed into Jump away from *here* to an equally impossible *there*....

Sharing Val Con's eyes, she saw Theo, somewhat older, possibly wiser, standing before a potted tree tied into the Jump seat on a ship's bridge, just as the legends and diaries said the Tree they leaned against had once traveled. And there...

...there were cats curled around and against them, and a man's laughing voice, quite nearby and not at all dreamlike.

"Sleet, I can't get so many, and hey, some of them live with me!"

With one breath Miri woke, and Val Con did, and so, too, did Liz/Lizzie/Talizea yos'Phelium wake, still laughing from whatever her dreams had been, and seeming as fresh as if she'd had a full night's sleep.

At their feet stood Yulie Shaper, with Mr. pel'Kana in attendance.

"Apologies, Lord and Lady," he offered. "It happens that the smoke is clear, with both Jeeves and Nelirikk declaring the house suitable. I thought it best to clear away. Mr. Shaper is on his way home, and wished to properly take his leave."

"That's right," said Yulie, with a nod. "An' I need to talk at you a minute, too."

Lizzie laughed again in Miri's arms, admiring the myriad of cats in the garden, some in their own orbit, some in Yulie Shaper's orbit, some in her orbit, and about her mother's feet as Miri stood, Val Con's hand under her elbow.

"We are at your service, Mr. Shaper," he said. "How may we serve you?"

Much to their surprise, Yulie laughed.

"Oh, no, you don't gotta serve me! Mrs. ana'Tak's done that—got some cookies to take home, too!—and your Mr. pel'Kana, he's done right by me too...more'n right. But I gotta ask, since you been busy: what're you gonna do about your branch?"

The waking delm shared confusion. Miri asked the question.

"Our branch?"

"Sure—that branch out front. Getting to be time to do *some*-thing with it. Got itself a nice covering of mulch leaves now, but it's broke in three, and they oughta get themselves settled. 'Nother ten or twelve days we'll be seeing autumn. Oughta get roots in before winter hits, you know!

"Now, here, lemme show you, since I'm my way home..."

The cats led the way, foreknowing Yulie Shaper's direction and intent. Perforce, Val Con and Miri followed, until at last they stood in the last rays of the setting sun, surveying the branch that had been the Tree's answer to their tourist problem.

Like Yulie'd said, the branch had broken into three sections, and on each section grew a tiny spike of a tree, while green fuzz covered the rest of the log.

"Now, see, this'n here, on the piece nearest my place, it looks to me that one's most along, and I was wondering, if you're not needing it, if I can take it over to my far field. Give it twenty or a hunnert years and it'll do like your big one's doing—pulling in some warm, sucking in the water, keeping out some of the cold and breeze! I'd be pleased to have it with me—and it'll give yours some company!"

"Indeed," murmured Val Con. "Take it and plant with our goodwill, Mr. Shaper."

Yulie nodded, and waved his hand at the log.

"These other two, see, they're almost twins. If your brother's coming home like you said he was, you might wanna take and plant 'em down on that piece o'land I'm gonna sell 'im. I think they'd like the sea air—an' they'd make a good present, a—a *welcome home* present!"

The Delm of Korval looked at each other and, as one, extended a hand in response to small rustlings overhead.

Miri's catch was two pods—one large and firm; the other small and soft.

She gave Lizzie her pod, and smiled when her daughter laughed.

Val Con's catch was four pods. One, he knew, was his. One was Father's; the third belonged to Mother. The fourth...

...was for Yulie Shaper.

He held it out and his neighbor took it without hesitation.

"Welcome home, Yulie Shaper," Val Con said, and raised his pod, as if it were a fine glass of wine.

Miri raised her pod, Yulie raised his, and Lizzie raised hers.

"Welcome home," Miri said. "All."